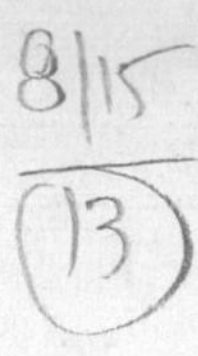

Advance Praise for Keija Parssinen's *The Ruins of Us*

"*The Ruins of Us* tells a gripping story about Saudi Arabian princes and bureaucrats, wives and extra wives, sons and daughters, fanatics and exiles, whose appetites and beliefs have been, until now, unavailable to readers of contemporary American fiction. Keija Parssinen uses her firsthand knowledge of the crossroads where U.S. and Saudi Arabian interests intersect and sometimes collide, and she directs the human and historical traffic with a maestro's sense of pace and a true storyteller's sense of consequence."

—Scott Spencer, author of *Man in the Woods*

"A big, brave novel, Keija Parssinen's *The Ruins of Us* takes us behind the compound walls of Saudi Arabia and into the secret passions that threaten to tear one family apart. Step into Parssinen's sensual prose and be transported."

—Anna Solomon, author of *The Little Bride*

"In *The Ruins of Us*, Parssinen carries the reader from Texas into the Saudi Kingdom in the grip of a story that is both entertaining and wise. Through an expertly drawn cast of characters and a suspenseful and timely series of events, it poses the universal questions: how much do we really know about the ones we love, and how far will that love carry us when the earth below our feet starts to shift? *The Ruins of Us* marks the debut of an enormously talented writer who is unafraid to lead us on the greatest adventure of all—into the wilds of the human heart."

—Lise Saffran, author of *Juno's Daughters*

THE RUINS OF US

KEIJA
PARSSINEN

THE RUINS OF US

A Novel

HARPER PERENNIAL

NEW YORK • LONDON • TORONTO • SYDNEY • NEW DELHI • AUCKLAND

HARPER PERENNIAL

FIRST EDITION

Designed by Fritz Metsch

Library of Congress Cataloging-in-Publication Data

Parssinen, Keija.

The ruins of us : a novel / by Keija Parssinen.—1st ed.

p. cm.

ISBN 978-0-06-206448-6 (pbk.)—ISBN 978-0-06-206449-3 (e-book)

1. Americans—Saudi Arabia—Fiction. 2. Saudi Arabia—Fiction. 3. Domestic fiction. I. Title.

PS3616.A7845R85 2012

813'.6—dc22 2011028519

12 13 14 15 16 OV/RRD 10 9 8 7 6 5 4 3 2 1

For my mother, the root.

For my father, the wanderer.

For my sister, the poet.

For my brother, the peaceful heart.

For Michael, fiery joy.

Be in this world as a stranger, or as a traveler passing through it.

HADITH, OR SAYINGS OF THE PROPHET

❧

When I wiped you from
the book of memory
I did not know I was striking
out half my life.

NIZAR QABBANI ("FOOLISHNESS")

THE RUINS OF US

ONE

AT THE AL-QASR souq, Rosalie al-Baylani stood beneath one of the many date palms that lined the marketplace. She had positioned herself behind the trunk of the largest tree to avoid the blast of wind off the al-Dahna Desert, but nonetheless, the heavy breeze blew her scarf back, the tiny pins she used to secure it popping off and flashing copper before disappearing into the sand. Rosalie set her handbag in the dirt so she could rewrap the scarf around her head. The absence of pins forced her to tuck the fabric's long edge close to her chin, making her look like a tourist who had never learned to properly veil herself. She was tempted to let it blow away altogether. Her red hair was shining and straight for once, begging to be looked at—a result of the olive oil she had started to mix with her conditioner, the trick Lamees had recommended when Rosalie had complained about the winter's dulling effects on her hair. She picked up her purse and dusted it off. She should have known better than to attempt a winter-white handbag in Saudi Arabia, where sand was always the victor. Sometimes, though—and Rosalie firmly believed this—in a place as harsh as the Kingdom, you had to do frivolous things to prove you hadn't forfeited the fight.

She waited patiently for her daughter to come back from the

toilets. Rosalie had told her driver to stay in the car. *We'll only be a moment. Just some small business to take care of.* Today was Mariam's birthday, and Rosalie wanted them to take in the morning alone. Hard to believe it had been fourteen years since the everlasting night at al-Salama Hospital when Mariam had extended her spongy arms and legs inside the womb and refused to emerge. She was smart even then, choosing to stay inside her protected world rather than emerge into one lit by the explosions of Saddam's SCUDs. Overnight, Desert Shield had become Desert Storm, Rosalie's labor marked by the whine of air-raid sirens, and the Eastern Province shuddering beneath the boots of the half-million American troops massed there. During the days that mother and daughter spent recovering, Rosalie had practiced putting on her gas mask as she held Mariam to her breast. There wasn't a mask small enough for the girl's infant head. In the neighboring room, a baby had howled unrelentingly. When Abdullah went in search of an explanation about the crying, he returned and informed her there would be no peace until the Bedouin parents decided to return and collect the girl, who had been half turned to rubber by a grease fire. Days passed with the screaming, as if the baby knew she had been abandoned for the weakness that her melted skin would bring into the tents. Even in the time of oil, the desert was about survival.

Rosalie was glad Faisal had come two years earlier. He had arrived much as he existed, quietly, with barely a cry to register his easy, if premature, emergence into the world. And so her wartime baby was loud and brave, and her peacetime baby lived his life like a breeze through palms—a whispered presence.

Now she glanced around the market for Mariam, missing her daughter already, whose years seemed so full of the girlish bravery and devotions that Rosalie remembered from her own childhood. Her abaya moved around her body, the material silken against her bare arms. She had not dressed for the weather. It was midwinter, and the dates were now small and green, closely bunched at the tops of the palms. They wouldn't begin their turn from green to red to ripe brown until early summer. When they started to drop like falling amber, she would be back to collect them from the merchants. Around her, the shoppers moved quickly through the cool afternoon, the Eastern Province sky bright and empty above them.

Mariam returned and took Rosalie's hand.

"You looked like you were daydreaming," Mariam said.

"In a way," Rosalie said. Memories were their own kind of dream, after all. "I was remembering the day you fought so hard to stay inside my belly. All of a sudden, you went from this calm little ball to a ten-armed monkey."

"I'm glad I finally decided to come out."

"Me too, badditi." She angled her chin toward the beautiful mess of the marketplace. "It's not so bad out here, is it?"

When speaking with Mariam, Rosalie found herself adopting her daughter's rapid speech, so that she felt like the girls she overheard in the mall, their Arabic fast and sure, its flow interrupted only by their giggles.

Today, they had already purchased a few items that Mariam carried in a large canvas sack. As they passed the spice merchant's stall, Rosalie moved discreetly toward the neat conical towers of spices that rose out of the tops of the barrels. She liked to rub a few grains between her fingers as she passed from barrel to barrel. If Abdullah was home when she returned from the souq, he never failed to tell her she smelled like a fortune-teller's floor.

"Just one more stop and then we'll go home," Rosalie said.

She steered her daughter toward the Yemeni's stall; she was determined to leave with something more than bread and spices. She would buy an intricate bangle from the Yemeni for Mariam to spin on her thin wrist. Adornment started now, in the fragile adolescent years when love was nothing more than a kiss exchanged between harried parents, the promises of songs and movies. It was a good age, fueled by hope and unrequited crushes, uncomplicated by the harder reality of another person. A husband, for instance, who was gone six nights out of seven. Business, he explained. Business is an unkind mistress, she said.

Abdullah, her occasional husband, her true love, was not very interested in birthdays—perhaps because he had lost enough young brothers and sisters that birthdays were not so much celebrated as marked with a sigh of relief—so he had asked her to choose Mariam's present. Something nice but not ostentatious, he'd said. We don't want her weighed down by expectations in case she decides to be like her fool father and marry for love, he joked, pinching Rosalie's hip. She'd puffed out her cheeks and raised both hands in a shrug. It was true. For the most part, they'd been fairly happy fools, in a time and place when marrying for love, and outside the tribe—*far* outside the tribe—were seen as liabilities, or worse, insulting.

The crowds thinned as people prepared for the late-afternoon Asr prayer. Rosalie walked faster, pulling Mariam along behind her. They needed to get there before the jeweler closed for prayer.

"Just a minute," she called out to the Yemeni as he stepped outside the shop to pull down the security grating.

He put up both his hands as if telling her to slow down.

"Closed for prayer, madam. So sorry."

"But it's my daughter's birthday. You wouldn't deprive her of the chance to choose her present, would you?"

Reluctantly, the jeweler pushed the grating back up and unlocked the front door.

"No, madam."

Mariam danced through the cracked door and began to survey the glass cases. Her headscarf fell halfway down her hair, but Rosalie didn't move to fix it. It was Mariam's birthday; she should have the carefree moments of the day.

"Let's not make the gentleman too late for his prayers," Rosalie said, waiting by the door to indicate that they would make an effort to leave as quickly as possible.

"This one," Mariam said after a few minutes of careful scouting, pointing to a wide bracelet with roped edges and large flowers etched into the metal. Pretty, but not anything Rosalie would have chosen. That's all right, she thought. Mariam is growing into who she will become, which is not me. Rosalie felt surprisingly calm in this knowledge. She squeezed her daughter about the waist, then removed her credit card from her wallet and placed it on the glass.

"I'll wait outside for you, Umma," Mariam said, kissing her lightly on the cheek. "I want to see how it looks in the sunlight." She grabbed the bracelet and ducked out of Rosalie's grasp, the door sighing shut behind her.

"Oh, madam!" the shopkeeper said with delight as he scrutinized the name on the card. "Baylani. You are family to Sheikh Abdullah, then?"

"Yes, as a matter of fact. You know him?"

"Who doesn't know the sheikh? He is my favorite customer. He always has a good joke to tell when he comes in, and his taste is exquisite. You are his wife, then?"

"Yes, I am."

"Then I must ask you something." The Yemeni clasped his hands and smiled. "What did you think about the onyx pendant? I had the setting specially made just for that stone. Oh, and how could I forget? Happy anniversary! It was December, wasn't it? Your wedding anniversary?"

"I'm sure the pendant was lovely, but I'm afraid you have me confused with someone else," she said. "Perhaps one of the sheikh's brothers bought it as a gift?"

"No, madam, there's no mistaking Sheikh Abdullah. But perhaps I have spoiled his surprise for you. I could swear the sheikh said the anniversary was in December. Please don't tell him I've ruined the surprise."

Abdullah knew she despised onyx—it looked too gothic against her pale skin, and Rosalie considered the stone's patent-leather sheen gaudy. The jeweler's befuddlement made her want to correct him again, this time with greater specificity. For me, Abdi buys amethysts because the color so closely matches the sky that day when we had to park at the rest stop, just east of Marble Falls, and wait out the tornado warning. It stormed for three hours, the heavens a grayish purple, like dusty plums, with us crouched by the roadside. His mouth tasted of the blueberry pie we had eaten in a late-afternoon fit of indulgence.

But never onyx, Abdullah knew her too well for that. She felt queasy. The shop was hot; she was aware of the sweat forming by her ears, where the veil met her hairline. Were they starting again? The affairs that had eaten at her insides like a parasite? No, they had moved beyond those days, they were years beyond those days. Abdullah had realized he could not satisfy his hungering heart with trifles. Still, he knew her too well for onyx.

"So sorry, madam." The jeweler pushed the credit card receipt across the glass case. She signed it and then paused. Her name was there at the bottom of the receipt; she could help the Hadrami solve the mystery right then.

"When did the sheikh make this purchase? Can't you find the receipt?" she asked. Her throat was dry. She'd been suffering nosebleeds at night, the air was so stripped by the north winds.

"Oh, no. My mistake, madam. As you said, I am confused." A blush had risen on the man's cheeks, deep enough to reveal itself against his olive skin.

"Me too. So why don't you help clear up some of my confusion."

Their anniversary wasn't until May, when the heat in the Kingdom was building and they had to escape to the mountains of Asir for a few days. It was what they did to reward each other for another year, twenty-seven in all. They did not exchange lumps of minerals. Abdullah had an aversion to clichés, preferring instead to give her jewelry on any old day of the week. It was best that way, when, sleepy-eyed with routine, she uncovered on a kitchen sponge a vein of pink fire nestled in an egg-shaped opal.

Now, the dust in the air, her incapacious lungs; she coughed to calm herself; she felt lost, and it was something to do. She coughed again and again, held up her hand asking the man to give her a moment. She was buying time to collect herself. Her heart hammered in her chest, the way it used to before she took the stage at the Lazy Lion. Then, Abdullah had watched and adored her, courted her shamelessly. From beneath the register, the jeweler procured a tiny bottle of water. She thanked him, then took a sip.

She watched her daughter standing outside the heavy glass door and holding her bracelet up to the sun. Each time it flashed, Mariam smiled. Rosalie turned back to the jeweler. There it was, caught in her lungs, tangled around her heart: anger.

"How many pieces of jewelry has my husband bought from you in the last year? I want to know. Pearls? Gemstones? Necklaces or bracelets?"

"I . . . I don't really know, madam . . ."

"Surely you have a record. Abdullah al-Baylani is an important man and you said yourself he's your favorite customer. I know you remember every time he's been in your shop. Come on now, tell me. Maybe I'll become your best customer."

The Yemeni laughed nervously, his eyes darting from side to side as if looking for another merchant to step in and save him.

She locked eyes with him. "You're already involved in this, sir. You might as well cooperate."

The call of the muezzin broke over the tops of the trees, the nasal call to prayer that Rosalie could recite in her sleep. The Yemeni picked up his prayer rug and stepped through the door, ushering her forward with a wave of the hand. Reluctantly, she stepped outside. He fumbled with the lock, and when it finally clicked into place, he raced away from them in the direction of the central mosque. As she watched him go, Rosalie felt the muscles in her neck relax. She took Mariam by the hand.

"Let's go," Rosalie said. "Let's go home."

She thrust the small maroon gift bag containing the empty jewelry box into Mariam's hand. As they walked toward the side street where Raja was parked, Mariam swung it back and forth, humming a song Rosalie didn't know. Silently, she dared any religious policeman to tell her that she should be at home praying. She clenched her fists and waited for the confrontation, but no one bothered them. They probably sensed the anger in her step, each stride long and purposeful. In the dry air, she could feel the bags under her eyes, which no night cream could hide. Perhaps it was best to walk in ugliness today. The day she learned that her husband was celebrating wedding anniversaries with someone other than her.

Raja got out of the car and opened her door, then Mariam's. It was an hour-long drive home to Al Dawoun and she didn't want to start back. There was nothing but the tomb of a house waiting for her. Last winter, after returning from a trip to Italy with trunks of new things, she'd begun to realize that she was decorating her house as if she were to be mummified in it. A crypt discovered thousands of years later with her perfectly preserved gems, hammered gold pots, and her wrinkled, eyeless face.

Rosalie stared out the car's window while Mariam occupied herself with texting her friends. One of the girls was planning a party for her, complete with a DJ who was the girl's twelve-year-old brother.

All those years living side by side with Abdullah, not effortlessly, certainly, but contentedly most of the time. She had granted him his other indiscretions, moving beyond them in a way that had made her proud. At the end of the day he had belonged to her, their marriage a place they could retreat to, a bond that had set her apart from the unknown others. But how do you react to the discovery of another *wife*? The jeweler had said wedding anniversary after all. It could only be *wife*.

She undid her seat belt and slid across the backseat until she was pressed against her daughter. Taking Mariam's hand, she gave a hard squeeze, brought it to her mouth, and grazed her lips across the knuckles. "Umma," Mariam said, annoyed. She squirmed free and resumed texting.

But maybe not. Maybe she was being paranoid. Abdullah had lots of brothers, and they were all rich, all with wives, many with mistresses. Abdullah might have made the purchase for one of them, to surprise one of the wives, or for discretion's sake. He was her Abdi. They were playful with each other. Perhaps they lacked fiery passion, but after more than twenty-seven years of marriage, who didn't? But the love was there, the deep affection.

Outside the car's window, the low dunes stretched to the horizon, broken by tufts of gray desert plants. Near the Gulf, the dunes had been whittled down and swept by the wind, grain by grain, into the sea. There was patience evident in the desert. It moved slowly, spreading over ancient trade routes until one day, centuries later, the frankincense route through Arabia was buried under a matrix of sand, whole cities lost along the way. History happened that way—slowly, each small human devastation crushed by its slow-rolling weight. Off on a far dune, Rosalie spotted a single camel moving lazily along the ridge, evoking an ache for something lost. It was the feeling she used to get while reading *National Geographic* in her doctor's office in Texas. All those photographs, so terribly exotic, didn't bring the far worlds closer to her. Instead, they made her acutely conscious of her difference and distance. Her awe was uncomfortable and her quiet appreciation lonely. She knew she would never be a part of a naming ceremony or a tribal coffee; she could only have it two-dimensionally, for it wasn't rightfully hers. The camel continued its plod across the horizon. Rosalie looked away, but the ache remained.

Heading back toward the Diamond Mile along the old Airport Road, the car rolled past the huge State Oil compound where she had grown up before moving to Texas. She would find him first thing, ask him directly. Secrets need shadows to thrive, and she would shine a spotlight on the onyx pendant and see what lived beneath it. As she watched the compound pass outside the car window, she felt a jolt of anger. If he had compromised what they'd built, she wasn't positive she could stop herself from reaching for the nearest kitchen knife. How foolish she had been to return to the Kingdom with him all those years ago. She had allowed her nostalgia for a place and time that no longer existed dictate her life's most important decision. Yes, she'd been in love with Abdullah, but how much of that love had been predicated on the idea that he could take her back to that distant place of her childhood? Look where chasing after memories had gotten her—stuck between worlds without a strong footing in either one. Rosalie closed her eyes and felt the *ca-thunk*, *ca-thunk*, *ca-thunk* of the car as it passed over the bumpy road.

As they neared home, dread settled in her stomach. She knew what he was capable of—Abdullah, with all of that life in him. The jokes, the looks, the money that simply would not stop reproducing itself. Women noticed those things. They appreciated those things. And Abdullah had trouble denying himself. Entitlement reigned in him. How could it not? For a moment, she thought she would be sick. She cracked the window and waited for the feeling to pass.

She wondered if Abdullah had come to her with his shared body, wanting comfort. What was the woman's face like? Had Rosalie passed her in the market or the mall? She could barely consider these questions. She dropped her head into her hands, her shoulders heaving silently. A sob emerged from the deepest part of her chest. The crux of the problem was, she loved Abdullah.

Mariam looked up from her phone.

"Umma, what is it?" She undid her seat belt and slid across the slick leather seat, putting her hand on the back of Rosalie's neck.

"It's nothing," she said, wiping at her eyes with the sleeve of her abaya. "I'm just happy you're here."

ABDULLAH WAS IN his study when she found him. He was bent over an open desk drawer, his back to her. She went around to the front of the desk, like a secretary come to announce an appointment. She would be businesslike, at least until she had confirmed her suspicions. She cleared her throat and he turned to look at her.

"You smell of za'atar," he said. "Come here, za'atarooni." He waved her over to him.

"You always knew how to flatter a girl, didn't you?"

She said this without a smile.

"What did you find at the market this time?" he asked.

"No, I think the question is, what did you find at the market? I hear you've been buying ugly onyx pendants there, and I imagine it's not to punish me. You're too cheap to spend that kind of money just to make fun."

Abdullah's face fell, and she knew then that it was true.

"Did you find her at the market, too? Buy her like a little slave girl?"

"Habibti," he started.

"It hasn't been that long since men could do that. Are you keeping a concubine, Sheikh Abdullah?"

Her voice was filled with cruelty and contempt, which surprised her. She had never spoken to her husband in that tone before, but then again, she had not known that she was to become the senior wife, mother of his children, or whatever title he would give her as appeasement. Abdullah was silent for several minutes. Outside, she heard a lawnmower kick on. She closed her eyes, willed herself to faint. It was too painful that the rest of the world kept moving while her life was ravaged.

"Rosie, I was waiting for the right time to tell you. And she's not a concubine. Please don't insult her. She's my wife, before God."

" 'Before God?' Don't you dare hang this on religion, Abdullah. The world would be an ugly place if we all did the things our good books say we can." She paused. "How long has it been?"

"Two years."

"Jesus."

She felt bile rising in her throat. She wanted to run at him, shove him back against the bookshelf, to make him hold her or push her away. But the large walnut desk was in the way, and she felt bound to where she stood, exhausted by his confession and all that it meant for their family. The sun spilled into the room, just like it did every other day. She fixed her eyes on the empty sleeve of her husband's shirt, where she knew his arm stopped just before the knob of his wrist. She didn't even know how he'd lost his hand all those years ago. For a while, she'd probed for an explanation, but he was secretive about the circumstances. Now it seemed like further proof that she had absolutely no idea who her husband was. For all she knew, a furious mistress could have sawed off his hand.

He'd been married to another woman for *two years*. Her next question no longer mattered. She smoothed down her skirt, then turned and walked toward the door. That question was *why*, but after two years, it was too late to ask why. Instead, she grabbed a jade bookend from the shelf, turned and heaved it toward him. He moved easily out of the way, which only further infuriated her.

"Pig!" she shouted. Then, more quietly, "You've ruined us."

UPSTAIRS IN HER bathroom, she locked the door and then lay down on the thick, cream-colored rug that covered the tile. It smelled of the rose-scented detergent that Abdullah insisted they use because it reminded him of his mother. Rosalie turned her cheek to one side and waited until she no longer felt like vomiting. This took two days.

HER NAME WAS Isra: nocturnal journey, after Muhammad's midnight journey to Temple Mount before his ascent into heaven. She should be named for shadowy things, Rosalie thought. After all, Isra agreed to live in secrecy for years.

After two days on the bathroom floor, Rosalie moved to her room and called for Mariam. Rosalie started to explain about Isra.

"Baba told me," Mariam interrupted. She shifted her eyes to the floor and folded the hem of her sleeve into a point.

"Tell me you didn't know about this before, Mariam," Rosalie said.

"La, Umma. But I know who she is, I think. Isra is not a common name."

Rosalie was impatient. "What do you mean, you think? Either you knew of her or you didn't."

"I didn't, I swear. But last summer . . . I thought she was Baba's business partner."

"Where?"

"Doha. When Faisal and I went with Baba. You were sick. Remember? You didn't come."

"My God, he has no shame."

"She gave me European soaps."

"From hotels?"

"Yes. I still have them under my sink."

No doubt from the fine hotels that Abdullah and Isra had stayed in all over Europe. The Grand-Hôtel du Cap-Ferrat; Claridge's; The Empire Palace. Rosalie could practically feel the crisp linens; hear the clink of Limoges china in the vaulted dining rooms. She could see them lying together on seaside recliners, clutching sparkling water and wearing broad, comical sunhats, as she and Abdullah had done for countless summers. There would be Champagne and late dinners served on tables docked in the sand. There would be lamp-lit streets haunted by the faint music of buskers. There would be lovemaking, and small, expensive soaps in the shape of shells or stamped out in perfect squares, bearing the imprint of the hotel name and smelling of an herb garden in late summer. She would make Mariam show the soaps to her so she could map out Abdullah's travels, marking each city in which he had betrayed her.

"I canceled my birthday party," Mariam said.

In her misery, Rosalie had completely forgotten. What kind of mother forgot her daughter's birthday party?

"Oh my sweet girl. I'm so sorry . . ."

"I was glad to do it. I can only dance when I'm happy, anyway."

"Your sixteenth will be amazing, I promise. We'll do something really special."

"Can we go to the States so I can get my driver's license?"

"Uncle Randy still has the old Mustang that I learned on. You'll take driver's ed and then we'll do a road trip across Texas." Rosalie reached out and put a hand on her daughter's cheek. She paused.

She knew better than to ask, but she couldn't help it. "Habibti," she said. "Tell me. Tell me about her face."

FROM INSIDE THE darkened car, through the window that she had asked Raja to roll down to get fresh air, Rosalie stared at the Star of Arabia Mall looming at the center of the parking lot. It was evening, and the mall was lit up like a casino. Raja had killed the motor and was flipping through a magazine. Rosalie's friend Lamees was always late, and Rosalie often contemplated building an extra fifteen minutes into her own schedule. Inevitably, though, she could not overcome her near-fascist insistence on punctuality. She believed once you had lost your respect for time, you might as well rocket straight up into the sky, into your daydreams.

Besides, Rosalie appreciated these idle moments in the car. She could sit unseen and watch the women gliding by with their daughters, the older men with their portly wives, and the bands of teenaged boys in Western clothing who gathered together in the parking lot before dispersing to any of the mall's five entrances. There, the teenagers would try to circumvent the mall rules against unaccompanied single men by coaxing an auntie into posing as their mother. Inside, the mall promised shining marble floors, cascading fountains, and also an abundance of soft-smelling girls wandering unescorted from shop to shop. In a way, she wished her son, Faisal, would join in their loitering. Instead, he seemed content to spend all his time driving around with his friend Majid, or listening to tapes of the Koran's suras being sung in clear, mournful tones. As a lapsed Baptist and, more recently, a nonpracticing Muslim, she didn't feel equipped to handle the complications of adolescent piety—hormones, yes, but religious fervor, not as much.

Here, out in the parking lot, sheltered by the silver and black bodies of the cars, the boys' faces were etched with a distinguishing anticipation. Rosalie wondered about her husband's boyhood and how he had satisfied his young desire in Saudi Arabia's climate of oppression. Al Dawoun had been a fishing village then, a half-civilized outpost with many places to hide and many daughters to watch secretly, from the accounting room of his father's first store, along the shallow canals that watered his cousin's date palms in the Hasa oasis. Yes, there, Abdullah had honed his appetites.

Leaning back in her seat, Rosalie pressed her cheek against the cool leather, watching other people come and go, amazed at how effortlessly they catapulted themselves forward to their destinations. It had taken a cajoling call from Lamees to get Rosalie to slide into her sneakers and get into the car. Now at the mall parking lot, she observed the passing people, searching for signs of grief and loss but seeing nothing. We hide our feelings so artfully, she thought. Out of politeness or pride, we do not talk of the things that matter most. She wished she could dig into the beating hearts that passed her and unearth the sorrows that lurked there beneath the disguising flow of blood.

After finding out about Isra, she'd spoken to her brother Randy for the first time since their mother had passed away. Randy had refused to come to Rosalie's wedding, and she knew he still judged her decision as a foolish one. But she called him nonetheless, needing all the help she could get. When she told him the news, she had expected a lecture, but instead he'd just said, "I'm sorry, little sister. I'm so sorry. Come home."

Home, she'd echoed. But I am home. I've been in this place for more than twenty-five years. My children, my friends are here. Despite her parents' efforts to keep her fully expatriated during her childhood on the State Oil compound—just a traveler in their immediate dusty world for as long as it took her father to make enough on the Tapline to retire back to Sugar Land—Arabia insinuated itself in Rosalie. For years after her family left for good, when they were living in a thin-walled development house in East Texas, she could not hear a PA system crackle on without hoping the call to prayer would follow. She had returned to reclaim the place that had been taken from her with the swift motion of the consular officer's letter opener, which he used to remove each family member's visa when they left. Of course, there was also the matter of her love for Abdullah. Both reasons for returning seemed insubstantial now.

Divorce was out of the question. Her parents had passed away, she couldn't even remember how to drive a car, and who would hire a middle-aged college dropout? Furthermore, she loved so much about the harsh, relentless place where she'd spent most of her life. There was beauty in the people's insistence on survival. She dreamed in Arabic. And tucked within the sprawling Baylani family, with their rituals and gatherings and new babies and noise, she had felt more connected to their family than she ever had in the States with her parents. She loved the long Thursday afternoons spent in her sisters-in-law's sitting rooms, where they drank sweet coffee and tea, shared gossip, and marveled at all the beautiful children. When Faisal and Mariam were born, the family was genuinely delighted, and although they remained somewhat formal with Rosalie, at least they were with her, which was more than could be said of her parents, who were so intent on making their point that they'd died while still proving it.

And while her college friends were getting divorced and remarried, she believed she was genuinely happy with her husband and with her life in Saudi Arabia. He was the man she'd thought he was when they got married—charming, a little possessive, smart, ambitious, and confident. She'd surprised herself by how well she fit into his life in the Kingdom. So well that it became *their* life.

There was a rap at the window, and Rosalie glanced over. It was one of the parking-lot boys. He had probably noticed her red hair through the open window and assumed she was an American from the State Oil compound. Those women, housewives from Texas and Louisiana, were known to be more sympathetic to the boys, who were barred from entering the mall without family to reduce the threat that packs of boys would roam and flirt and disturb the order of things. The State Oil women often returned to the parking lot several times to help them get inside. Lamees, who lived on the compound with her husband, said she overheard them talking at the women's group meetings and in the commissary, saying, "Boys will be boys. I don't see what the heck the problem is." I'll tell you what the problem is, Rosalie wanted to reply. This country so deprives its men of women that, by the time they are old enough to marry, one wife is not enough.

Rosalie cracked her door slightly so she could better hear him.

"Aiwa?" she said. She enjoyed the surprise on his face when he heard her Arabic, which was nearly flawless after years shaping her tongue around the heavy Gulf syllables.

"Madam, are you going inside? Please help me to get inside. I just want to buy a pair of sneakers."

She stared at his face. He would not be handsome, his nose a bit too narrow, but there was a pleasing mischief in his eyes.

"Later, perhaps. I'm waiting for a friend."

"Yes, of course. I'll be right over there, if you change your mind." He pointed toward a cluster of young men in the next row. "Shukran," he thanked her.

"Afwan."

Would any of the mall boys marry their mall girls? Rosalie was curious. Was saying you met in a mall the Saudi equivalent of Americans meeting in a bar? She and Abdullah had met in a bar. He was a regular and she was a bartender. Though perhaps he'd become a regular because she was a bartender. These memories of what had come before Isra were painful now.

Lamees's driver honked at them as he pulled alongside their car. Rosalie removed her headscarf from her shoulders and wrapped it carefully around her hair. She was wearing her abaya with the silver embroidery because Lamees said it made her look regal, and she was in desperate need of queenliness tonight. Already, she felt her body become soggy, at risk of settling into her shoes like mud. As she stepped from the car, she turned back and gave a little wave to Raja. He knew the routine. She and Lamees were not there to shop.

They were there in white tennis shoes and sweatpants hidden under their abayas. They would walk the perimeter of the mall four times, or 3.2 miles. It took about an hour.

"Oh, honey," Lamees said, leaning in to give Rosalie a hug.

Rosalie let her body be held, though she didn't have the energy to squeeze back. It used to be that her husband was the one to hug her like this when something terrible had happened. She tried to remember if anything truly awful had happened in the last two years, awful enough for her to crumple into his arms. Thankfully, no. No deaths, no betrayals, not even any illnesses. Her father had died of cirrhosis four years ago. That was her last great tragedy and even that was not enough to make her flop like a fish into Abdullah's arms. Over the previous three decades of his life, Wayne March had gone through a bottle of Jack a day, paid for with his State Oil pension, so the death—a slow pickling—was not a surprise.

"Come on, now," Lamees said. She pushed Rosalie back and held her at arm's length, surveying her face. "Let's fight with a mutawa and flirt with the teenagers. We'll swing from those awful fake vines they've got hanging over the fountain."

"All right," Rosalie said.

Lamees took her hand and led her down the row of cars. The feeling of Lamees's hand brought a sudden clutch of tears just behind Rosalie's eyes, so that she had to widen them in the darkness to keep from crying. They had been friends for ten years. Rosalie had seen Lamees smoking a cigarette in the shadows outside of Safeway, cursing in English into her cell phone. Rosalie had waited until the call was over and then bummed a cigarette. It was not often you saw a woman smoke in public in Saudi, and Rosalie desperately needed someone to talk to. Rosalie had just found out her mother had died, her gangrenous, diabetic body finally rotted to the core.

Inside the mall, the light was golden, expensive, originating from spotlights and melting over the moving people. Behind shop windows, outsized bottles of perfume were elevated on pink boxes, and heavy sequined dresses shaped themselves to faceless mannequins. Even though it was winter, the air-conditioning whooshed through the long corridors, the cold air catching in Rosalie's abaya to reveal her sweatpants beneath. Usually, for modesty's sake, she would tug at the runaway folds of the robe, but tonight, she didn't mind the eyes of the men watching her from the coffee stands. Rosalie and Lamees walked briskly, sidestepping the window shoppers and pumping their arms. Under her layers of clothing, she felt her heart rate rise, the slow spread of heat moving outward from her core. She breathed loudly, in and out, so that people turned to look as she passed.

"Khaled can't believe it," Lamees said after they'd settled into a rhythm. "He just keeps saying 'Abdullah al-*Baylani*?' as if there's been some misunderstanding. He's always seen Abdi as a mentor. A model businessman."

"Oh, he's still a model businessman. No question."

"You know what I mean. A great man, period. Progressive, educated, ahead of his time. Not to mention funny. Khaled loved him. But then, this. It's so messy. Very unlike him."

"Are you done?" Rosalie interrupted. "Because I really don't need reminders of how terrific Abdullah is. I was in love with the man. Am in love with the man, for God's sake."

"Well, we all were, to a degree. He had us fooled. If the diplomats ever find out, they'll be snickering behind his back."

Rosalie shook her head silently in reply and kept her arms moving. They passed a high-end lingerie store, where mannequins wreathed in satin stood on tiptoe and thrust out their breasts. A male salesman was helping a female customer, who was completely veiled; even her hands were gloved as she reached to touch the negligees and corsets. As Rosalie peered into the store to further examine the sight, she collided with a young man who was standing fixed in the middle of the walkway. Recovering from her stumble, Rosalie tried to apologize but he was too busy staring after a group of girls who had just brushed by. The girls glanced back at him but didn't wave. After all, one must be coy. Anything too audacious and men will turn away, ashamed for you.

Vulgar, she thought. Eminently vulgar and pitiable, these girls and boys. Striving after love that would end in heartache and betrayal. Rosalie felt her mouth tighten into a grimace. She felt sorry for them, these girls who saw their destinies in the eyes of the mall boys who would only repay them in suffering. The anger returned in waves. She could see that Abdullah's betrayal of her would live inside her for years.

"You can come and sleep in our guest room anytime," Lamees said. "You just let me know."

"The kids," was all Rosalie could manage by way of explanation. She was not the only one affected by Abdullah's decisions.

Lamees and Khaled were what the Saudis called "liberalayeen." They had a perfectly modern marriage that Rosalie had never thought to be jealous of until now. They both worked, and despite pressure from their families, decided that they didn't want children. When they went abroad, Lamees drove everywhere, trying to make up for the time she'd lost in the Kingdom. They jogged together around the perimeter of the State Oil Compound inside the chain-link fence, where a woman could wear whatever she pleased. Staying with them for a few days would be lovely, Rosalie was sure. Though she'd never stayed over, she knew what kind of host Lamees would be. Gracious, generous, and doting—the kind to leave a carefully selected stack of books on the nightstand in the guest room, alongside a cool glass pitcher of water. Khaled and Lamees's house was not large, but it was filled with luxurious carpets and sophisticated art. An entire wall was covered in gold-and-white damask wallpaper that made Rosalie feel as if she'd entered a ballroom.

They'd nearly completed a full lap and were approaching the gaudy fountain that sprayed three stories into the air as colorful flashing lights formed patterns on the pool tiles below. A few women paused to watch the display, their children peeking from behind their robes and racing between the overlaid benches that ran the length of the fountain. One of the older children chucked a silver coin into the illuminated water before a man in a checkered headdress—a father or an uncle—scolded him.

The light show ended and the families scattered, pushing strollers and guiding the circles of running children slowly down the walkways.

"I thought the hardest part about raising my children was going to be the first years of their lives, protecting their little eggshell heads and feeling like death could swoop in at any moment," Rosalie said, looking into Lamees's face. "But now I think the hardest part is that they will always connect me to their father."

"They are that bridge, regardless of whether or not you want to cross it," Lamees replied. "But our attachments are not only blood and bone. Your life is entwined with his." She paused. "It's not just marriage and children, it's love. Even if it ends, even if you cannot bring yourself to love him anymore, you won't be free. The people we've loved are always with us."

"I don't know if I agree." Rosalie said. "I never think of my old boyfriends anymore, and I'm pretty sure I loved them."

Lamees laughed. "'Pretty sure.' You know how ridiculous that sounds when you put it next to 'love,' right?"

"I suppose. I was happy with them, at least."

"Not the same thing. To me, love is mostly discomfort and melancholy. Realizing you can't escape it, even if you tried."

"Hmm."

Did Abdullah see her as the gatekeeper of his emotions? An intolerable idea for a powerful man, but love does not discriminate. Kings are made into fools who give up their gods, their treasure, their sanity.

Almost overnight, as soon as he took over his father's company, Abdullah had become something larger than anyone had predicted—a being whose thoughts and deeds meant a great deal to an ever-widening swath of people. During his rise, Rosalie had experienced some unease knowing she was becoming just one of many people to whom he had obligations. She felt his adulation fade as he was forced to devote more and more of himself to the princes in Riyadh and the investors in New York and Dubai. But she never considered that he would start to see marriage as an investment, one that should be diversified for his greatest benefit. For that is how he put it to her: *My dear, we will profit by this. We will have greater happiness. You'll have more freedom in your own home. I will treat you with even greater tenderness, because I will remember your generosity to me in my old age.* Now he spoke to her with a certain formality that said, *Our relationship is something recognized more by the state than by me.*

"You know," Lamees said, "Khaled and I both considered having affairs. We'd been married for several years and there was huge relief in the consideration of it. We liked these other people—people we worked with—and the questioning made us feel more normal." She tucked a loose strand of hair back into her casually wrapped headscarf. "The world is filled with cheaters. Even the word 'affair' makes it sound glamorous. Lighter than air. But after we thought about it, we knew it wouldn't be light. It would be heavy, even while it seemingly freed us from the intensity of our bond."

They had completed a second turn and were rounding back toward the fountain. There, Rosalie recognized the boy from the parking lot. He was typing rapidly on the keypad of his cell phone.

Recently, she had watched the bright moon of Abdullah's adoration waning, until it seemed to only reflect light from dying planets—a dull secondhand light. For years, they had been a comfort to each other, but somewhere along the way their marriage had grown functional. Now she could only acknowledge that the devotion upon which she had built her world in the farthest province of a desolate land had dissolved under her feet.

She was sweating as they passed the group of boys. Her abaya fell heavily on her shoulders, the silver thread giving it extraordinary weight. Her feet tangled beneath her and she stumbled, catching

Lamees by the arm. When the boys turned to look, Rosalie stopped and stared back.

"Marhaba, Auntie," the boy said. "You see, I was able to find a friend to let me in."

"Where are your shoes?" she asked.

"What?" He was confused. How quickly he had forgotten his lie to her. She was not in the mood to be lied to, not after being the rube fooled by lies for years.

She reached over and knocked the phone out of his hands. It skidded across the slick tiles at the fountain's side before slipping beneath the water.

"Hey!" he shouted at her. His friends laughed. One of them bent down to fish the phone out of the fountain. A few people standing around the fountain watched with casual interest.

"Leave it," she said. "Leave it, or I'll bring a mutawa over here. You'll be kicked out so fast your head will spin."

The friend dropped the dripping phone back into the water, where it fell with a satisfying *floop*. How pathetic they were, these poor boys who thought that love was something transmitted from a phone, or understood over an instant message.

She thought of the affairs they would have outside their loveless marriages, these electronic marriages arranged for themselves in the air-conditioned, sparkling shopping corridors of this mall, this great and groaning monument to human appetites—greed, lust, envy, all available to these boys.

"I think it's time to go," Lamees said.

Rosalie took Lamees's hand and strode toward the exit. Though her body was porridge, her mind was surprisingly clear. It reminded her of the times she had stayed up all night in college. On the walk home from wherever she had been studying, her body would melt with the force of gravity while her mind nimbly skipped over the events of the previous evening, her senses on hyperdrive. Large dew droplets slipping down blades of grass; a sneeze from somewhere on the fourth floor of a dorm; the dawn moving from black to gray to all the fresh colors of the born day. Dawn had a very distinct smell, not unlike the soap smell of just-washed hands. Vastly different from the choking floral perfumes of the Star of Arabia Mall on this, the fourth night of her new life.

IT WAS MORNING. Rosalie stood on her balcony and surveyed the block. For the fourth night now she had slept alone, while Abdullah vanished to the shadow lands of his second life. She eyed the houses along the Diamond Mile, the strange little country of money peopled with Al Dawoun's elite. There was the Zeid family palace on the right, with its garage of glass bricks; the Amoudi estate; the Sherif compound roofed in red tile imported from Spain. She'd once gone to a wedding party there and had gotten so lost that she'd walked right into the men's sitting room. She managed to squeak, "Excuse me, gentlemen," in her most American Arabic—people tended to forgive social missteps if they knew you were just an American dunce—and steal a look at her bemused husband before backing into the door and then fleeing. She had found her way back to the women following the smell of Chanel perfume and the rustling of elaborate gowns.

Now, looking at the houses, Rosalie had to consider if her co-wife was also a neighbor. Abdullah's father, Abdul Latif, had founded the Diamond Mile neighborhood, so where else would a Baylani live? Rosalie liked to imagine that her husband was not so foolish, but again, how can one gauge the foolishness of a man who has decided he could manage two wives?

On the other side of the sliding-glass door, Yasmin, the Bangladeshi maid, was making the bed. Rosalie hummed an old Emmylou Harris song, quietly. She couldn't remember the words but the melody came back to her; something from her gospel days at Sugar Land First Baptist.

"Yasmin?" she called through the cracked door.

"Yes, madam?"

"Come out here for a moment."

The maid hesitated before stooping to pick up her slippers by the door. She slid the door open, dropped the shoes on the concrete, and stepped into them.

"Yes, madam?" she repeated.

"Tell me. Where does she live? The other madam?"

Yasmin took in a quick breath and put her hand to her ear, a nervous gesture.

"It's all right," Rosalie said. "A good maid serves the family, and you're the best. You were just serving the sheikh, I understand. But now I need you to tell me. Which house is it?"

Yasmin shuffled across the concrete to the pillared ledge of the balcony. She glanced first north, then south along the street, as if to make sure nobody was watching. Then, she lifted her thin arm and pointed south toward the smaller houses clustered at the end of the street.

"The one with the blue tiles?"

"Yes, madam."

DOWNSTAIRS, ROSALIE BEGAN washing a bunch of parsley, moving her hands gently so as not to tear the leaves. These were the small tasks she could still manage. Earlier in the day, close to dawn, she'd heard the garage door slam. It was Faisal, gone again before she could talk to him. She wondered where he and Majid went together so often. It seemed that she hadn't had a proper conversation with her son in months. Now, with the news of Isra, she thought she should sit with him in case he wanted to talk, but she was afraid of what he might say. Since becoming more religious—a shift she hoped was just a phase, the way the popular high school kids in Sugar Land went to sleepaway church camp and loved Jesus because everyone else did—Faisal seemed to glide through the house with an air of haughty superiority about him. He came and went, and when they were in the same room together, she felt the weight of his disdain. She was sure that he'd known about Isra, that it had only fueled his inexplicable but robust contempt for her. Lamees told her it was nothing, just a sixteen-year-old boy setting his boundaries, and Rosalie realized she needed to stop being intimidated by his solemnity. Those contemptuous eyes were half hers, after all. She missed the excitable boy who had lisped out his stories to her, thrilled for the audience generally and glad of her company specifically. Since returning from boarding school, it was as if each word he chose, each step he took, was an audition for the role of *man*. Still, if they had their moment alone, what would she say to him? She had not yet started to weigh her options, and to tell him she would stay and everything would be all right would be an exaggerated smoothing of the waters for his benefit alone.

She glanced at the calendar hanging on the wall by the fridge. It was mid-January, yet she found herself longing for Ramadan, for the pleasures of its deprivation. Its asceticism would match her mood. In addition to not letting food or water pass their lips during the daylight hours of Ramadan, Muslims weren't supposed to have sex. Rosalie never understood the need for this rule. Sex meant sweat, and the igniting of that terrible existential hunger that lovemaking evoked but could never fully satisfy. No sane person would try to have sex while starved. It just wasn't practical. Who could enjoy an act that, by its very nature, required the players to give so completely of their bodies? To let someone else steal your dwindling energies, well, that was just inviting disaster. She finished washing the parsley, dried it, and plucked off a leaf to chew. Despite all that had transpired, Rosalie still had a sexual appetite. Abdullah had been absent so much lately, and she was hungering, though she knew from experience that sex was hardly the cure for desire. It could curb it but not fully satisfy it. She felt that was where people got it wrong, seeking communion, completion, with another broken being. The resulting dissatisfaction was why people smoked or fell asleep or got up to see what was in the fridge after sex. After the disappointing absence of transformation, people needed *things* to fill them up. In her early days of sexual activity (for that was the perfect word for it then, "activity," as it implied the regimented way she approached sex during her early missteps), she'd tried to find fulfillment through any number of these things, sometimes in combination with one another. It wasn't until her first night with Abdullah that she was able to just lie there afterward. She didn't go digging in her fridge or slide out onto the fire escape for a Lucky Strike. She had just felt full and happy, putting her hand on his chest and falling asleep. Maybe that was the problem now—that she'd grown too accustomed to getting that feeling of fullness from someone else. Maybe it was time to admit she needed a crutch, a substance, rather than a single person. Didn't everyone?

Overwhelmed, she put her head down on the cool marble countertop, letting her back sway out behind her. She felt a vein in her forehead throb against the pink veins of the marble. Through it, she could feel the slab from which the stone came, and through that, the entire quarry and, even faintly, the pulse of the sea beneath the boat that brought it over from Italy. She felt small, her connectivity tenuous. Resting there, she tried to forestall the building agitation and gather the stillness.

Another beat passed. She took up the vegetable knife that lay by the sink. Then, she strode to the front door. Once past the door, she walked to the end of the driveway, under the magnificent wooden gates that Abdullah had taken from a centuries-old coral house that developers had razed in Jeddah. She took a left at the road, walking briskly, as if she were going to ask for butter or milk. The sharp Bermuda grass along the roadside poked through her sandals. She marched in time with the steady tick of the sprinklers that lined the planting area in the middle of the street. She thought: "*I am doing. I do.*" The movement felt good, the purpose of one foot going in front of the other. She stopped in front of Isra's house.

Feeling faintly queasy, she pushed the gate open. It groaned on its oversized hinges. She clenched her fist around the vegetable knife, which had grown slick with sweat. She checked the windows, then the garden's layout. An overgrown fig tree shadowed the driveway, creating darkening, gibbous places into which she could slip unnoticed. She stole through the shadows, until she was at the tree's base. She stopped for a moment and stood in the tree's deep shade. Then she plucked a fig from the lowest branch. It was not fig season, so the fruit was withered, folded in on itself. White-knuckled, using the vegetable knife, she cut a large, thin *X* across the fruit's wrinkled belly. She stuck the knife through it and walked to the front door, where she left the fig on the bamboo welcome mat. She turned and started to jog down the driveway.

Just as she reached the small wooden gate, a voice called out.

"Rosalie? Is that you?"

So she knows my face, Rosalie thought. All this time and she's known my foolish, ignorant face. Then, remembering advice her father had given her when they were vacationing in Yellowstone—if you don't move, it can't see you—she stood still, panic starting its slow climb up from her stomach in all languages. Shit. Khara. Merde.

"Rosalie? Is everything all right? Would you like some of my figs? They're not in season now, but when they are, they just fall to the ground and rot. I've no one to eat them. Abdullah hates . . ." Isra's voice trailed off, as if she knew she shouldn't have mentioned his name.

Slowly, Rosalie turned her head, then her shoulders, her hips, her feet, until finally she faced Isra. She called up her best beauty-queen smile.

"Hello!"

"How are you doing?" Isra asked, her head tilted in that warm way that some women had.

The bitch speaks perfect English, she thought. She'd heard from Mariam that Isra was well educated, that she spoke four languages and had been an interpreter for Arafat when she was a student. In another life, Isra would be a woman Rosalie admired. She took a few steps back toward the doorway, wishing she hadn't left the knife stuck in the fruit, evidence that proved her insanity beyond reasonable doubt.

"Figs. Yes. I—I was just coming to ask you for a bushel or so. I'm making . . . a dessert for tomorrow night. But I forgot they aren't in season."

"Oh, it looks as though you've forgotten your knife on the doorstep," Isra said.

She was so polite. So dignified. But she could afford restraint, couldn't she? Isra had the luxury of even-temperedness for so many reasons: her beauty, her relative youth, the fact that she slept with Abdullah most nights. Rosalie looked at her. That beautiful, calm face, elegant in its lines. The sweep of black hair. Rosalie marched up the slight incline of the driveway until she was a few feet from the woman.

"Now, you listen to me," she said. "I won't call you by your name. I didn't come here for your figs. I came here to let you know how much you are truly despised. I know it may not seem like much. To be hated by a single person. But I want you to know that you have stolen a life."

She watched Isra's face change. Yes, there it was: pain. Or, at the very least, discomfort. Rosalie continued.

"How could you do it, knowing about his family?" She gestured violently with her right hand, her voice rising. "You'll never be anything but a second helping, taken by Abdullah when he got greedy. Remember that. You were chosen by a man having a life crisis."

A figure appeared in the doorway. She blinked. Her husband. *Their* husband. Wearing a silk robe that she had given him on their twentieth anniversary. The robe, bought for him out of love and anticipation of many mornings together when they would dust sleep from their eyes, don fine robes, and drink strong coffee in the courtyard.

"Rosalie?" he said. "What on earth are you doing here?"

"I decided to take some figs from this tree. After all, we don't have a fig tree, and according to the Koran, you are supposed to provide for all wives equally. So I am just taking my share."

"In January?"

"Is there a problem with that? Because I'm sure the mutawi'in would be happy to know about such unequal treatment. It wouldn't be good for your image at all, dear."

She turned on her heel and went back down the driveway. "I'll send Yasmin for the figs. Expect her within the hour."

BACK AT THE house, Rosalie collected herself before calling for Yasmin.

"Would you please go to the other madam's house and pick the figs from her tree?" she asked.

"But they aren't in season . . ." Yasmin hesitated.

"It doesn't matter. Take whatever you find."

"Yes, if you say so. Does she . . . ?"

"Yes, she's expecting you."

After Yasmin left the room, Rosalie laughed bitterly to herself. Plenty of neighbors screwed around with each other in the States, but there was something infinitely kinder in a culture that recognized such behavior as shameful. Where unfaithful lovers stole back and forth under cover of night, admitting that their behavior caused damages. In the Kingdom, it was legal; her suffering was sanctioned by the government, by the Prophet himself. If she became angry, she would be seen as graceless. If she yielded to sadness, then she would be pathetic. Impossible moments like this made her wonder if, all those years ago, she had sacrificed too much.

Still, she never would have guessed he would go and do a thing like this. Not Abdi, who hated conflict. It was utter madness, and she could only imagine what his sisters and the brothers' wives were saying about it. No one of his generation in the family had taken a second wife; the family considered itself beyond such things. What could have possibly possessed him?

But of course, she knew. Love. Only love made you into such a fool. And she knew it better than anyone, didn't she? Before Abdullah, she had been shrewd. Since Abdullah, it had been about feeling, the way of the senses, of instinct. It was a dangerous way, but at its height, it had been glorious. Love had made her let go a little. But she could no longer trust her heart, her body, herself so wholly. Now she had to try to fetter her passions, to reintroduce wariness. To once again lie in a narrow bed, a single body, complete in itself.

TWO

WHEN DAN WAS buzzed into the driveway in front of Abdullah al-Baylani's mansion, he looked at Rosalie al-Baylani standing beneath the front archway and hesitated. Perhaps he should turn the car around. He didn't want to witness this transformation of a living, breathing love into something more spectral. Because that's what was happening under the archway. He knew it, and the thought saddened him.

When Abdullah called him that afternoon, there had been such desperation in his voice that Dan had gotten into his car and driven the five miles from his apartment at the Prairie Vista compound to Abdullah's Italianate villa. He'd rarely heard Abdi so worked up, going on about figs and how Rose had just embarrassed herself terribly and he couldn't stand to be in the same country with her anymore and would Dan please come drive him to Bahrain so he could get soused?

It was after six o'clock on a Thursday evening, which in Al Dawoun, Saudi Arabia, meant the heart of the weekend. Dan did not feel like taking part in Abdullah's personal fireworks display. Dan would prefer, in fact, to strip down to his undershirt and spend the night eating buttered macaroni drowned in rooster sauce and watching *The Sopranos* on illegal satellite. But he went, impelled partly by their thirty-odd years of friendship and partly by his sympathy for Abdullah's wife, or rather his *first* wife, Rosalie.

Dan got out of the car and shut the door quietly behind him. He walked up the long driveway toward the house, noticing how the windows had caught fire in the rose-colored light of the waning day. Such an authoritatively grand house spoke fluently on behalf of the family inside, and Dan felt a twinge of jealousy. He felt sure that a family, no matter their trouble, could cast no shadows within such walls. In fact, he might go so far as to argue that it was the exonerating beauty of the estate that was keeping the Baylani family together at the moment, when they seemed so close to breaking open like a geode, exposing all of their jagged edges. As he approached, Dan walked close to the flowerbeds that lined the driveway. Sprinklers ratcheted along their coils, misting the lawn so that it gleamed under the January sun.

Dan felt that it was a shame to disintegrate the peace of such an evening with anger, but he supposed that people did not really choose how and when they got angry. It just happened. In the three years since Carolyn had filed for divorce, it occurred with discomfiting frequency. To escape the disintegration by anger of other beautiful things, and for the paycheck, Dan had moved back to Saudi Arabia. Still, anger and regret had a way of trumping geography to work on a person; some mornings, he felt chewed over, as if rage, like some sort of attack dog, had set on him in the vulnerable moments of sleep so that he awoke already ranting with all the artfulness of the groggily embittered. He would lie in bed, staring at the ceiling and listening to the movement of the world outside the condo. In those moments, he felt alone and very far from his children, Eleanor and Joe, so lacking in energy or direction that he even contemplated a passive form of suicide—starvation, sun exposure. He could drive out to Jebel Al Dawoun, lie down at the lip of a cave, and just wait until his heart stopped beating.

As he neared the Baylanis' front door, Dan could hear the growl of their voices, punctuated by Abdullah's shushings. The two of them looked small standing in the lee of the enormous arch, where the evening shadows played against their faces and made their teeth glow white. Abdullah was glancing around as if he thought the neighbors might be peering at them over the fifteen-foot walls. If paranoia was the Saudi pastime, then Abdullah was their Roger Maris. But Dan didn't give him grief for it, because he knew that Abdullah had perfected the game out of necessity. In the Kingdom, reputation was everything, and the country's rich built empires on it.

Rosalie jabbed her finger repeatedly in the direction of Abdullah's chest. They were both talking at the same time. Seeing Dan, Abdullah threw up his arms.

"Alhamdulillah. You're here. Let's go."

"Dan Coleman, you go home right now. Don't take another step this way. Things are fixing to get rough here in a minute."

Rosalie had slipped into her Texas drawl, an accent that she used like a shield when dealing with bad situations. Tough girl, Panhandle mama, rodeo queen. How could Abdullah have done this to her? This woman who had given up everything—family, religion, homeland—to marry him. Even now, standing on her front step in the unflattering light of the desert sun without a spot of makeup on her forty-seven-year-old face, she was striking. Her strong jaw gave way to a soft mouth whose upper lip peaked in a perfect cupid's bow. When they'd all hung out in college, he'd often found himself staring at that mouth. It was something a man couldn't help, noticing the features that made a woman beautiful. Now Rosalie smiled a tight, mocking half-smile. Her hair, dyed red to hide the gray but once naturally the color of molten lava, fell over her shoulders in a tangle. She had on a blue cotton robe cinched tightly at the waist. Dan could tell that she wasn't wearing a bra by the way her breasts gently sloped downwards, and it brought forth a wanting in him, more for the familiarity of a robed female body than for the breasts themselves. Sometimes the longing was too much. He closed his eyes for a moment and let the feeling pass.

"Dan, stay. We're going to leave in just a minute. As soon as I can get my wife to calm down."

"Yes, like you; you're always so calm, aren't you?" she said. "So cool and collected, surveying the messes you make. Dan, can you believe it? He doesn't blink, though he can see what this is doing to me. I had to learn about this mess from a jeweler at the souq. *A jeweler.* All because my husband didn't have the guts to tell me himself." She paused, put a hand on her hip. "And what about you, Coleman? How long have you known about this? How long have you been chuckling about what a fool I am?" Anger bloomed a blotched red on her cheeks.

Dan shifted uncomfortably. He felt implicated through his friendship with Abdullah, even though he'd only learned about Isra a few weeks before. Abdullah had kept her in a seaside condominium in Doha for the last couple of years, making monthly trips under the guise of business. He'd been busy all right. It must have been exhausting, maintaining the lie for so long. Last month, around the time he finally told Dan about his double life, he'd moved Isra into a house a block away from this villa because he was tired of traveling back and forth between countries, and he'd been trying to figure out a way to tell Rosalie about her new neighbor. Now it seemed someone had done the dirty work for him.

"Listen, I don't want to get involved, Rosie," Dan said.

"My God, this country is infuriating. No one wants to get in-fucking-volved!"

Dan was scared for her now, her body shaking from the force of her anger.

"That's enough, Rosalie," Abdullah said. "Go inside."

"You know what happens when no one gets involved?" she said. "When no one tells the truth? People wind up splattered on the wall, and then all the people who were so busy minding their own goddamn business get to act sorry while cleaning up the mess. I think it's disgraceful. And Dan, if you knew about this, then by God, you ought to be ashamed. And you," she pointed at Abdullah. "You've been hiding at your other house out of cowardice, too scared to face me."

Abdullah raised his hand in the air to silence her. He glowered. It was clear that whatever he had permitted by way of verbal abuse from her, whether out of guilt or sympathy, had just become impermissible. "If you ever speak to me like that again, you'll be on the first plane back to Houston. Do you understand me?"

Rosalie was quiet, but she held his gaze. She had pursed her lips into so thin a line that they almost disappeared from her face. Without them, she looked cruel.

"Now, if you will just calm down and think about this like a rational person, I know that you will see that I've done nothing outside of my rights," Abdullah continued. "When you chose to marry me and move here, you told me that you were ready to accept my culture. You said you loved my culture. Well, this is my culture."

It was early evening, and the neighborhood was silent save the *ch-ch-ch* of the sprinklers. It seemed Rosalie was barely breathing. Finally, she spoke.

"No one takes a second wife nowadays. Not one of your brothers or friends has taken one. It's what villagers do!" She paused. "What's happened to you, Abdullah? What's happened to my husband? My husband was an honest man. A loving man." Her voice cracked.

Dan should not have come. It wasn't his business, this private sadness. It really wasn't, no matter how many times Rosalie might accuse him of negligence. He knew better than anyone that once a marriage springs a leak, there's not a soul in the world to put a patch to it except the two people involved.

"Please, Habibti. I am still those things," Abdullah said. "You must understand, Isra doesn't change anything between us. I will give to you both equally. You will not want for anything, I swear to you."

"No. You're wrong, Abdullah. That's where you're wrong. You're not a cake. You can't be divided up. Love has to be more whole than that."

He reached for her hand, but she turned away and walked toward the door.

"It can never be what it was," she continued. "It won't ever be that pure again."

She seemed resigned now, small-shouldered in the shadow of the archway. She turned and went inside, the sound of the lock loud, as if punctuating her statement. Abdullah exhaled. They stood and listened to the sounds of the night: frangipani flowers opening up; sweet beans falling from the branches of carob trees; the chattering of larks, bluethroats, and wheatears. Nature had an infuriating indifference to human entanglements. Sometimes, a blue sky was enough to make Dan smash a glass.

"I need a drink," Abdullah said. "Let's try to get to the causeway before the rush."

"Too late for that. Every sucker in the Eastern Province is heading to happy hour in Bahrain."

"It doesn't matter. We'll use my pass and take the VIP lane."

They drove in silence for several minutes. Dan waited for Abdullah to say something about Rosalie, to excuse himself, or her. Back in Texas, they had always fought loudly, as if by making it a show and inviting other people to witness it, they could distance themselves from the actual struggle. Rosalie had been a fairly popular performer on campus, with her deep, stripped-down voice that reminded Dan of the great torch singers. On Saturdays, she sang in the dive where she also tended bar, the Lazy Lion. There was a guy on sax and another on piano. It was never a studied pursuit of hers, just something she did for fun. So many people had loved her—the tall, pretty girl with the mass of red hair Even though he was two years in with Carolyn by that point, he had felt a tug toward Rosalie, a little crush he'd never needed to confess because everyone shared the same feelings.

Rosie's taste for the dramatic raised her arguments with Abdullah to a form of high art, both of them gesturing wildly. Sometimes, Abdullah would just spank her, in utter seriousness, right in front of everyone, and then they would collapse all over each other with laughter. Dan and Carolyn, and whoever else happened to be around, would applaud the slapstick but roll their eyes about it later when they were alone.

"So I guess you told her, then," Dan said, pausing for a reply. When none came: "I thought you were going to wait until Faisal had gone to university."

"Yeah, well, an idiot Yemeni jeweler was bragging to her about what good friends we were, what a good customer I was. And he made the mistake of asking Rosalie how she had liked the anniversary present that I bought for her. Only, our anniversary is in May. She's not stupid."

"The man was understandably confused."

"The man is a meddlesome Hadrami fool."

"Fine, ya Sheikh."

"Yallah."

ON THE CAUSEWAY, hundreds of cars were backed up, the line reaching almost to the halfway point between the two countries. Suburbans brimming with families and sleek sedans packed with single men were gunning to get to Bahrain to start the weekend in a place where the religious police weren't going to be looking over their shoulders. There, they could go to the movies or a restaurant where unrelated men and women could sit together, or a one-star hotel where easy virtue was the house specialty. Horns blared loudly and music came in bursts as Dan and Abdullah whizzed past the stalled cars. Using Abdullah's VIP transit pass, they made it quickly through security. Abdullah looked at Dan.

"Princeton Club?"

Dan shrugged, then steered the car down the coastal road to the abandoned Gulf Oil compound, where the dilapidated clubhouse served as an old boys' club that came alive every weekend, its sliding-glass doors lit from within, casting golden rectangles of light on the sand outside. It had been named by one of the earliest and most notorious of the old boys, Braxton Neel, who decided to honor his alma mater by slapping her name on his little Gulf fraternity. The compound's current role in the community solely depended on the continued apathy of various governing forces. Dan didn't ask questions. After spending the better part of twenty years working in Saudi Arabia, minus the years when he'd gone back to the States to watch his marriage fail and his savings evaporate, Dan had learned that the curious and the questioning were the first to be surplused, the last to attend the consular dinners for the petty diplomats and businesspeople. At one point in his life he had taken pride in his contrarian ways, but now, at the age of fifty-two, he was content to be a company man sitting in a company chair, banking his small but untaxed paychecks and dreaming of the cedarwood cabin abutting the Pedernales River that would be his first purchase upon returning stateside. A place where he'd have a fridge just for beer and a cabinet just for whiskey and sturdy bookshelves that he would fill to the top.

"I don't know how you do it," Dan said. He couldn't *not* bring it up, although he was sure that Abdullah didn't want to talk about the fiasco.

"What?"

"Two wives. Must be exhausting."

"I enjoy both of their company. I love them both equally."

"Abdi." He paused, glancing at his friend, who looked back, eyebrows raised. "Have you lost your mind?" There. He had finally said what he'd been thinking in the weeks since Abdullah had told him.

"If I wanted angry accusations, I could have stayed at the big house."

"I mean, what gave you the idea in the first place?" Seeing Rose's shock and anger had produced a stronger reaction in Dan than when

Abdullah had first told him about Isra. Then, it had seemed an abstract thing, like it would somehow come to make sense. But of course it couldn't. Watching Rose grasp after words, watching her crumple with hurt, Dan saw it for exactly what it was: absurd cruelty, a total fuck-you to rational thought, an act of extreme cowardice.

"I fell in love with Isra. It's permitted, Dan. In Riyadh . . ."

"Hell with Riyadh. You and I both know the Najd is a different story. Some people are living in the eighth century there."

"I'm just saying, it's done, and it's permitted." Abdullah was talking toward the glass of the window, avoiding eye contact, his voice tired. "And I didn't want to say good-bye to her."

"It's selfish, you know that?" He paused. They had an easy relationship, lots of jokes and bullshitting and remembering when they'd been young and dumb. He knew he was crossing some kind of line with this talk, but he couldn't help himself. "I wonder how Rosalie's going to cope with everything."

Dan rolled his window down farther. The car suddenly felt too small for the both of them. He rested his left hand on the door so his fingers hung outside the car, a gesture that always made him think of long summers in Texas and the red-striped Chevy truck he drove in high school.

"It's not as though someone died."

"Why didn't you just get a divorce?"

"Divorce is a scourge. It would reflect badly on the family."

"What does that even mean?" Dan said.

"Look, I still love Rosalie. She's the mother of my children. But with Rosalie, I always felt like I was lacking some sort of understanding. And after 9/11, I couldn't even travel to my wife's country."

"Don't go blaming politics for the bust-up of your marriage. That's straight horseshit and you know it."

"OK, you want to know the truth, wise guy?" Abdullah stretched his good hand along the car door, strummed his fingers, and stared out the window.

"Yeah. I do."

Dan had a deep affection for Rosalie. To him, she would always be the redhead with the Chiclet smile serving them Heineken at the Lazy Lion, laughing while Abdullah recited Qabbani with all the melodrama of a lovesick fool: *When I love you, I march against ugliness, against the kings of salt, against the institution of the desert!* The cowboy patrons who were watching the Longhorns on the television had been completely befuddled by the poetry-spouting man in their midst, and rustled their boots nervously against their barstools. Dan had laughed until his eyes watered.

"The truth is, I feel like I hardly know who she is anymore. I hardly recognize her."

"Maybe if you dug out that old leather jacket she used to wear . . ."

"I'm serious. Don't turn this into a joke. She's become"—he paused, then looked at Dan—"a Saudi wife."

"Wasn't that the idea, though? That after a while, she'd adapt?"

"If you're a Saudi man and you marry an American woman, the last thing you want is for her to become a Saudi wife. Otherwise, why would you go through all the trouble with the family?"

Abdullah had defied his entire family, battled them tirelessly for months to gain their approval for his marriage to Rosalie, the Amreekiyah. In May 1978, the month Abdullah earned his second master's degree, they got married. He was twenty-eight, she was twenty, just another coed dropping out for love. His family had been furious. They'd had a wife picked out for him for years and only gave their permission for his continued studies in the States because they trusted him to come home and marry their pick immediately. And Abdullah had kept his word, secretly dating Americans, Iranians, even a Spaniard, but never entertaining the idea of marriage. To him, marriage was for Basma or Nura or whoever it was his family had waiting. But then Rosalie had roared into his life with all the subtlety of a Mack truck, and he'd discovered promises were harder to keep when love was part of the picture.

When the two of them arrived in the Kingdom in September of

that year, after Abdullah's student visa officially expired, he had made it his personal mission to force each and every family member, no matter how disapproving, to look him in the eye and say mabrook: *congratulations.*

"It's just . . ." Dan paused. "You fought so fucking hard for her. You risked everything. Your dad was threatening to leave you out of the business. *The laws of the tribe.* Remember? You fought all that for her."

"What my family did was all a show. I knew they loved me more than they disliked my choice of wife."

An insect smashed wetly against the windshield. Dan thumbed the wipers so that blue liquid sprayed up to clean away the guts.

"I don't know, it seemed pretty real to me. You're telling me your dad flying all the way to Austin to try and bring you to your senses was just fun and games?"

"The old man had to stand up for propriety. But he knew love when he saw it, and he relented."

"Exactly. He knew true love when he saw it. You guys were a fucking galaxy back then. It's why I just don't understand this."

"That's what I'm trying to tell you, habibi. We *were.* Of all people, you should understand. Love changes. It fades. You think I couldn't have been happy with a woman like Rosalie? Of course I could. But over the years, she became less and less like Rosalie. She threw away that jacket years ago; she has her clothes made in Paris now. She uses the word 'summer' as a verb. She started to like the money a little too much."

"Abdi, *you* like your money. You can't fault her for wanting to enjoy what's hers."

"It's different. One of the things I loved about her in Texas was that she didn't give a shit about money. She was just Rosalie and I was just Abdullah. And I'm not divorcing her now, because I still love her, and I have hope that someday we'll be able to get back to that simple place."

Dan shook his head. Isra wouldn't exactly help in that regard, but his friend did seem to be in love. Was this way kinder? Seeking love elsewhere until the first love recovers its sheen?

"Did you really have to wait two years to tell Rosie?" Dan asked. "Why didn't you own up to it from the beginning?"

"The truth is, I didn't want to hurt her. I thought it would be easier to just keep going and pretend that nothing had changed."

Dan closed his hands tight around the steering wheel and gunned the engine a little. Yeah, it was easier. Carolyn had once told him that she'd fallen out of love with him years before she filed the papers. If she hadn't finally acted, they could have gone on living together out of habit, unhappily, unwilling or unable to do anything about it.

As they pulled in past the chain-link fence that surrounded the compound, the sun was setting over the finger of water that separated Bahrain from Saudi Arabia. There were a few other cars in the parking lot, but none that Dan recognized. When Gulf Oil had closed down the beach compound, instead of razing the old structures it waited instead for the region's unforgiving climate to demolish the rice-paper houses, pieces of the property disintegrating into the salt-white waters of the Gulf year by year. The roof of the clubhouse was a patchwork and the walls had joined in the slow erosion. The company left behind hundreds of heavy, wood-framed couches and chairs that had filled the temporary houses and offices.

This January night, there were ten habitués clustered around the room, forming small circles as people tried to make conversation over the sound of Fairuz's voice blaring out of the boom box by the door. Abdullah had brought the system with him on one of their trips out to the bungalow, and he kept an ever-rotating stash of CDs at the clubhouse—mostly old classics like Umm Kulthum and Fairuz, but also a few new Lebanese singers like Haifa Wehbe, whose cleavage provided fodder for Arab morning show hosts but whose music, in Dan's opinion, fell well short of tolerable. He recalled so vividly the night he and Abdullah had gone to see Fairuz at Jesse Jones Hall in Houston. They had met just a few weeks before when Abdullah was fresh off the boat, waiting in line for food at the student union. Abdullah was standing in a sea of people rushing around grabbing tacos and barbecue sandwiches, looking completely befuddled. "Avoid the Frito pie," Dan had advised him. They'd shaken hands, and he'd guided Abdullah to Mama Lopez's taco truck, where he'd bought him two tacos al carbon loaded with white onion and cilantro. At first, Abdullah had been suspicious, but soon he was cramming the food in his mouth as if he hadn't eaten in a week. Dan had waited until the following week to introduce him to Mama's infamous habañero salsa. Afterward, they'd had to stand on the sidewalk blowing their noses for a full fifteen minutes before they dared venture to class.

Soon, it was Abdullah's turn to shock Dan's system. When Abdullah invited him to the Fairuz concert, the Middle East was a cluster of countries on a map, a montage of sand and veils and camels if he stretched his imagination a little. The concert was part of Fairuz's huge 1971 North American tour, and when she sang "Le Beirut," her arms spread wide and the sleeves of her white dress cascading like gossamer, Abdullah had choked up. At that moment, Dan knew that this was a man to be friends with.

Things were dismal for Arabs then, Abdullah had explained. With the dream of unity destroyed in 1967 and Nasser dead, Beirut seemed to be the one promise Allah had kept. It wasn't until 1975 that the city fell to civil war, neighbors murdering one another and shelling the centuries-old buildings all to hell.

After the show, Dan and Abdullah had tried to sweet-talk their way backstage, fueled by fantasies of Fairuz's midnight eyes, her goddess voice. The Lebanese security detail had listened to Abdullah's plea before spitting on the ground and saying, "Khaleeji dog." Abdullah had attempted to coldcock the man, but the guard caught his stump mid-swing and then yelled as if he'd touched a stove, pushing the pale, handless arm away from him forcefully. The mysterious phantom hand. Abdullah had told Dan he'd lost the hand in a horse-riding accident—a bad spill in the desert, the horse rolling onto his hand before stumbling back onto its legs. It sounded far-fetched, but Dan didn't press him. The lack of a hand was story enough.

Someone had dimmed the lights in the bungalow of the Princeton Club so that the yellowing plaster walls, the painted concrete floor, and the faded company furniture took on a romantic, rather than desperate, air of dilapidation. Dan went to the bathroom, and by the time he came out, Abdullah had already made himself a part of the circle of revelers, his hand resting on a man's shoulder as he listened to him intently. After a few minutes, both men tipped their heads back and laughed. Abdullah had always been that way—eminently sociable and lighthearted. Rosalie teased him for his lack of Arab fatalism, to which he always replied, "Only an asshole could be this wealthy and develop an existential crisis." But his optimism often resulted in a failure to foresee consequences. Dan knew that despite Abdullah's attempt to seem unfazed, Rosalie's anger—its visceral power—had shocked him. And perhaps it was Abdullah's authentic self-expression, so admired by Dan at the concert, which had made it possible for Abdullah to rationalize his choice to take a second wife. Wasn't marriage the ultimate expression of that vaunted emotion, that truest love? And if one should be lucky enough to feel love twice in one lifetime, well, why not?

Dan couldn't hear anything over the tinny feedback of the boom box. He glanced over at Abdullah, who waved. Dan waved back, although he was annoyed to see his friend acting jovial after what had taken place in the driveway of his home. Since learning about Abdullah's marriage to Isra, Dan had attempted objectivity, tried to step back to see his friend's triangulated domestic scene through the telescopic lens of cultural relativism. Professors clearing their throats in great halls with cathedral ceilings used that telescope to watch the constellation of Arab lives blink and shine hundreds of light years away. However, most of Dan's Muslim friends agreed that polygamy was not Islam's finest allowance, especially in modern times, so he didn't feel too bad about coming down on Abdullah for it. Could it be that Abdullah actually believed that he'd done nothing wrong? It was pretty obvious that Rosalie would slice off Abdullah's ears if she could, a tithe for his betrayal. This couldn't be the life she had planned for herself when she left Texas for the Kingdom, hoping for adulation and homecoming. She'd grown up on the State Oil compound just outside of Al Dawoun and possessed that displaced expatriate child's longing—more like an illness, really—for a home that no longer existed. She had probably passed a teenaged Abdullah while on shopping excursions to Prince Muhammad Street, so that when she'd met him in Austin, she'd believed him to be the cure for her plaguing ache. Dan went into the kitchen and poured himself a tumbler of Black Label. Bottles were stacked eight deep on the plastic countertops. The green and brown and white glass covered in peeling labels created an accidental beauty that pleased Dan. The mess lent the scene an air of community, as if the clubhouse were a tiny sacked city, and they, the remaining citizenry, tasked with rebuilding. Pressing the cool glass against his forehead, Dan listened to the sounds of the party—the music of ice cubes clinking in glasses, the laughter that pushed its way up and out of the conversation. He moved to the doorway, where he leaned against the frame and watched the room.

Usually, the Princeton Club was a mess of testosterone: pent-up bachelors and bored married execs who just wanted to find the peace that lay in the bottom of a tumbler of whiskey. Dan recognized a few faces, but the three women were strangers. Word was that they were Syrian cousins of one of the men and were trying to find work or love in the Gulf, whichever came first. Their presence electrified the low-ceilinged room. Dan watched the most attractive of the three as she worked the shisha. She looked like she was in her early twenties, but the way she moved her mouth suggested a lifetime of experience. She'd removed her abaya and her beaded black headscarf rested about her straight shoulders. When she leaned in to take the hose from the Saudi next to her, she extended a single arm, milky as the inside of a halved almond.

"Ya Valentino! Bahibak! Why don't you come over here? We can be usdeeqa'a," the Syrian said, addressing him by the nickname that Abdullah had given him. She walked over and stood next to him. "Salaam," she said.

He could smell the scent of Coco Mademoiselle as she swung her hair to one side. In a place where women couldn't show their faces, perfume was vital, and Coco Mademoiselle was the fragrance of the moment. Every woman in Al Dawoun doused herself in it, and on the hottest days Dan could swear that a cloud of bergamot was visible hovering above the city.

"Salaamu aleikum," he said. "Aish Shishmik?"

"Fatima."

That was nearly the extent of his Arabic. Hello. What's your name? Two decades in a place and he still felt trapped in a Berlitz video: *Beginner's Arabic for Cursing, Carousing, Unbelieving Scoundrels.* But the Saudis he knew all spoke gorgeous English, so why should he bother? They'd already done the hard work, and he felt that there was something romantic about hearing the burble of unintelligible words. When taking coffee with his friends, he liked to lean back and watch their expressions and gestures as they argued in Arabic, the tiny, gilded coffee cups suspended in their hands like ornaments.

A new song came on, heavy on the bass, and Fatima started dancing. An Olympic-quality undulator, she moved effortlessly, her body gamine and beautiful in its iterations. He wasn't interested, though. Not really. Dan felt a sense of superiority to all the men out there who had affairs, married and remarried like it was sport. They must not have really been in love, he'd think. In the chaste years since his divorce, he'd started to fancy himself something of a Petrarch, a Florentino Ariza—someone not deterred by romantic futility. But Abdullah fancied him a bore, a eunuch, a big drag. That was OK. Abdullah had never had much patience for the classics, was more of a pulp man himself.

He watched Abdullah, who was talking to a man Dan didn't

recognize and sneaking glances at the young woman who'd joined the group. She had a mouth like a split-open black plum, and she wore a long, midnight-blue dress that tied in a halter somewhere behind the masses of hair that she pushed out of her face. He was annoyed with his friend, his bald desires. Suddenly, the Princeton Club didn't seem like the best idea. He wanted to be alone, back in his condo, not out indulging his rapacious buddy.

He flipped the lock and moved the sliding back door to the side. A weathered, low-slung deck stretched five or six feet outward before stopping abruptly. Beyond was a short strip of beach, the water moving in gentle, moon-pulled waves. It felt good to be so close to the water, the little South Seas–style clubhouse pushed right up against the shore so that Dan could see the small dark mounds of dying jellyfish on the beach. The air on his face was miraculous, and the lights of Al Dawoun winked along the opposite shore like stars in a tilted sky. To his right, the causeway stretched into the darkness, its concrete supporters invisible so that it looked like it was floating the cars back to the Kingdom. It was late and traffic had thinned out. Dan hunkered in a company chair, its wood cracked from the wet, salty air blowing in off the Gulf. The chair's cheap upholstery was coming apart to reveal foam cushions, and every time he shifted his weight, he could smell decades of mold.

"Daniel Coleman," someone said from the shadows along the wall.

"Who's that?" Dan said, his eyes growing lazy with tiredness.

He watched the glowing red tip of a cigarette flare and fall to the sand.

"Patrick Hastings."

Dan could see the man's outline now. He was tall and lean with stylishly unkempt hair, which, backlit as it was from where Dan stood, had clearly thinned since the last time they'd met. Pat had made a pass at Carolyn in the kitchen at one of those hooch-soaked State Oil parties, and Dan had broken Patrick's wrist in two places with a cast-iron crepe pan.

"Pat, how are you?" Dan said, extending his hand. "It's been an age."

"Bloody hell," Pat said, pausing before he took Dan's hand. "I heard a rumor that you gave up on this place years ago."

"Can't quite tear myself away," Dan said.

They hadn't spoken since the night of the party. Carolyn had been so embarrassed that night, she'd insisted they go home immediately, and she'd slept under a sheet on the couch. She had shamed Dan later, telling him he must be some kind of asshole to think that she needed protection from a Pat Hastings pass, and why hadn't he just tossed her over his shoulder like a caveman and stormed home?

They stood listening to the beach sounds for a moment. Pat lit another cigarette.

"You're not hiding any cookware in your pockets, are you?" Pat said, exhaling to the sky.

Dan gave a halfhearted laugh. Back in those days, he thought that was what finished marriages—a little grabass in the kitchen.

"Not my finest hour, Patrick. Thanks for the reminder."

"I wore a cast for two months. Bones just wouldn't knit right."

Dan decided to change the subject. He needed to get away from that memory of fighting like a fool, like an asshole, of letting his temper rule the day.

"I tell you what," he said. "Being back in the States about killed me."

"Yeah. Once you unlock the golden handcuffs," Pat said.

Pat didn't need to finish the thought. They both knew the cliché: Come out from under the covers of State Oil life and you can hardly stand the sight of the bright world before you. You barely know how to pay taxes. You miss the gold souq and the extravagant vacations. You miss the power of the income and the right to complain about it. Hell, you even miss the possibility of having it out with a cane-wielding mutawa over the length of your wife's abaya. On the outside, too much was uncertain, and company life was hard to part with. After college, he and Carolyn had come to the Kingdom at Rosalie and Abdullah's urging. *What will I do without you idiots around?* Abdullah had asked. The money was easy, no taxes, free housing, a pool, and great schools for the kids. Things were great until they weren't, when Carolyn started staring out windows for long stretches, sleeping through the afternoons. She missed her family, missed driving, missed the Pacific. So they left.

Now expats were leaving in droves. Not for the first time in Saudi Arabia, the religious freakos had started speaking with their swords, and everyone—Saudi, American, Brit, Lebanese, Bangladeshi—was anxious.

"Were you in town when they took the hostages over at Palm Court?" Dan asked.

"Yeah, at the office. They sent us home for the day, but I live in the Grove so I didn't feel much better there."

"Shit. I went to Abdullah's. A Saudi home seemed like the safest bet. Didn't want my ass within ten miles of anything expatriate."

"I went down to Ras Ayatin pretty soon afterwards and the compound was like a ghost town. People dropped everything and left," Pat said. "I almost did too. My best mate out here, Richard Cleig, lived next door to the English bloke who got dragged down the street behind the car at Palm Court."

Dan shuddered. Palm Court was the nicest expat compound in Al Dawoun, a heavily guarded city within a city that housed foreigners and served as the corporate headquarters of several global oil groups. Last winter, he had fought hard to get B-Corp to put him up there, dreaming of Olympic-sized pools and five-star restaurants. They'd shot him down, citing the prohibitive length of the waiting list, but Dan knew it was just too expensive for the company tightwads. So he stayed on at Prairie Vista, with its single National Guardsman keeping watch, its splintery, faded sign and constituency of rotund British and American men whose cynicism wilted the frangipani flowers as they passed the perimeter hedgerow. Thank God for those B-Corp tightwads, or he may have ended up with a jihadi smile—that toothless, bloody grin that gaped at the base of the throat. Nine people at Palm Court were killed when the radicals stormed the compound, separating Muslims from kuffar, unbelievers. With a shiver, he wondered if the heart stopped in moments like those, when disaster confronted the fragile body.

"What the hell are we still doing here, man?" Dan asked. "You forget things so quickly. Even a bloodbath. Just get lost in the work routine and you could be anywhere. If it weren't for the call to prayer, I'd think I was in Cleveland."

"Yeah, right," Pat said with a grin. "I'm going to head back across the causeway before I lose the will. Take care of yourself, Coleman."

Pat leapt back onto the deck and cut straight through the clubhouse to the front door. The clubhouse, much like the Kingdom, relied on a strict revolving-door policy. Dan remembered the warlike drone of the military helicopters as they scouted overhead the day of the Palm Court massacre. Calmly, he and Abdullah had left the office, driven to the Diamond Mile, and proceeded to get blitzed on Black Label while Abdullah placed dozens of calls to ministers, businessmen, and friends, trying to get a feel for how the fallout would affect B-Corp. Eleanor and Joe bought phone cards and called him, frantic, and even Carolyn sent a cold, electronic probe into his state of bein—living? dead? afraid?—while Dan watched the endless coverage of the Palm Court incident on CNN and the BBC.

About a week after the hostage incident, Abdullah had stomped into his office with a large Safeway bag filled to bursting.

"Listen to me, stupid American. I have some things for you."

He took a large white ball of cloth from the bag and unfurled it.

"Here, put this on," he said, throwing the white robe at Dan. "Tarek!" he shouted to the Egyptian who worked at the desk outside Dan's office.

Tarek came in, an AK-47 rifle slung over his muscular shoulder.

"Tarek is going to go everywhere with you for the next few days. He will even tuck you in at night," Abdullah said. "He trained in the Egyptian military and we don't want to send you back to America in a bag."

"But Tarek's an accountant."

"An accountant trained by Mubarak to put bullets into the brains of zealots. And troublesome liberals, for that matter." Abdullah left before Dan could reply.

Guns still scared him, and he barely knew Tarek. He could feel his quadriceps clenched tight against his leather office chair as the Egyptian stared at him, awaiting direction.

"Tarek, you're a good man, thank you for your concern. But I think everything will be fine. Honestly."

"Are you sure, Mr. Dan? Aren't you worried?" he said.

"Yes, I am worried, Tarek. I'm worried about what might happen if you and I are walking home one night and some shabab makes a wrong turn out of an alleyway and comes nose to nose with Big Bertha," he said, addressing the gun, which looked sorely out of place against the backdrop of Gary Larson cartoons hanging on his file cabinet.

"Well, if you change your mind . . ." Tarek said.

"Thanks, Tarek."

"You should think about wearing the thobe, uncle."

Dan said he would think about it. But even in a thobe, he would still be an American, a fact no amount of white robing could disguise. His gut, his height, his clean-shaven face. Blending in was not an option.

He closed the door behind Tarek and walked over to the window. Al Dawoun burned white beneath the midday sun, and from a few blocks away, he heard the muezzin calling the people to prayer, the words of the adhan falling on the ears of the faithful, the faithless, the fundamentalist, the questioning, the confused. Somewhere, the escaped hostage-takers were kneeling down toward Mecca to pray, their bloody hands washed clean.

DAN HEADED BACK to the clubhouse, sinking into the high drifts of sand with each step. Once inside, the burnt-fruit smell of the shisha's strawberry tobacco tickled his nostrils. Two of the Syrian cousins sat on a loveseat in the corner speaking in rapid Arabic, Fatima's Gauloise voice low and steady. Her laughter reverberated off of the linoleum floor, the bare walls. It was a rich and beautiful sound, something you'd hear at a Parisian cabaret, someplace where pleasure really belonged. Abdullah was sitting on the floor and fiddling with his BlackBerry, his back up against the frame of the company couch, where one of the young women sat and eyed him with a sad but hungry look on her face. Dan knew that she knew she was looking at Abdullah al-Baylani, a billionaire who was not opposed to polygyny. Dan could practically see the dollar signs flashing neon in her head. To be Abdullah's third wife would be a plum but fraught position. The female community would revile and ostracize her, projecting onto her the fear of their own husbands' potential polyamorousness. The male community would view her as a sharmoota, a prostitute. They knew that a third wife would probably not be a mother to any new children; she would be a purely sexual vehicle. But there'd still be the mansion and the designer clothing, the first-class flights to Rio and Rome, and the thrill and affirmations that accompany being the youngest wife.

Dan couldn't believe he was even thinking the words "third wife" with regard to Abdullah. He never would have guessed his friend would entertain the idea of multiple wives, still couldn't quite get it situated as fact in his head. Rosalie must wake in the mornings and wonder, *What in God's name is he thinking?*

"Ya Abdullah," she said, tapping him on the shoulder. He looked up at her, an annoyed expression on his face.

It was getting late and Dan was tired. He didn't want to get caught in Bahrain overnight. The thought of his hair commingling with the life forms in the couch cushions made him itch. He caught Abdullah's eye with a clipped wave, gave him the old saturated eyeball stare that signaled *enough*, and went into the kitchen to get some water. He took ice from the freezer—it was the one thing that was always in stock at the clubhouse, thanks to a gentleman's agreement that one should never leave a man without rocks for his whiskey—plopped it into the cloudy water, and sat down on a plastic folding chair to wait for the sheikh to extricate himself from the spider hug of the wannabe third wife.

From inside the kitchen, he heard Abdullah say "La, la, la." No, no, no. Alarmed by his friend's raised voice, Dan peered around the door's edge. The woman was reaching for Abdullah's forearm, bumping him as he turned away so his tumbler of whiskey fell to the floor with a clatter.

"Ana assif," the woman said, kneeling to pick up the broken glass. She looked up at them, her face a picture of despair.

"Dan, get in the car," Abdullah said while trying to shake the whiskey off his thobe. "Let's go."

Fatima was on her cell phone, presumably calling her cousin, who had gone into town for another bottle of brown. Dan mouthed *I'm sorry* to her before finding the keys to the Range Rover. He climbed into the driver's seat, the smell of leather comforting, like the tack room of an old barn. At this point in the evening, he was grasping for familiar things. With a short peel of tires, he set them on course back toward Saudi Arabia.

The wind at the cracked window made distant motorcycle sounds, steady, puttering. Dan loved driving across the causeway and losing sight of land for a little while. In the darkness, he could see the water moving in orange streaks, illuminated by the streetlamps. He loved living in a coastal town. Unexpected moments of beauty always reminded him of the greater world—a dhow whose wooden frame stabbed at the falling sun, or a low dune fully covered in purple flowers. But those moments were fleeting, short lifts of life; he wasn't really sure how to get back the sustained feelings of buoyancy he had felt when he'd been a family man.

"Got a little hairy in there for a minute, didn't it?" he said.

"I just met that woman tonight and already she was asking me when we would see each other next," Abdullah said.

"What did you say?"

"I said I'm married. But she wouldn't leave it alone."

"Your reputation precedes you," Dan said.

"What does that mean?"

"You're well known around here. You can't be surprised that women are trying to jump on the gravy train."

"I'm a married man."

"I can't believe you sometimes."

"What?" Abdullah said.

Dan rolled his eyes in the dark. They drove back through the VIP lane in silence. To the left, there were lines of cars waiting at customs to be inspected. Living in post-9/11 Saudi Arabia was like permanently residing in an airport, the authorities constantly scanning, examining, X-raying, and patting you down. The scrutiny sometimes made Dan panic, thinking for a split second that perhaps he did have a bomb in his trunk or a bottle of scotch under the seat. Did they itch and twitch beforehand, the young suicide bombers? Spell their mothers' names backward and forward before an intestinal amen punctuated their fragment of a life? Were they thinking about paradise and the houri, the dark-eyed virgins, like the American anchormen postulated in stern voices that betrayed a hint of titillation? Or were they just thinking, khara. Shit.

"Let's get home," Abdullah said.

"Which house?"

"The big one. It's the weekend. Rosalie gets the weekends."

On Thursdays, Abdullah usually hosted a luncheon for the extended family, though Dan imagined that family obligations were probably on hold for the time being. He thought of Rosalie straining to play hostess in the formal women's sitting room, where there was so much crystal on display that it resembled an ice palace.

The streets outside were empty, the only movement from the glowing hands of a huge Timex clock on the side of an office building. They drove a few more miles down King Khaled Street before pulling into Abdullah's driveway. If only Dan could see past the high walls, perhaps he might glimpse Rosalie pulling the curtains aside, dropping them back into place—the closed lids of the palace's dull eyes. Her presence oddly comforted him, made him feel less alone.

"Think she's up?" Dan asked.

"Yeah," Abdullah said. "She worries. She thinks I should have a bodyguard."

"Don't forget the king of soul's advice: Try a little tenderness." He paused, looked over at his friend. "It's good advice."

"Remind me, was that Ibn Saud or Fahd who said that?"

"Fuck you."

Abdullah got out of the car and walked to the front door, his gait still a little shaky from whiskey and fatigue. The house rose into the night like a mausoleum. It all made Dan feel inordinately far away from Austin and the University of Texas and Threadgill's, where he and Abdullah had first gotten drunk together.

Since he learned about Isra, Dan had felt a gap yawning between him and Abdullah. Perhaps it had always been there, filled with funhouse mirrors that were mostly invisible, but sometimes, like now, opaque with the smoke of their difference. Still, Abdullah was all Dan had in the Gulf, so he clutched at the threads of their former life together and barreled through, dreaming of oaks along the Pedernales, the boughs hung with ball moss, the roots mazing deep in the banks.

Dan rolled up his window, blocking out the heavy night. He hoped the sound of the engine wouldn't wake the kids—quiet Faisal, keen-eyed Mariam. He wondered about his own children, Eleanor and Joe, just starting their nights in Boston, San Diego. What were they doing? They sent e-mails, called every few months. When he'd left to go back to Saudi, he hadn't considered the children. With a true expat's disregard for distance, he had ventured forward. But as it turned out, proximity did have a thing or two to do with love, and he could feel a coldness settling between him and the kids. Not hostility, exactly, but a brittleness of manner that marked the interactions of strangers.

The walls of Prairie Vista reflected white as his headlights scanned over them, and a plain wooden sign with a palm tree painted on it welcomed him home. Between the compound's razor-wire fence and the oasis downshore, there was only wind-snaked sand, camels, burned-out trucks.

He rolled down his window and grunted a quick marhaba and tisbah al-khayr to Khalil, the one-man army keeping watch over the compound. He didn't feel much like exchanging pleasantries. More than anything, he needed a shower. Framed by drooping oleander branches, the compound pool glowed turquoise, gurgling softly as water moved in and out of the filters. Its familiar nighttime beauty reminded him of evening parties with perfumed women, and children playing shadow puppets against the underwater lights. God, how he missed the insular world of marriage, of family. There, in that world, it was bedtime, then waking, scrubbing, eating. He recalled the old Arab saying: *I against my brother. I and my brother against my cousins. I and my cousins against the world.* Without family, you were exposed, a clam on the half shell there for the drying out. Once he had commanded a small army forged from his own flesh and bone. In a tiny sandpaper-walled house with an overwatered St. Augustine lawn in the Eastern Province of Saudi Arabia, they watched the assassinations and wars and stampedes and massacres and floods on TV. He would fall asleep listening to the thump of Carolyn's heart while locusts smashed themselves against their bedroom window. A tiny, contented tribe wrapped in cotton sheets. They had created new verb tenses for their state of suspension, where the movements of the askew world didn't matter much at all.

He parked the car and walked to the pool's edge, looking for the moon in the murky sky, but the desert's debris had blackened out where the moon should have been. Kneeling down, he untied his leather-laced topsiders and sat down on the pavement. The concrete warmed the parts of his legs not covered by his khaki shorts. He let the heat work over his body before dangling his feet in the water. Coolly, it reached between his toes, giving the illusion of human touch. The compound slept, all the lights extinguished. He closed his eyes and sat in darkness.

THREE

IN THE DARK the swimming pool was lit from within, the water glowing a rich aquamarine so that as Faisal swam his laps, he felt as if his body were being bathed in liquid jewels. It was one reason he chose to swim at night rather than during the day when it was warmer. He also preferred the deep silence of the late hours, when Al Dawoun slept. At that hour of the night, Rosalie and Abdullah would never see him practicing his laps and think for a moment that he missed anything at all about boarding school or Bern. That is, unless Abdullah stayed out late with Dan, as he was doing that night. Whenever they went out together, Faisal gnashed his teeth but kept silent. He knew Dan was a bad influence, but what could he do?

In truth, Faisal did miss Bern, with its cold Olympic pool where he and the other boys had learned how to tread water and swim their paces. He'd always been good, swimming in a few meets, the judges' whistles echoing off wet tile and the stink of chlorine strong in the air as he collected medal after medal. His coach had been shocked by his natural skill and had loved telling a joke about Arabs and water that made Faisal smile. Lately, he was experiencing an unfamiliar insomnia, and he found that swimming a few dozen times end-to-end in the family pool was just enough to drain the last stubborn energy from him so that he could sleep. In the pool, there was no little sister pestering him, no mother to bumble and fumble around him, no father to miss, no father's second wife to despise and then defend, all in the same minute, all in his upside-down brain. In the pool, there was no one but him.

In the two years since Abdullah's secret marriage to the Palestinian, his father had made countless trips to Doha, where Isra had lived in a magnificent condominium with a view of the seaside. Faisal knew it was magnificent because his father had taken him along on one of his trips several months earlier. He had introduced him to Isra and told him that there were some things that were just between men. When Faisal met Isra, he could not help but wonder at all the things his mother must have done to make his father seek out another companion. Obviously, she had failed their family in some grave way, and so he carried the secret of Isra around in his heart, where the burn and weight of it made him feel both happy and sad, and therefore utterly confused.

Now, for all of those reasons, Faisal cut patiently and methodically through the pool, his arms brushing by his ears as he pulled them close to leverage himself through the water. Every second stroke, he turned his face to the side and sucked in a long breath. He felt he could go forever, or at least halfway through the night. Above water the only sound in his ears was the slapping of his palms as they met the surface, which by now, thirty-eight laps in, was churning and peaking with his movements. Underwater, he only heard the noises he made, and he found that comforting. He chose a prayer and repeated it in his head as he swam until the incantatory rhythms of the prayer matched the movement of his body.

As he closed in on the fortieth length, Faisal shut his eyes inside his goggles and waited for the edge of the pool to rise and meet his reaching fingertips. Few things were as satisfying as the moment when he put his elbows over the pool's ledge to hang there exhaustedly until he caught his breath. After his heart rate slowed, Faisal hoisted himself out of the water and sat for a moment, his knees tucked close to his chest, the wind off the Dahna wicking the water from his back. Shivering, he watched the water slowly return to stillness until nothing remained of his swim except the wet spot on the concrete where he sat. He stood and shook the water from his head, dried his face with the towel.

Inside, the house was silent. Faisal tiptoed to the stairs and started up. When he passed his mother's room, he listened for the sound of movement within. Over the last several nights, as he'd stolen downstairs to the pool, he'd seen the light beneath her door and heard her restless clattering. Now there was silence.

In the bathroom at the end of the hallway, Faisal felt the cool Carrara marble beneath his feet. He thought about taking a bath. Perhaps the laps wouldn't be enough, not with Ali's words rattling around in his head. He flushed, remembering the afternoon at Majid's house. The afternoon had started out harmlessly enough. Hassan had asked how Mariam was doing, so Majid and Ali had started making loud kissing noises, smacking their lips together and circling the blushing Hassan. Finally, they'd tackled him to the tile floor, mussing his hair and kissing his cheeks like overbearing aunties. "How *is* Mariam, ya Faisal?" Majid asked with exaggerated curiosity, folding his hands and putting his chin on top of them. "In Hassan's head, they're already engaged," Ali cackled. "He and Umm Hassan are already planning the wedding. Gulf Hotel. Big reception. All paid for by Abu Faisal, of course!" Hassan had loved Mariam since they had all played together in the yard of the big house while growing up, for so long that it no longer bothered Faisal.

But then, Ali had grown bored with their tired routine and veered into new, awful territory: "So, we heard that your father finally went out and got himself an Arab wife," Ali had said. "A Palestinian, no less. It seems Sheikh Abdullah is trying hard to make up for the American!" His cascading chins wobbled as he laughed.

"Shut up," Faisal said. "You'd better shut up."

"Or what? You'll beat me up? I could sit on you and squash you into the next world."

Majid's older brother, Jalal, was playing music upstairs. Certain notes and a heavy drum line drifted down to them.

"That's something to be proud of?"

"At least every roll of my fat is Arab fat!"

"Ali, stop," Majid said.

"I don't see why you waste your time with him," Ali said. "He's Amreeki through and through." He grinned, his chubby cheeks bunching into little round apples below his eyes.

"Q'us umich!" Without thinking, Faisal punched Ali in his soft stomach. After standing doubled over for a few minutes, Ali had straightened up and laughed at Faisal, right in his face. So his punches inspired merriment. That was the kind of man he was—a fool, a rube, an ineffectual loser. How, then, would he be able to resist taking over the family business that had made his father so morally soft? If he planned to deny himself the power of that money, he couldn't become a man whose punches set others giggling. At that moment, he was determined to make himself into something harder.

"You know I'm right or you wouldn't be so angry," Ali said.

Swiftly, and without so much as a sound, Majid's knuckles cracked against the bones of Ali's face. Ali thudded to the ground and lay squirming, his face turned toward the floor, saliva pooling on the tiles.

"I said, stop it," Majid said. He gave his right hand a shake, as if to relieve a cramp.

Although Faisal was supposed to stay for dinner, he left without finishing his tea. It was not the first time Majid had to stick up for Faisal, and he doubted it would be the last. Majid's mother, Umm Jalal, had made lamb because she knew how much he liked it. Now he felt like an idiot; she must have invited him out of pity. All of Al

Dawoun seemed to know about his father's second wife. Everyone knew that she was a Palestinian and a rumored secularist who had lived in Paris, and that her existence had purportedly made Rosalie so angry that she had ripped half of the hair from her own head. His friends relished being able to tell him the latest gossip.

But then again, Faisal was never spared their teasing. There was always his face, his not-quite-Arab face. *Amreeki*, they called him. He supposed they teased him because he was such an easy target—quiet and so very rich. But there was also Majid—Majid, who never said a word against him, who would break his own hand to stop the bullying once it had gone too far. After so many years spent in talk and silence, motion and stillness, love and anger, they were the truest friends, their little child hearts growing together until one day they had awoken to find themselves young men. Faisal trusted Majid more than he trusted anyone.

The moon was high and bright, and inside his upstairs bathroom, Faisal could hear nothing but the wind outside the window. In the shower, he rinsed the chlorine from his body, then dried himself and put on his undershorts. Back in his bedroom, he opened his closet door to look at the row of medals hanging there, the blue and red and yellow ribbons with their gold medallions flat against the wall. He knew it was prideful to keep them displayed like that, but in the end he decided it was all right since nobody else knew they were there.

Faisal walked to his desk and picked up his grandfather's dagger, which he'd taken down from its spot on the bookshelf in his father's study. He ran his hand along the dagger's blunt spine, back and forth, until he could feel a small heat building between the pads of his fingers and the metal. He was sixteen. Soon he would move out of his house and away from his family. He was eager for that day. It seemed, more and more, that he no longer knew these people who called themselves his parents. He glanced at the crumpled black-and-white photo of his grandfather, Abdul Latif, which Faisal kept as a reminder of where he'd come from. There was something reptilian to the set of his grandfather's face, his eyes far apart and his nose hooked like some sort of egg-cracking beak. It was the face of a pack leader, an alpha dog. Faisal hoped there was still time for him to earn some of Jadd Abdul Latif's fearlessness.

Outside, a car door slammed. Faisal peered out the window. The wooden gate that separated the Baylani compound from the road swung open, triggering the outdoor lights. From behind the gate, his father appeared, walking slowly toward the house. Faisal could see Dan Coleman's car backing up into the road.

Abdullah tripped over nothing, then stood examining the spot on the ground. When he straightened and started walking again, he looked blind, like a lumbering animal. Faisal didn't like seeing his father like that. Who else saw him in such a state of sin that he couldn't control his movements? It was embarrassing. Ya Allah, how much longer did he have to wait for his father to find his way back to the path? It was feeling lonelier and lonelier there without him.

Ever since Dan Coleman had moved back to Saudi Arabia with no family, he had taken to hanging around the house, and Faisal didn't like it. Abdullah had started going to Bahrain more, and Faisal found a small stash of liquor under the staircase, the gin bottle half-empty and whiskey unopened. He'd thrown them both away. Once, in the kitchen of the big house, Dan asked Faisal if he knew that Dan was the one who had introduced Rosalie and Abdullah. "Kid, if it weren't for me, you wouldn't even be around." Dan seemed confused when Faisal shook his head and left without a word. Lying in bed that night, Faisal had mouthed the name *Dan Coleman* and then the word *hate*, just to see how they sounded together.

Now the front door opened and closed. Faisal tucked the photograph of his grandfather in the band of his shorts and then moved silently along the corridor, thankful for the thick carpet. At the top of the stairs, he paused, listening for Abdullah below. He wasn't supposed to know that Abdullah slept downstairs, but one morning he'd risen early to pray and had seen his father emerge, disheveled and robed, from the spare room.

Faisal floated down the stairs and into the kitchen. On the counter near the phone, the letter about his sister's latest problem at school lay open, the headmistress's telephone number circled in red pen. He doubted Rosalie had called; she'd been far too preoccupied with her own issues.

Dear Mr. Baylani:
As you know, we were forced to send Mariam home from school because she refused to wear her abaya while walking to and from the school building. Now, please try to understand: we have this rule in place for the girls' safety. We do not want our students harassed or threatened in any way. Please speak to her and remind her that it is for her own good. Additionally, her religious studies teacher is concerned about the state of her faith, as she relentlessly questions Mrs. Zaynab during lessons and Mrs. Zaynab recently confiscated three books from Mariam's bag. We're not sure how she came by these texts, but we cannot have books of that nature in our school. Finally, we hear that she is going to start a Weblog. I'm not sure if you are familiar with such things, but I can assure you, it is not the proper forum for a young woman to express herself, as one can never be sure who is reading it. Please see that you attend to these pressing issues. Our school's reputation, and your daughter's, depends on it.

Sincerely,
Headmistress Shideed

It was funny to read about his little sister behaving subversively. Faisal had never considered that she was an actual person outside the home. To him, she lived a purely interior existence, her chattering of little consequence to either her or her family. To think of Mariam acting against authority made him laugh. He heard of a young man whom the police had tortured to death years ago after catching him with banned books, but Faisal doubted the same fate could befall a girl. One thing was certain: his mother had done her best to ensure that neither he nor Mariam would ever fit in.

Faisal moved toward the door of the guest bedroom door and pressed his ear against the wood. Carefully, he leaned down on the handle so it made no noise as he turned it. Curled into a ball in the middle of the expansive bed, Abdullah snored loudly. Faisal approached the bed, the light from the hallway falling in a stretched yellow triangle over the sleeping man. Before he could reach the bed, he stubbed his toe hard. He heard sloshing and then felt the cool of liquid against his bare feet, but his father slept on, peacefully. Faisal leaned down to try to see the mess he made, but before he could see it, he could smell it. Whiskey. The bottle had emptied completely, the stain a dark circle against the white carpet. His toes felt cold and clean, as if he'd performed wudhu. Kneeling on the carpet, he prayed for his father. He wanted to wake him from his drunken sleep so that he would be forced to try to stand up straight and explain his swimming eyes to his son. It took audacity to return to your family that drunk.

Faisal took hold of the now-empty bottle and stood up. His eyes settled on the sharp edge of the vanity's marble top. Abdullah snorted and turned onto his back, his stump resting on his stomach. It was a pitiable sight, making Faisal hesitate, loosen his grip on the bottle. Because the drinking happened secretly, because so many people did it and everyone looked the other way, the hypocrisy had become just another part of life in Saudi. But it was not enough. Other men could go to hell, but not Abdullah. Faisal was determined to save his father from his own habits, for wasn't God forgiving and merciful?

Faisal closed his eyes and listened to his father's wet breathing. He raised the bottle over his head and brought it down forcefully against the edge of the vanity. It broke loudly, and he felt a small shard hit his face. His father grunted awake and rustled the sheets as he sat up. He looked at Faisal, his eyes bleary with confusion.

"Shame on you, Baba," Faisal said, his heart pounding.

He raced from the room, shutting the door behind him, and

ran up the stairs, down the hallway, into his room, and then into his bed, where he lay still; his heart expanding in his throat. Dizzily, he pulled the photograph of his grandfather from the band of his shorts, looked at his coffee-stained teeth and hawk's nose. He thought of Abdul Latif as a child, living in a tent, eating nothing but goat meat and sheep's cheese, falling asleep beneath a velvet sky. Abdul Latif's story had become a fable, one Faisal had heard many times. How Abdul Latif had left the desert as a young man, turning his back on the sea of black Baylani tents stretched from Yemen to Southern Iraq; leaving Asir for the Arabian Gulf, the city, and the new money that had started to pour in from all over the world.

Closing his eyes, his head light as cotton, Faisal let Abdul Latif materialize from the darkness, carrying the old dagger he took with him everywhere. He recalled the bitter morning they had gone hunting for falcons, the sky dead with cold. Abdul Latif had wrapped him in a long black robe and handed him a Shebriya dagger, its jeweled handle a shock of color against the sand. It was Abdul Latif's prized dagger, not the simple Khanjar knife he used for slaughtering goats. Faisal could feel the burn of the handle's rubies against his cold skin. He was twelve at the time, and Jadd Abdul Latif had lifted up his thobe to reveal a smooth, pink island of young-looking skin in his sea of brown wrinkles. Taking Faisal's small hand in his, Jadd had run it over the knotted scar. To Faisal's young mind, it felt like a jellyfish washed up on the beach, firm and smooth.

"My father did this to me," Jadd had told him. "It was my first experience with real pain. I was twelve and spending most of my time with my mother and sisters. When I was with Umma, I was all in all. I was the youngest boy in my family, and I meant nothing to the men. Baba wasn't being cruel, just preparing me for suffering, teaching me to bear it with dignity. He knew as well as anyone that life in the desert was hard. Afterwards, the men welcomed me."

That day, Faisal had recoiled, thinking his grandfather had

brought him into the desert to teach him pain, but instead, Abdul Latif had handed the dagger to Faisal and hugged him close. In his bed Faisal thought of his grandfather's old wound and touched his abdomen. He remembered Abdul Latif complaining good-naturedly about his wives' teasing. He said that they laughed at him because he could never fall asleep on the expensive mattresses they imported from Denmark. Instead, he slept on the floor on a rough woolen blanket next to the bed. "Comfort is the devil's elixir," Jadd often said. How had Abdullah grown so louche with Abdul Latif as his father? The only scars Abdullah had were clustered around his stump, the flesh there spackled with gray from when it had absorbed some of the gravel from the Italian road where his father claimed to have fishtailed out of control on a borrowed Ducati. He had probably been drunk.

Faisal desperately hoped for sleep. He began reciting God's ninety-nine names: Al-Rahman, Al-Rahim, Al-Malik, Al-Quddus, Al-Salam, Al-Mu'min, Al-Muhaymin, Al-'Aziz, Al-Jabbar, Al-Mutakabbir, Al-Musawwir, Al-Ghaffar . . . He watched the bedside clock as he moved down the list. After several minutes, he was finished. None of his friends could do the whole list—not even Majid—but when Faisal thought of Majid's thin arms holding an automatic rifle, the only one of the boys who had ever *fought* for something, Faisal felt his own triumphs to be small and cerebral. He felt the sadness coming on again, sparked by the idea that Abdullah, the man who had first taught him how to kneel and pray, might not be able to save himself from eternal suffering. Faisal tried to clench his mind tightly against these thoughts, but still he saw his father tumbling in blackness, falling, a trail of howling demons chasing him down in the dark.

THE NEXT MORNING, Faisal awoke to a sharp rap on his door.

"Zool?"

It was Mariam.

"Leave me alone, I'm sleeping," he said.

"If you're asleep, how are you talking?" Before he could answer, she burst through the door. "Hurry and get dressed. Umma and Baba want to talk to you about last night. I think a robber came."

She was clutching the small press notebook that she carried everywhere with her. Recently she had purchased a poster of a towering Christiane Amanpour in field khakis and a flak jacket, as well as several long, thin reporter notebooks from a paper store in downtown Al Dawoun. She talked incessantly about Faizah al-Zahrani and Sabriya al-Seif, two of the Kingdom's most prominent female journalists. Sabriya wrote for the Western papers, but Faizah worked at *Saudi Times*, where their uncle was the boss, and where Mariam worked as an intern one afternoon a week. He'd heard A'm Nabil complain once that Faizah was the one to get them in trouble with the censors, always trying to get in a line or two of "too much truth," as Nabil had put it.

"You have an overactive imagination," Faisal said, rolling over in bed to face away from her. He waited to hear the sounds of her leaving, but she didn't move. "There's nothing to report here, so just put your little notebook down and go away."

Quickly she was at his side, her knee pushed hard into his back. "No. I'm going to sit right here until you agree to be interviewed. I want to know what it's like."

"What what's like?" he asked, swatting at her leg.

"To love God so much it rules your whole life."

"Simple. Without God, no life. Now, get off my bed!" He turned and sat up, swinging his arm to swipe her off. "I hate to tell you, little sister, but your life is not a news story. And if it were, it would bore everyone to death."

She stuck her lip out and gave him a hurt look. He waited for her to walk away, but his victory didn't last long.

"And if you did anything besides play video games and read the Koran, you'd notice that life was happening all around you."

"I've got plenty going on, things you couldn't imagine," he said.

"Yeah? Like what?" She had her hands on her hips, her head cocked sideways.

He'd never told her about the Sahwi websites he visited, about Lewis Attiya Allah and the other religious men who discussed Islam on the Internet. She didn't know about the plans he had, about Majid's big ideas.

"You act so superior just because A'mi gave you a job at the paper and now you get to go in and pour tea for people," Faisal said.

"I do more than pour tea," she said. "A'mi has me writing. And last week, Faizah al-Zahrani asked me to look over her editorial piece. At least I'm out there, trying to make a difference."

He rolled his eyes at her.

"If I did ever grant you an interview, I could tell you things that would make your head explode. It'd be the biggest scoop *Saudi Times* had ever seen." So what if it was a hollow boast at the moment? She would never know that, and besides, he was sure that one day it would be true.

His mother appeared behind Mariam.

"Zizi, did you hear anything last night?" she asked with the most urgency he had heard in her voice in a while.

He hated all the nicknames that his family used for him. He was almost seventeen years old, and still it was "Zool" and "Fez" and "Zizi."

"My name is Faisal."

"I need to know if your sister has been telling stories again."

"Umma," Mariam protested.

"What? Remember that time with the El Ali boy? Now be still and let your brother talk."

He couldn't take living there much longer, not with his mother and sister buzzing around like this. Since Abdullah spent so much of his time with Isra, the house had become an intolerable world of female squawking. He felt as if his already-sparse goatee was retreating entirely into his chin. He got out of bed and pushed past them.

Abdullah stood at the bottom of the staircase, and Faisal noticed that the smell of whiskey had traveled with his father from the spare bedroom into the foyer.

"Baba? What's all this about a break-in?" He would press the matter a little bit, just until his father squirmed.

"Your sister says she heard someone breaking in last night. I'm sure it was nothing."

"It's funny actually. I *do* recall hearing something downstairs. Late. Around two o'clock in the morning?" Faisal narrowed his eyes into his best glare. A week ago, he never would have spoken to his father this way, though he had wanted to on many occasions. But hearing his mother scream herself hoarse in the driveway last night had emboldened him. Since news of Isra broke, none of the old rules applied anymore.

"Never mind the noise you heard," Abdullah said, red-faced.

"But Baba, it was glass," Mariam said. "Breaking glass."

"Baba, tell me what you know about hudud crimes," Faisal said. "Adultery. Defamation. Theft. Public intoxication. Yes, I believe there's eighty lashes for public intoxication."

Abdullah turned to face him, his right hand clenched into a fist. He brought it down hard on the banister.

"If you do not shut your mouth immediately, I'll lash you myself," Abdullah said. "I do know how the Prophet, peace be upon Him, feels about insubordinate children. Now, I'm going back to bed and I don't want to be disturbed."

Faisal saw a vein pop from his father's temple. Faisal longed to keep pushing, but he decided against it. If he disrespected his father entirely, what then? He needed Abdullah, even Rosalie, but he needed them to be a certain *way*. Namely to be good, responsible parents who weren't always off doing anything and everything they pleased. It had been so long since he actually felt like either parent had looked at him and taken the time to *see* him for who he was. And wasn't that a parent's only real job?

"But Baba, what if the intruder . . ." Mariam said.

"Enough, I said. I want silence in this house, and if I have to bind and gag you all, I will."

Abdullah scratched his head as if he wanted to draw blood and walked off in the direction of the other guest bedroom.

"Why does no one in this family listen to me?" Mariam whispered.

"Hummingbird, I'm sure if anyone had tried to break in, the alarm would have gone off,"

Rosalie said. "And your brother wants to protect this family as much as you do. Isn't that right, Zool?"

She looked to him for affirmation and he nodded vigorously. In this house of avoidance, it was easy to go along with what people wanted to believe. His parents were in orbit—untouchable planets in a galaxy that was, very obviously, not his.

"Faisal, Mimou and I are going out. We'll see you later today." She patted him on the shoulder.

"I'm still going to get that interview with you," Mariam said as she walked past him.

"Whatever," he said.

His mother and sister walked to the garage, where the two drivers slept in an adjoining room. There should be a perfect symmetry to their family—a mother and daughter, a father and son. But now there was Isra, and there was always whiskey—both things that consumed his father's every moment, when he wasn't at B-Corp. Faisal exhaled and walked slowly to the bay window in the living room. Parting the heavy drapes, he looked out to the courtyard. Lately there had been heavy windstorms, and a layer of sand muted the day's colors. He would leave a note for Yasmin about the mess in the guest room. He never directly addressed the servants, especially not the women, but he appreciated their precise movements as they dusted the intricate teak screens and jade statues Rosalie brought back from trips to China. She had started with tiny Buddhas and forest-colored combs, then small jade horses. Now life-sized emperors in rippling stone robes littered the women's sitting room, their mustaches delicate, belying their obscene size. Since Islam forbade representational art, it was difficult to smuggle them into the country, but she told Faisal her secret: She had worked out a system with Miteb Biltagi and she had her statues shipped to Biltagi Brothers' Grocery in huge vegetable crates. Customs never explored beyond the "Eggplant" stickers.

While she had explained, he'd winced at every flat, foreign vowel that made it so painfully obvious she had not grown up learning Arabic in a Saudi school. For all her years on the State Oil compound, she might as well have been in Texas, so far removed from Saudi culture was the expat experience. Yet, there was a time when he had loved her voice and the way it tumbled over the words too fast. It reminded him of an oud played underwater, the notes full of feeling but garbled. When she read to him as a boy, it had been beautiful, her head moving up and down for emphasis, her red hair like God's burnishing. As a child, he remembered thinking the hair must have been how his father found her, glowing amidst a sea of dark heads. Umma, the lighthouse. Now he felt that her red hair was just another indicator of her extravagant taste. He could hardly blame his father for taking a second wife whose Arabic was flawless, whose hair fell dark as the night sky over the Rub' al-Khali.

The jet of a sprinkler machine-gunned its way across the sliding-glass door leading to the courtyard. He checked his watch. The house was still as dawn. He stood from the sofa, glided along the tile floor and through the Moroccan archway separating the living room from the foyer. The house had begun to frighten him. Its opulence felt contagious. If only he'd been born poor and pious in the mountains of Lebanon or the wadis of Jordan, life would be far less complicated. There, he would only have prayer, and America's presence would have been less strongly felt. In Switzerland, when he'd told the Turkish cabbie where he was from, the man had scoffed and said "America, Arabia, same-same. Same-same," shaking his hand like he was throwing something away.

During his nine months in Bern, he'd grown bloated eating

filigreed chocolate and cheese webbed like lace. He'd worn expensive watches and sipped Armagnac with the sons of Greek shipping magnates. He'd felt so far from home. Without the structure of family or Islam's guidance, he'd grown unmoored. In a place where anything was possible, where God was absent, he'd let himself be borne along, his body and mind bending easily into pleasure's many shapes. The pale boys called him le maghrébin or le cabot and they were always hungry for the worst stories about Saudi Arabia. He tried to explain to them that he had never seen anyone's head chopped off, and that women were not kept prisoners in their homes, but the boys would just laugh at him, at his halting French, and pour him another finger of Armagnac. "Drink up, maghrébin! None of this back in the tents." The name al-Baylani meant nothing to them.

The boys, pale as fish bellies in their starched uniforms, talked openly about the ripe bodies of the female students, and once, at the very beginning of the school year, when Faisal was still floating in a haze of disorientation, they'd dared him to sneak into the bathroom of a girls' dorm. He waited and listened, as if he could learn all of the girls' secrets by following their toilet rituals. He'd peered out of the crack in the stall door and had seen a girl, just emerged from the shower, standing before the mirror with a hand on each breast. Water ran down her neck, down her back, until it settled in the crack of her bottom. Her nakedness, so close and three-dimensional, had stunned him. Back home, women's bodies were inaccessible, nothing more than suggestions beneath black robes. He felt dizzy with awe to see the flesh of this girl rounding and dipping in contours only familiar to him from advertisements. Faisal held his breath to see if she would resume movement or if she had perhaps frozen in that position, a statue, a beautiful and dangerous memorial to everything he had ever wanted.

He thought about telling the boys waiting outside, but the next day, he was sick with shame recalling the girl and embarrassed by his own body's reactions. It didn't seem fair, really, that all she had to do was stand there and, through her nakedness, make him a slave. He'd gone to the men's room and stood staring into the mirror. Then he splashed water on his face, washed his hands three times, and went back to his dorm room. When the girls competed at the swim meets, their long hair tucked beneath caps and their bony hips pushing against the dark material of the suits, Faisal took to sitting in the highest corner of the bleachers, turning his back on the commotion in order to study. He told himself he was doing the girls a favor, sparing them the embarrassment of yet another pair of gazing eyes. Black ink on white pages was far less troubling than water down an unfamiliar body.

A week after the incident in the bathroom, fifteen Saudis flew themselves into the world's tallest buildings, and after the vigils and a week of drawn faces and watery eyes, some of the kids at school became relentless. One afternoon late in the spring term, an Italian boy rumored to be Versace's godson turbaned a dishtowel around his head and cornered Faisal in the tray-drop area of the dining hall. "When are you going to martyr yourself, Faisal of Arabia?" he asked. "Allah has called me personally and made a special request for you. He wants you to blow up the school, starting with Headmaster Ponsot's office." The hall erupted in laughter. Faisal gave an uneasy smile and tried to shuffle past, but the Italian cuffed him on the head. Faisal dropped his tray in the foam of pink suds, then turned away from the boy and raced across the marble floor and out onto the central green. The Italian followed not far behind, both boys running headlong down a hill until they tumbled, limbs thrashing, to the bottom. The boy sat on Faisal, pinning his arms to his side. Around them, a group of their classmates had gathered, whooping and hollering as the Italian punched him in the chest and slapped at his face with his suntanned hands until a teacher pulled him off.

But this was merely the opening act in a series of hateful pranks that made Faisal wonder if perhaps Osama Bin Laden and Ayman Zawahiri were right about Westerners hating Muslims and wishing for their decimation. Faisal did not stop to consider that the acts of a few oligarchs' sons were more indicative of youthful spite than a universal conspiracy against his people. He only had his school as a measure for the world, and on that day, he decided he'd had enough of the West.

After several heated discussions with Abdullah and Rosalie, who both wanted him to stay and see more of the world, they reached an agreement. His mother in particular had resisted his repatriation because she felt that he would not get the broad liberal arts education he deserved in the Saudi schools. "But habibti," Abdullah argued. "The boy won't be thinking about Shakespeare if he's being tormented by his classmates. We need to protect our son, even if it means he has to wait until college for certain things." When Faisal overheard his father say this, he felt a swell of love. Abdullah understood how hard it was and he was bringing Faisal home, booking an end-of-term Swiss Air flight to Bahrain.

When Faisal boarded the plane, a neat beard was sprouting on his chin. When he debarked, he felt the roughness of his father's goatee against his face and was certain of one thing: Abdullah would show him how to operate in the world of men, in their shared world of good Muslim men. It was the memory of that feeling of hope and safety that made Faisal's later disappointments bitterer than an unripe date. For his father had not taken him by the hand as he grew up, but rather had become more and more engrossed in his work at B-Corp. Except on the weekends, when Abdullah kissed Faisal with great gusto and spent a half hour talking animatedly to him about football or school, and Faisal would raise his face to the warmth of his father's radiance. But then Saturday would come, the first day of the workweek, and Abdullah would be gone once again, leaving Faisal to navigate the dark corners of adolescence on his own.

In the fall after his return from Switzerland, Faisal began his scholarship at a local private school. Order returned; his fear abated. At boarding school, he had been seen as an Arab Muslim and nothing more, and he was punished for it. But when he returned to the Kingdom, he embraced that identity with an appropriative zealotry that surprised even him. He worked hard to forget his other,

American, half, for it seemed, in this new world order, that there was no room for line-straddling or commingling. He had seen the enemy—the enemy had sat on his chest and pummeled him, after all—and decided he wanted nothing to do with the Western fish-bellies. It was most inconvenient, then, that his mother remained pale and that his Saudi friends continued to address him with their arsenal of anti-American insults—that, in fact, they had become so innovative with their various slurs that it made Faisal curse the Arab talent for poetry.

But what angered him the most upon his return was how eager Rosalie seemed to send him away again. On his sixteenth birthday, she'd showed him an old map, torn and faded, spreading it on the length of the dining table. Doesn't it excite you? she'd said. That there's so much more to know and see in the world? What's wrong with my home? he'd replied. And why should I try to know about people who don't care about me? Who might even hate me? Faisal knew his mother still wanted him to go away for college, and he resented her naïveté about the world. Just because she had fallen in love with a foreigner didn't mean all the people of the world were destined to intertwine their lives.

Still, even with all of these complications, he was home. If he felt sexual fantasy or covetousness closing in on him, he could run outside into the compound courtyard and fold himself up in a wrought-iron chair, speaking God's names and a few prayers. When he was done, he counted the 4,667 aqua- and palm-colored tiles in the courtyard's mosaic. It was a beautiful mosaic, so cool and detached from the trouble and heat of living things. Its vacant symmetry soothed him, edified and cleared the mind for contemplation of God. The smooth ceramic absorbed his panic, its bright blues and greens never reflecting his muddy thoughts. He always kissed the tiles of the mosaic, the cool colors at his lips, moving down his throat, dousing the fires around his ignited heart.

This meditative activity allowed him to hope that maybe his mind wasn't as polluted as he thought, even though he imagined it scorched, black as the sky the day Saddam's retreating army lit the Kuwaiti fields on fire. He'd only been a child, but he could still remember the wells like torches against the blackening sky. He believed that a person could not yield to those sparks peculiar to the human heart. From his mother and father he'd learned the consequences of such relenting. He felt it disgraceful that the adults of the family were the acid disintegrating the Baylani name. One day soon, he would leave their house on the Diamond Mile and never return.

FAISAL WENT TO the guest bedroom and wrote his note about the broken glass to Yasmin on a notepad by the side of the bed. He checked to make sure he still had the picture of Abdul Latif in his pocket. Before leaving, he grabbed a large piece of the broken bottle, touched its sharp tip. Perhaps he'd wave it at Dan a little, just to show him evidence of his crimes against the Baylani family. In the garage, the odor from the drivers' tiny unventilated apartment hung in the air. Faisal got in his car, laid the piece of broken glass on the passenger seat next to the smoothed-out photograph of Abdul Latif, and started the engine. In spite of himself, he enjoyed the vehicle's powerful thrust. Ornamented and gleaming, the BMW divided the air steaming off the asphalt of Al Dawoun's streets. It was a shame that it stood out so egregiously among all the old Japanese trucks and rusted white hatchbacks. It could be a great getaway car—fast, night-colored. He turned out of the driveway and cruised slowly down the Diamond Mile. The quiet of the weekend morning extended all the way down the street, so that the mansions' resplendence resounded like a shout. The noon sun fell hot through the windshield, and he squinted against its blinding reflection off of street signs.

Once outside the Diamond Mile, traffic picked up. Laborers slept in the back of tiny pickups and dump trucks moved along, elephantine. He let the noise wash over him, the white concrete apartment buildings on either side of the street bandying the noise back and forth. Gripping the steering wheel, Faisal moved deftly between the mad lines of cars. It was always a circus of near misses—old trucks and vans careening forward, pirouetting around traffic circles on the thin line separating control from disaster. Still Faisal preferred the ruckus of the busy streets to the stifling quiet of his house. The gathering prompted by the "break-in"—he laughed now, remembering Mariam's confusion—was the first time they had all been in the same room in more than two weeks. Even when Abdullah came home for meals, Faisal preferred to eat upstairs rather than face the strained silence in the dining room. Before she knew for sure, Rosalie must have suspected something, for in the last months, as Abdullah grew more careless about dividing his time equally, she'd presided over those family dinners like a toppled queen in exile, with equal parts pride and despair.

B-Corp owned Prairie Vista, the compound where Dan Coleman lived. Because Faisal often spent much of his weekends alone, driving around Al Dawoun and out to the beach and back again, he had passed Prairie Vista hundreds of times. More often than not, the front guard was asleep in his booth, his tiny television blinking soundlessly through the glass. Now Faisal pulled the car up to the gate, where the guard spotted his B-Corp sticker and waved him through. He'd stolen the sticker from his father so that he could access the company swimming pool, but it had proven useful in other instances. Policemen generally left him alone, and he could gain easy entrance into any of the company-owned compounds. Parking the car, he checked the glove compartment for his sunglasses, slid them over his nose, and eyed his reflection in the rearview mirror. Tough guy, he thought. Bruce Willis. Harrison Ford. Tom Cruise. He admired those men for their boldness. It was too bad they were all kuffar, unbelievers.

Down the row of cars, Faisal spotted Dan's Hyundai. Good, he thought. It meant he was home. Faisal placed his hand on the BMW's door, the leather hot and soft from the sun. He hesitated. Maybe it would be best to wait in the parking lot and conduct surveillance. After all, there was power in watching. Then again, Majid would do more than watch. With a heave, Faisal got out of the car, his thobe sticking to the backs of his sweating thighs. The glass was heavy in his hand, and sticky. It still reeked of whiskey. He shut the car door and pressed the glass tight against his body so that nobody could see it.

The pool at the center of the compound was empty, save one red-shouldered man hulking along through the water, back and forth. It was close to noon, the white hour, when the sun managed to bleach the landscape so entirely that everything seemed dead. Objects took on the fuzzy quality of overexposure, their outlines blurred by the heat-expanded molecules pushing for escape from form. Faisal's neck was sweating beneath the stiff collar of his thobe as he stood at the door of Apartment 118. The blinds browned out the window—company-issued metal strips that blocked all signs of life.

Pausing momentarily, Faisal listened for movement within and then rapped twice on the door. A few beats passed before the door swung wide and Dan Coleman stood before him in a yellowing undershirt and a pair of wrinkled blue wind pants. Out of his khakis, he looked old and tired.

"Faisal. This is a surprise. Do you want to come in?"

Faisal nodded and stepped inside, mostly because he couldn't think of what to do next. Dan's graying hair was matted down on the left side, as if he'd been sleeping. The TV was on and the sour smell of old sweat permeated the room. Faisal pretended to scratch his nose so he could catch the faint scent of soap on his hand, but he only smelled whiskey. Besides the television, the only pieces of furniture in the room were a pulled-out futon that didn't look big enough for Dan's frame and a small particleboard coffee table. On the far wall, a tacked-up poster hung, the lower half faded from where the sun had hit it day after day. Faisal didn't recognize the man on the poster. He was sweating and gripping a trumpet in a smoky shaft of light. Miles Davis? Coltrane? These were names he'd heard the boys throw around at boarding school. From a shiny frame on the coffee table, Dan's two children and his former wife beamed out at Faisal. The woman (what was her name?) with a smile like a movie star, wide and white; the girl with hair the color of butter; and an apple-cheeked boy with a dusting of freckles. The photo was at least ten years old because Faisal knew that the girl was roughly his own age, maybe a few years older.

"Can I get you some Mirinda? Water?" Dan asked.

"OK," he found himself saying. "Mirinda."

Dan disappeared behind the refrigerator door then reemerged with a frosty can of orange soda. He motioned toward the futon. "Guess I have to put it up before you can sit on it," he said with a laugh.

Faisal watched him bend over and fuss with the sofa's stiff wooden frame.

"Damn thing gets stubborn sometimes." Dan's downward-tilted face was getting red from exertion, but Faisal didn't want to bend down and help him out.

"There we go. Have a seat."

"I'd rather stand."

"Suit yourself." Dan went back into the kitchen, where he started rustling around in the cupboard.

Faisal resumed examining the photograph on the coffee table. When Dan's family had lived in the Kingdom they would come to the Baylani compound some weekends. Faisal and the children had spent hours chasing one another around the pool until their feet were black and ragged, and at night they would sprawl out on beanbags in the upstairs toy room and watch American movies. "Is it all yours? All this?" the little boy asked him every time they saw each other, like there was something in the scale of the house, the expansive pool, and high-ceilinged toy room that he couldn't quite believe. Faisal had been sad when Abdullah told him the Colemans were leaving for good, since it meant no more nights of lying side by side, the girl's golden hair falling on his shoulder as she shifted her sleeping head. The memory came back to him with force. When he remembered childhood—his parents, their hands a trellis of joined fingers, his little sister like a wobbling goat kid, all knobby joints—he got a hollow feeling.

It was all gone now, that family in its purity. When he looked at his mother, he felt as if he were peering at a distant country on a map. She was New Zealand or Greenland—far-off, separated from him by fathoms and fathoms of sea. Before she learned about Isra, Rosalie had annoyed him with her badgering and advice, but now in the face of her foggy quietude, he found himself yearning for her presence. With his father gone most of the time and his mother in a state of continual self-pity, he and Mariam were left to fend for themselves. Luckily, he had Sheikh Ibrahim and Majid and his brothers in the Koranic study group. They were his family now.

"Hope you aren't feeling too picky," Dan said, setting a bowl of peanuts down on the coffee table. He took a handful of them and started eating.

"Um," Faisal said. He broke the metal tab off the top of his Mirinda can. "Well."

He swallowed. Silently, he ordered himself: *Say something. Something angry.*

"I want you to stop buying alcohol and giving it to my father."

A pause as Dan tilted his head, scratched his stubble-shadowed chin.

"Son, in order for me to stop buying hooch for your dad, he needs to stop asking me to buy it. He's the boss."

Where was his anger? In the dim light of Dan's desolate apartment, it had left him. He clutched tightly at the piece of glass until he could feel the broken edge digging into his palm. Dan was watching him with a perplexed look on his face. What was he even doing there? What had he hoped to accomplish? He set his soda can on the coffee table. His hand had been cut by the glass and was bleeding a little bit, round drops falling on the beige carpet. Switching the glass into his other hand, making sure to keep it out of sight, he stood up and started walking. He opened the door and let himself out.

"Faisal, why don't you finish your soda?" Dan called out after him.

But he was already outside, rushing back toward his car. He slipped inside, where hopefully no one would see the mess he had made of things.

FAISAL HESITATED ON the street outside Majid's house. On the corner, a dark-skinned man, Pakistani or Indian, worked a jackhammer against the concrete of the sidewalk. The walls around Majid's house cast no shadows. The air was dusty and hot. Faisal hadn't eaten anything for more than twelve hours, and he felt dizzy and tired. He rang the bell and, after a minute, heard the familiar click of the door being released from the inside. A deflated soccer ball sat in the middle of the short pathway to the house, a plain two-story unadorned by greenery of any kind.

A few years earlier, Majid's father had died of a heart attack. His mother had not remarried and said she no longer had the energy to make things nice. Each time Faisal came over, the house seemed to droop a little lower, and inside something was always broken. Faisal and Majid often spent their afternoons fixing the toilet or unclogging the kitchen drain. Umm Jalal and her family were poor but close, and Faisal envied them that closeness—the way Umm Jalal would get squinty-eyed with pride whenever Majid managed to fix the unfixable in the crumbling house. And when she was in the room, Majid was different. He lost his sharp edges, stopped forcing himself on the world. He made room for her. It seemed so simple, the bond between mother and son. But when Rosalie walked into a room, Faisal always felt on guard. What would she do or say that would differentiate her? What wrong gesture or turn of phrase would she give people to talk about?

Washed in the color-sucking light of the afternoon, Majid's house looked especially depleted. Faisal wished they could meet at his house from time to time, but Majid refused. "You won't catch me within ten kilometers of the Diamond Mile. Sorry, Faisal, but those people put their souls on and off like a necklace. You're different, of course, but let's just stay here. My mother makes the best ma'amul anyway."

Once inside, they went down to the basement and Faisal told Majid about going to Dan's condo, how he'd clutched the piece of glass but hadn't managed to say the right thing.

Majid examined Faisal's hand, tracing a finger along the inflamed edge of the cut. Without saying a word, Majid pulled back the sleeve of his thobe to show off the deep scar that ran, banana-shaped, from his hand to his elbow. The skin was pink and shining, like already-chewed bubble gum. Of course, he didn't need to tell the story behind it. It was local legend among the teenagers of Al Dawoun. Faisal had heard at least three different versions since Majid's return some months before, so trying to conclude just how he'd been injured became like a game of Clue: The American devil dog in Ramadi with the grenade; the British paratrooper in Fallujah with the long-range firepower; the red-faced Polish sniper outside the Green Zone.

"Now, this is a scar," he said. Then: "You don't want to go through your life passively, ya Faisal."

"I know that," he said, wiping his damp forehead with the sleeve of his thobe. "I was an idiot at Coleman's. You think I enjoy feeling that way?"

"Don't worry, brother. I'll help you learn the right words. I'll toughen you up. You can't change the way you were raised."

"What do you mean by that?"

"I mean that you're a little soft. You've always had everything you wanted. You've been an obedient schoolboy, just like your country and your mother asked you to be." He paused as if giving

Faisal time to react angrily, but Faisal kept quiet. He knew there was some truth to what his friend was saying.

"Like I said, you don't need to worry," Majid continued. "Whatever we do, we do together. You're a brother to me, and you think I'd let my brother play the fool?" He smiled his big broad smile. "We should play some more tricks on Coleman. Get him thinking about moving back to Texas."

"Yeah, maybe," Faisal said. He touched the tender skin on his palm. "I follow him around from time to time, when I get bored. It's pretty sad, actually. He doesn't seem to *go* anywhere. He just drives around Al Dawoun until it gets dark. Sometimes, he goes to the beach or the Gulf Hotel. Mostly he stays at the compound."

The windowless basement, with its cracked plaster and dim lights, depressed him. Once, when Majid had tried to host a group meeting at his house, the hamam had broken and flooded the basement, leaking piss and shit all over Sheikh Ibrahim's sandals. Majid had been mortified, and but for the scar on his arm, would have been the laughing stock of the group. It seemed that poverty was only noble in the Koran—in the physical world it provoked ridicule. The basement still smelled vaguely of urine, or perhaps it was just the mold of damp things, and he wondered how Majid could bear to spend so much time down there. He claimed it was the only place where he could surf Al Battar and other websites without Sahar or Jalal or Zahra looking over his shoulder.

"I'm going to go," Faisal said. "I'll see you for the meeting on Monday."

"Sure, little brother."

Faisal was already at the staircase, jogging up and out, back toward the street and the light. He considered Majid's idea of his destiny. The thought of speaking out in front of anyone terrified Faisal. All through his schooling, teachers had cajoled and scolded him in an effort to get him to participate in class, but his lips would not open. Only after Majid had convinced him to join Sheikh

Ibrahim's Koranic study group had Faisal learned the pleasures of a mouth filled with words. In school, the Koran had felt different to him, a heavy book read by paper-skinned, onion-hearted old men. But in Ibrahim's hands it came alive, the words strung together in musical verses that made Faisal's heart expand and contract with a force that felt like love. "This! This!" he thought. He thought of Majid, so tall and tough, so highly regarded by the other boys. And Faisal was *his* best friend. Of all the people Majid could have picked, he'd chosen Faisal.

As Faisal drove away from Majid's house, he decided not to go straight home. He couldn't stand the thought of going back to the house and its waiting silence. He needed to stay in the sunlight a little longer. Instead of turning home, he drove along the Corniche, the windows rolled down so he could feel the hot salt breeze. If he could just hold his problems up to the desert, the sea, they could be altered, absorbed, destroyed. Beneath the seaside palms, families picnicked, their trash floating out over the water alongside the gulls. Faisal felt his beard cutting hard under his chin from the force of the wind, and he opened his mouth to the sea air. He glanced down at the photo in the passenger seat.

Abdul Latif wasn't older than twenty in the picture. Faisal liked the shot because it captured the bravado of the man who left his tent and his tribe to wrangle his fortune when Saudi Arabia was a baby of a country. Here was a man who knew what it meant to be both modern and faithful, a balance that Faisal sought in his own life. The photo bore the date *September 30*, *1948* in faded handwriting. From what Faisal had gathered from his father, the picture was taken about a year before Abdul Latif's odyssey to the Gulf Coast and the riches awaiting him there. According to Abdullah, the wealth accumulated so quickly that locals claimed to witness golden-fleshed mangoes and topaz pitted dates fall into the lap of the fortunate young man from the Asir. Treasure had built homes outside Abdul Latif's door, walls of gold brick and dinar-tipped nails.

Here, with the sun in his face, the world a blur of primary colors under the doming sky, Faisal could close his eyes and imagine himself galloping next to Abdul Latif on his white camel. Hoof beats absorbed into the sand, orange saddle ropes flying out behind them, his grandfather ululating as they streaked across the desert. In the days before fortune. In the days before breach and compromise.

FOUR

TWO DAYS AFTER Faisal's bottle debacle and Rosalie's fig mutilation, Abdullah made a trip to the office. On his walk from the car to the door of the building, he missed the morning's many small moments of beauty: the sun glancing off the dewdrops that had settled on the lawn's green blades overnight, a low-hanging nest in the branch of the banyan tree outside the B-Corp building, its tiny, life-filled eggs cupped within. He had no eyes for the freshly washed windows that reflected the shwarma cart and its minder like a flawless silver mirror. Even the perfumed honeysuckle draped on the trellis in the office garden escaped his gaze, which he now fixed wrathfully on the sidewalk in front of him. Once he arrived at the office and realized that he'd overlooked all of the things that made his morning walk worthwhile, he became even angrier with his family.

"Farouk?" he said, addressing his secretary, a birdlike Tunisian with olive skin and eyes the gray-green color of the Mediterranean under a weak sun.

"Yes, Sheikh Abdullah?"

"I'd like you to send someone over to the big house and have them confiscate the Playstation and all the video games."

"Yes, Sheikh Abdullah."

"Shukran, Farouk."

"Ahlan wa sahlan, Sheikh Abdullah. But sir?"

"Yes?"

"What should I do with the video games?"

"Bismallah, Farouk. Send them to someone in Tunis. I don't care!"

Madness had lately afflicted his family. Rosalie was a corpse one minute and a banshee the next. Faisal was an enigma, with his furtive movements, his shadowy friends, his bizarre declamations. He created secrets that he guarded with militancy. Even Mariam was in trouble. They had received so many letters at home regarding her behavior at school that Abdullah couldn't keep track of her misdeeds—removing her veil on the playground, skipping class to read smuggled books in the library, passing out EQUAL RIGHTS FOR WOMEN NOW bumper stickers to her classmates. His once-sweet daughter was becoming a revolutionary. He would have implicated Rosalie in his children's oddball antics if they were not so utterly divergent. There appeared to be no one to blame, and that piqued Abdullah's fury.

As a consequence of his family's distracting behavior, he'd not given a single thought to his meeting with Prince Abdul Aziz, the yearly conference at which he blackened his tongue licking the prince's boots. Later in the week, somewhere in between talk of the weather (unseasonably warm) and the prince's sons (Ahmed was the favorite), Abdullah would guarantee Abdul Aziz a healthy percentage of any contracts that he granted to B-Corp. Usually, this required several hours of mental preparation on Abdullah's part; toadying did not come naturally to him.

He walked into his office and made sure to close the door with a convincing slam. How could he prepare witty banter about the prince's family when he was far too preoccupied with thoughts of his own disobedient lot? Why should a man stoop to work a fire that should blaze effortlessly? A woman should love her husband, as long as he provided a suitable life for her and gave her an equal share of his attention. The Koran said, *You may put off any of your wives you please and take to your bed any of them you please.*

Of course, Rosalie wasn't just a woman. She was a hellion, a sylph. In truth, he'd been terrified to tell her about Isra, worried that she would tear out his thinning hair in tufts or suffocate him in his sleep. Even while she'd become more of a Saudi wife than he'd ever thought possible, he knew that her spirit wasn't dead. The heart wants what it wants, he'd told his brothers, and they had nodded at him and shrugged, but in the back of his mind, he heard Rosalie saying *hogwash.* When it came to women, a yellow stripe of cowardice ran down the backs of the Baylani men. They owned provinces, ran villages, opened their hearts before Almighty God, but they could not bring themselves to be entirely honest with their wives. He knew it was in him, too, and so he'd decided to ride it out and see what happened rather than stick his hand straight into the hive and wait to get stung.

He sat at his desk, swiveling in his high-backed chair until he faced the windows. He wished he were the CEO of some American corporation, so he could keep a bar in the office—a neatly organized cart filled with the clear and amber liquids that helped take the edge off. "To life management," Dan said whenever they clinked glasses. At that moment, he could use a bottle of at least twenty-year-old scotch.

As he watched the morning unfold outside his window, twirling a pen between his fingers, Abdullah tried to recall any fig-decimating or hair-pulling or other forms of feminine vengeance occurring among his father's four wives. He couldn't. But then, he'd rarely seen Abdul Latif's other wives, and as everyone liked to say, it had been another time. Things had changed; he knew that, but tradition didn't change overnight. Tradition was the slow accumulation of centuries, and he was his father's son. His first experience of the world was as a child of Abdul Latif, a man who took wives as easily as he took his ghawa in the morning. It was what some powerful men still did. To hell with everyone and their tsk-tsking, their high-minded visions of modernization.

By the time his father took his second wife, Abdullah had been ten, too old to spend his afternoons in the care of women. While Abdul Latif worked at empire-building, Abdullah went to school, learning how to write neat classical script, perform ablutions, twist ears, and spit with vigor. If there had been trouble among the wives, the ripples had never reached the surface. Abdullah's mother, Khadija, bore the same slit-mouthed expression until she'd died, when he was seventeen. She'd been his father's first wife, his only Bedu wife, her body and mind built for hardship, her skin leathered and eyes lightened by the sun, hair a blackish red that seemed to contain all life and death, blood and soot, within its thick waves. The fact of her people's centuries-long survival in the Rub' al-Khali meant that she wasn't a woman to question destiny and she wouldn't have dared to oppose Abdul Latif's decisions. But it had been a different era, and having multiple wives was a more accepted way of life. Now the Kingdom was filled with monogamists who said, "Oh, I believe it is every man's right, by the Koran!" and then, with a false humility that grated on Abdullah: "It is just not for me, alhamdulillah."

He wished his mother were still alive. She would have loved Rosalie, after the initial shock of it. They were both tough as the desert, survivors. And they both laughed full-force, heads tilted back, teeth showing. Abdullah always enjoyed the way people in restaurants and movie theaters would turn to look at them whenever Rose had laughed that throaty laugh. He tipped back in his chair and surveyed his office. A large mahogany desk custom-made for him by a Dutch carpenter, deep built-in shelves where various plaques and trophies spoke of his years of triumph, two walls of long windows through which he could view the city where he had spent his young adulthood, his middle age, and now, his later years. Yet his well-appointed workspace was nothing in comparison to the homes he'd given his family. He was most proud of Rosalie's house on the Diamond Mile. It was a family house from the start, and he and Rose had given the children the run of it. The pool was always filled with bright toys, the makeshift soccer pitch in the backyard littered with homemade obstacle courses the kids and their friends would set up and race through, the competitive looks on their faces reminding him that children were not so far removed from the pulls of the adult world. Rosalie was always down on the floor or out in the grass, playing with the kids. They'd never had a nanny, though she'd consented to a housekeeper and a cook. He'd loved that casual, hands-on American way she'd mothered their children. Over the years, though, as her clothing got finer, she preferred to watch from the patio, a tall glass of iced tea in her hand. And maybe that was her right, as a mother—to one day refuse to get down in the dirt with her kids, to feel as if she had done the hard work and could now sit back. Or maybe it was the country changing her, since mothers in her social circle just didn't behave that way for the most part. But he missed the rambunctiousness, the energy. The years of money and ease had made her more refined and to him, less recognizable. When he had married Rosalie, he knew that the only way for a non-Saudi woman to be fully happy in Saudi Arabia was if she came ready to surrender to the culture and religion. Such was the strength of the country's orthodoxy; there could be no other way. But he had loved her so desperately that he ignored his misgivings. And at the time, he felt that their passion was enough.

Now her energy was returning, just not in the way he had hoped. When he was being honest with himself, he knew that he hadn't told her about Isra out of fear. Fear and sadness. In Texas, she'd had a notoriously bad temper—Jalapeño Rose, they called her at the Lion—and certain customers refused to come back to the bar after run-ins with her. Of course, she was usually in the right. Someone had failed to tip, and so she'd publicly shamed him, or some drunk had tried to grab a part of her she was determined to share only with herself or Abdullah.

But he'd also been sad at the predicament he found himself in. He'd fallen in love with Isra. While he hadn't admitted it to Dan in the car the other night, he agreed with him that a man could really only love one woman at a time. So what did that say about him and Rose? He knew the answer, and it was a punch to the gut.

And now that the truth about his second marriage was out, he could feel Rosalie's love transmuting into something ugly. He knew she would not cooperate with his efforts to incorporate Isra into the Baylani family, though they *were* all family, especially now that Isra was pregnant, due in early summer. Rosalie, Isra, Mariam, Faisal—all connected through him, bound by blood the moment the baby arrived. He was going to tell Rosalie the other night—babies mitigate anger; he'd seen it himself when Faisal and Mariam had been born, the new softness in his father's face—but he found he couldn't get the words out.

Farouk knocked and then opened the door. He set a tea tray down on the small table in front of Abdullah's desk.

"I thought you might want a tea," Farouk said. "They say it has soothing qualities."

The earthy scent of the tea filled Abdullah's nose.

"See that some gets delivered to everybody else in my family then, will you?" Abdullah shook his head. He watched as Farouk carefully poured the amber liquid into a small, gilded cup.

"Shukran, ya Farouk."

"Afwan, Sheikh."

"Farouk?"

"Yes, Sheikh?"

"Pour one for yourself. Sit down for a moment, take a little break."

Farouk looked confused, probably because Abdullah had never said more than "hello," "good-bye," or "thank you" to him in the decade they had both worked at B-Corp. The man poured himself a cup of tea, then perched on the edge of one of the showy leather king chairs that Abdullah had had brought in from Italy.

"Are you a religious man, Farouk?" Abdullah watched him shift uncomfortably in response to the question. "The truth, now. No lying to the boss." He meant it as a joke, but he saw there could be no joking between the foreign office manager and the CEO.

"Not particularly, sir. My father was a philosophy professor at the University of Tunis."

Abdullah laughed. "So, you had your own problems growing up, eh? Nihilism? Existentialism? All those isms could drive a man as mad as any suras."

"True enough, sir."

"Are you married?"

"No, Sheikh Abdullah."

"Ever been married?"

"Yes, once."

"What happened? Did she die?"

"In a way. We divorced after fifteen years of marriage."

Abdullah tried to appoint his face with the proper expression, but he wasn't sure what that would be in this case. Sadness? Concern? Anger?

"And why was that, if you don't mind me asking?"

"She met someone she loved more than me, sir."

"Hmm. Children?"

"No, sir."

"Ah, see. There's where it gets complicated, doesn't it?"

"I suppose so, sir."

They each took sips of their tea, the silence stretching out into the next minute, and then the next. Abdullah did not feel comforted by their talk. He wasn't sure what he'd expected to feel, but now it was something akin to annoyance. There should be some sort of training before you got yourself mixed up in such things—marriages and divorces and children and second marriages. He had trained for every other part of his life, football as a youth and then business and economics as an adult. Even driving required training. Yet when you married, what advice did people give? Only congratulations, and what good does that do anyone?

"I've taken up too much of your time already, Farouk. Please." He gestured toward the door. Farouk rose, lifting the tea tray from the table. He had a certain grace about him, and what Abdullah had previously, and a bit resentfully, mistaken for austerity, he could now see was sadness. He had just never taken the time to notice before.

"One final thing," he called out, just as Farouk was closing the door.

"Yes, sir?"

"Please call Mariam's school. Tell them she'll be leaving at lunch. A doctor's appointment."

Even though she was a scamp and trickster, or perhaps because of it, Mariam always cheered him up. They would go to lunch at the Gulf Hotel, eat shrimp cocktail on the promenade overlooking the water. After the blow-up at the marketplace, Mariam had canceled her birthday party. She'd not gotten a proper celebration, and he wanted to make it up to her. He knew that she shouldn't have to suffer as a result of her parents' problems.

He switched on his computer, counting the beats until the reassuring start-up sounds resonated through the quiet room. Thank God for the office, his cool refuge from the tumult of the big house. He thought of the house he shared with Isra, which was still an oasis. Her newness. Her firmness. Her cute Palestinian way of saying things. He neatened a stack of papers on his desk, pleased with thoughts of her.

AT NOON, ABDULLAH pulled up outside of the Al-Watan Modern Girls School. He parked at the curb and then rolled down his window to tell the guard his purpose. After a few minutes, Mariam appeared, her eggplant-colored abaya flapping open around her legs, revealing the long woolen skirt beneath. She clutched a stack of books to her chest and moved to open the door, but the security guard lunged at the handle, as if insulted by the idea that she would open her own door. She gave him a withering look.

Once she was inside the car, Abdullah again rolled down the window.

"Tell the man thank you, habibti."

"Shukran," she said with a little wave of her hand.

He rolled up the window and turned to look at her.

"I've never known you to be impolite, Mimou."

"Ali and I are fighting an all-out war, Baba, and you just forced me to surrender the day."

"War? What kind of war could my sweet daughter possibly be fighting?" He said this with a chuckle because everyone in the family knew that Mariam was always stirring things up for some cause she'd adopted.

"He calls Headmistress Shideed when I arrive every morning and reports my 'inappropriate dress.' I think my abaya is elegant."

"Try to be a little understanding, badditi. The man's old. He's never seen anything but black abayas. He's old-guard."

"Times are changing. Why can't *he* be understanding? His time is in the past. *We're* the future, me and the other girls."

She pulled her scarf off her head and smoothed her hair. He noticed her hands had lost their baby fat, her fingers long and thin, her nails painted bright pink. She was fourteen. Soon, after the baby was born, she would no longer be the youngest in the family. She would be a good sister. She already was.

"You're right," he said, pulling the car out into the street. "Patience will only get you so far." He thought of Rosalie, how she had wanted to change things back in the States—the way women were treated by professors and in bars. When she'd gotten to Saudi, though, she was intent on fitting in, eager to please his family and friends. There was no place for her women's lib ideas in a country where women couldn't even drive.

"Where're we going?" Mariam asked.

"I thought I'd take you for a birthday lunch at the Gulf Hotel. I know how much you like their shrimp cocktail. You can even order a virgin daiquiri."

When she didn't respond, he glanced over at her. She was staring out the window, her cheek resting against the car door.

"Love? Doesn't that sound like fun? Playing hooky with your baba?"

"Not really," she said. "Umma wouldn't like it."

"She won't mind. She knows you didn't get your birthday party, and besides, it's only one afternoon of school . . ."

"I'm not talking about school. I'm talking about being with you. Like everything's OK."

"Everything will be OK, Mimou, I promise. Let me take you for lunch. Please?" He knew he needed it more than she did, and he felt badly for pressing the issue, but he'd been so excited to see her. He hoped her optimism and energy would spread to him, make him truly believe that everything would be OK. "I won't tell her if you won't. It'll be our secret."

"But that's the problem. You keep too many secrets, Baba."

After a few minutes of silence, Mariam reached over and turned on the radio, flipping channels until she came to some Lebanese pop music. As they drove, she hummed along, folding the edge of her abaya into peaks and then unfolding it again.

When they arrived at the hotel, a valet took the car and drove off. Doormen greeted him by name and smiled at Mariam. She hadn't rewrapped her scarf, but it was OK. The hotel was lenient about those things, their restaurant popular for its mixed dining room, where men and women sat together freely.

Since it was cool and sunny outside, they chose a table on the promenade. He let Mariam have the chair that looked out toward to sea, which was uncommonly blue that afternoon. She ordered a mango lassi, shrimp cocktail, and a whole grilled branzino stuffed with lemons. She smiled at him after she finished placing her order, as if to let him know that his attempts at diplomacy would cost him. He ordered the fillet with a side of broccoli. Since Isra, he had started to watch his waistline again, picking at his food like a bird. He'd forgotten the energy it took to be in love.

"And how is the internship going? A'm Nabil says good things about your work ethic."

"He would say good things even if I were lazy. You're his brother."

"I don't think so. You know he has no tolerance for fools and loafers."

"That's true. He told me some stories about you from university. The time you two stayed up all night, studying for your rhetoric final—how you kept wanting to take a break and buy a beer, and he got so annoyed that he started a running tab for every time you said the word 'beer.' He said you still haven't paid him the hundred dollars you owe him."

Abdullah smiled.

"Nabil was the better student, no question. But where did all his studiousness get him? I could buy his whole neighborhood."

"Baba, don't be crude. A'ami doesn't care about money. He's fighting for bigger things."

"The luxury of the youngest brother. Not all of us can afford to work on our vanity projects."

Abdullah could feel his face getting hot. He shouldn't get angry, especially after he'd dragged her there in the first place, but it was hard. Sometimes, a person could be *too* right. Mariam and Nabil were both that way, and it grated on his nerves.

"I have over four hundred followers of my blog now," she said, gracefully changing the subject. That was another thing he loved about his daughter—she would drive you to the edge with her questions, but she would never push you over it.

"Really?"

"My blog. You know—*True Confessions of a Saudi Teen*?"

He couldn't remember anything about it, but he didn't like the sound of it.

"Don't worry," she continued. "It's totally anonymous. I wouldn't want to get anyone in trouble."

He raised an eyebrow at her and made a mental note to read the blog at some point. As a father, he was pretty easygoing, but the name of the blog sounded like a soap opera. He didn't want to wake up one day as the father of the next big reality television star, or worse, have his daughter made an example of by the government. He knew they'd jailed a blogger a few months back, but the man's site was political, always digging at the royal family.

"What's it about, this blog?" he said.

With the help of his prosthetic hand, he popped open a pistachio nut from the small wooden bowl on the table. Whenever he went out, he made sure to wear his prosthesis. His stump was fine for home and family, not for restaurants. He chewed and, while his daughter talked, kept his eyes closed for just a moment. The sound of the waves lapping against the piles that kept the restaurant suspended above the water and the sun on his face made him think, for just a moment, that if he could bring Rosalie here, if they could sit together on the promenade, they both might find their way back to love.

"Fashion. The good abayas I've seen lately, the new ones I sew for myself. It's also about school and my war with Ali. I think my stories are pretty funny, and that's why people read it. I also talk about things I hear at the *Saudi Times*, about Hisham al-Sabah and the work he does for people put into prison without any reason. Faizah al-Zahrani and I talk a lot. I write about her, too, though I use a code name. It's Sheytana, since A'ami is always calling her a devil for the trouble her stories cause him."

He watched his daughter talking. People never said she looked like Rosalie, since their coloring was so different. But he saw it, in her broad mouth and deep-set eyes. Could he have done something to make things different? How could he have even begun to explain to Rosalie that, even though she'd become exactly what his country demanded her to be, it wasn't what *he* wanted her to become, and now he no longer loved her as he once had? Or maybe it had nothing to do with Saudi Arabia or with the money. Maybe it was just that people changed over time and love vanished without warning, without mercy.

"It sounds great, habibti," he said.

"You're barely listening." She looked at him with exasperation. "What are you thinking about?"

"How you may have gotten my black hair, but everything else belongs to your mother."

"Really?"

He could see that she was pleased with this assessment. They'd always been close, Rose and Mariam, so close that he'd felt a little jealous; it made him more aware that he lacked that closeness with his son. The food arrived, and Mariam didn't hesitate to hack off the head of the branzino, stabbing at the white flesh with her fork and making little noises as she ate that showed her happiness. She grinned at him over the table, pulling a fishbone from her mouth and standing to flick it out over the railing and into the sea. "I return you to your brothers!" she said, giggling. Her appetite was also her mother's.

When she sat down again, her face grew serious.

"I think this is just a phase you're going through," she said.

He looked out over the water. An orange buoy bobbed on the surf. He'd heard of dolphins, and even sharks, swarming the shore occasionally, but today the water was quiet. How to explain adult love to a girl, when he himself couldn't understand its fluctuations?

"Isra isn't just a novelty," he said. And then, before he could stop himself: "I'm in love with her."

They were both quiet for a moment.

"You're not, though." Mariam insisted. "You just think you are. You're in love with Umma. You had me and Faisal with Umma."

And he was going to have a child with Isra, too. If that was what the world required to make love legitimate, then by God, they were legitimate. He saw, though, that Mariam was on the verge of tears, so he kept that last thought to himself. He had indulged enough already with this lunch. He needed to stop looking for absolution from Farouk, a stranger, and his daughter. Before God, he had done nothing wrong.

"Shall we get dessert?" He said. "Crème brûlée?" He knew how much she liked it.

"Sure," she said. She didn't meet his eyes, as if she had betrayed her mother for a custard.

"Happy birthday, my little duck," he said, patting her knee beneath the table.

BACK AT THE office, at the day's end, Abdullah watched from his window as the city of Al Dawoun changed into an alien territory of lights. The white concrete buildings glowed in the blue light, neon flickering on above the stores—al-Shabab Barber Shop; Good Yum Chinese Restaurant; al-Sabah Grocery, where Abdullah bought the sweet-smelling strawberry tobacco for his shisha and the pistachio nuts that he kept in the pockets of his thobe. Running his good hand through his hair, he felt his heart beat slowly in the silence. Everyone had gone home, but Abdullah stayed, dreading a return to the big house. He rubbed his stump as he watched the moon rise, its halfway shape engorged on secondhand light. He had only a few moments to himself before he would have to go to the mosque for the Maghrib prayer, and then to the big house for the night's dinner. Tonight was the first evening he and Rosalie would host the family since Isra's existence had been uncovered, and he knew his brothers and sisters and their wives and husbands would scrutinize everything, down to the temperature of the sweet tea, in order to see just how Isra had affected things at the big house. Cold tea or overcooked fish or dry dates spelled disaster, for only a struggling family would overlook the run of its kitchen. He was suddenly glad he had spoken in advance to Yasmin and Anisa about the importance of the meal's preparations. Of course, there were variables he could not control. Rosalie, for instance.

Abdullah considered his stump an accessory. He polished his interrupted pink wrist with a soft cloth and occasionally used it for cheap parlor tricks. He thought it sad that some limbless people felt inclined to hide their handicap with long shirtsleeves or strategically placed bandages. To make up for the self-consciousness of others, Abdullah was an exhibitionist. He used his stump as a prop to enthrall children at family gatherings, rounding them up and telling stories of the fearsome horseman, Sa'dun, leader of the Bani Khalid, the largest tribe in the Hasa oasis. He spun stories of Sa'dun's battles against the Ottomans as the warrior tried to protect eastern Arabia and its yellow pearls from Suleiman the Magnificent's men. Unveiling his stump, claiming that he lost his hand in battle fighting alongside Sa'dun, Abdullah wheezed his thin laugh as the children stared, mouths agape. Never mind that he was neither a member of the Bani Khalid tribe nor several hundred years old. The elimination of mystery and wonder implied by the very uptight, scientific word "proof" was all that Abdullah stood against, for mystery and wonder were the bedrock upon which he'd built his faith in God and the world.

Tilting back in his chair, he ran the old, soft cloth over the rounded flesh of his stump. The blue vein in his wrist pulsed. He closed his eyes and tried to remember life with two hands. Now, where did the dead-ended blood go when the vein tapered out? Abdullah looked down at his stump and thought of the young boy he had been when he'd lost his hand. Funny how the absence of one thing—a hand, or an old love—could lead to the presence of so many memories. Memory was like that, taking advantage of a certain color, a trodden street, a known perfume, the cast of light in morning or evening, to catapult its way back into your head in order to spread its pallet and stay awhile.

He'd been pensive since his lunch with Mariam that afternoon. She reminded him of hard truths—the love that had produced her, for one. Instead of energizing him, their lunch had made him nostalgic, so that all afternoon he'd fiddled unproductively in his office, digging up memories of the early times with Rosalie. The "foreign exchange" party they'd hosted, when she'd forced him to make brisket for fifty of their friends and she, in turn, had to make a similarly outsized kabsa. They'd spread newspapers all over the floor of their tiny place, topping it with bed pillows and couch cushions and whatever else they could find to fashion it into a makeshift majlis. They stole a keg from the Lion—Rose claimed they owed it to her in tips—and Nabil rounded up several shishas from the other Arab students on campus. Miraculously, both meals were succulent and perfect, and everyone stuffed themselves full, then fell asleep in piles around the living room, sauce on their faces, their fists still full of the basmati rice that Rosalie had cooked for days leading up to the party. And there were the Texas football games, when Rosalie would paint orange stripes on his face and they'd go and shout themselves hoarse from the cheap seats at Memorial Stadium. He remembered driving up to Dallas to watch Earl Campbell run like crazy against a mean Oklahoma team. Afterward, Rose had pushed her way to the front of a long line of fans waiting by the team bus. When Campbell finally came out of the locker room, she'd shaken his hand, rattling off his career stats and telling him he was a shoe-in for the Heisman. Campbell just beamed, and when she'd finished, he said he had to get a photo with the girl who knew his stats better than his mother. They'd all three posed together, and then he'd signed their program. Abdullah wasn't sure where that program had ended up, but the photo was framed and set on the bookshelf of his office at the big house, Rosalie's red hair in loose Farrah waves, like all the girls wore back then.

In that photo, her smile practically took up her whole face. A shit-eating grin, Dan had called it. That girl, that grinning, bold girl. He closed his eyes and felt his heart beating a little faster, sending warmth through his body. Perhaps he and Rose could get that feeling back and it could be as he'd initially, foolishly, imagined his life with two wives—a different, deep love with each woman. How naïve he had been, how impulsive in marrying Isra. And how cowardly. He saw that now, acknowledged that he had not wanted to deal properly with the distance opening up between him and Rosalie and so had fallen back on the laws of the tribe to avoid it.

Abdullah leaned forward in the chair so his arms hung down between his legs and touched the floor. It was an exercise his doctor had told him to do whenever his back ached. He wished the doctor had told him what to do when his whole body hurt, when his brain cramped up from too many memories. Old man, shaybah, he admonished himself. He sat up and kneaded the fleshy muscles along his spine, recalling one of his father's sayings: *A sore back means a heavy load is coming.* Abdullah smiled. To Abdul Latif, the idea of a heavy load wasn't ominous; it merely meant more gold bullion was on the way. The man had never known a day of depression, earning his riches through the force of his optimism, and Abdullah tried hard to emulate him. But in Abdul Latif's time, things happened backward and upside down. The Americans pulled out the earth's insides and a Bedu boy walked out of the desert seeking his fortune. Anything was possible.

If Abdullah didn't leave soon, he'd be late for prayer and have to suffer the condemning glances of the Imam. Abdullah checked his e-mail one last time. There was a new message from Faisal, some sort of video. Squinting at the badly pixelated images, he thought it was the same terrorist video he'd seen on the news. As he focused on the video, he realized that the fuzzy-featured terrorist was actually a white man, and he held up a book before repeatedly plunging it into the toilet. When the camera zoomed in on the text, Abdullah saw that it was the Koran. It was overacting at its worst, the man's stupid grin incapable of expressing the paler shades of malice fundamental to desecration. Abdullah was not sure what feelings the video was meant to provoke. Clearly, Faisal wanted him to get angry and would probably bring it up at dinner that night, indignant. Kuffar! Faisal would growl, the poor boy's idea of cocktail conversation.

But anger eluded Abdullah. He just felt sorry. Sorry for the fools responsible for the video and the imbeciles who perpetuated its message by forwarding it on to others. Perhaps it was his old age and the comfort of his wealth that allowed him to be so calm. To him, the video was farcical, one goofball committing a single, outrageous act. The man couldn't touch the verses that Muslims all over the world had known by heart since they'd learned to read. A book was just paper and ink, a bit of leather.

In Texas, he'd made the few requisite political overtures that the time period and his age demanded. He'd been halfheartedly involved with the Arab Student Union, but gradually he found himself choosing Rosalie's quilted double bed over the hot concrete of Congress Avenue and the poster-board signs of the union. They'd been dating for several months and after a while, she'd told Wayne and Maxine about him. Her parents had spent thirteen years in the Kingdom, but their time overseas did not mean they would accept him as a suitor for their daughter. They'd feigned tolerance until Thanksgiving, when she asked them if she could bring her new love home with her to Sugar Land. Why sure, honey, they'd said. But just know that we will try to convince Ab-Dallah to accept Jesus Christ as his personal Lord and Savior.

Instead, he and Rosalie stayed in Austin, eating enchiladas verdes, drinking shakers of Mexican martinis, and making love. They'd lived cocooned away from his world and hers. When they finally emerged a year later they were engaged, their love resplendent as a butterfly wing; he'd told his family that he'd found a bride and began the preparations for Rosalie's introduction and the wedding. He finally met Wayne and Maxine March and faced their uninspired proselytizing. When Rosalie converted to Islam, her parents stopped speaking to her, breaking their silence only when she gave birth to their first grandchild. Interestingly, that was also when *his* family became more accepting of her. Abdul Latif had never made it hard for her, exactly, but neither he nor Abdullah's sisters and brothers had gone out of their way to help Rosalie find her way in the beginning. He still recalled Rose coming home from the Biltagi Brothers' market in tears. It was back before she'd become fluent in Arabic. She'd been looking for dried oregano for a pasta sauce she wanted to make, and when she couldn't find it on her own, she asked her sister-in-law, Nadia, to help her ask the store clerk in Arabic. But Nadia had pretended she didn't understand what Rose was asking, though Nadia's English was flawless. "That bitch," Rose had said to Abdullah when she got home. Instead of sympathizing with her, he'd yelled at her for insulting his family. "I'm your family now too!" she'd shouted back. Later, after they'd calmed down, she'd looked at him and said, "You better be on my side, because you're all I've got." With the help of a private tutor that she hired using her savings left over from the Lion, she'd learned Arabic in less than two years—an astonishing rapidity for the tricky language. But Rosalie didn't waste her Arabic or her English on prayers. After witnessing, with great annoyance, both sides of the family try to ruin love with their versions of faith, she told him she had decided to forego bossy religions of all kinds. Instead, she did her yoga, and each morning, when she was done, she looked so serene that he accepted her form of spirituality as unusual but good.

AT THE MOSQUE, Abdullah hurried to his spot, prayed, and raced out before he could be waylaid by any of his friends. He wanted to try to talk to Rosalie before the guests arrived for the feast. In the car, he hummed nervously, tapping his fingers against the mahogany console as the car bumped over potholes. Ayoub, Abdullah's driver, wasn't known for finesse, but for a few extra riyals a month, he kept his boss's whereabouts quiet. It was a bargain well worth the few clips and dents they'd ratcheted up on Al Dawoun's crowded roads. Unlike Ayoub, the German hardware could be trusted to keep secrets regardless of its treatment.

Normally, evening was a slow time of easement and reflection when Abdullah could say his most honest prayers. At dusk, his mind became loamy again, ready for new seeds, and so he read his favorite suras over and over, working toward memorization. But now, instead of smoothing over the prayers in his mind, he found himself fixating on the video Faisal had sent him. His son was restless, anyone could see that. There were tides moving in the boy. Abdullah rattled his prayer beads, imagining Faisal's hands growing redder and redder from anger at his father's tardiness and the scalding water he used when performing wudhu. He was at the traveling age; the age when every young man wants to go out into the world. Most of his schoolmates had graduated and gone on to study in America or in one of Saudi Arabia's improved universities. Yet Faisal wanted to stay right there in Al Dawoun, rooted to this old familiar ground. Odd boy, Abdullah thought. Odd, serious boy. My boy.

Colors hung in the evening sky. Abdullah remembered his father telling him the story of the sunset once, when he'd asked why the sky always caught on fire. Abdul Latif had replied, *It's the color of a million hearts exploding from God's beauty*. Stay, light, Abdullah willed. He didn't want dark to fall just yet. Dark meant another night of choosing which of his wives' beds to sleep in. He hadn't thought of that when he married Isra. He'd been too fixated on her lemon breasts, the shape of her eyes, her words spoken like poetry.

One last peaceful year, he'd think with each anniversary of the marriage to Isra. He'd counted two before the afternoon when Rosalie had confronted him after her weekly trip to the al-Qasr souq. With time, he came to justify his marriage to Isra as zakat, charity—one of the five pillars of Islam. After all, she had been lonely, widowed. A woman needed a man's care. So what if he was susceptible to women's beauty. Who wasn't? What was the difference between a heart exploding at sunset or at the sight of a beautiful face? Both were signs of God's presence in the world. Still, he missed Rosalie, her ritual disrobing, the way she shaped her body to his. He missed examining the deep blue vein visible just under the skin of her left breast. Abdullah had always imagined it pumping blood directly to her heart, animating her as they made love. Isra's body was new to him; he was still learning its geography. It's what drove him wild about her: the opacity, the quality of the unknown that Rosalie had lost after their many years together.

AYOUB SLOWED THE car just enough to prevent it from careening into the ditch in front of the wall which surrounded the Baylani compound. They hadn't beaten the other guests, after all. Mercedes and BMWs crowded the driveway. A single champagne-tinged Rolls shone out from the dark mess of steel. Ayoub parked and then opened Abdullah's door for him.

"Enjoy the feast, sir."

"Shukran, Ayoub. Tomorrow at eight a.m.?"

"Certainly sir."

When Abdullah reached the house, he took a breath and collected himself. Tonight had to go well. The family must see that everything was all right.

He opened the door to the familiar chaos of a feast night. Children darted about and the strong smell of cooking onions hung in the air. He felt his shoulders loosen and his stomach tighten in anticipation. In the great room to his right, the men were gathered, waiting patiently to eat.

"Abu Faisal! Salaam waleikum. Keyf al saha?"

"Alhamdulillah, ya Dan."

Abdullah allowed himself to be borne around the room on the tide of familiar greetings and faces. Usually, when it was just the family, everyone ate together, but tonight Dan joined them, so the women ate in the next room. Abdullah made the rounds and kissed his brothers in greeting before taking a seat on the low-lying burgundy sofa that ran the perimeter of the room. The mood was good, boisterous and easy, and a steady stream of grand-nieces and grand-nephews came in to say marhaba and kiss Abdullah's forehead. He felt the dull throb of his stump, a natural metronome keeping time to the conversation's movement. Faisal approached him, walking erectly but with an awkwardness that showed his youth. Eyeing Dan, Faisal took his seat on Abdullah's right. Laughter sounded in the next room.

Taking their seats around the elaborate meal, the men mumbled bismallah. Quiet fell over the room as they began to eat the first course. Abdullah slowly chewed a cube of meat, letting the spices open up his nostrils. Cinnamon and cardamom clouded his palate, and he tasted the faint flavor of wormwood leaves, each spice distinct and alive on his tongue. As the men ate, Abdullah felt a low ecstasy burning in his stomach. He was grateful for the food, for the family around him. Thanks be to God, he thought. Prayers said from the stomach were always the truest.

Abdullah watched Dan attempt to roll rice into a ball to eat with the meat of his stew, but the ball kept falling apart in his hand. Around him, the other men balled the rice and meat together expertly before popping them into their mouths. It wasn't sticky rice, and it had taken most of the men a childhood of practice to properly roll up the long, uncooperative grains. Abdullah chuckled to himself as he remembered Dan's first time in the Kingdom decades ago. Saudi traditions eluded him and he had embarrassed himself at more than one dinner that Abdullah threw in his honor. He sat with the soles of his feet facing people as they tried to eat; he inhaled his food using both hands, probably thinking he was being polite with his zeal. He took his cups of sweet tea with his left hand, not knowing that Saudis didn't use their left hand to eat or drink because it was unclean. *The left hand is for ass-wiping, or it was, back in the day*, Abdullah had finally told him. Fortunately for Dan, they accepted him as a well meaning, if rough-hewn, person. The Baylanis didn't have anything against Americans, as long as no one in their family wanted to marry one. They'd loved Dan even more after he married Carolyn, fathered two children, and revealed the devotion to family that Saudis held most dear. Unlike many Western expatriates in the Kingdom, Dan counted Saudis and Arabs among his best friends, and he went to more kabsas than compound barbecues.

Just as Abdullah decided against teasing his friend for his rice-balling deficiencies, Faisal stood and began to speak in his clear, slightly accented English.

"Before we begin the next course, I would like to say a prayer for the man sitting to my father's left, Daniel Coleman. You all know him well and he has shared my family's hospitality for a number of years now. But we should never forget that Mr. Coleman has not yet accepted God, nor has he accepted the teachings of the Prophet Muhammad, peace be upon Him."

Abdullah felt a piece of meat sticking in his throat. Faisal continued.

"I cannot enjoy this meal knowing that I sit beside a man who will know hellfire when he passes from this world. The Koran says *Believers, do not make friends with any but your own people. They will spare no pains to corrupt you. They desire nothing but your ruin. Their hatred is evident from what they utter with their mouths, but greater is the hatred which their breasts conceal.* I fear for my family, and so I take this opportunity to speak directly to God on this unbeliever's behalf, in hopes that He might help Mr. Coleman."

Yusef, Abdullah's middle brother, cleared his throat and stole a quick look at Dan, who was sitting with his legs crossed, his ruddy face turned politely toward Faisal. Rashid and Ibrahim, Faisal's cousins, were quietly repeating na'am and wallahi, nodding in agreement. Abdullah had always believed that the two boys' faith was more the result of boredom and a pushy mother than anything else. He fixed them with a silencing look.

"Allahu Akhbar. Bismallah al-rahman al-rahim. Alhamdulillah wa shukru lillah."

Abdullah interrupted his son before he could continue.

"Bas, Faisal. Bas. That's enough. You've shown Mr. Coleman a great deal of disrespect. Apologize to him immediately."

A few of the other men nodded in support of Abdullah.

"Ya Faisal, sit down," Yusef said. "We just want to eat. We're all friends here." He twirled his beard nervously.

"For God's sake, yes," Nabil said. "Sit down, boy. Some of us spend all day working. We don't want fighting when we come home." Nabil was not known for his patience. His short temper and quick tongue caused issues at home, but were what made him one of the best news editors in the region.

The rest of the men remained still, the absence of their voices amplifying the tension in the room. Faisal's cheeks, which were almost as fair as Rosalie's, turned a deep red, whether from fury or embarrassment Abdullah couldn't tell. Yet Faisal went on, his voice quavering slightly.

"I think it is my right to say a prayer for an unbeliever, should I find myself sitting next to him at a meal."

"Faisal . . ."

"Especially after watching that awful video I sent you. Father, please."

"Now is not the time to talk about the video. See how you've made everyone silent? No one else is as ungenerous to Dan as you are. It's your right to refuse your meal, if you're so offended by his presence, but the Koran states that the Prophet, peace be upon him, took pleasure in the company of all men. You should treat our guest with the same respect."

Abdullah's voice was firm and left no room for protest. Faisal left the room quickly, an angry sigh stretching out behind him until he had disappeared beyond the doorway.

"Dan, please eat some more," Abdullah said. "Women hate

skinny men. Unless you have some more kabsa, you're never going to get married again."

Dan countered with a weak grin. The good mood had evaporated, and the men sat solemnly, not eating as they watched the maids clear the dishes away. Some of the more conservative men, the men who'd never really grown accustomed to Dan, with his loud laughter and jokes, looked stern. Abdullah could almost hear them writing their own fatwa banning laughter. While the Filipinas placed platters of steaming hamour and rice in the center of the table, Abdullah rose, told the group to continue eating, and went in search of his son. His heart worked double-time. His stump roared with blood.

HE FOUND FAISAL standing on one of the house's seven balconies, the one that overlooked the compound playground and garden. Beyond the garden, the desert bloomed. The sky was clear, the moon radiating dully behind a cosmic dust. Abdullah remembered that when Faisal was young and the moon was ringed in yellow, Rosalie would tell him that fairies were dancing around it. When Faisal returned from boarding school, angry and defensive, he had asked her to stop using that expression because one of the mullahs at school had taught him that fairies were just superstitions created by Western shayateens and that being superstitious was defying God's will.

Faisal stood at the wrought-iron railing, his back to the house, and dialed someone on his cell phone. Abdullah eavesdropped from behind the heavy drapes at the sliding-glass door.

"He humiliated me in front of everyone." Faisal's voice cracked. "My own father won't listen to me. He's so weak."

Though he'd suspected that Faisal felt that way about him, it hurt to hear it spoken aloud. Abdullah was taken aback by the anger in his boy's voice. There was a pause as the person spoke back to Faisal, his voice coming across deeply but indecipherably in the still night. Abdullah stepped quietly onto the balcony, his thobe catching the wind off the desert and expanding like a blanched parachute around his skinny legs. With air like this, they would have to go camping soon. Closing his eyes, he gathered the image of his tent at Abu Hadriyah, a thunderstorm speaking its thrilling language to the campers as it rinsed the dust from the air. Somehow, he knew he would need the peace of that image later. He watched Faisal mewling into the phone, his talc-white thobe fluttering, whiter than just-bloomed jasmine against the moon's dirty yellow. Faisal stood in the pour of moonlight stomping his foot at the stars like a child.

"Faisal. Hang up the phone." Faisal started when Abdullah stepped out of the shadows.

"I'll be done in a minute."

"You will hang up the phone at once."

Abdullah paused to think of a sufficient punishment. He rarely confronted his son, and it took him a moment to come up with something.

"Hang up or you won't drive for a week."

It was the best he could do, the only thing he knew that Faisal cared about, besides his Koran. Abdullah knew better than to try to take that away—he didn't need Faisal, the state, *and* God against him.

Faisal sighed deeply and murmured something to the voice on the other end before snapping the phone shut.

"There. Now, do you think you can manage to show some respect for the guests of this family?"

"I think that the guests of this family should show God some respect. In fact, I think this entire family could be better at that."

"Don't speak to me like that, or you can be certain that you won't be going to any university, here or in America. I will not tolerate this kind of behavior from my son."

"Come to mosque with me tomorrow, then, Baba. Let's pray together."

"You think that B-Corp runs on prayers alone? What do you think I do every morning, when you're praying? I'm busy making sure that this family, and that your children, and the children of your children, will be supported for the rest of their lives. Faisal, if there's one thing that you should understand, it's that, here on earth, a man must rely entirely on himself. Neither a king nor an imam can feed you. Remember that."

Abdullah turned back toward the glow of the patio door. He went inside and waited beside the curtained door. Beyond the backyard in the spill of desert, Abdullah heard a pack of wild dogs come alive.

LATER, AFTER EVERYONE had gone home, Abdullah pulled on his nightclothes and watched his wife's outline moving through the shower's beveled glass. He'd stolen into the bedroom because they needed to discuss Faisal.

Rosalie washed herself with choreography still so familiar to him. Right arm soaping the left arm, sweeping across the chest and under the right breast. Then, the same movement led by the left arm. Both hands over the face, behind the ears, encircling the neck. Then down, down over the stomach and the inside of the thighs. He imagined the soap frothing around her body, wrapping her in a halo of foam. His confusion and anger about the confrontation with Faisal vaporized. He would do what he always did when troubled by something; he would lay his troubles at Rosalie's feet. They must put aside their problems and manage their son, together.

"Rosalie?"

"Abdullah? What are you doing in here?"

"Forgive me. It's important."

"Hang on, I can't hear you."

The faucets squealed and the towel disappeared over the edge of the glass. A minute later, Rosalie walked out bundled in her bathrobe. Her body, which she tended so carefully through yoga and walks around the mega-mall downtown, was still impressive in its lines. He remembered when she used to come out of the shower naked, gleaming, rivulets of water cutting paths down her flat abdomen. He would think, my goddess, my statuette. He would bend and lick the droplets from her hipbones. He had wanted to possess every inch of her, colonize her from the inside out. She'd turned him into an idol worshipper, and he in turn left gifts of gratitude for her—bright gold bangles filigreed like miniature palaces, skeins of jewel-toned silks, and piles of golden brown steaming sambusa. The Prophet, peace be upon Him, would not have been pleased. Sometimes Abdullah had been scared to even look at her. At her beauty, her foreignness, the mothlike quality of her skin.

Now she swaddled herself in monogrammed terrycloth, protectively, as if she thought that her difference had become a burden for him. Could he tell her now how much he loved that difference? Would it change anything for them, if she could reclaim it? He looked away and took off his prosthetic hand. Perhaps she would soften toward him if reminded of his handicap.

"It seems our son wants to start his own Committee for the Promotion of Virtue and the Prevention of Vice," he said.

"Tell me something I don't already know."

"Rudeness is not becoming to you."

"You are not exactly one to lecture on decorum."

"Rosalie, please. Now is not the time to be childish. Our son worries me."

"Childish? You've been nothing if not a greedy little child yourself these past years."

Abdullah felt his face grow hot.

"I raised my voice to him." Abdullah looked at Rosalie, hoping to see some glint of sympathy in her eyes, but she still was not looking at him.

"Well, you probably should have done that when he got back from Bern. Now it will just fuel him."

"I thought he'd grow out of this, but it seems I was wrong."

"Yes."

Abdullah watched her mouth carefully shape the words, her lips raw pink from the shower's heat. He worked his stump furiously. He knew he should stop abusing his limb, but since he'd given up smoking a decade back, it had become both his social prop and anxiety absorber. Rosalie returned to her routine as if he wasn't there. As she smoothed lotion over her body, his eyes wandered from her lips. Her hair fell wet around her shoulders, and he could see thin streaks of gray around her temples. She was trying to hold the robe around her body, clumsily, while applying the lotion. The tie unknotted, revealing her odd hooded belly button. She rewrapped herself tightly and disappeared into her closet, emerging after a moment wearing a pair of silk pajamas that he had never seen before.

"Faisal doesn't like me," Rosalie said matter-of-factly, as if she were talking about laundry or a car problem.

She fidgeted with her pajama buttons. She had nervous habits that accompanied her most confessional moods. When angered or thrilled, she was confident, turned her mouth from a bow into the most unforgiving line, the most expansive smile. But when saddened, lost, or in love to the point of pain, she didn't know what to do with her lips, her hands, her eyes. Abdullah knew that now, at this moment when her lips stayed stillest, when she didn't know how to shape them, was a moment of great need. He wondered when their conversation might again reach the echelons of intimacy. He couldn't imagine it. He listened. After a long pause, she continued.

"It's just . . . I feel my own son is a stranger. He's hard. There's so much anger in him, and I have no idea where it's coming from . . ."

"Habibti, of course the boy loves you. Loving your parents is not a choice. Remember how you loved Wayne and Maxine despite everything. At the end, you cried for those bastards." He wanted to reach out, stroke her arm, but she hadn't invited it.

"He can barely hide his contempt for me."

"Yes, but what can we do? We can't bar him from studying the Koran; I wouldn't dare do that. He's young. He's just trying to learn to be a man. He needs to push against us. " He reached for comforting words but realized that he didn't really know the first thing about Faisal's current state of mind.

"You aren't even around for him to push away."

She was sitting on the bed now, her left hand massaging her temple, her right arm tucked under her robe defensively across her stomach. He laughed softly out of discomfort. Rosalie's pale skin flushed.

"Habibti . . ." he said.

"No more habibti, Abdullah. It's too hard. Halas."

"I've confronted Faisal. He's too young to know how to hate anyone."

From the shower there was a steady drip-drip-drip onto the wet tile.

"What about Dan tonight?" She rested her hands on her hips accusingly.

"Dan? Faisal just wishes he accepted God. Even I wish he'd accept God. I've invited him to mosque at least a hundred times. The man had faith in one thing, one thing that was strictly of this earth, and look where that got him."

She stared at him, and then started toweling her hair dry.

"You have to come home to us, Abdullah. Faisal needs more than a warning. He needs his father. Come to dinner with us tomorrow. Just you and me and the kids."

Her words were muffled as the towel fell over her face. She threw it on the edge of the tub and left the bathroom. In the bedroom, she pulled down the comforter, sweeping several gold-embroidered pillows onto the ground. She climbed into bed and lay on her side, her back to his empty place on the mattress. He moved toward her. They should be together tonight, after all that had just happened. He was almost grateful to his son for giving them this chance to speak like husband and wife. He lay down beside her, putting his hand on the soft place where her hip gave way to her waist. Instead of turning in toward him as he had expected, as she had done so many times before, she pushed his hand away.

"Please go," she said. "You can't sleep here."

"Sweet . . ."

"I said, leave. At least allow me the space that you've taken for yourself."

She said it all with her back to him. He sat up and then slid off the bed. To his surprise, he wasn't angry. Her stubbornness was starting to wear on him and a strange coldness had filled him. If that was how she wanted to behave, then he would let her. He would be patient. He had all the time in the world because he had love available to him. It was she who would grow lonely night after night in an empty bed.

He shut the door loudly behind him and made his way to the downstairs guest room. He felt a pain at his wrist and, looking down, realized his stump was bleeding from his nervous rubbing. In the guest bathroom, he rinsed the blood away, covered it with ointment, and wrapped it in gauze. Since he had tenderly dressed his limb dozens of times in the months following the accident, it was as natural as brushing his teeth. Funny, it had been years since his stump had given him so much trouble.

Abdullah left the bathroom and entered the guest room. He took off his thobe and lay down in his undershorts, alone as a boy. The sheets were cold against his exposed legs. When he finally fell asleep, he dreamed he was the largest star in a constellation shaped like a whale, his light growing ever more white as the small stars threading through and around him burned out, one by one. He started awake in the unnatural darkness created by the thick, expensive drapes. He knew Rosalie wasn't on the other side of the bed, but he reached his hand across the sheets anyway.

FIVE

THE DAY DAWNED muddy brown, a dust storm blowing down from the mountains in Turkey. Dan was headed out of Al Dawoun to the North Compound, a company outpost that stood like a last-chance Texaco against the desert. Between the small encampment and the Kuwaiti border, there was nothing but cracked-tar roadway, rusted and mangled car bodies, and a smattering of camel breeding pens. Clouds of dust passed over the car, a welter of wind and sand and the occasional Pepsi can. A few high, brave clouds sat above the toss of the storm, ridged so precisely they looked sculpted. Earlier in the day, before the shama'al had settled over the Eastern Province, Dan had gone to the beach. It was always empty in winter, and as he walked the shore, he stooped to pick up a spotted shell. It possessed a naked geometry that made sense to him, and he was glad to hold something so perfect in his hand. He used it to poke at a dead jellyfish, then put it in his pocket for a talisman. When he looked at a shell, or at the clouds spread with such impossible precision, Dan could see an argument for God's existence, for then, it wasn't a leap of faith but a conclusion he could reach empirically. Dan wasn't a religious person—he hadn't picked up a Bible since grammar school—but in Saudi Arabia, amid the vast desert and the everlasting sea and sky, he felt closer to God than he ever had before. There was something holy in the rawness of the land, and it was not surprising that an entire religion had been revealed on the Arabian Peninsula.

Ahead about a hundred yards, he saw a checkpoint, the makeshift wooden booths looking rickety in the winds off the jebel. He slowed his car and got his iqama out of the glove compartment. "Keep your work papers with you at all times or you can be arrested," Abdullah had warned him when he'd returned to the Kingdom two years earlier. Since 9/11, the Western expatriate community had diminished rapidly, and Dan felt his foreignness every time he went out of the apartment.

Like many Americans, Dan remembered where he had been on the morning of September 11. But what had etched that day in memory was his marriage coming apart, the grotesqueness of two people falling out of love. How could he be expected to give a damn about some extremists' large and abstract hatred for him when he had Carolyn's to contend with? The night before the towers fell Carolyn had kicked him out of the house. He hadn't known where to go, so he fell asleep in his car, which he'd parked in the ditch under the oak in front of their house. When Carolyn went to get the paper the next morning, she'd found him red-eyed, slumped over the steering wheel. She rapped firmly on the window. "Something terrible has happened," she said. Yeah, no shit, he thought.

"Terrorists. Fifteen of the nineteen hijackers were Saudi." He had been furious with her, thought she was trying to change the subject, to ignore the fact of his broken heart on her doorstep. He might have raised his voice a little, might have called her an empty-hearted shrew. He might have been loud enough to rouse the blue heron that slept in the trees near the creek behind their house. He watched as it rose above the aspens, so slow and elegant. Then he had stormed the house looking for his electric razor and she'd called the cops. "You were always so goddamn self-centered, Dan. They're saying ten thousand dead and you're screaming about your razor."

With that phone call to the police, it was no longer "you and I." They'd had to bring in third parties. The lawyers. The cops. The kids. But despite the inevitable violence of such triangulations, Dan still wished for Carolyn something fierce: on stars, on wishbones, on birthdays, before sleep, in prayerful whispers.

Carolyn. She was so much like her moniker, a bit haughty, sometimes Germanically cold—the kind of woman brought up to appreciate sealskin cloaks and marble, who knew that satin was for beguilement and tulle for surrender. She had once told him those sartorial truths while he waited for her to finish trying on cocktail dresses at Neiman's. She'd whispered, as if giving away some precious secret kept by the glass-boned dowagers of Pacific Heights, among whom she'd been raised—women who'd managed to dye their pioneer's blood as blue as the bay they looked out at from their French windows. At that very moment, Dan should have realized that he was in up to his neck, that whatever beatnik salary he could cobble together during the nomad's life he'd planned for himself would never be enough for such a woman. But she possessed a face that belonged in a blueberry patch or at the edge of a lake about to swan dive, and that freckled warmth hoodwinked him into believing that Carolyn was just a simple girl looking for a way to forget about finery, to taste the salt from the neck of a florist's son. Perhaps he'd doomed them both at that very moment of willful blindness.

There were two lines of vehicles at the checkpoint, cars on the left and a mile-long line of trucks with bald tires and tattered mud flaps on the right. The dust in the air was so thick he could barely see two cars in front of him. A thin layer of sand had settled on his dashboard. He wondered what the police would do if one of the men on the watch list rolled up. How did you distinguish the terrorists from all of the good and faithful Saudis when they all wore the same white thobes, the same checkered ghutras, read the same Koran, went to the same mosque as you or your cousins? Hell, maybe they *were* your cousins. As he approached the guard booth, he started to roll down his window, but the two fidgety young men perched atop the truck waved him through, barely glancing his way. One of them had his hand on the automatic weapon mounted on the truck's top. Dan raised his hand quickly, a shukran and masalama. Reflexively, the kid jerked the gun around to face him.

"Shway shway," Dan said, putting his hand down slowly. Hold it. Hang on. Slow down.

The guard shot him a contemptuous look. They were jumpier than normal. Perhaps they were after a particularly big fish, a fugitive Crazy Sheikh, as Abdullah called the firebrands. Abdullah always laughed a bit too hard when he dismissed the radical element in Saudi culture. "Look around—these are boom times. Why do you Americans always have to focus on the negative? You have Timothy McVeigh, we've got the Crazy Sheikh."

Dan let the wind blow his hair off of his forehead for a few seconds as he drove away from the checkpoint. Nothing like a gun in the face first thing in the morning to get the blood going. Dust rimmed his nose, stung his eyes. He liked to let the dry air suck the life out of his skin. Sometimes, he went to the beach, put on a face mask and goggles, and stood in the middle of the shama'al. The stinging felt good. It made him feel as if he was exercising his right to pain. The highway dipped beneath power lines that stretched to the horizon like some futuristic arbor.

He thought about last night's feast at the Baylani home, one of the hundreds he'd enjoyed in their living room, with its stained-glass ceiling tessellating natural light and the twenty-seven chandeliers transmuting electricity into crystal starbursts. When Faisal had stood up before the meal to say his piece, Dan had been far from offended. In fact, he had welcomed the discord. In Faisal's rebelliousness, Dan witnessed the teenage moods he'd missed experiencing from his own son.

They'd served the main course at ten o'clock and people had talked late into the night, forgetting Faisal's untraditional blessing. Dan ate sweet-fleshed whitefish and delicate egg-stuffed pastries, bell peppers bursting with spiced ground beef, and teardrop almond cookies. When he went to wash his hands at the sink next to the kitchen bathroom, he had crossed paths with Rosalie. She was dressed in a sky-blue djellaba, her slim figure lost in its clean lines. It was the Saudi housewife version of the muumuu, used to hide bloat and paunch, neither of which Rosalie had to worry about. He knew she woke to do yoga in the courtyard every morning. Abdullah prayed beside her at dawn as she did her asanas, though probably not anymore. Those tender acts of habit were surely destroyed now.

"Delicious dinner," he said.

"Ahlan wa sahlan, ya Dan."

"Your son was very entertaining tonight."

"Oh, no. Whatever he did, please forgive him. He's young."

"He tried to convert me," he said. "I wish I felt that strongly about something."

"Misdirected passion can be dangerous."

"Yes, but to feel passion at all. Must be easier to get out of bed in the morning."

Dan thought about the look on Faisal's face when he had stopped by Prairie Vista the other evening, his green eyes alight, giving him a look of ardor. When Faisal had issued his warning, Dan hadn't been afraid. It was just Abdullah's boy, Zool, who'd graduated early and was probably bored out of his mind. What teenager wasn't eager for rebellion? At least Faisal hadn't taken up drag racing like the kids in Jeddah, where the bored teenagers got themselves arrested or killed every other weekend. Faisal looked more like the type given over to romantic abandon. Dan had been overseas for most of Joe's high school years. Had there been moments of fervor, the kind only teenagers are brave enough to show, to allow into their pink, unmarked hearts? He would have to remember to ask Carolyn.

He turned back to Rosalie. "I feel like I just receive information now."

"Welcome to middle age."

"Yes, but Abdullah . . ." He stopped himself, glancing at Rosalie to see if she grasped his implication.

"Abdullah is never satisfied. I pity him." She paused. "I'd better get back to the other room. If I'm gone for too long, they start gossiping."

"About you? Still?"

"Some things never change. And they have been eager to see how I'm doing since the news."

"And?"

"I've been better."

"Rosie," he said, then hesitated. What he was about to say was definitely a breach of loyalty, but he didn't care. Abdullah was a fool who took love for granted. "I've been through it. Just know that I'm here for you."

He looked hard at her, trying to read her face. She was still so damned beautiful. Carolyn, who was not exactly homely, had always been jealous of Rosalie's perfect, wide features.

She took his hand in both of hers, squeezed hard, then turned and left the room, her perfume lingering. A shiver passed through him. It struck him suddenly that he wanted to know Rosalie's thoughts. It had been so long since he had conversed, really *talked*, with a woman. On his yearly vacations to Europe or America, he struck up conversations with bartenders or waitresses, trying for those little sympathies that only women can give.

He'd spent so long with his family as his four walls and a roof that when it all burned to the ground, he was left exposed. In the settlement, Carolyn took almost everything, and he hadn't wanted any of what she didn't take—objects that had filled the houses they'd shared for nearly three decades. With each item he left behind, he felt his heart fired and cooled, annealed by each rejection of the symbols of the life they had made together. He hadn't planned for the memories to dislodge from the material things and follow him into his empty condominium on a desolate stretch of desert on the outskirts of Al Dawoun.

Now, on the drive to the North Compound, Dan found his

thoughts returning to Rosalie. They'd been good pals in Texas, but in the Kingdom, their lives had been lived separately. Guiltily, he found that he was glad to have a comrade in heartbreak, especially a woman. He had been starved for company, but the guys never actually wanted to talk about anything. Rosie was perfect: tough but compassionate. She knew Carolyn and he knew Abdullah. They would be each other's confessor.

He made up his mind—he had to get in touch with her. Nobody could treat Rosie March the way Abdullah was treating her. But he didn't have her cell phone number or e-mail address. Abdullah was a true Saudi and believed that any male-female contact was inherently sexual. To ask for Rosalie's cell phone number was equivalent to saying "I want to sleep with your wife." If Dan had a message to pass along to her, he had to call Abdullah, like a grown-up game of telephone. Tradition always trumped efficiency. A craving rose up strong from his belly. If only Rosalie would just take his hand again. Touch was so important. It took so little to pacify the body, to meet its needs.

Out of nowhere, the low-lying compound appeared, tan trailers against the khaki-colored sand. The desert always dispatched distance extremely. Either it took light-years to reach some prayed-for, quavering marker on the horizon, or a destination stunned the traveler with its immediacy. Nothing was to scale. It was a rabbit-hole world in which size and proximity meant little. The LEGO-sized buildings mushroomed to full size in half a minute. Dan flexed and pointed his feet to get the blood flowing again. It was midweek and the compound had a hivelike energy. Come the weekend, the workers would recharge by watching bootleg DVDs of Bollywood films whose extravagance lent the dingy camp some razzle-dazzle for a few hours. As the Bangladeshi and Indian and Sri Lankan men watched the films, thoughts of distant wives and lovers thickened the air as the desert's yellow light poured in through the windows. The compound residents didn't have alcohol to bring the out-of-reach back to them, but they did have the movies. Dan felt kinship with the men, marooned together as they were.

He opened the door to the front office, and before he could set foot inside, Yaser descended on him.

"You're late. Two messages for you. Abdullah and Eleanor. Who's Eleanor? Are you keeping some piece of ass out in Bahrain? Because if you are, then I guess I'm going to have to stop feeling sorry for you."

"For chrissakes, Yaser. Eleanor is my daughter. Ellie. You really don't listen to anything I say, do you?"

"I try to avoid it."

"Fuck you."

"You're not my type."

"You're a real asshole, you know that?"

"Dan?"

"What?"

"You look like hell."

"Thanks."

"Dan?"

"What?"

"I changed my mind. You're definitely not getting laid. You look like hell."

"Jesus H. Murphy. Can't a man just come to work?"

The way Yaser mouthed off, it was hard for Dan to remember that he had grown up in the Hijaz and not on Atlantic Avenue in Brooklyn. When he'd asked Yaser where he'd learned his accent, his slang, since he had never studied in the States, he'd replied, "American television. Movies." Dan was sure that the Ulema loved the idea that the enormous Saudi youth population was learning verb conjugations from Johnny Depp.

He sat down in his tiny office. Sand pinged the plastic windowpane. Same old bullshit. Always the same old bullshit conversations. He felt so alone. He thought of all the boring things that husbands and wives absorbed from each other. Large things. Silly things. Desperate things. The dialogue of love was nonlinear and utterly unimportant to the greater world, but the intimacy created was vital to a person's survival.

It was still too early to call the States, so he dialed Abdullah first. He picked up on the second ring, his voice tinny.

"Salaam, ya Dan. Guess where I am?"

"Hopefully somewhere with a wider cocktail selection than the North Compound."

"Dubai. Poolside."

"Puta madre. What's the occasion?"

"After last night, I needed to be reminded why I married Isra. She's helping me remember. She's really good at jogging the memory. We're only gone for two nights. But I need you to do me a favor."

"Shoot."

"I didn't tell Rosalie, and she's expecting me at the house tonight. A small dinner with the family."

"So call her and tell her you won't be making it," Dan said. He didn't like where the conversation was headed.

"No wonder your marriage fell apart. I *can't* just call and tell her. Then she'll ask me where I am. And then when she finds out, she probably won't speak to me again. I need you to tell her that I was called away on an emergency business trip. Go in person. Take flowers."

"I'm not going to lie for you, Abdullah. Not to Rosalie." He clenched his fist around the phone.

"Tell her I'm in . . . I don't know. Muscat."

"We don't even have dealings in Muscat."

"Who cares? She's been there several times and won't ask questions about it."

"Abdullah . . ."

"*Do not* mention Dubai."

"But . . ."

"Also, call the Al Dawoun office and update them on the story, in case she calls there."

He sighed. "Anything else?"

"Yes. Isra's family owns an apartment here. Never, *ever* mention this to Rosalie. She'll think I bought the apartment and then it'll get messy. Understand? Also, Dan?"

"Yeah?"

"Don't forget to stress that it was an emergency." Abdullah hung up the phone before Dan could protest.

The son of a bitch. Of course there was no need for Abdullah to wait for an answer, no reason for him to expect anything but compliance from the man whose ass he had saved with a job. Though he dreaded lying to Rosalie's face, he couldn't wait to see her. They would talk for hours about how hard life was. His heartbeat kicked up a notch, like it used to before a date. Of course. Now he and Rosie would really understand each other. Life was long, but too short for the bullshit—being taken for granted, or getting bogged down in the mud of nostalgia. He would wait a couple of hours before calling Ellie, enough time for the sun to rise over Boston. It had been so long since they had talked. He felt a pang of guilt. When he'd realized he and Carolyn weren't going to reconcile, he'd fled back overseas to what was familiar, and to what was far away. Truth be told, he hadn't thought much about the kids and how such a move might affect his relationship with them. Heartbreak and the need for a paycheck had conspired to make him a deadbeat dad, or at least an absentee one.

Getting up from his office chair, he stretched his hands over his head, felt the familiar pain in his lower back from his year—the worst year—working as a stock clerk for MegaSavers. The year of reeling, of making his way without a sail after Carolyn had cut him loose. The terrible irony of it was, she had wanted to leave the Kingdom, go back to the States to be closer to her family. She grew tired of the desert, bored with life on the compound. But then when he couldn't find a job after they left, when he had to spend his days doing laundry and picking the kids up from school, she'd blamed him for it.

When he'd moved out of the family house, he'd rented a duplex just blocks away. He liked to think that Carolyn could smell the ceiling rot, hear the roof as it sagged ever lower. He let his lawn die; he was not above cheap metaphors. With his useless back brace on, he'd arrange bulk boxes of cereal from midnight until nine a.m., go home, and sleep the day away. After ten months of this—of praying for asbestos poisoning, of standing beneath creaking scaffolding, of crossing low-water markers during floods—he'd gotten the call from Abdullah. He had a job for him. At a desk. It was summertime. Dan had left Joe and Ellie to clean out his house and gotten on a plane, taking nothing but a pair of topsiders, a couple of shirts, his wallet, his well-thumbed passport. Austin to Houston, Houston to London, London to the Kingdom. To sanity, to salary, to worth.

AFTER LUNCH, WHICH he'd eaten hastily in the dusty canteen, Dan returned to his desk. He hesitated a moment before picking up the phone and dialing Ellie's landline. It was Sunday morning. He realized he had no idea what her Sunday ritual was. Did she go get the *Globe* and a small, bitter coffee from a neighborhood deli? Did she jog along the Charles, counting bridges or the oars of rowers?

"Hello?" A male voice. Momentarily surprised, he tried to recall if Ellie had written anything about a boyfriend.

"Ellie there?"

"Just a moment."

From ten thousand miles away, the rustling of sheets, of two bodies realigning themselves to accommodate his intrusion.

"Dad?"

"Hey, kiddo. Staying warm out there?"

"Oh," she laughed nervously. "Yeah. Well. That was Sean. Remember? The guy I wrote to you about?"

"Sure, hon. What kind of accent is that?"

"Irish. Sean's from Dublin. He's here doing his PhD in comparative lit. Anyway, I called because we have some news."

His heart started pounding. He knew what was coming by the way she giggled. Then she said it—*marry*—and his stomach fell away, far from his center, and his heart continued to test its casements. He mumbled some pleasantries, some jokes as he tried to be overjoyed, but mostly he was still stuck at the word, the idea. Marriage. Twenty-five years before, he had leapt too, and landed on his ass in a chasm so deep he was just beginning to claw his way out. Ellie was only twenty-four.

Mabrook, *congratulations*, he said. And, *I've gotta run*, *love you*, before hanging up the phone. From his desk drawer, he took out the photo he kept stashed there. Carolyn, her blond hair a mane falling on Joe's bald baby head as she leaned over him, and Ellie, tenacious, her four-year-old face just beginning to lose the openness that goes away forever once you start to learn things about the world. Now she knew so much more, but not enough. He worried at the pain she would come to know, the heartbreak, the abandonments that accompanied the togethernesses. She was leaving the boat. Ellie and Carolyn, men overboard. He placed his head in his hands.

Quietly, he grabbed his mask and shouldered out into the storm. Yaser shouted something behind him that got muffled by the wind. The sun was low and uneasy, moving from orange to red in an ombré ball over the distant jebel. He could not properly process the news alone. He would go to Rosalie with Abdullah's message and then tell her about Ellie.

HE'D DRIVEN THE last hour in near-darkness, the newly installed streetlights not yet operating but standing in the median like an army of sleeping giants. He should have stayed overnight at the camp or departed earlier. Driving the route at night, with its unmarked detours and potholes, invited disaster. But he had to deliver Abdullah's message before the family sat down for dinner. When he finally saw downtown Al Dawoun's fuzzy halo of lights, he felt relief. The idea of getting stranded on a dark and remote road did not appeal to him. Though most of the recent kidnappings had been in or near Riyadh, nearly four hours to the west, he was still wary. He didn't want to be the guy who was seen, posthumously, as just asking for it.

Cars packed the curbs of the Diamond Mile. The storm had been carried south and the air was now remarkably still. After parking on the side street adjacent to the house, he stood and listened for a moment. Car doors slammed, people shouted salaams and marhabas to each other across the wide boulevard. But from inside the houses, nothing. Behind the twelve-foot walls, each home was a world unto itself, each garden the moat to catch all stray voices and secrets. Though there was a sense of neighborly camaraderie, at the end of the day, the Saneas ate with the Saneas, the Rashids with the Rashids, the Gosaibis with the Gosaibis, the Zamils with the Zamils, and so on and so forth, down to the smallest, least-powerful family in the Kingdom.

At the side gate, a maid buzzed him in and he made his way down the long path to the door. Anisa, the Baylanis' tiny Indonesian maid, swung open the heavy door and invited him inside. She motioned for him to wait on the foyer couch and poured him a tall glass of apple juice before leaving to fetch Rosalie. He could hear voices coming from the dining room, probably Mariam and Faisal. He did not feel like exchanging pleasantries with Abdullah's kids, did not need further reminding of Abdullah's familial glut. No matter what he did, Abdullah could never be excised from his family. "What a stupid life," Abdullah had said to him after learning of his divorce. "Listen to me. I'm old and ugly. Rosalie is old and ugly. You are *very* old and ugly. The Ugly?"—his nickname for Carolyn—"Of course, she too is old and *very* ugly. We should all be old and ugly together. It's as simple as that. You can tell her I said so." Marriage advice from a serial husband.

"Ahlan, ya Dan." Rosalie stood at the room's entrance, her red hair pulled back into a loose ponytail.

There was a moment of awkwardness as he tried to decide on the appropriate greeting. Since she'd left the States in '78, he'd never been alone with Rosalie for more than a minute. A hug? A kiss on the cheek? A handshake? He reached out his hand, an inelegant gesture, as if she were a colleague and not an old friend. In Saudi, rules were rigid but not often articulated, leaving him on occasion to stumble through blindly.

She laughed and took his hand.

"Abdullah won't be able to make it tonight."

No lies.

"He's tied up."

Still, no lies.

"Doing what? We've got the family here. Even Faisal. We're expecting him."

"He's . . ."

"Where is he?"

"It's business." And there it was. The big fat one.

"Business?" She paused, examining his face. "Dan, don't tell his lies for him. It means he assumes we're both fools." Her mouth turned down at the corners, and he could see her cheeks reddening.

"I'm so sorry," he said.

"I suppose I ought to go tell the kids. You know, this would have been the first time we've eaten as a complete family in God knows how long."

He didn't know what to say, so he kept quiet.

"I'm so tired of this," she said. "Of the deception. It's bullshit. I can't go out there and participate in this charade in front of my children." She gestured toward the sitting rooms, her voice a harsh whisper. "We need him. His son needs him. Doesn't he understand that?" Her head dropped and she began kneading her forehead with a fist. A momentary pause and she looked up.

"Let's go," she said. "Let's drive out to the beach. I've got to get out of this house."

Before he could protest, she called Anisa into the room and asked her to tell the kids that she felt sick and was going to lie down. Then she grabbed her abaya off the hook by the doorway. Before they got into the car, she slipped the niqab over her face, something he'd never seen her do.

"The neighbors," she said.

THE DATE PALMS stood black against the young night sky, the branches pulled sideways by the wind so the trees resembled a line of dancers with arms outstretched to the heavens. They pulled past the empty guard booth and into the parking lot of the private State Oil beach. The guard was probably eating his dinner with some of the other guards of neighboring beaches. Nobody went to the beach in the chill of winter. Getting out of the car, Dan felt the gust against his face and looked out to the water's edge, which glowed orange from the lights that stood over the empty picnic shelters lining the shore. Some three hundred miles east over the water, Iran lay hulking in the night, the two rival countries forced to stare at each other into eternity, with nothing but the salty Gulf to dilute their mutual mistrust. Earlier in the day, he'd pitched rocks into the low waves before driving to the North Compound. He was back, only now he would talk; not with the curses and insults that comprised his daily banter but with real words, and it would be glorious.

"Let's climb to the top of the dune and count the ships passing," she said.

She kicked off her slippers and pulled off her abaya, leaving it in a heap in the sand. The beautifully embroidered abaya had probably cost Abdullah four thousand riyals, and he would be furious to know it was being treated with such carelessness. That his wife felt he had shed her in much the same manner would be incomprehensible to him.

Dan knew she would get cold and wanted to tell her so, but she was already gone, running full-speed toward the dark mass of sand that divided the clean stretch of beach from the public one that was littered with fast food containers and watched over by a massive concrete fish that had once housed a snack stand but now served as a graffiti canvas. Huffing to the top of the dune, he felt every one of his fifty-two years. Rosalie was sitting at the edge that sloped down into the sea, her arms wrapped around her folded legs. The smell of salt was in his nose, the moon was half in darkness, and he could hear the flag by the guard booth snapping in the wind.

"Rosie."

"Yes?" She looked up at him. The shadows fell just right across her broad face, and for a moment she was a charcoal portrait whose inner life was only to be guessed at. She turned back to the sea as he sat down beside her.

"You'll be relieved to know that pain suits your features."

"I'll thank my Nordic grandmother for that. I got her suffering eyes."

"Not at all."

"I feel like I've been atomized, turned to dust."

"Ellie is getting married," he blurted.

She paused briefly before saying, "Dan, that's wonderful."

"You know better than that."

A large cargo boat slunk along in the distance, its red light blinking slowly. It was the saddest thing he had seen in a long time. So slow, so far away, sending out its warning to a silent sea.

"It is, though—wonderful. It was for me and Abdullah. And I remember how you and Carolyn grinned when those kids were born. There was wonder in those days."

In their pillows, the smell of Carolyn's perfume mixed with the oil from her hair, her hand at the back of his neck, Sunday mornings on the deck. Then, the tiny, squirming bodies that bound them together forever, no matter what the courts said.

"Yes, but it can get taken away, and if it does, it's an amputation. A death."

"They have to try, though," she said. "Give them a shot at joy.

You know, they say this generation of couples is going to learn from our mistakes. I read an article."

Your mistake was marrying a Saudi, he thought, but bit his tongue. Had he fared better? Had he the right to criticize?

"Why don't you divorce him?"

"You know as well as I do how that would go," she said. "He'd keep Mariam and Faisal, I'd see them maybe once a year. You know, even if Abdullah suddenly died, custody of the children would go to a male custodian before me?"

"Yeah, well. This ain't Sugar Land, as I'm sure you're aware."

"You know the State Department posts a warning nowadays? *Read Before Marrying a Saudi.* Guess they got tired of all the pissed off ex-wives trying to get custody and blaming the U.S. government for not doing more. But I came here with both eyes open. I grew up here; I knew what it was like. But I wanted my home back. I wanted it back so badly. And of course, I loved him. You know how he is. He put a hand on my shoulder and looked at me with that quizzical expression. He just said, 'What are you doing here, my destiny? I wasn't expecting to run into you in a bar.' And then the Qabbani. Remember? And that was it."

"Yeah, but is this it for Mariam? For Faisal?"

"They've lived here all their lives. They're Saudi. I couldn't take away their home. Mariam wants to stay and change things. And Faisal . . . I have no idea about Faisal. Not a clue. He'd rather die than tell his mom anything. He was never a talker, but I used to be able to ask him questions about his life and get an answer. Now he just stares at me like I've violated some code by speaking to him. But Joe must be the same way. It's got to be the age."

"I don't know about Joe," Dan said, looking down at his hands. "That's the worst part of divorce. You lose the everyday experiences that tell you what your children are like, what kind of people they're becoming."

"You didn't have to move half a world away."

"Huh. You never were stupid, Rose. No one ever accused you of that." He paused. "You're right. After she kicked me out, I couldn't cope with seeing the kids just on weekends. And I was flat broke. When Abdullah offered me this job, I fled."

The wind shifted direction, bringing with it the shushing of the waves below.

"I can't just get a condo in Sugar Land," she said. "Not after this. I bet I couldn't even get a job as a secretary. I haven't worked an honest hour in more than twenty-five years." She laid back, her hair blending in with the sand. Her face looked bare, exposed, as she stared straight up into the netting of stars. "I'm trying to figure out if I can get by without him."

That was the worst part of it, thought Dan. Six months after the divorce, when he was sulking in the duplex and keeping up his angry silence, Carolyn had written him a note asking if he would ever speak to her again, and how can two people go from meaning everything to each other to meaning nothing? He'd crumpled the note and kept his silence until the anger almost burned him alive. But six months later, he'd gone looking for relief, for her. He'd driven to the old house, barged through the front door, found her in the kitchen and tried to kiss the life out of her. She'd kissed back—that kiss must have lasted five minutes—but then pushed him away and started crying. He said, Let's forget about all this crap and try again; and she'd said, I can't, I can't, so he'd driven away, his whole body on fire. He didn't know how people managed to get divorced twice, three times, even four. How did they not die from the sheer pain of it? Humans were not built to bear it; we are cruel in heartbreak. Better to cling with a slippery grip than to wreck yourself so thoroughly in the letting-go. Because when love ends, when you let go, you always lose a part of yourself that you can never reclaim, that the other person keeps, greedily, the toll for their love, the tax.

"Stay with him, Rosalie. It's not worth it."

"I'd only stay if we were in love. Any kind of love. And I'm just not sure that's the case anymore."

Far below them at the foot of the dune, the water moved endlessly against the shore.

"I can't imagine what it's been like for you here," Dan said.

For a minute, she didn't say anything. Then she answered, "It's not the place, if I'm being honest. It would be too easy to blame the place. It's just that . . . I was so young when we got married. You have an idea of love as being this all-powerful force that will just sweep you along. But it's not that way at all. It's *hard*. And it changes shape without you even noticing."

Dan lay back and felt the sand rise to meet the base of his spine. He closed his eyes, counted his breaths. He turned his head to look at her, only to find her already staring at him.

"You're beautiful," he blurted. He looked away, embarrassed. He sounded like a teenager. As he pulled in a long draft of air, at first he felt only her hair as it fell on his face, then her lips against his, and finally the weight of her body as she sank on top of him. He did not push her away. In fact, he pressed his face into hers. Her skin was white with moonlight. His head grew hot, a pressure he hadn't felt in so long. But there was something else, too—a pang he hadn't felt in the few cold kisses with the French flight attendant last summer.

Staring down at him, she said, "You're the first man, besides Abdullah and my father, that I've been alone with in years."

He knew that he should stop her, that she wasn't thinking clearly. What if someone saw them up there? There'd be hell to pay. And she was sick with grief and the kind of hurt that makes people do mad things. He didn't want to poach from her broken heart. There was danger in it for her, for both of them. He pushed at her feebly, but she was so close. He didn't subscribe to the Saudi theory that men and women couldn't be alone together without screwing, but he did think that danger was imminent once someone of your preferred sex had climbed on top of you. When she had touched him moments before, he had wanted to give in to his animal instincts, but he knew that in doing so he would somehow fail her.

"We're proving them right, you know," he said. "That we can't be alone together."

She sat up and he watched the dark grooves of her nostrils expand as she breathed heavily. "I'm disintegrating in that house."

She lay back down in the sand next to him, but far enough away so that they were no longer touching. He turned on his side, put his face near her neck, where her hair met the base of her skull. That old familiar smell, oil from skin and hair mixing with fragrant shampoo. Breathing her in, he wanted more. He was afraid he wouldn't get enough; that he would never get enough. He felt nauseous with the wanting. He felt the roughness of the sand that clung to her wet skin. Suddenly she was crying, long sobs like the lowing of an animal. Dan moved away from her, watched her as she turned on her belly and rested her face on her folded arms. Even the air and the sea and the moon could not give her what she needed, so Dan kept quiet. After several minutes, she grew calmer, her breath coming in uneven hiccups. At last, she turned to face him.

"Let's not, Dan. I don't want to destroy what little I have left."

"I understand," he said, though really, he felt surprisingly angry. Abdullah had already wrecked things, and when Rosalie had kissed him, Dan had felt a stirring in his heart like hope, like he was no longer alone.

"I have to be able to look my children in the face, you know? They're confused enough about what's going on between Abdi and me."

"Sure," he said, but he felt like someone had kicked him in the gut.

They went down to the water to wash the sand off their legs, her ankles bare and white beneath her djellaba, her collarbone like a shell's edge. While she cleaned herself, her face turned out toward the sea, Dan pulled out his cell phone and snapped a picture, quietly.

Something was happening, a change, and he wanted to preserve the moment. Up close, the water glowed with millions of phosphorescent particles. He could see the fat white bodies of jellyfishes moving like orbs.

They might have been walking on the moon, so strange was the tableau. Stunned by their restraint, they moved slowly, like walkers in a garden. She smoothed her hair.

"You're so good, Rosalie," he said. "You're a good wife."

"But the crime is in the loving, Dan. Not the physical acts. Now he says he loves both of us. Love, and her name uttered right after it. There's the crime. And I don't give a good goddamn what the Koran says. If you're a human being, you know you can't love two people, not wholly, not at the same time."

At the parking lot, she picked up her abaya and slid into her sandals while he shook the sand out of his hair. He watched as she draped the niqab over her face. Now he was involved. In-fucking-volved, as Rosalie would say.

"DON'T PULL INTO the driveway," she said. "Just leave me right here."

The house was dark. It wasn't late, but dinner was over and the cars that had been parked along the street were gone. She took a piece of paper from her purse and jotted something on it.

"I'm going to call you soon, but here's my cell number, just in case."

"Doesn't Abdullah get the bill?"

"Yes, but not until next month. Who knows where I'll be then. I've got to do some serious thinking, Dan. I'm going to need your help. I'm not going to divorce him, not yet anyway. But I want to get out of here for a little while. Get my head on straight."

"OK. I'll do whatever I can. I'm here for you, remember that."

"I'm glad someone is," she said. "I'll call you soon." She got out of the car and headed toward the house.

Without waiting to see her through the gates, Dan drove off. He didn't want to risk being seen by one of the neighbors, or the kids. They hadn't done anything too terrible, but by Saudi law they were criminals. The warmth of Rosalie's body was gone. He wondered how Abdullah could only want that body every other night, that perfect body of nerves and muscle and that heart that loved him. As he drove toward his condo, the night's events replayed through his mind. Part of him, the schoolboy part, felt a rush of pride. Rosie March had kissed him. She had wanted him.

The dust storm had left small drifts of sand along the perimeter road that led to Prairie Vista. The moon had risen to its highest point, far away in its cold silvering light. In Boston, it was Sunday afternoon. Ellie and Patrick would marry in the summer. They would live together and never be alone. At night, they would hold each other, feel the other person twitch in sleep. Ellie would sleep knowing for certain she would not be like her parents. In the beginning, you are always so sure. Though he was not a praying man, Dan said a prayer for his only daughter: that she would be right in her gamble—steadfast and loved, always.

SIX

AT NIGHT, YOU can be brave with resolutions. In the dark, emboldened by the late hour, you build cities of hope, elaborate grids for the restless mind. But mornings, you wake without a map, trying to reimagine the cityscape with the same audacity as the night before. When Rosalie went to bed, she felt certain she would leave the country. But the moment she awoke and turned over, felt the cool of the sheets, the roughness of the raw silk pillows that she left piled on Abdullah's side of the bed, her certainty faltered, wavering just enough for her to notice it, like a heart palpitation. She felt heavy in the bed and imagined the planes leaving Al Dawoun without her, bright, metallic spots in the sky, and she, the little girl standing and waving, her hopes slender as a crane's legs. She used to have nightmares about being forced from her home, ripped from Abdullah's side and ushered into the wilderness. Now for the first time, the prospect of remaining had become terrifying.

Rosalie did not know exactly when she'd fallen in love with Saudi Arabia, but now she found herself searching for the definitive moment. How? She asked herself. How did I come to be back here, in this land so unlike the place of my childhood memories?

That love, that mysterious child-love for a left-behind place, that's larger than time spent there or the remembrance of distant, long-ago faces. It is not innate; it didn't solidify during her birth in her parents' temporary home on Dalia Street on the State Oil compound, for that had been marked by struggle—her mother passed down an explicit version of events that left harsh words echoing in Rosalie's head. Nor did it happen during the afternoons spent feeding mongooses to the alligator that Jimmy Ruweedle kept in a pit in his backyard, although that did inspire the first thought that perhaps she was not living a normal childhood. And Rosalie knew that it didn't happen at the compound pool, where she and the other company brats dove for halala coins in the deep end, feeling their ears pop and their eyes rage with chlorine as they searched for the glint of silver against the tiles. No, those moments, even taken together, were not love. They were simply memories that she had of an irregular childhood. Love is built of more peculiar stuff, she had learned, and so Rosalie searched her memories for those moments in which she might have constructed her obsession with Arabia—a land that did not want her, that perhaps did not want anybody.

One day erected itself in memory. The day of the birth. Not her own, but a stillborn child of the desert who nearly took his mother with him. The desert was like that. The dead, not satisfied in death, often tried to take the living, too.

The day of the birth was an especially hot one. Kids were warned off the pools: The sun would melt them as they walked from the lounger to the water, fry their little feet like sliced ham in a skillet. Well, what am I going to do with you all day if you can't go to the pool? Maxine March said to her daughter. Maxine was chewing her green weed again, khat, which always made her restless in the long Arabian afternoons—afternoons that went on and on like seasons. On afternoons like these, while Wayne worked the Tapline, Rosalie often overheard Maxine talking to a shadow as if it were her father or some other man her mama was angry with. Pacing the small temporary house from front to back, Maxine had whole conversations with the sun's smudge on the living room wall.

Rani, the houseboy who brought the khat up from Yemen on the first of every month, was ironing clothes in the corner of the Marches' house. The house was propped up on cinder blocks like all the other hastily erected expat homes on Dalia Street, and when the windstorms came, Maxine prayed for deliverance. Lord, don't sweep us into the Gulf. Lord, we're sinners but we deserve better than the bottom of some heathen sea.

If you left the khat unchewed more than a couple of days, it spoiled, so Maxine spent those first days of every month circling the sitting room chewing, spitting her green spit, and lighting cigarettes between the long chews. Now she had the radio going, tuned to an American military station that played Benny Goodman, Tony Bennett, and others whose voices seemed radically misplaced on their flat, fenced stretch of desert.

What fool closes the pool because it's too hot? Maxine wondered aloud. Rosalie knew that she didn't want an answer; she just wanted her daughter out of the room so she could wear out the carpet and talk to shadows in privacy.

Rosalie had her watercolors out because it seemed like the sensible thing to do on a hot day when the pool was forbidden. Worse came to worst, if the sun did burn down the house, she could always dive straight into her brush cup like in the cartoons, her eyes wide and blinking from between her crunched-up legs. But she never had a chance to try because before she could make her first stroke, Zainab came slamming through the front door.

"Rosie, my father's going to deliver a baby from a Bedouin woman outside camp. Come on!"

On most days, Maxine didn't like Rosalie playing with Zainab. Maxine didn't think that Americans should mix with the locals, even if Zainab's father was a trained professional—a doctor who had saved Wayne March's life, in fact, when he'd gotten potted on siddiqi out at the Tapline and fallen face first on a small hill of fertilizer that the gardeners hadn't yet spread over the traffic medians. The chemicals, ingested through his gasping mouth, should have killed him, but Dr. Salawi gave him an elixir that made him vomit up every last bit of wet in his stomach, including the sid.

"Mama?" Rosalie asked.

"Go. Give these leaves to that desert mother." Maxine handed her a bunch of khat. "Lord knows it can't feel good to deliver a baby on a day like today, in a country like this one."

By the time they arrived at the tents, Rosalie had snuck at least three leaves into her mouth. When she slid out of the car, she spit the remnants into her palm and dropped them into the sand by the jeep's tire. Her heart was beating rapidly in her chest and, despite the heat, she felt the urge to bound from dune to dune, popping all the tiny polyps of the succulents that grew there. The world seemed rinsed, as if plunged in water and rid of its dull tea colors. She could see the heat shimmering in waves across the air. Palm fronds crackled as the leaning trees reached out to touch one another. Somewhere a woman screamed, the sound high-pitched, cutting through the shimmering air like a blade. Rosalie was twelve years old plus a few weeks, but in the last minutes, she sensed the earth had galloped past the sun at least twice, and she felt her skull pulse with new wisdom. She could feel the desert shifting beneath her feet—not a groaning, as she'd expected, but a quick movement so that she had to dance to stay upright.

"Come on," Zainab said. "This way." Her father had already gone ahead.

Inside the black goat-hair tent, a girl lay on her back in blood. Rosalie staggered at the smell. Dr. Salawi was on his knees near her hips, inspecting between her legs like she was a broken-down automobile. The women surrounding the girl spoke gruffly in Arabic, and Zainab looked eagerly from face to face. Rosalie gave the rest of the bundled leaves to one of the grannies, who sniffed at them before kneeling at the girl's head. When the granny tried to feed her a leaf, the girl spat and went back to screaming, but soon, she was chewing leaf after leaf until they were gone. Her screams did not stop, but they became more rhythmic, as if she were trying to make a song from her pain. If she had known any prayers, Rosalie would have said them, but Wayne and Maxine were Southern Baptists in name and prejudice only; it meant they used whatever prayer-speak they knew to protest Abdullah's presence in her life, years later. Their prayers were not for the grace of babies in a heathen land.

Finally, Dr. Salawi pulled the baby out. It was wet and silent, its tiny limbs pressed tightly to its chest. Even though it did not breathe or squall, the girl took it in her arms and rocked it. She kissed its small head and called out a prayer. She smiled at Rosalie.

"Why's she smiling?" Rosalie asked. "That baby's dead."

Zainab asked the girl, who answered in a few words, still grinning.

"Because she is alive," Zainab translated.

Her baby had not killed her, though it had tried.

The grannies buried the baby under a weeping carob tree even though they knew that some creature would come for it in the night. They were not angry in this knowledge. It was only the desert replenishing itself. In their careful movements, Rosalie saw love but no sadness. When you are born to a mother who talks to shadows, you see beauty in simplicity: a land that greets death with solemn silence; a mother who smiles simply because she is alive.

Look: a short jeep ride between me and this existence, she thought with wonder, sensing the enervating desert close at hand. There was no chain-link fence or glittering pool standing like a moat between her and this life. She felt suddenly dizzy, shaken by the enormous quiet of the grove. She could hardly believe that life existed there. Nobody had told her that whole families created worlds for themselves in the nothing sweep of the desert outside of the compound. She felt excluded and fascinated. She felt a pinching at her breast, like discovering a secret room in a house you thought was your home. There was so much more to know.

Yes, Rosalie thought. In that moment, Arabia was irrevocably part of her.

But there is a trouble peculiar to expatriate children who fall in love with Saudi Arabia. Their visas expire when they leave, and they quickly discover that the place they have loved so long does not want them back. There is no room in a closed Muslim society for nostalgic American children. With no possibility of return, these boys and girls, at first melancholy with their loss, soon create in memory the perfect homeland, a suitable object for all the yearning sadness in their quiet American lives.

Rosalie was thirteen when she and Wayne and Maxine and Randy left for good. And so in Texas, Rosalie began her slow fixation on the peninsula, singling it out on the maps in her high school textbooks, touching its outline tentatively, wondering how it was doing, that faraway country where she was born which did not want her back, though she would never stop loving it. Let this be a lesson to you, someone should have warned her yearning heart. Let this be a lesson in love—that you do not always get what you want. That sometimes, you must watch your love across a murmuring sea, nevermore to be close.

THREE SHARP KNOCKS came at the door. Rosalie buried her face in the pillow, annoyed at the intrusion.

"Rosalie?"

It was Abdullah's voice.

"What?" she said.

A pause.

"I . . . Would you like to go shopping in Bahrain? We can go this afternoon. I'll take off work."

It was his peace offering for the missed dinner, and perhaps more. He would buy her finery. A new bracelet, or a sapphire set in a tree of gold. Perhaps even an Italian silk dress. Undergarments made from French lace so elaborate and dense that they would hang off of her naked body like chain mail. She would accept the presents, but only to add to her war chest. According to the Koran, all gifts given in a marriage were the rightful property of the recipient. When she left the Kingdom, she would take her jewels and designer clothes.

Then she would pawn them, hire the best international lawyer, and try to gain custody of Mariam. Though it broke her heart to admit it, she knew that Faisal would never leave his country or his father. In fact, she was probably ambitious in her hope that he would want anything to do with her at all if she divorced Abdullah. Perhaps she should start training her heart to function without the love of her first child, the miracle child who had insisted on being born a full six weeks early, pink and wrinkled as a skinned possum, so ugly that the nurses laughed every time they saw him.

"Give me one hour to get ready," she said.

"OK. Dan's on his way. He wants to go in for a beer."

She held her breath and counted the beats of her pulse. She exhaled. Would Dan feel a twinge when he saw her with Abdullah? What had happened between them on the dune—she had been acting out. She hoped he realized that. Today, Rosalie would practice indifference. It would be the first step toward detachment from her current life. She would lay her fear and her love on a bed of ice until they were both gray as the dead-eyed hamour in the souq. She rolled off the mattress and dropped her nightgown to the floor. She pinched the soft flesh of her belly hard. Pain was one way to quell desire.

ON HER WAY out of the bedroom, Rosalie glimpsed Faisal in the courtyard. She looked down at her son's face through the window, his cheekbones spreading wide and high, creating an openness that made him look like a Pashtun. His was a mountain visage, defying gravity. How handsome he was. Like his father, but more unusual—the result of the two continents mixing in his blood. She waved, and he nodded solemnly. Whenever she passed him in the house, she wanted to squeeze his cheeks in her hands, squash them around to see if the blood still flowed there.

She heard the swish of the sliding-glass door, the click of the lock as he moved it back into place. Leaning over the banister, she looked for him in the sitting room below. Their eyes met.

"Faisal? Would you mind coming upstairs for a minute?" She

wanted to have a moment alone with him. It was hard to be angry with people when you were alone with them, hearing them breathe, watching the clumsy movements of their fragile bodies. That was one reason why Rosalie couldn't handle being alone with Abdullah. When he'd found her in the bathroom last night, she'd felt a softening toward him, a feeling that ran so contrary to what was in her heart that she hadn't known quite how to react. But she had listened to her husband because she was concerned for her son. Faisal's religious outburst revealed to her the stark truth that her boy, the one she had spent sixteen years raising, controlling almost everything down to the hue of the oranges that he consumed, had found his path away from the family and was now in the world, where either he would be in control of himself or others would be. She studied Faisal's face as he mounted the stairs.

Before he made it halfway up, the doorbell rang and Abdullah charged out of the guest bathroom. He swung the door wide to reveal Dan Coleman. Rosalie watched Faisal's face turn cold.

"Coleman! What, did you fly here? I guess I should never underestimate your need for a beer." Abdullah looked up at her. "Habibti, hurry up. We want to make it before noon prayer."

Faisal gave Dan a withering look, then turned and went back toward the courtyard. Rosalie considered following him outside but decided against it. She wasn't sure she could control her tone in talking to Faisal. She suspected he'd known of Isra for some time now, and she worried that her bitterness over his knowledge would transform her concern for him into a retributive bark.

"Shut the door, you're letting the AC out," she said. The relief of the previous days' north wind had disappeared, replaced by a damp stillness that made breathing difficult.

"You'll be needing your gills today," Dan said. "Got to practically swim through this air."

IT WAS MIDDAY as they made their way across the causeway. Whenever they went anywhere together, Abdullah had Dan drive. The

Gulf, milky with salt, stretched out on either side of them. There was no wind, the water glassy as a lake, so that a single windsurfer kept capsizing, his red sail slowly tipping into the water. Inside the car, the air-conditioning blew loudly. Rosalie wanted to close her eyes and sleep. When she'd climbed into the backseat, she was so jittery that she almost leaned forward to tell Abdullah that she'd been alone with his friend. She had even kissed him. Did she still have the power to make her husband jealous? She wanted to see Abdullah's features blanking in confusion, then the contorting effects of his anger.

"We'll stop at a barber first. I should get cleaned up before we go to the shops," Abdullah said.

Rosalie assessed the backs of their heads. Abdullah's was bare, his graying hair cropped close to the neck. He was meticulous about upkeep. Dan, on the other hand—his hair was thick, a deep brown. A few white hairs had sprouted around his temples, and on top the hair was mussed, as if he'd forgotten to comb it that morning. It had grown shaggy, falling over his collar in tufts. Bachelor hair. He looked as unkempt as in his grad school days, except the lank hair was charmless now that it sat on a middle-aged head.

At the inspection station for vehicles reentering the Kingdom, blue-uniformed policemen and National Guardsmen moved between cars, checking in backseats and trunks. There were more of them than usual. Dan eased the car through the VIP lane and paused momentarily at the booth. A policeman with a patchy goatee and crooked teeth that gave him an underbite greeted them. Instinctively, Rosalie's hands moved to her headscarf to make sure it was in place. In Arabic, Abdullah asked him what the commotion was about.

"The jihadis are acting up again," the guardsman said. His eyes twinkled.

She supposed it was a good sign if a National Guardsman could joke about extremism. To him, the thugs were children, naughty children. Nothing to see here, just a bunch of amateurs with firecracker bombs. It was a risky comment to make, but she could tell that the man was not risk-averse. His eyes were small and hard, and he had fading bruises on his neck. Here was a person who had seen violence in some form, and their effete party—men with soft hands and shaggy hair and she with the carefully embroidered abaya that exposed her vanity—were another species altogether. Abdullah gestured to let the man see into the car but the guard put up both hands and shook his head as if they were old friends and inspecting the car would be insulting.

Abdullah nodded his thanks and climbed back inside. She noticed, not without pleasure, that he had grown rounder in recent days. She pursed her lips tightly, saw Isra prone beneath him, head thrust back, breasts protruding, heard her half-cries of pleasure, and as suddenly as it had flared, Rosalie's affection vanished.

"You're the one who needs a haircut, Mr. Coleman," she said.

He turned in the driver's seat, as if to confirm that she was addressing him.

"You got a pair of scissors?" Dan asked.

She saw him looking at her through the rearview mirror. He was flirting; she could tell by the subtle way he moved his head to one side, as if asking her to take something from him, an invitation for her to touch him. Abdullah was reading something on his BlackBerry. She stared back at Dan, hoping to squash his boldness. She couldn't deny that something had passed between them, but it was more like commiseration than anything resembling love. She needed him to think rationally. Making the proper arrangements for her flight out would require lucidity.

"Didn't you cut hair back in Austin?" Dan pressed.

"Nope," she said. "Must've been one of Abdullah's other girlfriends."

"Habibti, why do you say that?" Abdullah cut in. "You know you were the only one." He said it as if his fidelity was a ribbon she could hang on her wall, a memento of a glorious past.

"I'm sure you could do a fair job of it," Dan said. "You've got to be better than the Filipino guy I go to."

"There is no way in hell that I would allow my wife to touch your head. Who knows what's growing there?" Abdullah laughed, and Rosalie knew that was the end of it.

At one time his voice and his laugh had been hers, listening to Hank Williams at the Hole in the Wall on the Drag, the vent wafting fry fumes at them; at Zilker Park, under the Christmas tree. "Who's the infidel now?" she had shouted at him as they spun dizzily beneath the lights. A private world where they made their own noise. But she would not allow herself to be overcome. Out the window, there was one of the Khalifa palaces, a concrete monstrosity of towers and cupolas, soulless as a new shopping mall. They drove around a traffic circle, Dan craning his neck in search of a barbershop. The blues and reds of traffic signs in Arabic and English. Narrow jewelry stores jammed between shoe shops and teahouses. Through her window, Rosalie watched people moving—Indian men in ragged pants, women shuffling on sidewalks, their feet like two flicking tongues beneath their abayas.

"Over there," Abdullah said. He pointed out a corner barbershop where two men and a yellow cat sat in the shade of the building's upper stories.

They parked and got out of the car. She noticed that Dan stood a couple inches taller than Abdullah, his broad back stretching the shoulders of his polo shirt. Both men were large, with athletic strides. Abdullah had once been the keeper for an intramural soccer club at UT, his extra inches of height helpful in sending the ball safely up and out of range of the net. She didn't know Dan's history—maybe six-man football on the dusty fields of West Texas, or basketball. She imagined him thinner and younger, loping up and down a brightly lit court where the air smelled of concession-stand hot dogs.

They stopped in front of the open door of the barbershop. The men outside had identical faces, wizened and brown as mahogany. They spoke with Egyptian accents. The yellow cat lifted its tiny head, its fat body stretched out behind, a feline odalisque. Dan said a few halting phrases in Arabic and the men smiled in appreciation. Abdullah looked at her, rolled his eyes. He felt that Arabs were too easily impressed by the cultural overtures of Westerners. In spite of her desire to freeze out care, Rosalie could not stop the low-level telepathy that they had developed through thousands of shared days and words exchanged.

They pushed past the waiting-area curtain and into the shop. A radio buzzed in the corner playing a Lebanese pop song, all habibti and everlasting love. The tiles on the floor were chipped and yellowing but clean, and there were two large chairs set before mirrors. Rosalie looked at herself in the one closest to her. With the headscarf pulled tightly under her chin, her face protruded, pushing against the edge of the scarf like a body caught beneath too-tight sheets. She looked squeezed, slightly puffy. In a single motion, she undid the tuck she had created on the side of her head. She pulled off the scarf, her red hair wild with static beneath it. Through the mirror, she saw the barbers staring at her.

"Put it back on," Abdullah said.

"No. My ears were sweating. Besides, it's Bahrain. I'm allowed."

"These men think you're a whore." He said it in English.

"That's their problem, isn't it?"

"No, it's my problem."

He moved to tug the headscarf back into place, but Rosalie dodged to the left. "La. No." He took her hard by the wrist, so that she could feel the pinch of his fingers, the cool flat of his palm against her skin. For a moment, she thought he would kiss her. How often had he taken her roughly by the waist, the shoulders, the wrists, scaring her with the violence of his desire, while she pressed back against his embrace, a wordless mock struggle. Now he held her at a distance. There would be no gratifying capitulation, as when she would stop her back-tread and move hipbones-first into him, when he would dig at her limbs with his nails, run his fingers through her hair as if he expected to find gold there. Abdullah made a noise in his throat and dropped her arm. His eyes lingered on her face, and she felt awkward beneath his inspecting glance.

"But we're in Bahrain, Abdi," she said.

Behind them, Dan's eyes stared through the muddy mirror. Emptied of his usual jokiness, they were the still blue of twilight. His lips were parted slightly, as if he were on the verge of speaking. Normally, he would have come to her aid, made a joke about Abdullah's bossiness. Now she saw that he was scared of giving something away.

One of the barbers wiped down the red vinyl of a chair. Abdullah sat down. At its peak, their love had had an edge that depended on the fear she felt whenever she considered a life without him. She was sure he had sensed it. Power is always clear between two entangled people. Still, she'd felt safe within her marriage. Part of her anger at him was for jolting her out of that safety, for making her feel, once again, like she had to fight for a love that was owed her.

With his good hand, Abdullah waved the barber toward him. She thought of her jealousy-limned dreams. The time she dreamed that Abdullah's courtship of Isra had followed to the word his courtship of her, every "fuck" and "love" exactly positioned so that his love for the second wife perfectly overlaid and eliminated his love for the first. She had gagged in her sleep and awoken choked and panting. It was not the physical connection that she had imagined having with her husband twenty-seven years into their marriage. She thought of the moment on the dune with Dan, the way they had both pawed hungrily at each other. The way he had looked at her with a kind of boyish reverence, the look she'd grown used to from men when she was a student. On that dune, she had remembered what it was like to be adored, and it was a powerful feeling.

"Come on, yallah," Abdullah said to the barber. "We need to make it to Gold City before they close for prayer."

"Don't rush him. You want a clipped artery?"

"Worry more about your own arteries, Coleman."

"I'm svelte by American standards."

"King Fahd is svelte by American standards."

"That man's lucky he looks so good in a dress."

She watched the barber move his fingers through Abdullah's hair, drawing it out more slowly, pausing against his scalp as he surveyed the hair.

"I'm going to give you a shampoo," he said.

"Ma'alesh." Abdullah fanned his stump out in dismissal.

The barber guided Abdullah to the sink on the other side of the room. She often forgot that her husband was a cripple, because he carried himself like some ten-armed Hindu god. As soon as the water opened up, she turned to Dan, placed her hand on his knee. Under her palm, she felt his warmth. He looked at her, eyes questioning. She felt the thinnest fracture of desire breaking through her. Could they? Back in the States? *Habibi habibi habibi*, the woman sang on the radio. One of the barbers had fallen asleep, and his teeth caught each exhale, creating a soft whistle. She felt fragile as an egg, as if she could split apart at any moment, her organs exiting rapidly as a slippery yolk. Dan stood and her hand brushed his upper arm.

"Yallah, yallah," Abdullah said to the man who had tilted him back, plunged his head beneath the spray of water.

Dan spoke to her in a low voice.

"Have you given any more thought to leaving?"

The smell of anise filled the room from the suds of Abdullah's shampoo.

"Yes, but I'm nervous, Dan. I've never been good at lying."

His eyes were beseeching. He had a shadowy scruff around his jaw. She felt charged by his desire for her.

"I'm on re-pat next month. Going to Corsica. I'm going to hike across the island. Maybe you could find your way there, after you get your visa. We could drink that liquor they make from myrtle and jump off the calanques."

His voice had a dreamy quality. She liked the fantasy. Maybe she would stop in Corsica on her way back to Houston, relearn what it meant to be adored.

"You'll have to forge Abdullah's signature on the permission documents," she said. "See if the Tunisian can dig up some old forms so you can see what it looks like. Buy the ticket. Yes. I think . . ." She paused. "I think I'm going to leave him."

At that, Dan placed his hand over hers just as the barber guided Abdullah into a seated position. Abdullah's eyes lingered on them, a towel draped around his shoulders. She yanked her hand back.

"Almost done?" she called across the room.

Her voice sounded too cheerful. Abdullah stood and walked toward them, drying his ears with the towel at his neck.

"I'll get the cut some other time. It's time to leave."

Abdullah smoothed the towel over his head. It was something he'd done thousands of times in her company. The intimacy of certain movements—those you've practiced since birth in the maintenance of your body. It had been one of her favorite things about married life—watching him shave, memorizing how he stood while taking a piss. She had shadowed him for decades, at times feeling as though their spirits crossed bodies in the night—out with a snore, through the nose, the way the Egyptians removed brains. It was incredible to her that another man's body could present the same promise of earned familiarity. Impossible. Even if she did divorce and remarry, she was certain that she would only be able to see the next man as rehearsing to play the part of Abdullah in the theatrical production of their epic love—trying to get his tics down, never quite uttering his lines with the same gusto. Abdullah balled the towel and tossed it at Dan's chest.

When Abdullah looked at her, she could see his jaw bulge slightly. He was clenching his teeth, his lips thinned into an ungenerous line.

Abdullah paid for the shampoo and then they were back out in the street.

"Gold City," he said.

GOLD CITY SAT in the heart of Manama, and as they made their way down Government Avenue toward the Bab al-Bahrain, the white gate marking the souq's entrance flashed brightly. The century had been unkind to the surrounding buildings, some of the last standing traditional structures from Manama's early days of development. The gate had once abutted the sea, and the pearling vessels that supplied the gold souq had moved along the near horizon. But over the years, the government had reclaimed much of the Gulf waters to expand the reach of the island, and the gate was now far from the waterfront. When Rosalie bought antique pearl jewelry, she imagined the sun glancing off the bare chests of the pearl divers as they hauled their treasure up out of the sea and into the souq, the jewelers fitting the still-dripping pearls into gold settings.

Dan parked the car, and as they walked toward the shops, Abdullah took her hand. Dan walked several paces ahead, almost skipping. With a shake, she freed herself from Abdullah's grip.

"So it's jewelry before hand-holding, then?" Abdullah said. "You're a smart woman, zowjti."

"Hmm," she said. She wondered if she could be called smart. Since she was twenty, she'd allowed herself to be led by the hand.

In the souq, ropes of yellow gold hung against red velvet, glittering like metallic flames, cold and brilliant. Medallions large as Aztec suns burned behind glass, and necklaces long enough to join the Gulf to the Red Sea folded in on one another to create curtains of twenty-four-karat gold. The shoppers' abayas whispered along the marble floor and people spoke in low, awed voices, the gold's glow falling across their worshipful faces.

"Let's go to the gems," Abdullah said. "We'll find my friend Abdul Wahab." He hurried ahead, gesturing impatiently at them to follow. When they arrived at the shop, Abdullah asked for a loupe, then bent over and inspected a pair of diamond earrings.

"One carat each. Platinum setting. Feel how heavy," Abdullah said, placing them in her palm.

"They're beautiful." The stones would pay for a car when she got back to Houston; she followed the blue flame that she could see moving in their depths.

"Sixteen thousand dollars," Abdullah said. "For you."

Dan snorted, and Abdullah turned toward him sharply. His eyes held the appraising look of a man about to make a wager.

"Dan, I think you should buy these for my wife."

Rosalie gave a nervous laugh. "Don't be ridiculous," she said.

"By way of apology."

"What are you talking about?" Dan asked

"I think you know the answer to that."

Dan looked at Rosalie with confusion, his face flushed.

"I saw the way you touched her hands in the barber shop."

"Abdi, be reasonable," she said.

"Go on. Buy her these earrings. You're making what, seventy or eighty thousand now, after that last raise?" The gold merchant looked uneasy, glancing frequently toward the earrings that Rosalie still had cupped in her hand.

"What the hell is your problem?" Dan asked

"Keep your hands off my wife."

"You're insane," Rosalie said.

"Are you kidding me?" Dan said.

"Be a gentleman, Dan," Abdullah said. "At least buy her a present if you're going to flirt with her like that." Abdullah smiled a mean grin, then said flatly, "Go on. Buy the earrings."

She'd seen them go to extremes to humiliate each other in the past—elaborate practical jokes, physical pranks played out for the amusement of the other Baylani brothers. But now Abdullah seemed serious.

"Abdullah," Dan said.

"I don't want them," she said.

A small group of shoppers had stopped to gawk.

"Here, how about I give you a loan until you can afford it."

Abdullah put down his credit card with enough force to rattle the display case. The merchant ran it and presented the receipt to Abdullah with a shaking hand. She wanted to toss the earrings on the floor, make Abdullah stoop to search for them. She no longer cared about his bad back. It wasn't her place to care anymore. But she needed the earrings. Releasing a heavy breath through her nose, she slipped them under her abaya and into her pants pocket.

"Why don't you go ahead and get Isra a pair, while you're at it," Dan said.

"You son of a whore."

"Just a gentle reminder of your obligations. That's what you keep me around for, right? Trying to be the best Jeeves I can be for Sheikh Abdullah."

"You have an odd way of showing gratitude, Coleman."

"Remind me, what exactly am I grateful for?"

"That I don't fire you right now."

"Or maybe the fact that I'm not the asshole who destroyed a perfectly good family by fooling around," Dan said. "I guess I'm grateful for that."

"You were content to destroy your own family by less obvious means. And after all this, my wife still *respects* me. Carolyn sees you for exactly what you are."

"And what the fuck is that?"

"A beggar."

Rosalie had heard enough; Abdullah's cruelty astounded her. She turned and hurried back toward the souq entrance, the breeze from the air-conditioning billowing her abaya out behind her like a cape. Shoppers stopped midstep to watch her pass. Abdullah called out, but she did not slow down or look back. She wanted to keep going. Out the white gate, west over the great brown boot of the Arabian peninsula, west over Eritrea, straight to the churning spread of the Atlantic, where she would use her abaya as a sail to drift out and away. There would be no permission forms or backward glances, only forward momentum.

MEMORY GATHERING: SOME Saturday night at the Lazy Lion. B.A.—Before Abdullah. Talking to a wire-haired guy who's been reading at the bar. Some tattered paperback with the cover torn away. It's OK. She doesn't need to know the title. She doesn't need anything from this guy. She doesn't find him to be attractive, and from the way he talks to her, the feeling seems mutual. That always makes her more relaxed behind the bar. It makes her banter more interesting because she actually thinks about what she is saying, rather than whether or not she will fuck the guy at the bar whose face pleases her. She does not find herself wondering about the wire-haired man's chest and what it might look like in the shadows of her small apartment. Does he even have a chest? She cannot tell. It has gotten lost in the tent of his shirt.

By now, she has seen nearly a thousand Saturday nights at the Lazy Lion. She works every weekend, and during the week she goes to class at the University of Texas. She knows exactly how many work hours equal an hour of class. She never goes home to Sugar Land. Maxine has gotten fat and diabetic, and now she is bedridden and the whole house smells like cauliflower. Wayne says it's her rotting limbs. Her older brother Randy drives out from Houston to check on them and leaves messages for Rosalie to let her know how they are doing. Though she is close to graduating, Rosalie feels like a drifter. She is young, anything is possible, and that is precisely what scares her.

As he is getting up to leave, the wire-haired man checks his pockets dramatically. Never trust a Marxist, he says. Why's that? She asks. I don't have enough for the tip, he says. She waves it off like it's no big deal, but it is kind of a big deal because that money would pay for at least one or two minutes of class, and she's not even going to get laid. Here, he says. He pulls something out of his back pocket. Have this. It means more to me than a dollar, anyway. After he's gone, Rosalie lights a cigarette and wanders over to see what he's left on the bar. It's a world map. Careful to wipe away the wet spots first, she unfolds it on the bar. Even in the dim light of the Lazy Lion, she can make out its brilliant blues and greens. She moves her fingers over a tan, boot-shaped peninsula. Saudi Arabia. She lived there once. In her chest, an ache. Her throat closes. It is like seeing a photograph of an old love.

THAT EVENING, AFTER returning from Gold City, Rosalie welcomed the clean simplicity of her daughter—her floral smells, the nakedness of her teenaged wants. At nine thirty p.m., Mariam materialized at Rosalie's door, having halted her furious typing to allow Rosalie to mother her. It was wonderful to be called to purpose like that. It happened so rarely now that the children were nearly grown, so when Mariam arrived with her need to be stroked and soothed, Rosalie approached her duties with a religious earnestness.

"Tisbah al-khayr, Umma." Mariam stood in the doorway. She was dressed in a red cotton shalwar kameez. Against it, her hair fell in a deep chestnut curtain.

Rosalie patted the space in front of her on the bed, and when Mariam sat down, she stretched a leg on either side of her daughter's body. While Rosalie combed through Mariam's hair, she considered her situation. Her adrenaline flared whenever she remembered the scrape of Dan's stubble against her cheek, the pressure of her breasts mashed against his chest. It had been so good to feel another body against her own. Afterward, her limbs were supple, her skin prickled with the slightest breeze. She was a boxer, a champion racehorse, her strength present in the muscles coiled hotly beneath her skin. Her underwear was damp. It might just be physical, but physical was a hell of a lot more than what she had currently with Abdullah. And in her gut, she was surprised to feel a longing for it to be something more than just sexual. Leaving someone was always easier when you had another person's arms to fall into.

"Dear one. Tell me more about your internship at *Saudi Times*."

"My teacher wants to give me school credit for it, if she can convince Headmistress Shideed," Mariam said, her feet swinging back and forth at the end of the bed. "It's just once a week, but since A'm Nabil paired me with Faizah al-Zahrani and I'm doing so much writing, it should work out."

"That's wonderful, sweetheart. I'm thrilled for you. You have to be sure to send A'm Nabil a nice gift. Maybe we can bake something for him. He has that sweet tooth, and A'ma Nadia complains it's killing her; she's eating so many pastries, she's getting fat. Maybe you can give them to him at the office so A'ma isn't tempted."

Mariam laughed. Nadia was Abdullah's middle sister, the smartest of all of them according to Abdullah, who occasionally entertained the idea of making her a partner at B-Corp. Once, he'd even pitched it to her, but she'd responded with a cascade of her famous giggles. "And who will take care of my six little ones, then? Nabil? I can barely get him to come home at night, he's so in love with that newspaper."

Nadia had definitely tested Rosalie's patience with her little mind games at the beginning, but once she was convinced that Rosalie wasn't just some gold digger after the family coin, they'd become close.

Rosalie spun Mariam's hair into a coil, twisting it tight and looping it upward. The hair was shining as crude oil, a sober frame for her daughter's face. Mariam's hazel eyes had a green fire through the irises that burned in a quiet way. As a baby, she would sit upright in the night and deliver prophesies in babbles. Even then, Rosalie listened. There was wisdom in the child. Now she was off, seeking her path, pursuing her heroes that she might learn from them.

Rosalie lacked her daughter's seriousness. Perhaps she should have approached her life with more sensibility. Instead, she felt that she had grown merely decorative. Letting her daughter's looped hair fall loose, she combed her fingers through. She didn't have to look to know that Mariam's eyes were closed. She could hear it in her breath, which came steady with the even thrum of a sleeping baby. It was their pre-bed ritual, this head massage and hair comb, and Mariam tilted her head back, her narrow brown throat moving up and down as she swallowed. With each press of fingertip to scalp, Rosalie felt the electricity that exists between a mother and the child she has carried, the little buzz and shock of once-joined flesh touching again. If only she could put her hands through Faisal's hair, touch his cheek. Perhaps he would feel that primitive tug, his muscles remembering when they fed off her blood. Perhaps he would be less angry with her. Despite Mariam's protests, she found that she could not help gathering the child in her arms and drawing her close, her daughter's upper body fitted to her mother's, a shell folded into the sea bed.

Rosalie thought of making a life in the States. She would be a secretary in a dental office, go home at five to an empty condominium, phone the children twice a week, perhaps create a profile on one of those Internet dating sites. The thought of wading through the pools of potbellied, sunburned men with their fixed swagger and their middle-aged intransigence, made her wince. They would have powerboats, play poker and weekend golf, take vacations to Corpus and Cancun. They would speak loudly, full of bluster and the determination that life's disappointments ingrain. They would be well past the pleasing pliancy of young manhood. It would all be so ordinary, so unbearably mundane, while her children would bloom like exotic plants somewhere far across the world—unknown and unknowable to Rosalie in her Sugar Land condo.

She got a panicky feeling in her chest, her heart racing at the thought of unmooring herself so entirely. And of course she had to consider the fact that, if she left, Abdullah would belong entirely to Isra.

"Mariam, my heart," she said.

"Yes, Umma?"

"How would you feel about going to school in America?"

"But I am going to go to school in America, for college. I told you that already. I'm not going to a King Whatshisname School for Girls. They don't even teach all the proper subjects. Lina's sister goes to one and every time I talk to her, she gets stupider and stupider."

"No, honey. I mean now. For high school. Would you like that?"

"Boarding school?" Mariam said. "I thought you said I was too young to be away from my family."

"I would go with you. We could live in a house near your school. I could get a job and keep you company. And Faisal might be nearby, for college."

She said it flinchingly, as though she realized that the idea was ludicrous.

"I don't know," Mariam said hesitantly. "That'd be cool, I guess. Would Baba come?"

"No, hummingbird. Baba would have to stay here and work. This is his home. But he could come and visit us. You could be on the school newspaper and play sports. You'd like that, wouldn't you?"

This child bribery was probably ill advised, but Rosalie couldn't help it. She had a powerful need for her daughter, especially when she considered leaving everything. And Mariam would have a freer life at an American high school. There would be dances in gyms, the sound of sneakers on waxed wooden floors, the banging of lockers in the hallways, Homecoming floats and football games, the smell of popcorn and wood smoke on late November evenings at the stadium. There would be so much for Mariam's senses. If she stayed in Saudi Arabia, they'd keep an abaya over her, just the first of the many things to come between her and the broader world.

"Let me think about it, OK?" Mariam said.

"Yes, of course, habibti."

"Umma?"

"Yes, dear?"

"I might have suspected. For the last year."

"What are you talking about?"

"Ever since Doha. Ever since I met Isra in Doha. Even though she was wearing a navy blue suit and had her hair pulled back tight. I think I knew. I should have told you." Mariam's voice cracked quietly.

"Oh, my darling. No. Don't be upset. Your silence protected both of us for as long as possible."

She wrapped her arms around Mariam and rested her head against her back. From there, she could hear the thumping of her strong heart. Unlike Faisal, Mariam had been born with a robust body, nearly twice as big as her premature brother's. Rosalie counted several more beats, then shifted to the side so she could see her daughter's face.

"It's just that . . . Baba is never wrong," Mariam said. "He never makes mistakes. My teachers talk about him like he's a prophet. And I know he loves us, so I trusted him. I kept silent."

"Mariam, you were right to do that." Rosalie cupped her daughter's cheek in her hand. "To believe. Don't ever feel foolish when your trust has been betrayed. Hurt and angry for a time? Fine. But a trusting heart is a gift."

Rosalie always felt wiser as a mother than as a woman, so that she often listened to her own counsel as if she had something to gain by it. Unsurprisingly, she did. Why is it, she thought, that what we expect of our children is greater than what we expect of ourselves?

She shifted back behind her daughter, weaving Mariam's hair into a loose braid, unwinding it, weaving it again. She massaged her daughter's scalp where her hairline met the skin at the base of her neck. These nights of touch with Mariam were not enough to sustain her. She remembered Dan's warmth on the beach. She had never had to survive very long in her adult life without sex, not until Abdullah stopped staying at the house as much a few months earlier. From the moment she had let her virginity go on the hard sand behind a tin hutch in Port Aransas, her body's own climate mirroring the salt and wet of the beach, she had thought, yes, this is what it feels like to be alive.

The children's birth affirmed her feeling that sex was not only spirit leavening, but life-giving in that most base, literal way. The moment she held her babies, felt the glory and the mess resultant from sex, a bolt fired through her, life splitting her wide. She had been thirty-one and then thirty-three years old, and she felt a communion with the universe so strong that she became grasping, wondering how she could maintain that feeling always. Five years into their marriage, she'd yielded to Abdullah's pleas to start trying for children—she'd been so lonely in the Kingdom, so tired of trying to preserve the timeline she'd created for her life before she'd met Abdullah, which had *not* involved getting married at twenty, and certainly hadn't involved children before twenty-five. But then it was like life was playing a cruel joke on her—they couldn't conceive right away, and when they eventually did, she'd miscarried. They'd had to see doctors in Germany, all the while the Baylani family thinking they'd been right, that this Amreekiyah was a dud. Then finally, thankfully, Faisal had implanted and kept growing until he'd emerged wrinkled and shrieking. She hadn't been afraid, as she thought she would be with a newborn baby. Rather, she'd felt with certainty that she'd never be lonely again.

But then Abdullah had used it all against her: *You are the mother of my children.* It was how he saw her now. When he'd said it, she'd tried to cry, but she was stuck in that bleak room of depression that is not big enough to be sadness. *You are the mother of my children;* he said it as if it were enough. But she knew it only meant that she was no longer all and one. And what about during their honeymoon, when she told him that she wanted to be buried in the same coffin as him so that their bones would become dust, their bodies indistinguishable? Now he would be buried with Isra. Their hearts would grow gray and feathery as moths' wings, collapsing side by side. Hers would mold in its cage of bones. She put her hand to her chest.

Mariam had fallen asleep and was leaning heavily into Rosalie's shoulder. She pressed her nose into her daughter's hair and breathed deeply. It smelled of the lavender shampoo Rosalie bought for her on the previous summer's vacation to Provence, and of something deeper, the skin of her scalp, plain and earthy as oatmeal. Rosalie remembered the time they'd gone to France, walked around the sunflower fields of the Luberon, sunned themselves on beachside recliners in Cannes. She'd sipped from sweating glasses of pastis and rosé, and Mariam had finished one Shirley Temple after another, the grenadine staining her lips pink. At night, they'd eaten bouillabaisse and tiny calissons, whose nuclear sweetness kept them buzzing until well after midnight. There in the fortifying light of the Mediterranean sun, she had been happy.

She wanted to lay Mariam in her bed undisturbed. It seemed only right that when a child falls asleep in a mother's arms, she should awaken in the light of morning with a sense of peace and no recollection of being deposited in her sheets. With a heave, she tried to lift Mariam in her arms but her daughter was too heavy. Her leg slipped from Rosalie's grasp, and Mariam woke, blinking and starting, half in and half out of her mother's embrace. Rosalie sighed, felt her uselessness settling around her like dust.

"Umma, what're you doing?" Mariam laughed.

"I thought I'd put you to bed."

"That's OK. I'll put myself to bed."

Yes, she remembered. This is our family now, each person putting themselves to bed, striving and struggling and aching behind bolted doors. When would they let each other in again?

"Good night, then. Think about what I asked you, habibti."

Mariam kissed her on the cheek. "OK. 'Night."

She watched her daughter exit the room, the sway of her slim hips, her step buoyant. Rosalie wished she possessed the confidence she saw in her daughter. Mariam would never allow herself to be someone's first or second wife. She would have been on a plane to Houston the moment she learned about Isra. She would be *wife*, or nothing. She belonged to a new generation of Saudi women. Things were changing, but not as rapidly as Rosalie had thought. She pushed her heels into the thick carpet, straightening her legs. Yes. She would leave. And she would try to take Mariam.

It was late, but she called Lamees to tell her she wouldn't be able to go walking for the next couple weeks. Something had come up that needed her attention. The voice mail flipped on and she left a message. After she hung up, she wondered if she would ever see Lamees again. Perhaps after she left the Kingdom, she could meet Lamees and Khaled on one of their vacations, on a safari or a beach on the Indian Ocean. Even as she thought it, she realized it was impossible. The love could not be shared. And Rosalie knew her bitterness over their happiness would kill the friendship. It had already started to.

She needed to talk to Dan. He would provide answers, tactics for departure, bullet-pointed itineraries. He was a nomad. He knew how to come and go without disturbing the landscape, letting the horizon absorb him. One night when he had come over to drink with Abdullah, he'd told her that he was always ready to disappear. For months after the divorce, Carolyn had tried to contact Dan through Abdullah but somehow his name was never known, his information never shared. Always a bad connection or an issue of translation: Dan Coleman? Ma hua? Who's he? This global Houdini. He would know how to help her disappear from the Magic Kingdom.

SEVEN

HERE WE ARE, thought Faisal, two candles dying between us. It was the candles that so thoroughly depressed him, the glowing red wax and bright flames and polished silver candlesticks out of accord with the distinctly noncelebratory mood of the diners. Mariam drooped. Faisal could hear Rosalie swallow her lentil soup, each spoonful going down leadenly. Three nights had passed since the botched family dinner, when Abdullah had failed to show up and his mother had disappeared before they started the salad.

Even after returning from his trip Abdullah had mostly stayed away, leaving Faisal with a weary mother and a fidgeting sister. Faisal tried not to look at Rosalie's face, fixing his gaze instead on the puckering candles, the chandelier, a small red stain that looked like a bindi against the pale carpet, the badly done oil painting of his father in which his legs looked like large sausages coiled around the midsection of an Arabian stallion. He wondered what Abdullah and Isra were talking about at that moment as they sat at her dining table, just a few hundred meters away. He wondered if they too endured such moments of subterranean silence.

He'd seen Abdullah and Isra drive up to her house, just returned from the trip, their faces rosy, the car filled with duty-free bags from

Dubai International. Isra whooshed out of the car, her white dress shocking against her tan shoulders, her abaya crumpled in a heap on the floor of the car. His father honked at him and waved with his good hand. Faisal didn't wave back, instead fixing his eyes on the crane suspended over the top of the half-done skyscraper going up behind Isra's house. He stared at the building's skeleton long enough to make sure there would be no eye contact with them, and long enough to be pleased by the Windex-blue of the skyscraper's reflective windows.

He was angry with his parents. They had to do everything noisily, misbehaving like children. Knocking on Isra's door! Isra had gossiped to an acquaintance, and within days, the Diamond Mile was electrified by talk of Rosalie's antics. Every time he passed by the neighbors' homes, he imagined the burble of courtyard fountains to be low-throated snickers coming from behind the high walls. In some of the more outrageous versions of events he overheard from Ali and Majid and Hassan, the fig became a bottle of Chanel No. 5 smashed into a thousand shards against Isra's door, a decaying chicken's heart black with flies, a fat mongoose with a red ribbon around its neck, sharpening its teeth on the concrete. He wondered if women could keep nothing private—if the great secret of their days was, in fact, that they had none.

"You're wearing me out with all this chatter," Rosalie said, her fork poised over her lamb.

He grunted.

"What's the matter? Did you and Majid have a fight?"

Faisal was surprised. She rarely asked him about Majid because she said she didn't trust boys trying too hard to be men, so Faisal never told her anything about him. It was for the best, anyway, as Majid had a family network as complex and secretive as a walnut shell. Because Rosalie had never asked, Faisal never told her about Majid's uncle, a Sahwi scholar imprisoned by the al-Saud in the late nineties, still floundering in jail because he refused to go on TV to confess his mistake in declaring the royals to be apostate. Neither did he tell Rosalie of the twenty-centimeter scar that snaked from Majid's elbow to the back of his hand, earned in some back alley in Fallujah, where, Majid said, the acrid smell of smoke was counteracted by the sweet pungency of rotting garbage. And it was Majid, with his warrior's heart, who had led Faisal to Sheikh Ibrahim, the man who spoke God's truth and was unafraid of the al-Saud. She never asked. He never told. He liked keeping these secrets from her, and from Abdullah—liked the way the mysteries bunkered in his heart; the business of possessing knowledge that no one else in the family did.

"Majid's a jerk," Mariam said.

"Why?" said Rosalie.

It was a game they had started playing together, and it made Faisal twitch. One of them asserted something, and the other one made her justify the opinion. Rosalie claimed it would teach Mariam to make statements that were "clear and true," whatever that meant. Rosalie said that, too often, and not just in newspapers, people lied or said fuzzy things, things they didn't really mean or understand.

"Well," said Mariam. "For one thing, he told me that after a certain age, a woman should never answer the front door. And he doesn't smile. I almost preferred when he used to throw me in the pool."

Faisal laughed; he couldn't help it. When they were younger, Majid had made it his habit to throw Mariam in the pool behind the house, clothes and all, until one day Rosalie had seen him do it, charged from the house, and angrily shoved him in. At the time, they were twelve, and Faisal wasn't sure if Majid had ever forgiven Rosalie that humiliation. Now Faisal was letting Rosalie entertain her vision of Majid as an ill-tempered child because if she knew the real reasons behind Majid's scowl, she would try to squash their friendship. He didn't want to sneak around in order to see his friend, and he had learned that defending something only led to further scrutinizing. Without Majid, his days would be tedious. He saw boys all over the streets of Al Dawoun: in the malls, throwing their phone numbers at passing girls, at the mosque answering text messages in the middle of prayer. He didn't want to be like that—one of the mall boys with nothing to do but eat and fantasize about girls and money. That life reminded him too much of Bern and all he had endured there.

"No, it's nothing to do with Majid," he said.

"Well, you're sulking about something," Rosalie said.

He took a long drink of the apple juice in his glass and finished the fattoush on his plate, waiting for her to continue. He picked the pieces of parsley from his teeth.

"Who told you?" she finally asked.

"What?" he said.

Now, apparently, she even read his scowls. There was no privacy with her.

"About the Isra incident."

"Hassan told me."

"And who did he hear it from?"

"He overheard his mother talking about it."

Rosalie brought the dull end of her knife down hard against the tablecloth, so that it thudded against the dense wood beneath the cloth. He felt the shiver of the massive Norwegian beams. Two grains of rice jumped off of her plate and onto the tablecloth. Yasmin bustled in and cleared them away.

"There are no secrets in this town," she said.

He remained close-lipped. It hadn't taken him long to learn the power that came from ignoring his mother—her questions, her jokes, her outbursts. After draining his water glass, and then his juice glass, and then his glass of laban, he stood to go outside.

"Faisal," she said, pausing. "I know you might be upset with me, but you must understand . . ."

"I already understand."

"But . . ."

"You've embarrassed us," he said. "Besides, Isra is a fine wife."

"Pardon me?"

Mariam gave him a cold look, and he felt a moment of regret, but his mother needed to hear it. She'd been behaving like a child about Isra, as if she didn't have a fine life, a better life than most women.

"I don't understand why you're so mad. Baba did nothing wrong."

"Your father lied to me. For years."

Since Isra, Rosalie had become obsessed with the act of Abdullah's lie—when and where it had first occurred, how many people in the family had known and kept it hidden from her.

"The Prophet, peace be upon Him, said 'The sons of Adam are accountable for all lies with these exceptions: During war because war is deception, to reconcile among two quarreling men, and for a man to appease his wife.' Baba was only trying to keep order in our family."

She shook her head and laughed a small, tight laugh, her usually broad mouth pulled small.

"I shouldn't have expected any different from you," she said. "I can't see even the littlest bit of me in you."

She laughed again, and it sounded hollow, like echoes along the wall of a cave. Because she never asked, he also never told her that the boys at school called him *Amreeki*, how much he hated it when Fat Ali shouted it out across the school courtyard—Ali, whose skin was Nubian dark and who, in turn, got called *takrooni*. Rosalie was staring in the direction of the front door, like she was waiting for someone to walk through. Faisal pushed his chair back and walked to the sliding-glass door. Through his hand, he felt the *whoosh* of the door on its tracks, an easy movement that made him feel, momentarily, that everything would be as it should be. Then he saw reflected in the glass his mother's head in her hand. Perhaps he had been too cruel, but if he had to be the one to hold people accountable, he would.

Stepping into the courtyard, he breathed in the evening, fragrant with the frangipani flowers that glowed blue-white in the darkness. He sat down on the edge of the fountain. Through the glass door, he saw Rosalie rise and walk upstairs. She moved like an old woman, each foot heavy on the wide staircase. Would it always be like this now that his father had Isra? The quiet of the house deepening, as if they had all dived under the water and were trying to mouth words to each other? Would they no longer make the noises that families made? Even when they'd been whole, theirs had been an unusually small family, and he had ached for more siblings, brothers in particular. He blamed his mother for this, because he knew that most Americans had small families. It was unnatural, and he felt the silence in their house to be God's rebuke. No wonder Abdullah had married again.

Earlier in the year, after visiting his friend Hassan, who had eight chattering brothers and sisters, Faisal decided that he was going to have at least six children. One wife. Six children. Breaking dishes. Honking toys. Quarreling. He knew God would give him this because at night when he prayed about it, he felt an exaggerated heat around his heart as he articulated the words, as if God was placing his hand there in reassurance: *Please, give me a beautiful Raja or Lamees or Hanouf or Rheem. And give us six children. Though five will also do. Even four would be OK. And make them beautiful and black-haired like their mother. Give them skin the color of a heated date. Do not make them halfway. Shukran Jazeelan.*

He settled into the patio chair, its mesh firm against his back. But as he closed his eyes and began to meditate on the meeting, he heard the door again, and even before he could see her, he smelled Mariam's perfume, some potent stuff that she picked up at the women's market. He didn't turn around, waiting for her to speak. Instead, she cuffed him on the back of the head.

"Ow."

"Hamar. What is your problem? I've never seen you treat Umma and Baba this way."

"Did you just hit me?"

"Umma should have hit you too. You're worse than a donkey. You're a donkey's dirty little bum."

"I'm glad to see all those books you read are helping your vocabulary."

"Shut up. Just because you grow your beard long and wear those ugly old sandals doesn't mean you're a man. Two summers ago, you still had all of those stupid Star Wars statues above your bed. I haven't forgotten."

"A lot can happen in two years. I stopped wanting to be something that I wasn't."

"A geek?"

"No. An American. You'll learn someday. The way they shove their culture down our throats. They're bullies, that's all."

"So you think they should all read the Koran and Ibn Khuldun and work to understand us, but we should ignore their culture?"

"No, not at all. They just shouldn't bother and leave us alone."

"You're jealous of them." She arched her thick black brows.

"Jealous?" He sighed. "Pathetic people want to be something that they're not. But I wouldn't be surprised if you ran off to New York one day."

"At least I wouldn't have to wear a garbage bag to school."

"See? They've already made you ashamed of your culture. You should be proud of it. You know, it's possible to have modernity and faith."

"No, it's people like you and your stupid friends and the religious police that make me ashamed. And I'm not going to leave. I'll go to college, but then I'll come back. I don't want to *be* American. I just want to be myself, which is impossible here. That's why I started my blog. I'm going to make a change for myself."

"Now you're being ridiculous. You think words make any difference at all? Words are just letters. They don't affect anything."

She threw her hands up.

"There's no talking to ignorance." She sighed loudly. "Just try not to be so rude to our parents. *That's* un-Islamic."

She went back into the house, leaving the sliding door open. He heard her bedroom door slam at the top of the stairs. She would probably waste an entire evening typing away at her blog, exchange a few angry IMs with Dalia, her best friend from school—a poor, confused girl with a Saudi father and a dead Lebanese mother who was rumored to have been something of a whore with the American men over on the State Oil compound. He made a note to try to find more suitable friends for his sister. Maybe, down the road, Hassan would be a good match for her after all. His stomach growled. At dinner, he'd eaten only a bit of fattoush, some soup, and a piece of za'atar. The taste of sumac on his tongue made him hungry.

FAISAL WAS GRATEFUL for the sound of the doorbell when Majid came to pick him up for their study group. He climbed into the front seat of Majid's car, which smelled faintly of cigarettes and stale fast food. Majid's older brother, Jalal, with whom he shared the car, smoked two packs of Marlboros a day. Majid never mentioned Jalal, but Faisal would often see him cruising around Al Dawoun, his windows down, some European pop group on the stereo, all synthetic beats and sterile harmonies.

Faisal's phone vibrated with a new text message: HASSAN'S HOUSE. They organized meetings this way to lessen the likelihood that group members would be followed. The group was relatively small, just twenty-five men, and casual guests were not allowed. They couldn't risk dealing with men who were not loyal or discreet, not with the government as paranoid as it was. Faisal thrilled at the thought that he and Majid and the sheikh were part of their own mini-rebellion. It made him feel purposeful, part of something grand. Yes, the Koran and the sheikh spoke to his heart and he believed, but he was also glad of the companionship: Majid's respect, the sheikh's large, calloused hand placed just so on Faisal's thin shoulder. As they waited for the light to change at the intersection of King Abdul Aziz and Al Quds, a beggar approached the window. She cupped her left hand and dipped her right hand into it, gesturing for food or money. The beggars, always women to elicit more sympathy and avoid shaming the men, moved like wraiths through the lines of cars along Al Dawoun's busiest streets, their eyes and mouths covered, their abayas blowing into car grills with each hot gust. She knocked on his window, but Faisal kept his gaze fixed on the road.

The woman waited. The light lasted. Faisal looked to his right, through the thin pane of glass separating him from this woman who surely smelled of urine and burnt garlic. She had no eyes for him to look into, she had no face. Finally, the light changed and they were moving again, down the wide central boulevard, six lanes of traffic accelerating together with a roar before becoming staggered, the red taillights of vehicles blurring as drivers shifted in and out of lanes. In the glow and whir of the highway, amid the urgent horns, Faisal felt that where he was going, and even who he was, were issues of the utmost importance, and that these people around him somehow had a stake in his passage. He saw the three-story palm tree covered in yellow lights that stood outside of the Mercedes dealership, the glass storefronts showcasing expensive dresses, rugs, chandeliers. The Italian coffeehouses with their men-only sections crammed right up against the low-lit windows so that Al Dawoun seemed to be a city populated entirely by men. The American chain restaurants with their neon signs and brimming parking lots. The Corniche stretched long and dark in the fallen night, the blinking lights of tug boats and oil vessels slowly crossing far out from the land. He rolled down his window to hear the low crashing of the waves and smell the salt. On its more moneyed periphery, Al Dawoun was a crystal city by the sea—diademed buildings, surfaces gleaming with the transparency of modernity, all oiled chrome and glass brick, bevel and sheen.

It was exactly what men like his father wanted in a Saudi city. A haven to do their business, so that the city became a place to send and receive faxes, no longer a place to be *from*. Faisal suspected that this was why Abdullah left Al Dawoun at every possible opportunity. He could sense his father's relief, and even pride, that Saudi Arabia was now a place that looked more like the rest of the world and less like the limited world it had been, known only to Bedouin, traders, and soldiers. An "Arab backwater," as a drunk Syrian businessman had once called it while tipping back a white and tonic in their living room.

Now they were headed into the city's interior, toward Hassan's neighborhood. Hassan lived in an area that seemed closer to the heart of the simple fishing village that Al Dawoun had once been, that Faisal had seen in his father's photos from the fifties. Away from the glittering Corniche and the moneyed neighborhoods, Al Dawoun was a place of neutrals, everything fashioned from clay and concrete, the houses cheaply stuccoed. Faisal was surprised that such places still existed, there and all over Saudi Arabia—places stunned and shrunken by the awesome development around them. Places where the people still lived on the Peninsula alone, with no ties to London or Houston or Dubai. In those sheltered locations, Faisal felt the preservation of culture. What Abdullah would call poverty or ignorance or just stubbornness. Faisal wondered how much longer those neighborhoods, those villages, could withstand the strong tide coming in to sweep away the sandstone fortresses in which the people housed their purely Arab lives.

The neighborhood was right in the middle of the city, in one of the oldest residential districts. It was middle-class, the streets riddled with potholes, some of the street lamps broken, their shards fallen in the street and then broken a thousand times by the tires of passing trucks. Despite himself, Faisal felt a wave of gratitude for the wide, clean streets of the Diamond Mile, where the medians were planted with palms and frangipani trees, surrounded by well-tended grass. To avoid drawing attention to the meeting place, members staggered their arrivals. He watched as they trickled in a couple of minutes apart. He knew that in men, these glints, these slight shivers of the eyeball, the light and dark of respect and jealousy, determined power. If you could convince men that righteousness and fearlessness existed in you, then you were master of your fate.

Hassan's house was a large white concrete structure, utilitarian, the outer wall topped with cut cinder blocks. Oleander grew through the cinder blocks, the broken leaves oozing their clear poison. Three stray cats circled a garbage can that sat near the front gate, batting chicken bones along the sidewalk. One of them paused to watch Faisal as he made his way through the gate, its single eye glaring from its mangy face.

Inside, he and Majid descended the narrow stairway, and Faisal felt his stomach contract. Though he'd been in the group for more than a year now, he still felt excited to see the sheikh. In Ibrahim's narrow but muscle-knotted shoulders, Faisal could see the accumulated tension of time spent inching along the frozen paths of the Hindu Kush. In the slope of his skull, the hundreds of nights spent flat-backed on cave floors, lying in wait for the Russians. Next to such indisputable physical testimony, Faisal felt like a pretender to faith.

The sheikh greeted them warmly, placing a hand on Majid's shoulder and gesturing for them to step into the room. With Ibrahim, Majid was like the mischievous son who asked too many questions, which caused his father fits, but whom the father loved the most of all his children because of his sheer talent for both trouble and glory. Faisal was jealous of the easy rapport that Majid had with Ibrahim, of the bond they shared through their mutilated flesh. Once, when Faisal had found himself alone with Ibrahim in a corridor of a group member's home, he had gotten a catholic urge to confess all of his father's failures, and Ibrahim had listened patiently, nodding his head. At the end of Faisal's sputtering, Ibrahim had said only "Trust in God" and walked away. Theirs wasn't the familiar relationship of fathers and sons because Faisal could not overcome his crippling sense of reverence for the sheikh.

Faisal left Majid and Ibrahim to their playful greetings and went in search of Hassan. Hassan was younger, closer to Mariam's age, and Faisal knew he looked up to the older boys. He knocked on his bedroom door, then opened it and stepped inside. Hassan turned around, startled. The room was dark except for the pale glow of his computer screen.

"*True Confessions of a Saudi Teen*?" Faisal said, squinting to read the screen. The font was all different colors, bright and garish. Hassan could act so young sometimes. "What's this garbage?"

Hassan quickly closed the screen and stood up.

"Nothing," Hassan said, blushing. "Some dumb thing my sister reads."

He steered Faisal back out to the meeting space. They both sat down.

"Salaam ya shabab," Sheikh Ibrahim said. "Keifa halikum alayyum?"

"Alhamdullilah."

Ibrahim leaned against a near wall, his crutches resting next to him. His foot had been blown off by a land mine during the Afghanistan jihad of the eighties. In the study group, there was no greater symbol of righteousness than the missing limbs of the weathered Afghan Saudis, as those early jihadis were known. Faisal stretched his arms and legs, shook his wrists loose. He didn't like to feel watched, so he was particularly annoyed when an older man with a lupine face sat down in the seat right across from him. A neat gray beard grew from the man's narrow chin, and Faisal saw the flash of silver caps when he opened his mouth to yawn. He'd noticed the man on two previous occasions; he was probably an uncle or an older cousin of one of the group members. The man looked at him, but Faisal averted his eyes, embarrassed to be caught staring.

"Allahu Akbar," Sheikh Ibrahim intoned.

At home, Faisal often tried to imitate the quiet resonance of the sheikh's voice. In front of the bathroom mirror, or when he asked Mariam to give him the television remote. He could never get it exactly right and determined that it must be like singing. Either you could do it or you couldn't.

"Men, I am here to assure you that I will not be turned into a menstruation sheikh. The al-Saud have made us into a country obsessed by these small issues, the better to keep us from mulling over the real problems plaguing this country. Listen to our radio programs. Listen to our television shows. Everyone wants to know: Can I sleep with my maid, since she is like a slave, making relations with her permissible under Islam? Can my wife buy lingerie from a strange man in the mall or is it haram? If I fart, do I need to repeat my ablutions?"

A few people laughed, including Majid.

"We obsess over these issues of family, of relationships, of private worship," Ibrahim continued. "But these questions have little to do with our Almighty God.

"What we should be asking is, 'Why does my country, a supposedly Islamic state, align itself with the infidels, the Americans, and welcome them into the Arabian Peninsula when the Prophet has said we must expunge them?' and 'Why must I be completely obedient to this sultan, this king, when the Prophet, and Abdul Wahab himself, both say to serve God and God alone?' "

Faisal moved to the edge of his chair, his right foot tapping in time with the murmurs of affirmation making their way through the crowd. The tea and coffee lay untouched, every face turned toward Sheikh Ibrahim like heliotropes to the sun. The sheikh was not much past fifty, the features of his face dramatic—heavily lashed eyes, unruly caterpillar eyebrows, surprisingly feminine lips that protruded pinkly.

"Why is it, I ask you, that the imam is no longer permitted to say the word *'America'* in the mosque? It is because the al-Saud are scared to upset our masters. So I will say it to you now: America! May that country know that we criticize them, that they are harbi, aggressors waging three wars against Muslims, and that our opposition to these injustices cannot be ignored. The most conservative estimates say twenty-five thousand civilians were killed under the occupation in Iraq, and the Americans dare to lament four thousand dead on the eleventh of September, or fifteen hundred American soldiers dead in Iraq? Those numbers are laughable compared to the people that they have slaughtered in Iraq, in Afghanistan."

It was warm in the basement, and Faisal could feel a thin line of sweat spring from his hairline and along his upper lip. The sentences ran through him like blood, warming him, moving through him to his core, settling against his viscera. Frequently, he would fast the day after hearing the sheikh speak, not out of piety but because he could not fill himself up any further. His body felt like a conveyance for power, for will, not just a bony, tendoned mass waiting to be rested and fed. On the days with the sheikh, he barely noticed his body.

"Or the twenty-two people who died at the Palm Court compound, or at the Dorrat al-Jadawel. The newspapers and the television stations love these events, but why do they not give the same attention to the Muslim children dying on the streets of Basra, or in the Gaza Strip? Why do they not call the soldiers of the occupation murderers, as they do the jihadis who are working to reclaim Muslim lands for the believers? And they call them terrorists, the men who defend the bilad al haramayn, the Land of the Two Holy Mosques. But what greater terror than having this holy land ruled by al-firqa al-dhalla, those who have strayed from the path?"

Ibrahim asked so many questions that Faisal could not answer. The sweat moved down his face and settled around the top of his thobe's collar, soaking it to transparency. Sandals sussed against the linoleum floor. The smell of body odor moved through the room as the men shifted in their chairs.

"And remember that the Prophet Muhammad, peace be upon Him, said to eliminate unbelievers from the Arabian Peninsula, so these 'criminals' are merely following the Prophet's directive. Why do the al-Saud encourage jihad outside of our borders, in Afghanistan, even in Iraq, but here at home, they discourage us from fighting by the Word? Again, they are afraid. They fear the strength of the truly pious, because they themselves are corrupted. It is as the martyr Sheikh Issa al-Oshan said: that we must first fight the forces of evil here in our own country before we can dream of combating it elsewhere. When will it end? I ask you, King, you of the al-Sulul, the hypocrites, when will it end? We are slaves to American interests. We send our young men there, and they return with American whores for brides. In this way, they break our bloodlines and compromise our faith. They return, ready to sell their countrymen on a dream of progress created in Washington, DC, among the imperialists, in New York among the homosexuals, in Hollywood among the Jews. I say: La!"

Though he stared straight ahead at the sheikh, Faisal felt as if every man in the room was looking at him, pitying him his interloper of a mother. He stood up too quickly, knocking the tea service over. It clattered to the floor, and the others turned to look. The sugar cubes disintegrated in the pool of tea. He rushed to the door, up the stairs, hurrying past the maid and Hassan's mother to the courtyard gate. Outside, the three cats were still there, resting against the concrete blocks of the wall. The street was empty and dark, so he sank against the wall until he was sitting in the dust. He crossed his arms over his knees, then rested his head on top of them. The sheikh's words were like a hand across his face: *American whores.* In the taunts of his classmates, he could imagine jealousy of his family's power, but Ibrahim's contempt for families like his was fueled solely by the belief in their moral degradation.

Sheikh Ibrahim knew his family situation—everyone in Al Dawoun did—so the comment was not made coincidentally. Was he angry at Faisal for some reason? He wished that Rosalie had been part of the bride exodus of the eighties, when the novelty had started wearing thin for the Americans who had married Saudi men in the seventies—when they realized that the Ghassans or Muhammads they'd met and loved in Phoenix or Los Angeles were not the same men at home in Riyadh. So the American women packed their bags and fled their ill-conceived lives. They left their children behind because it was the law, and even the FBI couldn't help them get them back. Their departure had been all over the papers. Rosalie kept the clippings; he'd found them one day while going through the hall closet in search of corkboard for a school project. He was certain the fault lay with America's relentless openness, its insistence that all people could commingle and intermarry and have children of all colors. In America, it seemed that there was no sense of tribe, no respect for blood and tradition. People ran around falling in love with all types of people and ruining lives in the process. But no one ever seemed to consider the consequences that the children, the products of these marriages, faced.

From behind the wall, Faisal heard the front door slide open against the tile and the sound of women's voices. He tried to rub the tears from his face but they were already dry. He hoped they hadn't left tracks against his cheeks. Scrambling to stand, he felt the rough concrete of the wall rubbing hard against his skin, pressing through the thin material of his thobe. The courtyard gate opened and there was Umm Hassan and her daughter Nura, followed by the cook, who was also their driver. Nura was still in the process of putting down her niqab, and he felt guilty for catching her unaware. Umm Hassan gave him a vexed look and mumbled something to Nura, who stood there holding the veil in front of her face, waiting for him to go away. Behind them, the new group member slipped out the gate, nodded to them, and hurried down the street.

"Ana assif," Faisal apologized.

He turned and walked quickly toward Majid's car. He didn't want to see any of the other group members. All of the little things he had done to secure their respect over the last year seemed meaningless now. He moved to the passenger side and leaned against the car. A breeze moved the leaves of the banyan tree that grew out over the sidewalk. The moving leaves made a *wish* sound that reminded him of the summer his family stayed outside of Damascus with Dan and his wife, who had rented a large house there. They'd gone to visit the Americans and had stayed for a week, the adults drinking wine on the roof of the house while Faisal built towns from the rich mud beneath the *wish-wishing* grape arbor. Mariam was three years old. Rosalie had developed a habit of holding his face between her hands and giving him a kiss on the nose each morning. *Wish-wish.* Back then, Faisal had loved his mother so much, he had nightmares about her dying.

"That was quite an exit you made."

He turned to see Majid, teeth glinting like a half moon set in the dark sky of his face. He was trying to think of something to say in response when they heard a scream. Without a word, Majid turned and ran back toward the corner. In the darkness, his head and hands and feet were lost, his movement marked only by the whiteness of his thobe. Faisal glanced the other way down the street and then followed his friend toward the corner. He heard Nura and her mother shouting before a flurry of male voices drowned them out. Then, breaking glass, a car alarm, slamming car doors, and engines screeching to life. Now he could definitely hear Umm Hassan shouting La! La! Hassan! As he got closer to the corner, he saw Majid waving him back.

"Go! Get in the car," Majid hissed.

Faisal ran, careful to keep his sandals from flapping against the pavement. He opened the passenger door and fell into the seat, and with a spin of the wheels, they were off, going the wrong way down a one-way street, away from Hassan's house.

"Al-Mabahith," Majid said. "The secret police. I'm pretty sure. They loaded them all into a Suburban and drove away. One of the policemen smashed the windshield when Hassan tried to get in his family's car."

"Was Ibrahim still in the house when you left?"

"Yes. He was answering questions."

Faisal covered his face with his hands and spoke into his palms, his breath hot against his face.

"So they have him. He's going to jail, then?"

"It's impossible to know. The Interior Ministry doesn't exactly broadcast these arrests. They could keep him for months before anyone verifies that he's in custody."

"Do you think someone tipped them off?"

"Maybe Hassan's maid or driver, if they were unhappy. It could have been someone in the group."

"They'll torture him," Faisal said, his voice wavering. "Just like they did with your uncle. We should follow their truck and see where they take him."

"Are you crazy? We won't be able to help Ibrahim if we get arrested too. Tonight, we'll go home. We don't want to arouse suspicion from our families or anyone else. But tomorrow. Tomorrow we will make a plan."

"Should I call the National Society for Human Rights? Or the Arab Human Rights Group? They are always trying to monitor these arrests. You know, keep the pressure on the authorities."

"Where do you think you are? Switzerland? You think the royal family listens to anyone telling them when and how they should arrest people? No, you shouldn't call them. We don't need them interfering with our problems."

Majid was driving fast toward the Diamond Mile. The big boulevards had emptied out, the urgency of streaming headlights gone. Al Dawoun was stern in the darkness, resigned to the quiet of the dead hours before dawn. Faisal's heart was still somewhere up between his ears, thumping loudly. He tapped his fingers against the car door, wondering what would become of Ibrahim. Would they beat the soles of his feet until they bled? Would they pull out his fingernails or shave his head? Would they keep him in jail for months, years even, without telling anyone that he was in custody? Faisal was afraid, but he would never show this fear to Majid. It would be like laying your neck down before a tiger. Faisal sighed, long and shallow so that it made no sound but clouded the window where he pressed his cheek. He wished he could tell Abdullah, since he would probably know who to talk to about Ibrahim's situation. He wished for the long-ago time before his parents had become unknown quantities. For that moment when he'd stepped off the Swiss Air flight and felt his father's whiskers against his face, when Faisal had thought he knew how his life would be.

As they pulled into the long driveway of his house, he caught a glimpse of another car tucked into the shadows growing across the concrete from the base of the house. The moon had risen, exposing a slice of silver hood. Majid brought his car to a stop. Faisal knew who owned the car. It was Dan Coleman's. After spending dozens of slow Al Dawoun nights tailing Dan as he made his sad rounds around the city (Safeway, the barber shop, the camera repair shop, and saddest of all, the Gulf Hotel, where he sat alone in the lobby reading what appeared to be, from Faisal's lookout behind the valet station, outdated guidebooks to world capitals), Faisal intimately knew every scratch on the car's body. Bumper: a thin one, long and white as a bone. Windshield: a crack like fractured ice. Passenger door: teacup dent. The car's body was always white with dust, and B-Corporation was stenciled in green on the driver's door.

"We should probably try to stick close to home for the next few days," Majid said. "They might be looking for others."

"Call me if you find out anything about Sheikh Ibrahim. Masalama."

"Wallahi. May God protect him. Good night, brother."

Faisal slammed the car door. Surely Dan knew that his father was at Isra's house.

Behind him, he heard Majid roll down the car window, bang twice on his car door. "Hey," he said. "Whose car is that?"

"No one. Probably A'm Nadia's."

"Since when does a Baylani drive a Hyundai?"

"Go home, ya Majid. Don't let your imagination get away from you."

To Faisal's relief, Majid backed slowly out of the driveway, waved, then turned east toward his neighborhood.

As he opened the front door, he heard the low movement of voices, and then he saw two figures come out from behind the colonnade that separated the foyer from the dining room. There was his mother, comfortable enough in the presence of a man who was not his father that she could stand around chitchatting with him without even putting on her headscarf. Faisal dug his nails into his palms. He switched on the foyer light. Dan Coleman stared back at him, his mouth pursed, his large body eating up the space between Faisal and his mother. Dan scratched the bone of his nose, as if he needed a minute to think about why Faisal might be standing there in his own house at that particular moment.

"It's after ten o'clock," Rosalie said. "Where have you been?"

Her voice was anxious in a way he'd expect from mothers, but it sounded overwrought coming from her. Over the last week, as things had gotten worse between her and Abdullah, she had been wholly preoccupied with his father's whereabouts, not Faisal's. Before he drove up, she probably hadn't even noticed that he'd been gone. Something was wrong in the way she was standing, shifting nervously from one foot to the other. She was holding a blue file folder.

"Out. I've been out."

"I just came by to give some papers to Abdullah," Dan said. "I thought he'd be home."

"Well, when you found out that he wasn't, you should have left."

"I was just about to."

"Sure. Ma'alesh."

Faisal put his chin at an appropriately indifferent angle, though in truth he was disturbed. Whatever had happened, Faisal didn't like this secret meeting with Dan. What did his mother expect him to think?

"Faisal, it's OK. Look at me. Dan just drove up a few minutes ago. He brought this with him, for your father." She brandished the file folder.

Faisal turned toward her. She had a sphinx face. Expressions moved across it like cloud shadows over the dunes. He looked at Dan, whose permanently sunburned skin made him look agitated. He had tiny veins around his eyes that seemed about to burst. Where was Abdullah when he was needed? The constant monitoring of his family's actions had tired Faisal out. If he were Majid, he would assume a calculating look, let them know who was in control. He would have some sharp, witty remark that would shame both of them in a way that still left them somewhat grateful. But he was not Majid. No matter how hard he tried. He walked past them into the kitchen where the air was cool and smelled faintly of sandalwood.

The voices did not resume their hum, and a minute later, a car engine tripped on. Faisal listened as it grew fainter. He waited to hear his mother walk upstairs to her bedroom. When he heard her door shut, he went to the garage. From the recreation shelves he grabbed his swimsuit. For a moment, he thought about the driving ban that his father had issued, but then put it out of his mind. In a family that seemed to be breaking every rule, a quick drive across town almost deserved a medal, it seemed so valiantly harmless. And besides, who was there to remark on his absence? He ducked into the cool, dark interior of the car, waited for the garage door to lift, then coasted down the driveway and drove straight for Majid's.

From the curb outside Majid's house, Faisal called him.

"I'm outside. Get your swimsuit and get out here."

After a few minutes, Majid appeared outside the gate, a baffled look on his face. He got in the car.

"Ibrahim gets arrested and you want to swim laps?" Majid asked.

"This day," Faisal said. He paused, took a deep breath. "I need some relief. We're going to Prairie Vista."

"What's wrong with your pool?"

"I can't stand to be in that house for another second."

Faisal was quiet. He put the car in drive and they rumbled away over the potholed road.

"You should have let me come in the house with you," Majid said. "It was Coleman, wasn't it?"

Faisal felt like a small, ragged flag snapping in the middle of nowhere, a flag whose colors were gone, its armies deserted.

"Was it or wasn't it Coleman?" Majid said. "Come on, why are you protecting them?"

Faisal closed his hands tighter around the steering wheel. Finally, he said, "It was him, all right? It was Dan Coleman. I got angry. I sent my mother to her room and told her I was in charge when Baba wasn't around. She looked like a little puppy, all ashamed." He was breathing hard, like he had just finished the last leg of a swim relay. "I took care of it."

Majid sat in silence. After a moment, he asked, "Were they doing anything?" He sounded excited, like he wanted the answer to be yes. Faisal weighed what to say. They *could* have been doing something. At this point, he wasn't sure what his mother was capable of.

"They *could* have been. Before I got there," he said. "That's why I got so mad. That's why I took care of things."

He felt good about this answer. Majid seemed to accept it with a disgusted huff, like it was exactly what he'd expected from Rosalie and Dan. Really, Faisal just wanted to swim and forget about the whole thing.

At Prairie Vista, he pulled past the guard booth, pointing to the B-Corp decal as the guard looked on. He parked in the visitors' section. Inside the car, he pulled his suit on underneath his thobe. Majid did the same, his knees banging against the dashboard. The pool was empty, its surface glassy save the gentle movements of a few frangipani leaves floating across. It promised weightlessness and cool forgetfulness. They pulled off their thobes and eased down the steps. Faisal felt the rush of the water against his legs and stomach, relishing the slow immersion as his swim shorts ballooned around his thighs. The filter gurgled. The night was pure stillness. Faisal ducked his head underwater and sank to the bottom, until he was sitting cross-legged listening to the muffled sounds of Majid's slow movements through the water beside him. When he could hold his breath no longer, he surfaced. He let his feet rise in front of him until his toes poked through. He floated on his back, his ears half submerged. He looked straight up into the doming darkness. It was too dusty for stars, but he could see the sky's black, and that it did not end. Standing, he brushed his wet hair out of his face and looked at his friend.

"Thank God for swimming pools," he said.

"Don't worry, brother," Majid said. "I have an idea."

"About what?"

"Coleman. Ibrahim."

"I told you, I handled it."

"You did well. But I think we can use what happened to get some good results."

"OK." Faisal waited, nervous about what his friend might suggest. With the sheikh in prison, his mother with that idiot American, and his father probably getting drunk somewhere, Faisal felt as if his whole world were sliding into the foaming sea.

"Trust in God," Majid said. "Which apartment is Coleman's?"

Faisal drew his hand out of the water and pointed: 118.

"Good. Very good. I think he'll be able to do us a favor. Help us save Ibrahim. Considering what you saw tonight, it won't be difficult to convince him to help us with our plan."

Faisal tilted his head and shook it hard until the water came out of his ears.

"Go on," he said.

His mother could be a fool if she chose to be. What really mattered at that moment was the sheikh.

LATER THAT NIGHT, back in his room, Faisal removed his thobe and ghutra and lay down on the bed. He said a prayer for Sheikh

Ibrahim. He said a prayer for his father. He said a prayer for his mother and one for Dan Coleman, that they might not be as foolish as they seemed. He prayed for Majid. He prayed for Mariam. After nearly a week of sleeplessness, he prayed for sleep. Faisal closed his eyes and saw all the electric lines of his life crisscrossing like neon in the darkness. He slept.

EIGHT

QUIETLY, ABDULLAH OPENED the French doors leading out to the balcony and stepped outside. He didn't want to wake Isra, who was sprawled inelegantly across their bed. On the balcony, the young morning was soft against his face. Later, the humidity would be oppressive—entire watery sheets of the Gulf made airborne. From where he stood, Abdullah could see the upper stories of the big house down the block. Was Rosalie awake and shuffling around the kitchen? Were the diamond earrings blinking beneath her hair? Occasionally, she prepared American breakfasts for the children—pancakes and beef sausages and fried potatoes. She joked that they needed a big farmer's breakfast to make it through their days in the Saudi school system. Out of habit, he would shush her. What? She would ask. Who's listening? *The maids. The drivers*, he would say.

Despite her years in the Kingdom, she still had that American naiveté, that belief that governments existed to serve the people. The al-Saud served themselves first, and then their people, and there was no room for criticism, no matter how hushed or private it seemed. After seeing his father lose contracts by failing to attend the prince's kabsa, Abdullah made sure to keep his thoughts to himself. On his watch, the Baylanis had hurdled the Sa'ads, the

Gosaibis, the Zamils, and others to gain a position so close to the royals that Abdullah could count their bright gold fillings. B-Corp had gotten the Pepsi contract, and Abdullah had laughed to himself as he left the meeting, triumphant, for what better way to be rich in the desert? He would never do anything to jeopardize his position. He would never take the royal names in vain. The prince had long wanted an excuse to hobble B-Corp, to seize some of its holdings and claim them for the Family. It was the largest company in the Eastern Province, and the fourth largest in the Kingdom, and the al-Saud could not stand that an unrelated merchant family had become so powerful.

After the disastrous events at Gold City, Abdullah had decided to stay at Isra's house for a few days. He needed to be well rested before his meeting with Prince Abdul Aziz, and he could not imagine finding much peace with Rosalie. She moved now like a coiled spring, and because he didn't want to face that kind of hurt and fury in another person, particularly not in Rose, he felt avoidance to be the best tactic.

The day's meeting with the prince would be casual, tea and dates, perhaps a card game or backgammon. There would be some talk of business, and millions of dollars would hang in the balance, so that with each roll of the dice, with each joke that passed between them, Abdullah would be advancing B-Corp's agenda. Frequently, he found himself wishing that Abdul Latif could be there to see how the company had flourished. His father would hardly recognize Al Dawoun, with its carefully tended Corniche and restaurants glittering from man-made islands. In a lifetime, Saudi Arabia had undergone centuries of change, and the Baylanis had played a significant role in that modernization. Abdullah pressed his tongue against the roof of his mouth and closed his eyes. The thought brought a pride so fierce that he had to pause and catch his breath. Yes, sometimes the Kingdom's feet were too big for its shoes, or the other way around, but it was to be expected in any teenaged nation.

Abdullah had already decided that he would invite Dan to join him at the meeting. Not as apology, necessarily. He found apologies useless, self-indulgent—a scramble to rewrite the past when all that really mattered was the future. They'd go to the palace, laugh about its extravagance, and then move forward. He wasn't actually threatened by Dan. Inviting him to the palace would be a distraction, but it would also serve as a reminder: I am Abdullah al-Baylani, the friend of kings, and you are Dan Coleman.

Of course, the invitation would also serve Abdullah in other ways. He needed Dan there to mitigate the prince's anger when Abdullah began his negotiations for a smaller royal cut of the Pepsi profits. With a third party looking on, the prince wouldn't dare fly into one of his storied black rages, fits that had once left a prominent businessman with nothing but a single segmented tangerine to show for his decades of striving. The man, formerly a host to dignitaries from around the world, had gone back to his village in the Najd and not been heard from in years. Abdullah was mildly afraid of Abdul Aziz. After all, the man's forefathers had managed to subdue an entire fractious peninsula. This taste for domination had not grown dormant in their grandson. Beneath Abu Turki's substantial flesh beat the heart of a warrior, except now he fought for money rather than land.

Behind Abdullah, the doors opened with a whisper, and he turned to see Isra, her lips still puffy from sleep.

"Isra," he said. He took his wife's face between his hands and kissed her eyelids.

"Sabah al-khayr. What a beautiful morning."

She walked to the balcony railing, then leaned over and looked first to the left, then the right, assessing the day.

"Mornings are my favorite time," Abdullah said. "Everything is new."

"Yes, darling. You can start fresh each morning. Now, if you please, won't you tell me what you were so angry about yesterday?"

"No, nothing of importance. Not worth bringing into your peaceful house. Would you please bring me some coffee and the newspaper?"

"Yes, my heart. Perhaps later you'll feel like sharing what is bothering you."

"Perhaps."

He knew that he wouldn't feel like it, though. To him, Isra's house was a place of forgetting, where he could let go of his troubles like so many colored balloons disappearing into the sky. Though two years had passed, theirs still felt like a new love, and Rosalie's discovery of Isra had only reinforced that feeling. They'd been caught like two youngsters courting in the shadows. For wasn't love most powerful when it was new and governed by its own wildness? If Rosalie had not been so nosy, she could have gone several more years safe from the knowledge of Isra. They could have remained neighbors who nodded politely at each other as their BMWs passed along the Diamond Mile.

A few minutes later Isra returned, carrying a small brass tray of tiny porcelain cups. After setting it down on the Kuwaiti chest next to the couch, she poured a glass and handed it to him. It steamed in his hands and he inhaled the bitter smell of the soil-black coffee. They did not keep servants at Isra's home because he worried about their chattering. Also, he did not want to share her. There was purity and simplicity to their interactions. Their love a lagoon, everything was stillness, blue with peace. He thanked her for the coffee and she smiled, resting her hand on his shoulder.

"Did you see the news?" she asked. "Hanieh announced that Hamas is boycotting the elections."

"That surprises you?"

"No, but it worries me. I'm worried about my family, with things openly hostile now."

"If anything happens, we'll bring your parents here."

"Abdi, please. They've stayed through everything else. They

aren't going to be pushed out by their own people. And you know my mother could hardly survive here."

"Wearing the abaya is more tolerable than living in constant fear of war."

"I suppose. But it's been so quiet in Hebron lately. Umma thought they might even reopen the Old Souq."

"Habibti, I'm sorry, but I really can't think about these things right now. I've got to prepare for the meeting with Prince Abdul Aziz."

"Fine, but we will continue talking about this later. You know people who can help. And we've only got six months to make this world livable for Kareem." She laughed and rubbed her stomach.

"You know I hate that name."

"Now you're paying attention. How about Mahmoud?"

"Too dour."

"Laith."

"Hmm. How about Noor?"

"Ah, so you're changing your bet?" She gave him a sly smile. "It's a girl now?"

"Either way, I'm a happy man."

"You'd better be." She smiled, kissed his cheek. "I'll go. You need time to think of jokes that will go over the old sultan's head."

"You know me so well."

"I have to. It's my job."

She leaned in, wrapped a few of his curls around her finger and tugged gently. He could smell her skin, the lingering morning smell of her, before she showered. Her stomach bulged ever so slightly. For now, it was their secret. As she turned to leave him, her bathrobe caught the breeze. He watched her departing ankles, thin as a child's, and wondered if Isra had ever gotten enough to eat as a girl in the West Bank. It had been part of her appeal, that refugee's thinness. He'd wanted to take her back to the Kingdom to feed her fatty meat and saffron rice and fried onions and thick stews until she became plump and radiant. No matter that she'd lived for years in Paris working for the United Nations, where she'd eaten foie gras and roasted duck with prime ministers, aristocrats, starched bureaucrats; her face had retained its look of deprivation, cheeks hollow beneath the bone, full lips rising dramatically from her gaunt face. And that was the difference, really. Isra held in her heart the essence of what it meant to be an Arab after 1948: suffering. How could he explain to Rosalie his need to be close to that?

After Abdullah finished his coffee, he rose out of his chair and stretched, reaching his uneven arms up until he could feel every bit of his frame, the muscles in his calves and thighs shuddering with the movement. With each passing day, it seemed that his body took a few minutes longer to transition out of sleep. The day had begun its plunder, the sun irradiating the neighborhood, turning the large windows of the Diamond Mile into white fire. In this climate, he would go to the prince, to the man whose family had drawn swords to possess the peninsula before they even knew about the fortune lying beneath the sand. It was not a bad destiny, although many argued that the soul of Arabia was destroyed when the first oil pump was put down. Abdullah had read the literature, but what was there to do? He was born in a place, and that place had rules, and by chance or God's grace, his father had known what to do and when to do it. Did it take soul-decimating labor and a betrayal of the land, and perhaps even the spirit of the holy peninsula to do it? Perhaps. But such questions were not for him to answer. He'd leave it for the poets and the muftis to decide.

With a final glance toward the roof of the big house, Abdullah went inside.

AT THE OFFICE, he pulled into his parking spot and glanced around for Dan's car. It was parked in a corner, unobtrusively, its color unidentifiable beneath a coating of dust. Dan always came early and stayed late, working Thursdays and Fridays when the office was silent save the hum of the copy machine.

Inside the automatic doors, a cool wall of climate-controlled air enveloped Abdullah. He greeted the security guard and breathed in the smells of the office—the bleach of the just-cleaned carpet, the cardamom coffee, the singed smell of the paper coming off of the copy machine. Whenever he walked into the building, he felt it in his marrow. Success. This busy office and five others scattered around the Kingdom, his brothers and his men, running hospitals, developing cities, tending rigs, distributing appliances, delivering crates and crates of icy Pepsi to his relentlessly thirsty countrymen. And all under the Baylani name, the logo on buildings in bright red neon, standing out against dust storms, tarred rain, darkness.

Abdullah took the elevator to the fifth floor and walked toward Dan's office. Expats had very limited access to the palace, and he knew Dan would be curious to see whether the rumors he had heard were true. Though the royal compound's streets weren't paved with Italian marble, there were many other gilded lilies to amuse his friend: cashmere-covered sofas, Swarovski crystal chandeliers whose light exploded off of wall-length mirrors, the sitting room as big as a football pitch, the enormous mural of the prince on camelback, his rolls of fat reduced to a rich man's paunch by some forgiving artist.

Hunched in front of his computer, Dan sat with his back to the door.

"Ya Daniel."

He swiveled in his office chair and, seeing Abdullah, spun back around to face the computer.

"Want to go have coffee with the four hundred and sixty-fourth richest man in the world?"

"Bugger off, Sheikh."

"Oh, come on. You're not still angry about Gold City, are you?"

"No, why should I be? It's Rosalie who should be pissed."

"Well, do you or don't you want to go? Last chance. I'll even drive."

"You really are an asshole. You know that, right?" Dan paused, turned back around. "But I wouldn't miss a chance to embarrass you in front of your boss."

"Good. We leave at two o'clock. And you might want to change your shirt." He gestured at Dan's faded green golf tee.

"I'll see what I can do."

A FEW HOURS later, they were in Abdullah's BMW on their way to the palace. Sand had collected in the road's potholes, and the car's impact sent up little coughs of dust. In the dirty sky, the sun was as bright as a pomegranate. In defending Rosalie from Dan's flirtations, Abdullah had felt closer to his wife than he had in months, and through that renewed desire, he had realized that he did still love her. It was hard to recognize it sometimes, because his love for Isra took such a different shape. It was newer, he felt it in his blood. But with Rosalie, it was in his bones, lodged deep. He had felt the same possessiveness years ago when he had asked her to marry him. He had spent the afternoon stalking her around campus, watching her drop men dead by the mere acts of walking, of putting up her hair. After she said yes, they'd fucked in an angry way, fueled by his desire as well as that of the hundreds of men who saw Rosalie in the streets and desired her too. But he'd made the mistake of removing her to a place where she was no longer subject to those starved looks; where it was, in fact, his duty to protect her from them. For a moment in Bahrain, Dan had returned that feeling to him—that curiously pleasant feeling of possessing something that someone else wanted. It had made him feel young again.

"So do I kiss his signet ring?" Dan said. "Do a little curtsy? Are we talking medieval, or Victorian here?" Dan said.

"Try to be serious for just a second, OK? I know this is a first, but I actually need your help today."

"Well, isn't this a day for the ages. Guess you should have thought about that before your tantrum yesterday."

"If you had a wife like mine, you'd guard her too."

"Hmm. That's what you've been doing, then? Guarding her?"

"Listen: Abdul Aziz is notoriously temperamental, particularly when it comes to negotiating contracts. So I don't want you disappearing on some tour of the grounds while we talk business. I want you standing right next to me as we negotiate. If he tries to slip into Arabic, just gently remind him that you don't speak it. His English is not the best, certainly not as good as most of his brothers', which means he won't be able to be as aggressive as he usually is."

"How aggressive are we talking, here?"

"Whole empires reduced to a single citrus fruit."

"OK, I'll do my best. But you owe me, Baylani. Big-time."

Abdullah drove fast, plowing across intersections, treating stoplights as gentle reminders. In the empty lots that lined the road, dust made tiny tornados that unraveled and settled over the broken glass and scattered trash. No matter how rapidly Al Dawoun developed, no matter how many construction projects sprouted up, the city seemed unable to rid itself of abandoned lots and feral cats. In the poorer areas, children set up makeshift football nets between discarded oil barrels. It was like North Africa or Ethiopia, places where children were forced to use the decay around them. When Abdullah had visited Addis Ababa, he'd been overwhelmed by the flies, the way people didn't bother to brush them from their faces. It seemed forfeiture to despair. How did a people, an entire nation, decide to stop struggling for decency? In Saudi Arabia, they ran paved roads over the Rub' al-Khali and extended the shoreline hundreds of meters into the Gulf. They irrigated. They built pipelines that got so hot in the sun that you could roast a lamb over them. It was an endless war, but what choice did they have? The desert was always there, ready to reduce them to their former existence. So it still surprised him when he stumbled across these small victories of the third world over progress—the oil-barrel goalposts, or the barefoot children. He made a mental note to donate nylon nets to the various community organizations around Al Dawoun.

"I heard that Abdul Aziz's son gets an entire floor of Caesar's Palace when he goes to Vegas," Dan said. "I heard he's lost several million dollars gambling."

"Whatever you hear, it's probably true. There is no such thing as overstatement with the son. He's the al-Saud's blackest of the black sheep."

"I heard Aziz is the worst in terms of bakshish. He's made over a billion dollars off of British contracts."

"I'm not denying it. I won't deny or confirm."

"I heard his latest girlfriend is Bulgarian and has a snatch so sweet he's thinking of overthrowing his brother just to make her queen."

"At least that would give him something interesting to talk about."

"I thought you and the prince were friends," Dan said.

"It's strictly business now. When I married Isra, he gave up on me. Barely gave me his blessing. But I'm telling you, I've never felt something to be so right."

Dan gave him a skeptical look.

"I thought that getting royal permission to marry a non-Saudi was only a formality."

"Oh no. It's very much real. And it's a pain in my ass."

With the prince, Abdullah had to tread carefully. When he and Abdul Latif had gone to secure permission for his marriage to Rosalie, they had joked good-naturedly: "What? Are Saudi women not good enough for you?" "I'm sure they're good enough, but I wouldn't know since I can't see them or talk to them!" His father had been mildly horrified, but he'd wanted to continue, to say that beneath their abayas, perhaps Saudi women had queenly shoulders and long thighs that flexed and softened beneath cut-off shorts as they walked, but as it was, they were all billowing black tents to him. Then, when he had decided to follow up his marriage to an American by marrying a Palestinian, his relationship with the palace grew strained. In the 1970s, Westernization justified everything, and Saudi men were marrying Americans in droves. But with Isra, the prince's face had turned purple. There was no joking, just an impatient dismissal, as if Abdullah were no longer worth the prince's time. But Abdullah had insisted on the marriage—anything less would have been an insult to Isra *and* Rosalie.

"Hey, Abdi. About yesterday . . ."

"Let's just forget all about it. OK? I'm sorry it ever happened."

"Let's not put Rosalie in that position again."

"You let me worry about my wife. Everything's going to be just fine."

They pulled abreast of the palace. On the right side of the intersection, the bright yellow "M" of McDonald's stood out against the dusty sky, and on the left, the palace lay unromantically sprawled over four city blocks. Palatial in size but not beautiful, the prince's residence resembled an Eastern Bloc fortress, thick-walled, low-lying, the gray of winter mornings in Kiev. Abdullah wondered if it had been made so ugly on purpose; if the royals had thought that, as long as it resembled subsidized urban American housing, the people might not notice that it was large enough to be seen from space.

"She's a real beaut," Dan said. "Lloyd Wright's finest."

Abdullah chuckled. Visiting businessmen were always disappointed when he drove them past the palace. They seemed to want royalty to err on the side of decadence, especially the Americans, who arrived with the most outlandish stories about the Kingdom in general and the al-Saud in particular. "It looks just like the engineering quad at Cornell," one had said with disdain. Did they expect turrets, rococo doming? *This isn't the Loire*, he wanted to say. *Or even Riyadh. A hundred years ago, we were all in tents!* The multitude of armed guards were the most impressive part of the façade. They were positioned in pairs every fifty meters, perched on and around the concrete barriers meant to protect against car bombs.

When Abdullah was giving his tours, the best part came when he warned his passengers against making any quick movements or staring too hard. "They've got their fingers on the trigger. Shoot first, if you know what I mean." They always knew what he meant, or pretended to, and the excitement of being so close to death seemed to make up for the lack of splendor. Even the biggest braggarts grew quiet and looked straight ahead, and it made Abdullah feel good to be able to instill in them a proper sense of awe for the Kingdom and what was at stake in a place that owned a quarter of the world's oil. Lives were at stake. Not the businessmen's, per se. In fact, he couldn't exactly say whose lives were in jeopardy, but he knew power when he saw it. In those moments, he experienced a shiver himself, for the stakes were not always apparent at the office, or at home quarreling with Rosalie or making love to Isra. But guns had a way of making it very clear that something was to be gained or lost.

They pulled up to the security gate. Abdullah rolled down the window and told the guard—an ugly, spindly boy—their business. With his hand resting casually on the thick neck of an automatic weapon, he spoke with an entitlement usually reserved for the rich, the beautiful, or the very old. With a nod of the chin that Abdullah would have taken as impudence from anyone else, the guard urged them forward through the opening metal gates. Slowly, he pulled the car forward.

"Look at this." Abdullah gestured to royal gardens beyond the car windows. He pulled to a stop and left the engine running.

Dan rolled down his window to get a closer look. "Ma would've gotten a kick out of this. She always tried to get exotic plants for the nursery. A bonsai tree was the closest she ever got. Bought it from a Japanese man in Dallas. He told her it was seventy years old, but when it arrived it wasn't much taller than her potted violets." Dan's mother, a reed-thin part-Comanche woman, had made countless suppers for Abdullah in college, and still, just at the mention of her, he smelled her peach pies, the clean laundry scent of the Coleman homestead outside of Marfa.

Palms lined the red sand walkways, and giant banyan trees with smooth trunks shaded the stone benches scattered throughout the garden. In the air, the smell of juniper hung like perfume. Smaller trees, tamarinds and ficuses and sago palms and acacias, formed a dense arbor along the nearest wall. Inside the perimeter pathway, a wide lawn glistened, the grass so fine that it appeared bladeless. Sprinklers counted out the slow seconds and silver cylinders of water from the central fountain caught the sun before splitting the surface of a small pond. Birds small as his thumb darted in and out of the vegetation, breaking flight to call out in urgent chirrups. The garden went on and on for miles. The Prince pumped in thousands of gallons of water per week to irrigate the grounds.

"Look at this. How do they get these rock roses to survive here?" Dan said, calling him over to where he was squatting next to a cluster of pale pink flowers. "Incredible. Just stick them in the ground and watch them go. Nine times out of ten, they'll make it. I remember getting off the train in Avignon to lie on a boulder that was surrounded by these things."

"Fascinating. Let's not keep the prince waiting."

AT THE DOOR, they were greeted by the prince's personal secretary, a young Saudi man whose goatee gleamed, framing perfectly white, straight teeth. Yes, Abdullah thought. One need only remark the changes in the average Saudi's dental hygiene to know that times were good and getting better. The secretary, probably a cousin or nephew, led them down a hallway whose gleaming whiteness always made him feel as if he were walking inside the smooth basin of a shell. Along the ceiling, crystal chandeliers sparkled and winked, marking their pathway to the point where he could see the hallway give way to the prince's majlis, the scarlet carpet spreading out from the marble like blood.

"Yep, this is about right," Dan said.

They arrived at the end of the hallway and entered the majlis. Abdul Aziz was seated at the far side of the room, large and magisterial in his black winter thobe and mishlah. They embraced like brothers, but Abdullah knew better.

"Abu Turki. It has been too long. Since the Kabiri wedding?"

He spoke in English so that Dan could understand, and also because he enjoyed watching Abdul Aziz stab at the words like a poorly trained spear fisherman. He remembered a time when he, too, lacked fluency, the English words as elusive as darting fish, but he had realized that there was power in the language so he had strained his eyes in darkened library cubicles and made a fool of himself at department beer socials in order to master it. Abdul Aziz never had the same hunger, never needed to. His power was his name, so no matter how many times he approximated his thoughts in elementary sentences that he'd turned to pulp with his clumsy tongue, people listened attentively. The man whose family could send the global markets into a tailspin by whispering about raising the price per barrel need not concern himself with the dull work of infinitives.

"Ya Abdullah, keif al-hal? That's right. Kabiri's eldest. Who is your friend? Ahlan wa sahlan, sidiqqi."

The room was built to hold hundreds of people, and the prince spoke loudly, as if he were addressing an entire majlis of men.

"Daniel Coleman, my oldest American friend. I hope you don't mind, but I thought he needed to see how much better the Saudis do it. This makes the White House look quaint, doesn't it, ya Dan?"

"Indeed. I bet Bush is on his best behavior when he comes to visit," Dan said.

"Yes, I have had the president here. He brought me a cowboy hat. My littlest grandson loved it."

The Prince laughed. If they'd caught him in a sour mood, Dan might have had to wait in the courtyard. But luckily the prince's camel had won the race or his girlfriend was putting on his favorite panties or the cook had made a particularly good seleek. He was downright jovial.

"Mr. Coleman, do you play backgammon? I hope you're better than your friend."

"I beat him every time, hands down," Dan said.

The prince smiled. "We'll play a game in a little while. So, Mr. Coleman, how long have you lived in the Kingdom?"

"Oh, on and off for about twenty-five years now. Mostly on."

"So you've seen the change, then. We've had great change in that time."

"Yes. Yes, absolutely. The other day in the supermarket, I counted five different types of lettuce. I remember back in the early days, the only green thing you could get were raw dates."

The prince laughed. "Perhaps Mr. Coleman would like to go on a tour of the palace with Ismail?"

"Oh, no, I think Dan would like to stay here with us," Abdullah said. "You see, he has a special interest in international business."

"But I'm sure your friend won't mind if we speak in Arabic? There's a private matter I'd like to discuss with you, Abu Faisal."

No doubt he was referring to the percentage negotiations. Abdullah nodded almost imperceptibly at Dan.

"Forgive me, Abu Turki," Dan interrupted. "But if you wouldn't mind, could you conduct the meeting in English? I don't want to miss anything."

The prince pursed his lips. "Fine. You're sure you don't mind?" he asked Abdullah. "As I said, I have a private matter I'd like to discuss."

"Oh no, I don't mind at all. As I said, Dan is like my family."

"As you wish. How often do you get to the mosque these days, Abu Faisal?"

"I try to go five times a day, alhamdulillah. But business is good. It's harder and harder."

"And your son. I hear he goes regularly."

"Yes, Faisal is a good boy."

"Does he make you proud?"

Abdullah glanced at Dan, who was accepting a cup of tea from the servant.

"You don't answer," the prince said. "I hope the boy doesn't bring you shame."

"As I said, he is a good boy. He is very faithful."

Abdul Aziz lowered his voice and began to speak in Arabic. "Have you heard him speak about a man named Ibrahim?"

Under the prince's scrutinizing gaze, Abdullah was embarrassed to reveal the thinness of his knowledge.

"No. No I haven't, Abu Turki. But I'm sure there are many things that sons don't tell their fathers. Wouldn't you agree?"

"Yes, but it is the things that they hide from us that we must be most vigilant about. For instance, I discovered that Turki was losing thirty thousand a month on the horses."

A cold smile spread across Abdul Aziz's face.

"But family secrets don't concern me too much," he continued. "I'm more interested in the secrets my people try to keep from me. They usually have greater consequences. Assassination secrets, for instance, or bombing secrets. My uncle got three bullets in the face for ignoring something that was both a political and a family secret. So now we have a whole police division dedicated to these secrets. I wonder why people are still so foolish as to try to keep them from me."

Dan made a subtle gesture with his hand, the palm upturned as if to say, *What the hell?* Abdullah shook his head curtly. He was suddenly grateful that Dan didn't speak Arabic and would be excluded from whatever humiliation the prince had in store for him.

"Forgive me, but I'm confused," he said.

"Your son. He's been keeping secrets from his father and his king."

"What has Faisal done?"

"Sheikh Ibrahim, as I mentioned to you, he's in our custody now, and a man gave us your son's name as being part of this sheikh's group. Apparently he has been studying with Ibrahim for many months. This is serious, Abu Faisal. Your boy seems to believe the worst of the Saud family, and you know that we can't have that kind of blasphemy here in the Kingdom. It is nothing more than fitna. My brother is the Keeper of the Two Holy Mosques. We do not take criticism of our God-given role lightly."

Abdullah did not know whether he should be surprised, angry, or ashamed. "With all respect, Abu Turki, I'm sure he meant nothing by it. He's only a boy."

"He's a young man. And young men carry out the bulk of killing in this world, don't they? Never mind the jihadis. Look at the armies of any country. Young men, all of them."

"I wouldn't know."

"Yes, but I would. The members of my family must wake up every morning and think about who is trying to kill us, who is trying to harm the people of Saudi Arabia. We cannot afford to exempt men for being too young. We will take action against anyone old enough to pull a trigger."

It was laughable, this talk of his son as some sort of criminal. The only violence in which Faisal seemed to have any interest took place in his video games. He never watched when they slaughtered the sheep for Eid, always making sure to stand on the far perimeter of the circle of men gathered around to see the first spurt of bright blood. He absented himself from falconing on winter mornings, as if the dead and dying desert rodents were too precious to see clutched in talons. Instead, Faisal seemed always to be folded up on his bed, reading the Koran. Abdullah was indignant, but he hid his feelings from the prince.

"What do you suggest that we do to help Faisal get back on the right path?"

"The problem is his anger," Abdul Aziz said. "In a boy, mafi moshkela, but it's no good in a young man. A Saudi man must learn to respect his leaders, isn't that right? Violence against my family is akin to violence against God. Send your boy away to school in England or America. Keep him out of the country for a few years, until he learns self-control. Until he learns to appreciate his homeland."

"Yes." It was all Abdullah could bring himself to say, and he mumbled it, teeth clenched. Even in the best meetings, he was never allowed to forget that he was the subordinate, and it disturbed him that Faisal had given the prince reason to talk to him in such a condescending manner. Abdullah could feel a tingling in his stomach. He wished that he lived a hundred years ago so he could go after his son with a camel whip and remind him that his stupidity had repercussions for his entire family. Perhaps the prince was right about one thing—that modern sons lacked an understanding of tribe and moved with the arrogance and ignorance of the unattached. What did Faisal gain from Sheikh Ibrahim besides false brothers who would turn him in to the authorities?

"Shukran, Abu Turki. I appreciate the warning. You have my word that I will take care of this situation as you have asked."

Deliberately, in an attempt to shock him out of his smugness, Abdullah reached for the prince's hand with his prosthesis, but Abdul Aziz was unfazed and drew him into a tight embrace. The prince was being generous in his victory.

"You've grown too comfortable, Abu Faisal. Times are good for you and for B-Corp. You've got a new wife. But power requires vigilance. Don't forget that. The police won't act against your son, for now. But you should get him out of the country as quickly as you can."

Abdul Aziz kissed him twice on each cheek. Abdullah seethed, stepping out of the embrace and running hastily through the litany of farewells. He motioned Dan to follow him, and they made their way back out through the maze of marble hallways without speaking, Dan's rubber soles squeaking. They pushed through the doors of the main entrance and into the sunlight.

"What was that about?" Dan asked.

"It's the sheikh that Faisal studied with. They've arrested him."

"Is there anything that I can do?"

"No."

"What about the sheikh? What's going to happen to him?"

"The police have carte blanche. Usually there's some sort of reeducation process. You'll forgive me if I'm not overly concerned with the sheikh right now."

"Right. Your son."

"That little shit."

He had no idea how he would convince his son to leave his home, his friends, his religious community. He didn't want to spook the boy. What did he know about the man his boy was becoming? Was he the type to disappear into the desert, the mountains, all for his beliefs? In twenty years, would Faisal be one of the bearded men known by a historically significant nom du guerre, speaking to his loyal men by electronic address, a leader within the vast and mythic network of extremists Abdullah only read about in the newspaper? In the last two years, just who had his son become? Faisal was at an age when some children left home and never came back; so much depended on this moment.

"Isra's pregnant," he blurted.

"Wow. When is she due?"

"June."

"Christ."

"No. Noor. And she'll need a brother who's not a fool."

"What are you going to do?"

Abdullah just shook his head. As always when he did not know quite what to do, he would ask Rosalie. They would talk together as concerned parents, with the familiarity of people who have spent half a lifetime together.

AFTER HE DROPPED Dan off at Prairie Vista, Abdullah drove to the big house. The day was dying, the sun reluctantly ceding its place in the sky. The pale pink stucco of the house blended with the colors of the sunset, and Abdullah thought of Portofino, where they'd gone to get inspiration before building, where Rosalie hadn't washed her hair for days, letting the salt and wind wick the oils away until the strands resembled the waves of the sea.

He would break the news to her in the courtyard. It would be hard for her to be angry if he could only get her out by the fountain, with its thousands of blue glazed tiles as calm and shining as the Riviera. He wanted to talk to her about their son. This time, she could not spurn him, for it wasn't just about them anymore.

He had seen Dan's hand on his wife's at the barbershop, and he knew with certainty that it had not been nothing. His friend, his unlucky but handsome friend, desired his wife, and the idea quietly thrilled him.

Once inside, he called out into the quiet of the house. He glanced upstairs toward the door of the master bedroom. "Habibti?" he said, louder this time, climbing the stairs two at a time, his stump pumping to give him balance as he huffed his way to the top. He threw open the door and Rosalie startled awake. The room was dark, save the purple light coming in around the closed blinds. He approached the bed.

"Oh." He paused. "I'm sorry to disturb you, but we need to talk about Faisal."

He pulled up the blind and a moody twilight filled the room. Out the window, he saw the yellow lights of Isra's house but he did not feel her pull. Here, now, it was only Rosalie. Seeing her face soft with sleep, he could practically feel the softness of her breasts beneath his hand. He took a seat on the Kuwaiti chest next to the window.

"You had your meeting with the prince?" she said slowly, still trying to process the information.

"Yes." He was impatient. "He told me that Faisal's sheikh has been arrested. He suggests that we send Faisal away to school for a few years. An order, really."

She sat up in bed, pulling the comforter up and holding it to her chest.

"What? That makes no sense. The sheikh is just a teacher."

"No one scares al-Saud more than the men who know their Koran too well. What should we do? You've wanted to send him away to university for a while now. I know this isn't what you had in mind, but it gives us a good reason to force the issue. Abdul Aziz strongly suggests that he leave within the next few weeks."

"Abdi, you can't be serious," she said. When he didn't answer, she swallowed and looked down at the floor. "Is Faisal in danger?"

"No. I don't think so. Abdul Aziz all but assured me that he would be left alone until his departure. I'm going to find him and tell him."

"He can probably stay with Randy and Amanda while he works on his applications."

Abdullah wasn't terribly fond of Rosalie's brother, Randy, but he and his wife lived in a large, empty home in Memorial, outside of Houston. Randy had hated it when Rosalie moved to Saudi Arabia, but he loved her and would do whatever she asked of him.

"I could go with him, just to get him settled. Maybe Mariam could come along. I'm sure I could get her an excused leave from school."

"Yes, it would be good for him to have the company. Where is he?"

"I have no idea. He leaves without telling me. I'll go get Mariam, she'll know." She threw the duvet aside. Her pale nightgown had bunched up around her thighs, and in the shadow cast by the fabric Abdullah imagined the world of heat there.

"Wait. Come here."

Surprisingly, she obeyed his request, padding over the carpet toward him. She moved to sit next to him but he pulled her onto his lap. He thrust his nose into her hair and breathed in and out, deeply, the air from his exhalation covering his face in warm dampness. He felt the two thin layers of cloth between them. She was still and silent.

"My love. I will take care of everything."

He made his voice steady. He wanted to be a comfort to her.

"I love you," he said.

She turned to face him, and her eyes had that drowning look that he'd first seen in them when she had confronted him about Isra. Slowly, she reached over and placed a hand on the side of his face. "I love you." And then, "Why did you do this to us?"

He kissed the inside of her palm and then gripped it tightly, guiding her to the floor. In his chest, his heart thumped loudly and he felt the sweet, lonely ache of the loves he'd known—Khadija's face pressed against his tiny child's face; Ghazi, his first friend, pitting dates before handing them to him to eat; in the souq, the nameless girl with eyes like pools of tar, lashes long as the legs of a dung beetle, whose image had stayed with him until he first made love to Rosalie; Faisal's red, ancient face opening in a wail when he arrived, messily, into the world. All of it was there as he laid his body over hers. No, he would not forget again. She clutched at his back, pulling him closer.

IT WAS PAST eight o'clock when he went to find Faisal. He had not wanted to leave Rosalie, and they'd lain on the floor for several silent minutes after they'd finished. In a way, they were again new to each other. They had not been together for so long.

Rosalie had kept her eyes closed the whole time. When he'd finally risen to leave, she had turned onto her stomach and rested her head in the crook of her elbow as if trying to avoid his face. It wasn't a posture of shyness, but something closer to sadness, or regret. He leaned down and kissed her on the back of the head, then ran his fingers down her long back. "I'll be back soon," he said.

Mariam's bedroom was on the other side of the house, and he turned on the hallway lights as he made his way there. Through the door, he could hear the faint sounds of music, something upbeat, a young girl's voice. He knocked twice and then opened the door.

"Tisbah al-khayr, ya Mimou," he said.

"I thought you were at the other house tonight."

He shook his head.

"Little beetle," he said. "How would you like to go on a special mission with your baba?"

"Where are we going?"

"We need to find Zool. Do you have any idea where he might be?"

She paused. "Is everything OK?"

"Yes. Now, where is your brother?"

"He has to be with Majid. He only has the one friend, Baba."

"Lead the way."

If Mariam was with him, then perhaps Faisal would be a bit more compliant. He was protective of his little sister. He wouldn't want to make a fuss in front of her.

Mariam turned off the music and grabbed her abaya from the hook by the door. Rosalie told him Mariam spent hours on the weekends sewing her own abayas, and he noticed that the latest one was midnight blue. His children, each poised at the opposite end of the revolution.

"THERE, BABA. THAT'S the house," Mariam said.

A wooden gate interrupted a low and badly plastered wall. From behind it, an oleander bush grew thick and wild, spilling over the top and obscuring the lantern above the house number. It was a neighborhood with which Abdullah was not familiar, and he struggled to understand what Faisal gained from spending time in such a shabby place.

He pulled alongside the curb and killed the motor.

"Wait here," he said, before sliding out of the car and closing the door.

At the gate, he pushed aside the sticky oleander and rang the bell. The street was empty save a few stray cats, the other homes looming silently behind similarly inadequate walls. Or perhaps these people, these hardworking men, felt that they had nothing to hide, and that further unnerved Abdullah. A moment later, the gate creaked open and Majid greeted them. Abdullah was suddenly embarrassed about bringing Mariam. Certainly this pious boy would think it irresponsible.

"Ahlan wa sahlan. I wonder if my son is here, enjoying your hospitality?"

"Ahlan, na'am. Ya Faisal!" Majid called out. "Nothing is wrong, I hope?"

He seemed serious, but his mouth tricked up on one side. His body was broad against the gateway, as if he were standing guard.

There was a shuffling noise behind him, and when he moved to let Faisal past, Abdullah noticed that his left hand was pink with burn. At the sight of the shiny skin, his stump ached. He knew what it was to be a young man with a compromised body. Before he could say anything further, Majid had nodded curtly and closed the gate. Leaves, backlit by the lantern, cast thin shadows on the broken sidewalk.

"Let's get in the car," Abdullah said. "We need to talk. We'll have a powwow. Do you know what a powwow is?"

Faisal didn't answer, just stared hard at Abdullah before moving toward the passenger side of the car. He did not get in.

"Zool, Baba says that we're going on a mission," Mariam said from the backseat.

"Habibti, this was the mission. To get your brother." He paused. "I have something important to tell you, Faisal."

He looked at his son's face across the car roof. It seemed to deflect everything that he said, to crumble the words to dust and scatter them on the still air. He had not noticed this hardness before and it startled him, this anger that sat like a stone among soft lentils. The night was quiet around them, the streetlights cutting perfect circles up and down the deserted road. No wind, just humid stillness. The night holding its breath.

Mariam opened her door and stepped outside.

"The prince . . ." Abdullah paused before deciding on a different tack. There was no need for Faisal to know that he was on a watch list. "Your mother and I have decided that it's time for you to go to America for school. We know that you've been bored, and we think that this will solve that problem."

"I already told you that I'm going to go to Mecca for university. And I'm not bored."

"I'm sorry, Faisal, but this is not a request. You'll stay with your uncle in Houston until you get into a school." Faisal looked flustered, shifting his weight from foot to foot and refusing to meet

Abdullah's gaze. After a long pause, Faisal looked up and folded his arms in front of his chest.

"I think you would be wise to tend to your own affairs before you interfere in mine," Faisal said. It was so dark that Abdullah could only see the white flash of his teeth as he spoke.

"Your mother and I . . ."

"Don't speak to me about my mother!" Faisal brought both hands down on the roof of the car, the metal absorbing the force of his open palms with a dull thud. At the disturbance, a bird stirred from within the oleander and flew away. The night, listening. "Baba, are you really so blind?"

"Zool," Mariam said.

"Mariam, I'm sorry you must hear this. I found Rosalie and Dan together at the house. It was late and they were alone. God help me, I do not want it to be true, but it is."

Abdullah's skin turned hot to the tips of his ears.

"My son, do not attempt to distract me from my purpose with lies. That is not a light accusation. Do you know the punishment for slander?"

"You're a liar, Faisal. Umma would never." Mariam turned toward the street and brought her hand to her mouth.

"I'm sorry, Mimou," Faisal said, pressing his sister's wet face into his side. "Baba, I didn't mean to tell you like this. But you're blind if you think that sending me away will solve this family's problems. I won't go with you."

"Our problems? You're the problem. Look at what you've done!" Abdullah shouted.

He had ceased to care about the watching houses, the eavesdropping night. In his stomach, nausea mixed with the perfect, postcoital calm he'd had when he left the house. No. Rosalie loved him; it was as constant as the moon. It had been as if no time had passed. He ran over to Faisal's side of the car. He pulled Mariam away from her brother, then opened the plastic fingers of his prosthesis and pinched Faisal's shoulder, hard. Faisal tried to push him away, but Abdullah jerked him closer. Then, swiftly with his good hand, Abdullah backhanded Faisal across the face. His son cried out, but the night did not respond.

"Listen to me, you little beggar. The prince wants you out of the Kingdom. You've picked your friends poorly."

He hesitated. He did not have qualms with lies told for a person's own protection. Still, he turned the words over in his head before he said them, trying to gauge their power to make Faisal obey. He wasn't sure, but he found he could not stop himself from saying them.

"Your sheikh is being tortured as we speak; Prince Abdul Aziz told me himself." He waited for a reaction. "The light of day won't look good on a dead man's face. If you value your life or your sheikh's, you will go to your mother's house and pack your bags."

Their faces were so close, the words dissolving between them. Abdullah released him from his grip and opened the back door of the car.

"Get in, Mariam."

Once she ducked inside, he slammed the door behind her. He looked at his son, whose face remained hard and empty. Quietly, Faisal spoke.

"I pity you." He paused and rubbed his hand over the red mark on his face. "You have forgotten what family means."

Abdullah felt the hard bone of his knee meet the soft flesh of the boy's gut, the delicate curve of his ribs, felt the give of a body that he had created. His mind was a scramble of impulses and, confronted by the stillness of the night and his son, he felt hysterical. He struggled for the cool head that had defined him through his career and much of his life. He walked quickly to the driver's side. Once inside the car, he sat very still, taking in large gulps of air through his mouth. He started the engine and pulled away from the curb.

"Everything will be fine, Mariam. Baba will take care of everything. OK?"

"Faisal is lying, isn't he? About Umma?"

"Yes, my beetle."

Abdullah had regained his composure, and he replied quickly because it was the only answer. Even if Faisal were telling the truth, it was the only answer. If Rosalie had trespassed, if she had invited Dan to take what was not rightfully his, Abdullah would have to divorce her. He hated the very word, its second syllable like the hiss of some green-blooded, love-killing creature. The trees lining the road moved slowly in the wind, their silhouettes dark in the crepuscular light. From inside the car, the world was soundless. Abdullah felt his certainty returning, along with a new calm. He turned the AC up, the cold, recycled air blasting against his face. In the rearview mirror, he saw Faisal and Majid standing in the road, watching as he drove away.

In the morning, he would tell Rosalie about Isra's baby.

NINE

FOR THE FIRST time in several years, Dan felt as though he were doing something that mattered. He was helping someone worse off than he was. He was glad to support Rosalie, and he was glad to know he was no longer the silt of the emotional world. But civic duty and bolstered pride weren't the only forces pushing him to help Rosalie get out of the Kingdom. There was still that little expansion of hope in his chest, so that when she texted him the night before and asked him to meet her at Biltagi Brothers' Grocery at seven thirty p.m.—Abdullah would be at Isra's—he felt revving adrenaline and experienced the fleeting thought that he should comb his hair and shower before they met. Biltagi Brothers' would be just right. The Committee never sent people there to monitor, and it had a dusty quiet disrupted only by the occasional housewife doing her shopping. The machinations required to meet Rosalie secretly thrilled him. *Out beyond the Mutawi'in and the al-Saud, there is a place called Mind Your Own Damned Business. I'll meet you in the dry goods aisle.* Rumi, Saudi-style.

Before he left his apartment, Dan gathered the plane ticket and the travel release form and folded them into his back pocket. In the end, the Tunisian had pulled a copy of an old form for Dan, but he wouldn't go so far as to forge Abdullah's signature. Dan had done that part, somewhat sloppily, knowing that he could probably spend years in jail for it but not caring—at least, not caring enough to put an end to the delicious, burning nervousness in his abdomen.

That afternoon, as he skirted the compound courtyard to get to his car, the swimming pool was empty, the men probably inside watching a Premier League game on satellite. Sometimes, if things got a little rowdy at the pool, the Brits full to their eyeballs with homemade siddiqi, he'd hear brawling or awaken to find a neighbor slumped against the cement pillar outside his door. He never learned names, just helped the fellow to his feet and guided him to whichever apartment number he managed to mumble in his drunken stupor.

At Biltagi Brothers', Dan bought cans of fava beans and cloves of garlic and a small bunch of scallions that still smelled of dirt. He also dropped into his basket a package of cocktail napkins and colorful paper plates with pictures of spaceships on them. For a moment, he considered buying the paper party hats that matched the plates. He was in a celebratory mood. To celebrate her escape out of love and into something a little less dangerous, he and Rosalie would throw a very private going-away party. She would go back to Texas, he'd work another year or two for B-Corp, save enough to retire, then move back too. When she got to Texas, maybe Rosalie would also buy property along the Pedernales and send Mariam to the local high school where Ellie and Joe had gone. Wouldn't that be something? Later, Mimou might end up at the University of Texas, roaming the same streets named for Texas rivers that he, Abdullah, and Rosalie had cased years before. There was the problem of Faisal and what would become of their connection if she left, but Dan would not press the matter; Rosalie was already hesitant enough.

It had been a mistake for him to try to deliver the exit visa information to the big house. He should have waited, but he'd wanted to see her again. When he woke up the morning after the episode on the dune, he'd felt a sudden jolt of devotion and protectiveness.

Even if circumstances kept them from acting on their feelings for the time being, he would continue to tend the fire. Life was long and strange, indeed. What he did know for certain was that, for the moment, he felt a spark of caring for a woman other than Carolyn, and he was grateful to Rosalie for it.

While perusing the vegetable crates, Dan allowed himself to imagine what a life with Rosalie might be like. Nights, if she decided to stay over at the cabin, they would open the windows and listen to the rush of the river in the ravine below. Together, they would remember Texas, feel the mythology of it all around them. Days, they would occupy themselves with small and undemanding tasks—go to the hardware store for lightbulbs, or the drug store to pick up each other's prescriptions. They wouldn't go in for big projects like bathroom renovations or child-rearing. They would have companionable bodies and the politeness that only two people who aren't entirely in love are capable of. They would age, if not gracefully, then at least not alone. They would not chew the bitter root of memory. They would talk and fuck and make dinner together, a real domestic scene. As the years passed, the Kingdom would become just a place where they had lived once. It would seem as foreign to them as Zanzibar or Timbuktu.

But if they did finally forget, where would all those memories go? Did they even have a chance, or were old lovers always with you, lodged in your body and mind like shards of calcium on arthritic joints?

He checked his watch. Ten minutes to eight and she still wasn't there. He knew Rosalie was always on time, so her tardiness unsettled him. Dan moved to the neighboring produce refrigerator and turned a lemon over in his hand, inspecting it for abrasions before dropping it into a plastic bag. He preferred to do his grocery shopping at Biltagi Brothers' even though the Safeway was worthy of any American suburb. Its endless aisles were white and gleaming with wax, stocked to the ceiling with boxes of Muesli and jars of Nescafé. Still, he couldn't bring himself to give up Biltagi Brothers', with its smell of paprika and cumin and coriander and its burlap sacks of coffee beans and the lighting that always made him feel as if he were inside a yellow balloon looking out at the brighter world. Hypercolored bags of sweets from Japan and Korea and dusty packages of dried goods from the subcontinent far outnumbered American and European products, and this suited Dan because he did not have to go out of his way to avoid the things that reminded him of his ex-wife: pumpernickel, Coffee-Mate, banana peppers, Kozy Shack pudding cups. He wondered what kind of food Rosalie liked. At this point in her life, she was probably rigid in her tastes. They wouldn't have the time to carefully acculturate the other person to themselves. That was for the starry-eyed and energetic. Should they just exchange lists detailing preferences and habits? It had been so long since he'd had to explain himself to anyone. What would he even write on his? *Dan Coleman: 2% milk. Folgers not Maxwell House. Cottage cheese. Oatmeal. Number 2 Blade. Size 14 shoe. 36 x 34. Wearer of boat shoes but not an owner of boats. User of fountain pens. Writer of letters. Taker of Paxil. Early riser.*

Around him, a couple of women, wide in their abayas, glided from aisle to aisle, avoiding eye contact. So strange, the absence of the women's faces. It made him sadder than the absence of their bodies, which still found a way to show contour beneath the abaya. But the faces. Dan had a feeling of missing several people at once—all the women in Biltagi Brothers', all the women in the street, all the women in the car on the way home, all the women preparing the night's meal, all the working women; all the women, everywhere. He didn't know them, but still, he missed them, missed the opportunity to know them. Their enforced separation from him made him feel terribly lonely.

It was nearly eight fifteen. The market closed at nine o'clock. The store was starting to empty out, and he'd walked three full circuits around the perimeter, zigzagging through the aisles for extra time. Something had come up. He didn't want to text, in case she was with Abdullah. He would ring up, then go home and wait to hear from her.

At the register, Kiran, the same thin-boned Indian man who'd been serving him every week for the last two years, smiled at him as he started scanning the goods.

"How are you today, Mr. Dan? You buy curry leaves. Making stew?"

"Yeah. Just something to freeze so I can eat it for the next few weeks or so. Then I'm gone, Kiran. Gone with the wind."

"A vacation, Dan sir?"

"Yep. For now. But in a little while, it'll be for good. And this time it's going to stick."

"Good for you, Mr. Dan." He gestured to his little radio. "Just now, I hear that they are arresting young men for trying to blow up Abqaiq Refinery."

"No shit. Today?"

"Two hour ago. They try to break the security gate with their truck, and when a guard start firing at them, whole thing explodes! Truck, gate, everything."

"I'll tell you what, Kiran, I'll be glad to get out of here. These guys aren't screwing around anymore. I try not to give a formal shit, but it'd be nice to keep my ass intact."

Kiran laughed. It made Dan feel good to crack a joke.

"These jihadis make trouble for everyone."

"They're a mystery to me. I've never cared enough about any one thing, except maybe my family, to cook myself for it."

"Be safe, Mr. Dan," Kiran said, handing him the grocery bags. "Things are not being like they were."

As Dan took the bags, the bell hooked over the door chimed, and in walked Rosalie, imperial in her black designer robes. The silver embellishments glinted as she walked, little sparks thrown from her moving body.

"Dad gum," Dan said. "I forgot something for the stew. I'll be right back." He hurried back to the canned goods corner, bits of spilled rice and dried insect bodies crunching under his feet.

"No problem," Kiran said. He turned back to his crumpled copy of the *Saudi Times*.

At the back of the store, Dan waited in front of a row of spices. After a few minutes, he felt the air around him move as she passed by. She settled in by the tahinis.

"Raja's circling," Rosalie said. "I told him I'd call him when I got finished."

"Good work. I've got everything you need here in my back pocket. Hey, you hungry? They've got good shwarma here."

She exhaled, shook her head. He liked the idea of nourishing her. He knew he was fantasizing now. Every day, if he and Rosalie made it out, they would build each other up and take each other down, piece by piece, starting new each morning. If one day they decided they were tired of the building up, they could shake hands and move on.

"Dan."

He looked at her. The store was completely empty except for Kiran, who was still engrossed in his newspaper, or pretending to be. They spoke in low tones even though the radio at the cash register was turned up loud. Dan was nervous. Al Dawoun was a small town, and even on the slow end of long day, you never knew who you could run in to.

"I'm just not sure," she said.

"About what?"

"The leaving." She fumbled with the sleeve of her robe.

"Hey, you pulled the KGB move at the barber shop," he said. "You seemed pretty sure then." He fixed his eyes on her mouth, which was quivering slightly.

He picked up a jar of paprika, then set it down carefully. He looked toward the window and out to the parking lot, where a couple of men were passing outside, their shadows black and large against the colors of the setting sun.

"I was angry. Haven't you ever done stupid things in anger?"

"Christ. Why'd you even bother coming, then?" he hissed, so that spittle launched from his mouth and landed in tiny bubbles on a spread of cans.

"I wanted to tell you in person."

"It's not like we're dating. It's not like what happened meant a goddamn thing."

But he wanted to ask her, *What about the river? What about the cypress trees and the bass swimming through the roots?*

"You should watch how you talk," he continued. "Because, you know, you say it, and it's out there. I mean, people build things on it and . . ."

"I can't leave right now. Faisal's in trouble, real trouble. Abdullah told me last night. We're going to fly him to Houston until things blow over. I can't be going to Corsica now to drink wine all day."

"That's what you think of it? You think there's something wrong in choosing to get up and live? Forget Corsica, then. Just go straight to Houston. *You're* in real trouble."

He thought of the moment on the dune, his hand on her wrist in the barber shop, and how good it had all made him feel. Then she'd just thrown a bucket of water on the fire. What foolishness. What a fool he had been, with his dreams for her and himself.

"Believe me, Dan, I want so badly to just say to hell with Abdullah and all of this. To run away. That's the easy thing, and it's been calling my name since I learned about Isra. But at some point, you can't just reset your life and start over. I can't look at my kids and say, 'I'd like a do-over, I made the wrong choice. Have a nice life.'"

"So you're doing it for the kids? You're sticking it out for the kids?" He picked up a can of fava beans, set it down again, loudly. "Honestly, Rosalie, when has that ever worked for anyone? You have to think about yourself, here, too."

"I am thinking about me. That bastard is the love of my life. My happiness is bound up in him. I'd rather have this compromised life with him than be alone up on my moral high ground." She looked at him. "He's a good man, Dan. You know that."

Dan glanced at his watch. Nearly 8:40.

"Yeah, unfortunately, I do," he said at last. "But he's damn selfish."

"Who isn't? And sadly, I think that this disaster with Faisal might actually mean good things for our family. It will force us to band together for a time." She paused. "I'm sorry."

At that moment, Dan wished he had something powerful to throw at her, like *What about us?* But for both of them, those words lay with other people. Had Rosalie pleaded with Abdullah? And had he said "I'm sorry"? These were the humiliations that people kept until death, the stories they never told. There was no redeeming humor in them, so people let the memories of them burn in their hearts, the private stories of heartbreak and endings, the futility of people negotiating failed love. He wanted to sympathize with her, this partner in sorrow, but now he found he had only anger.

"It's just, you got me thinking. I thought I could finally go back. To the States."

She turned to look at him. She looked exposed without her makeup on.

"You should move back," she said. "It's your home. You don't need me for that."

Was it true? That he could choose to return without an invitation from Carolyn? From Rosalie? For so long, he had moved in accordance with, or in reaction against, Carolyn. That was marriage. That was divorce. Could he now live in the world as a singular and mobile force? Could he take steps that were neither toward nor away, but rather just a means of forward motion?

"Dan," she whispered. "You don't need to pretend. It's better if we're just honest with each other about what this is. You don't love me, and that's fine. I don't love you. I can't. I can't love two people at once."

"I thought we could help each other out. Get out of Saudi. It's not much of a life here."

"For you, maybe. You belong elsewhere. It's more complicated for me. I still love my husband, and I think he still loves me."

"So he can love two people at once and you can't?"

"I know you think I'm being naïve."

"That's the polite word for it."

Isra's pregnant, he thought. He wanted to tell her, but that was a mess Abdullah deserved to sort out.

"Rosalie?" He raised his voice slightly, and she glanced anxiously around the store.

"It's my choice, and I choose my family. I have nothing without them."

"He's not going to change, you know. He's too old."

"I know. That's why I'm going to Houston with Faisal and Mariam. I'll stay away for a little while. See my brother, put Faisal in school. This is Abdi's country. It won't ever be mine." She said the last part hesitantly, like she was trying to convince herself. "If I decide I need to divorce him, then I will, but I'm not ready. When he comes to the States to see me, it'll be easier to pretend that it's just the two of us. It'll be easier to be two human beings."

Dan wished that Carolyn had done that, granted them some time to figure things out, even if it meant pretending for a while. But she'd given him no warning; she served those papers up cold on that snow-lorn January morning.

"I don't regret what happened between you and me," she said.

She was standing to his right on the other side of the aisle. He looked down at her, saw her smooth her right eyebrow with the butt of her palm as if trying to press the memory back into the darker reaches of her mind. "Abdullah would divorce me in a second if he knew."

"Yeah, well. After everything you've been put through in the last week, you're giving the man another chance."

Perhaps he was half in love with her after all, because at that moment, Dan felt the sharp pang of loss. The disappointment of nothing changing, but also the relief. It wasn't quite joy that he felt, but satisfaction knowing that he would once again be allowed the perverse pleasure of dwelling. It was kind of like falling in the mud and, feeling the warmth, rolling around, and making a good and satisfying mess, but knowing that when you got up you'd be cold and dirty and regretful. That was nostalgia. That was remembrance. He would give himself this last day of immobility, and then tomorrow—tomorrow, he would act. He would make his plans for Corsica, and maybe he wouldn't even come back. Maybe he'd pack a rucksack and head north for the continent, moving along the rivers of Central Europe, watching the lights of the cliff-top castles on fire from within the thick of the pines.

"What's on the other side for me, if I leave him?" Rosalie said, bringing him back to earth. "The kids grow up motherless or fatherless and I get old back in Sugar Land. Seems pretty dark to me."

Under the harsh fluorescent lights of the grocery store, she looked tired, the hollows under her cheekbones like little basins. He was overwhelmed by her goodness, her steadiness. He smiled at her, and she smiled back. Her signature wide smile.

"I think you're wonderful," he said.

She glanced toward the door. "I'd better get going. You go first."

"When will I see you again?"

"You know the answer to that."

He passed behind her and squeezed her hand, which was folded inside the sleeve of her abaya.

At the register, he paid for a small bag of oregano he'd grabbed.

"Good night for real, this time."

"Good night, Mr. Dan."

Outside in the parking lot, Dan could hear the noise of King Khaled Street a few blocks away, horns blaring and tires squealing. Life and activity that were not his. Where was everybody going, all the time, their lives such a big production of motion? Perhaps he'd go walk along the Corniche and try to learn the secret to movement from the streaming cars.

A car door opened, slammed shut again. A shuffle of footsteps off to his right.

"Mr. Coleman, we've been looking for you."

He turned around to see Faisal and Majid, Faisal's low-forehead friend who'd slunk around several Iftars that Dan had attended at the Baylani house.

"Boys. Evening. What can I do for you?" He hid his alarm in folksy tones, but one thought bolted through him. Rosalie.

"Would you mind?" Majid gestured toward a black BMW "We need your help with a problem. We think you can help us solve it."

"I doubt that," Dan said, turning to face the boys, who had walked around behind the trunk of his car. Majid rested one foot on the bumper.

"Give me your cell phone, Mr. Coleman," Majid said.

"Guys, I'm going to get in my car and drive home and make the curry that I was planning. You're going to get back into Faisal's car and go throw your phone numbers at girls, or whatever young people are doing these days." Dan forced a laugh to indicate that he'd made a joke. Jokes helped. He racked his brain. What was the one about the Shiite and the goat? George Bush and the three wise men?

The boys remained grim-faced.

"Cell phone, please." Majid flashed the barrel of a pistol from where it was cradled between his right arm and his side.

Shit. They were out of sight of the register inside the store, and Dan regretted choosing the Mind Your Own Damn Business side of town. He tossed his phone to Majid. He wondered if he could drop the documents from his back pocket so they'd be hidden under his car, but when he moved his hand, Majid stopped him. He pointed to Faisal's car with the business end of the pistol. "Get in."

Just as Dan ducked into the car, Rosalie appeared at the top of the shop steps cradling a paper bag on her hip like a baby. Even in the growing darkness, there was no mistaking her.

"What on earth is going on here?" she said.

Faisal and Majid stopped what they were doing and stared, but before they could speak, Kiran emerged and locked the front door. He glanced at their strange group.

"Everything OK here, Mr. Dan?"

"Sure, Kiran. Just a little family reunion."

"Very good, sir. Good night." He climbed on his moped, sparked the ignition, and it sputtered to life. Without glancing back, Kiran drove away, leaning into the turn toward the main road. Obviously, the man's practiced discretion could work for or against someone.

"Umma," Faisal said. He was shaking his head.

"More business papers to be delivered?" Majid asked, one eyebrow raised.

"I just came here to buy groceries," Dan said. "We bumped into each other by chance."

"We've been watching you from the parking lot," Majid said. "Was it chance that led you to talk for twenty minutes?"

"Look, you've got the wrong idea," Rosalie said.

Majid spoke to her in Arabic, gesturing toward her purse.

"Faisal, this is insulting," Rosalie said. "Are you going to allow your friend to disrespect your mother like this?"

"We came here to talk to Mr. Coleman," Faisal said. "I didn't expect you to be here too."

"Well, I am here."

"We just need a moment with Mr. Coleman."

"Faisal," Rosalie started. "You're not thinking . . ."

"No," Faisal said. "For once, I am thinking. I'm wondering what you're doing here."

"Who do you think you're speaking to?" Rosalie asked. "I'm your mother, for God's sake."

Again, Majid said something in Arabic. He spoke louder this time, his large eyes almost comically round in his thin face. He approached her and held out his hand.

"Ya Allah!" Rosalie was clearly shaken. She took her cell phone from her bag and handed it to Majid, who pocketed the phone, then moved toward Dan. "Turn around," he said.

"Ya Majid," Faisal said. He spoke to Majid rapidly in Arabic. His voice was tight, as if he were afraid of losing control of the words tumbling out of his mouth. Imploring. Dan felt a twinge of pity for him. Clearly, Rosalie had not been part of whatever cockeyed plan they had cooked up. Finally, after a few minutes of back and forth, Majid clapped Faisal roughly around the ear, not in a violent way, but in the way of an older brother telling a younger one to get back in line. Rosalie watched them closely. Dan felt a void opening up between him and the scene unfolding. It was a movie without subtitles, and he watched it with a sense of detachment. Someone would have to explain it to him.

"You've both gone entirely mad," she said, as if by speaking English she could make more sense of what was happening.

Majid took a step toward Dan and started to pat him down clumsily.

"Back off, kid," he said.

Majid grabbed him by the hair and yanked hard. Dan yelped. He felt a searing pain in his scalp and heard the unmistakable sound of hair coming out at the roots. That dull, ripping sound. Dan gritted his teeth. He breathed hard with the pain of it. With his head pulled back, he felt something like feathers falling over his hands and it took a moment for him to realize that it was his hair, those dead pieces of himself falling on his hands like goose down. Above him, the moon glittered cold as a cube of ice. Majid pulled the documents from Dan's pocket.

"What's this?" Majid asked, tapping the envelope against Dan's chest.

"I demand that we leave my mother here," Faisal said in English. He was looking at Dan as if for help.

"Have you forgotten the sheikh already? Do you want to give them more time to beat him in their prisons?" Majid was shuffling through the papers, squinting to read them.

"Don't make me act against God," Faisal said.

"Our God doesn't protect unrepentant sinners," Majid said. "Remember what you saw in your own living room?"

"Be kind to parents," Rosalie interrupted them. *"And, out of kindness, lower to them the wing of humility, and say: 'My Lord, Bestow on them thy mercy even as they cherished me in childhood.'"*

"You are hardly worthy of the Koran's protection, at this point," Majid replied. "Look here," he said to Faisal. "Look at what Mr. Coleman had in his pocket." He said this in perfectly enunciated English, with a ringmaster's flourish, as if he were set to unveil a flying elephant. Fuck me, thought Dan. And fuck those papers. It had been the ultimate delusion.

Majid held out the documents, the exit visa and the ticket, inches from Faisal's face. "The truth is right in front of you. Your mother was going to run away with this man."

Faisal took the documents and scrutinized them. His face grew scrunched, unreadable as it moved fast between varying emotions. He looked up at his mother.

"Get in the car," Faisal said. His voice was stony.

"Zool, please. Have a little faith in your mother. I was here to make things right. That is all I'm going to tell you."

"Get in." With a skip step, Faisal heaved the cell phones into the empty lot next to the store. "Now!" He crumpled the documents and dropped them in a nearby sewer grate.

"Where's Raja?" Dan said under his breath.

"I told him I'd call when I was finished. I never called."

"No talking," Majid said, guiding Dan's shoulders down into the car like a police officer loading up a drunk.

Once they were inside the car, Faisal started the engine and locked the doors. The dark tinting on the windows made the world outside look black. Faisal turned on the AC and idled while Majid pulled duct tape from beneath the back seat. Turning first to Dan, Majid taped his wrists tightly, and Dan could smell the faint floral detergent of his thobe. "Now you," he said to Rosalie. "Give me your hands." Leaning over Dan, Majid wrapped the duct tape around Rosalie's thin wrists.

Majid settled into the seat by the window and jabbed Dan in the ribs with the gun. Dan shifted his weight nervously. What would a bullet feel like, passing through the body? Even if it went directly through the heart or into the brain, would there be sensation before death? He remembered an interview with one of the Kingdom's top executioners in which he said that it took seven seconds for the eyes in a head to stop roving around, and nearly a minute for the body to die of massive hemorrhage. The executioner spoke of death with a vocational frankness.

"Don't do this," Rosalie said. "Whatever you're planning."

"Keep your hands down and be quiet," Majid said. "Yallah, ya Faisal. Let's go."

Dan was surprised at how ordinary it felt to be taken hostage. Over the past few months, when violence had become a truth of Saudi life that he couldn't deny, he had started to envision how he would react in a Palm Court situation. He imagined shitting himself or bursting into tears, begging or getting gunned down while trying to run away. But now that he was standing face-to-face with these armed kids ordering him around, he found it easy to do what they said and wait calmly for the next set of instructions. He considered the possibility that it was an elaborate ruse orchestrated by Abdullah. After all, they'd pulled stupider stunts before—the time he'd blanketed Abdullah's BMW with vintage Nasser bumper stickers. Abdullah's retaliation two years later—the midnight dhow trip out of the Kingdom to "save" Dan from arrest for his incendiary comments at an Iftar dinner. Or maybe it wasn't a joke at all. Maybe Abdullah suspected his wife's plotting and had sent the boys to scare them a little.

They hadn't driven far when Faisal pulled up in front of the *Saudi Times* building. Dan had been to a couple lunches there, the editors all well-educated men who liked quick jokes and cutting judgments, both of which Dan could provide. Leaving the car running, Faisal walked to the entrance of the building, where he stooped to push an envelope under the door. If only Dan could open that envelope, he might learn the fate that the two boys had planned for them. But it was already inside, a small white rectangle on the dark carpet of the building's entryway.

Dan thought about opening his door and rolling off the road into the soft sand, running back toward town. But he knew that the bullets of Majid's pistol would outrun him. To be gunned down in the back, arms thrown up in surrender by the force of the bullets, was about the least dignified way to leave the world. He'd seen war footage.

Faisal got back into the car and angled it onto the road. Dan sat still, watching the road unspool before the headlights. Faisal spoke rapidly into his phone, the tone of his voice escalating so that by the time he snapped the phone shut he let out a frustrated bark. He and Majid spoke, and Rosalie clucked her tongue.

"Apparently their friend, Hassan, refuses to let them use his house as their hideout now that they've brought me along," Rosalie said. "At least someone still has a conscience."

Dan rubbed his head where Majid had pulled his hair out, feeling the sticky mixture of pus and blood that oozed out.

"If either of you says another word, I will shoot you and dump your bodies right here." Majid said it through his teeth, jamming the butt of the gun into Dan's ribs.

They drove for a while until they reached the poorer section of Al Dawoun. Faisal pulled up in front of a shabby home and parked. The gate opened and a boy no older than thirteen or fourteen stepped out. Dan watched as he and Faisal spoke for several long minutes. Finally, Faisal threw up his hands, nodded his head. He and the other boy disappeared behind the gate before reemerging, their arms laden with bags. The trunk popped open and the car sank ever so slightly beneath the weight of the load. As Faisal got back in the car, he and the other boy were both shaking their heads.

SOON THEY WERE outside the city, heading south. The roads were empty. Dan wondered if Abdullah had remarked Rosalie's absence yet, if he knew, or cared, where his first wife was on that January night. He let his face go soft, resting his head on the cold glass of the window. Darkness hid the desert's sweep. It was a bleak land that did not remember, sending its topmost layers always into the sea. The lights of Al Dawoun began to disappear behind them until the city was nothing more than an orange haze on the horizon. South. What was south? Yemen? He'd read that Yemen housed the largest number of al-Qaeda members, outside the mountains along the Pakistan-Afghanistan border. In his stomach, he felt a tiny tickle of fear. Was this it? The face of extremism? But of course terror happened that way, with a quick jump from the mundane—in a weekday marketplace, a mosque filled with supplicants, a busy office building, on a commuter train. The people in the Twin Towers had been wiping cream cheese off their chins from their morning bagels, taking conference calls, straightening ties, spilling coffee when their walls gave way to fire and metal and blood.

The boys were arguing again, this time in Arabic. Dan turned to his left to try to get a glimpse of Rosalie. His fingers were wet with his own blood. They were speaking a language he couldn't understand. He was traveling through a country he knew like one knows the coatroom at a party. Already, he felt his old life separating out from him, leaving him suspended inside the dark little capsule of the car. The boys fidgeted, cleared their throats, directed the car farther into the night. They were going somewhere. Dan wondered where, and how much of himself he would leave there.

TEN

FAISAL WAS NOT sure how he came to be where he was at that moment, hurtling down a dark highway with two hostages, one of whom was his mother. Sweat beaded across the bridge of his nose. He'd seen her airplane ticket, Manama-London-Houston, and an exit visa, which showed a signature that was most certainly not his father's. As a boy, he'd stared at his father's many impressive framed certificates and memorized every straight edge and curlicue of Abdullah Baylani's calligraphic signature, and the collection of lines and dots on the paper beside him bore a greater resemblance to Tibetan than Arabic. Regardless of whose signature it was, it meant his mother was trying to leave the country. Had she planned to tell them, or would he and Mariam awaken one morning to an empty house? Did his father know, or was it just one more thing to pass like water through his open hands?

It was late now, the side roads dark and silent. Hassan had been skittish, and rightfully so. He'd been released by the secret police after they took Sheikh Ibrahim because he was only fourteen years old. After Hassan heard they had Rosalie, too, he'd immediately backed out of the plan. He had said, "What about Mariam? Have you considered her?" which was not what Faisal wanted to hear at that moment, so he'd ignored him. Instead, Majid had decided to take the hostages to Qut al-Wisoum, fortress ruins along the Gulf two hours outside of Al Dawoun. Before leaving town, they'd stopped at Hassan's to gather the supplies they'd stocked in his basement—a sack of rice, a woolen blanket, a small radio so they could hear the authorities announce the sheikh's release. Hassan had also provided them with a propane stove and water to drink and to boil the rice, enough for two days. That was the worst part of the new plan—they could no longer rely on the indoor plumbing of Hassan's basement, or Umm Hassan's cooking. But the region surrounding the fortress was known for its natural springs, the threads of freshwater that made it an ideal spot for a port. If they were forced to hide for longer than expected, they could drink from the springs and be fine.

Once they got there, Faisal would have time to settle his nerves. He would have the fortress ruins, the bay like mercury beneath the full moon, the lights of Bahrain like so many yellow diamonds. He would sleep among the ghosts of the thousands of men who had first made Arabia great, the traders, the seamen, the tribesmen. They didn't need Hassan; they had the desert and all of its history waiting to make room for them.

Driving south into the darkness, Faisal longed to shut his eyes, to give in to the lolling forward motion of the car. Since Sheikh Ibrahim's arrest, he had not slept well. Instead, he had lain in his bed for hours, imagining the many ways in which Ibrahim was being tortured: through enforced sleeplessness, or by a loutish interrogator pulling the fingernails out of his clean and elegant fingers, the fingers of the hands that he had countless times raised up above their small group as if trying to protect the young men from some terrible force that would descend upon them. Ibrahim was short but broad, and with his arms winging out to his sides, he weekly made room for their small ecstasies. The sheikh knew the difficulties of believing—he had watched his country of devout and simple herdsmen, fishermen, and merchants run headlong into modernity, gaining material wealth while losing themselves. Ibrahim tried so hard to keep burning the flame of truth that Muhammad had lighted for all of the Ummah, the believers.

And yet the al-Saud wanted to punish him. Every day, the royals overlooked the misdeeds of blasphemers and unbelievers who cared more about money than truth but posed no threat to the monarchy. Only the men who believed in God more strongly than they believed in the al-Saud were punished, and it was the worst kind of betrayal coming from the family who had given itself the title of Keeper of the Two Holy Mosques. Faisal was tired of the hypocrisy, but before Ibrahim's arrest, he'd never considered that he might protest against it. In truth, it had never deeply affected him, and he was intimidated by what fighting might bring him—jail time, exile from the only home he knew. "Complacency wins the royal family decades," Majid had said when trying to convince Faisal that they should take Dan. "Why do you think jihad takes place in poor countries? It's because the people have nothing left to lose, and who can govern desperation? The poor, they're the ones that get things *done*. So for today, you're not al-Baylani, OK? You're some poor son of a whore with nothing left to lose."

After Faisal told Majid what his father said, that the morning light would not look so good on a dead man's face, Majid had taken him by the shoulders, hard, so that Faisal could feel his friend's panic moving through his fingertips and into his arms. "If Ibrahim dies, he will look down on the al-Saud from paradise and laugh as they are escorted to their special place in hell." Majid's face had been so close to his. When someone moved that close to you, it seemed like you should either kiss them or punch them in the nose. Faisal had never done either to anyone, and looking at Majid's set mouth, the urgency in his eyes, he had the desire to do both. He was afraid, and he was grateful for Majid's certainty. When Majid repeated the plan he had started to hatch in the pool, Faisal had said, *Yes, yes!* with a conviction that he didn't feel but hoped would come to him. He wanted to be the kind of man who stood up for what he believed in. With Majid's help, and through his plan, he could become that man.

Majid told him that they would be the eyes that watched the al-Saud, because when the royals thought that no one was watching, they were brutes, as if they forgot that God and the devil were always watching. Majid had watched over his shoulder as Faisal carefully composed the letter on Majid's computer, in Arabic and English, addressed to the king: *We demand the immediate release of our honorable teacher, Sheikh Ibrahim Ibn Sayid. We have taken one American hostage, Daniel Coleman. We will release him unharmed once we receive confirmation of the sheikh's freedom. You have twenty-four hours to respond. Do so via radio address.* Majid had wanted him to add a sentence about how they would harm the hostage and send the videotapes to Al Jazeera if they received no response, but Faisal had refused. "They will respond," he'd said. "They will do anything to avoid public embarrassment." Perhaps his A'm Nabil was making the call to the prince or the police right then. He felt nauseated at the thought, but whether from dread or anticipation, he couldn't tell.

It wasn't until the next day, hours before they were to set the plan in motion, that Majid had shown him the handgun, which looked like a toy until he felt the weight of it. "Take your jadd's khanjar," Majid had urged. "It's got a diplomatic blade. I know it'll do some negotiating for us." Faisal had tucked the sheathed blade into his boot.

But now that plan was ruined, and all because of his mother. After seeing the travel documents and feeling the sting of her betrayal, Faisal couldn't bring himself to say the words that would have saved her: *She's my mother*, and *I never saw anything at the house.* In the parking lot, she had watched them, her face filled up with a knowingness that Faisal had come to despise. *Poor young fools*, her eyes said. *I know*, *I know; you think I don't*, *but I know.* It was maddening, her knowingness. When he was a boy, she'd known everything: when he'd kicked skinny Bassim in the shins; when he'd eaten the entire tray of sweets that she'd been saving for her ladies' coffee; when he copied off of Sayf on his fourth-grade aptitude test. She'd used her knowledge as power, never punishing him outright but instead bartering with him: *Do your homework and I won't tell Baba about Bassim*, or *Eat your lentils and I will forget that I have no sweets left in my pantry*. But she didn't know him anymore. She didn't know a thing about him.

Just a few weeks ago, while his mother had moved through her grand house, Faisal had kept the secret of Isra deep inside like a jewel nestled in his guts. He knew that if he decided to reveal it to his mother, she would be forced to take it and wear it around her neck for all to see. But then the secret was out, spilled by some idiot merchant at the souq. *If you don't like it, then leave*, Faisal had wanted to tell Rosalie when she walked the house like a red-eyed zombie in the days after her discovery. And yet, when faced with the proof of her imminent departure, he hadn't experienced the joy or relief that he'd predicted. Instead, he felt a little sick to his stomach, as if he'd eaten too much on a hot day.

The car brimmed with the different silences of each person: Dan's anger, his mother's resigned stance, her shoulders curled forward. In his own silence, Faisal wanted to appear sure and strong. He wanted his to be the kind of silence adopted by righteous fathers reprimanding their water-hearted sons, or that of thin-lipped generals refusing to waste words on their quaking soldiers. During the two days since the sheikh's arrest, Faisal had said at least a thousand prayers for his teacher's safety, so perhaps this was God's answer. And what did Faisal care for Dan Coleman? He was nothing. He was less than nothing. Kafir. Hatab al-nar. A destroyer of families, his own and those around him. Besides, Majid was right—the only way to get the government to be reasonable with prisoners was to get the West to pay attention. The only way to get the West to pay attention was to threaten one of their own. Faisal remembered that fat, tattooed contractor up in Riyadh, Paul Johnson, who built Apache helicopters that killed Iraqi civilians and who lost his head because of it. Faisal remembered the photos, the body belly-down on the floor, the head propped on the back like a growth from some genetic mutation.

Faisal swallowed. This wouldn't be like that. Unlike al-Qaeda, he and Majid wouldn't make outrageous demands, like wanting the Americans to empty out Guantánamo or the al-Saud to expel all Westerners from the peninsula. This was going to be simple: a man for a man. Or at least, it *had* been simple, before his mother had gotten herself involved.

The road was deserted, and outside the car window the dirty public beach stretched for miles around a hook of land, marked by the moonlight on the water and the lighted concrete picnic areas that spanned the shore. In the reflected fluorescent light, he could see the soda cans and candy wrappers floating in the murmuring water. His family had never come to the public beach. The sand was too dirty, and his mother said what was the point in going to the beach if she had to keep her abaya on. They may as well boil her in oil, that's how hot she'd be, and besides, she wanted to wear her bathing suit. OK, OK, OK, his father always said. Before Isra, his father let his mother decide things, so much that Faisal was embarrassed for him. What man let his wife choose all things? It was no wonder Abdullah took a second wife. He'd let his first one take too much and he could never get his power back. Faisal was disgusted by both of them. In time, he would renounce them entirely; leave them to erode each other slowly with their words, like water that has come undammed. He would move to Mecca where he would study and build a family who would know each other as they knew God: from birth and to the very core.

In Faisal's boot, the Khanjar dagger pressed hard into his anklebone. In the rearview mirror, he saw that Majid cradled the gun between his legs. It had belonged to a cousin who'd left the National Guard but managed to hang on to his smallest gun. They'd decided it would be best if Majid handled the weapon, since he'd been trained. Though, there would be times when Majid would need to sleep and Faisal would then take the gun. Majid said that as long as you *appeared* to know what you were doing, everything would be fine.

Faisal's stomach growled audibly, and he thought longingly of the rice that they had brought with them. They would have to ration food and water carefully, but it was enough for the four of them for two days—double the amount of time they'd given the royal family to respond.

"We're almost there," Majid said. "Are you ready, brother?"

Faisal grunted. He was still angry at Majid for forcing the issue of his mother, and furious at his mother—for being where she shouldn't have been, for trying to leave them. Again, he glanced in the rearview mirror, but he couldn't see his mother's face. She was sitting directly behind him. He wondered if she was afraid, or angry with him.

In the distance, Faisal saw the outline of Wisoum, spread low along the beach. The lagoon was still, a shimmering extension of the land. Just decades ago, traders had docked their boums at the port and set off by camel caravan for Riyadh and Jeddah and Mecca. When Faisal was younger, his father brought him to see the fortress, and they had walked to the Portuguese watchtower and stood staring across the Dahna to the horizon. There was only the sound of the wind cutting around the sandstone tower. The dunes were not the smooth, endless red of the interior. They were coastal dunes, lighter in color and pocked by shrubbery, a sign of the saltwater nearby.

"This is your inheritance, Faisal," his father had told him that day at the watchtower. "There is no force greater than that of the desert. It conquered the Europeans, the Turks. Only your grandfathers knew how to manage it. They understood they must work with it, not attempt to control it. And now it gives back to us. How it has given back!" But Abdullah had forgotten that the grandfathers kept God by their sides when they took the Peninsula. They could not have done it without God, of that Faisal was certain. But now that the people on the Peninsula had so thoroughly tamed their surroundings, they felt free to forget their God. They had their piles of money and thought they no longer needed Him, their spirits growing impoverished. He often wondered when the desert would take it all back from them. It would not be long now if the Kingdom kept to its crooked path.

Faisal slowed the car and turned off of the paved road. The tires of the BMW spun in the desert's soft sand and he cursed under his breath. It wasn't the right car for the desert. They were unprepared. But they couldn't turn back, not with the note already under the newspaper's door. The car regained traction and they edged onto the rudimentary path that connected the road to the fortress. After driving several kilometers, and at the dark tidal line on the far side of the old customs building, they parked the car. The structure's porticoed doors gaped a dark black in the moonlight. Faisal got out, opened the rear door. Dan lifted his head from his hands and looked around, blinking.

"Get out. Stand against the car, facing us," Majid barked. He pushed at Dan as they squeezed out behind the front seat of the car. Next, he pulled Rosalie out behind him. Faisal opened the trunk and took out the food, water, and stove.

"We'll leave their hands taped," Majid ordered. "No need for blindfolds. Not much for them to see out here.

Just then, his mother stepped toward Faisal and swung her bound arms against him like a club. He staggered backwards.

"Faisal," she said. "This is real. It's not some game."

He stood there dumbly for a moment, holding her wrists and feeling his shoulder throb where she'd hit him. In the flooding moonlight, he could see Majid watching him, waiting to see how he would react. It was a test. Faisal looked at Rosalie's face, red from her exhortation, and made a decision: This would be his renunciation of her, standing there at Wisoum Bay. So many outsiders had been fended off there, why not Rosalie? Here she was, trying to stake her claim on him, trying to reduce him to *boy*, even while she was not being *mother*. He would not allow it. He leaned down and brought his face level with hers.

"Before God, I declare that I am no longer al-Baylani. I am not your boy; I am not your son. You were leaving anyway. I'll be Ibn Muhammad, and that's it." For a brief moment, his mother looked stricken and Faisal felt a regretful pang, but she recovered herself, putting her shoulders back like a soldier at inspection. That haughty strength made him quiver with anger. It was her selfishness, not her Americanness, that set her apart from other women. She was going to leave them. She was going to leave her family behind. He couldn't be son to that kind of mother.

"I'm sorry," she said quietly. "You can't change your blood." She paused, then continued, "You know this is wrong. We were only talking, Faisal."

"But he had your ticket and visa," Faisal said. "Don't treat me like an idiot."

"I wasn't there to do wrong, I promise you. I did consider leaving your father, yes, but I don't think you should have to try to understand that. In the end, I went there to make things right. Your father and I are going to be fine, please believe that. I want to give that to you . . ."

"We have no time for these family soap operas," Majid interrupted. He cut a strip of duct tape and secured it over her mouth. "We'll set up camp inside those archways."

Faisal wondered what other creatures had had the same idea. In addition to the ghosts of marauders and tradesmen and Bani Khalid sheikhs, there would be the husks of scorpions, the shed skins of desert vipers. For the first time, Faisal wondered if he might die there on the beach, or inside the building's dank walls. In a line, they moved toward the building. Faisal stepped in the large footprints that Dan left in the uneven sand. Near the door, his mother lost her balance and fell forward. With her hands bound, she was struggling to get up, so Faisal took her under the arms and set her back on her feet. Though he made sure to avoid looking at her directly, her expressions were embedded in his mind, so that he could sense the contortions that meant *anger.* Well, this was not cheating on an exam or kicking Bassim's shins. This was bigger than that, bigger than her.

Their group trudged on toward the customs building. Above them, a billion stars made a dim light.

FROM THE ARCHWAYS of the crumbling building, they had watched three sunrises and three sunsets. Sea birds sang and the waves made their breathing sound against the shore. Their cell phones were dead. They had already eaten all of the rice, which Majid boiled over the propane stove in the evening, giving a fistful to each person. The radio, which they played all day and into the night, switching between channels, waiting for the good news, became the backdrop to their days. Until they heard the announcement, they would have to stay hidden, biding their time until they could steal back into Al Dawoun, send Dan and his mother back to their homes, and embrace their teacher. After that, who knew? Yemen, maybe? Somalia? He heard there were places to go where only God ruled over men.

Majid had placed Rosalie and Dan far enough apart so that they could not look at each other. The quiet of their days was so complete that the sound of Majid's footfall in the sand set Faisal's heart racing. Dan Coleman's clean-shaven kafiri face had sprouted a fine salt-and-pepper stubble. Faisal thought that it suited him, and then was angry that he thought about Dan's looks at all. But he had never realized how long an hour could be at midday, when prayers had been said and there was nothing more to do but occasionally wipe the sweat from your forehead or drink warm water or urinate into the bay or take Dan to the bay's edge to urinate. He and Majid took turns doing this, and it always made him feel ashamed to be so close to another man during that private moment. When Rosalie had to relieve herself, Majid walked her around the side of an old stone wall and then turned his back to her and faced the bay. Five times a day, they prayed, everyone except Dan. To cleanse themselves, they said bismallah and performed tayammum, rubbing the purest sand they could find over their hands and faces. They could not spare any water for ablutions.

Three days without phones or video games or cars or the hundred other machines that filled his life with their meaningful *tack-a-tack* sounds—sounds of industry and accomplishment, sounds of information and transportation. There they were, spooning tasteless rice into their mouths like the ancestors, squatting to shit in the sand, hearing the sounds of an entire country carried by the wind off the Dahna. Then there was the radio, its constant crackling a comfort, the voices fading in and out with bits of news and shreds of song. They listened, but it gave them nothing. It got so that Faisal could not remember which hour was which, which meal was which, which piss was which.

Slowly, very slowly, he felt what had made him distinct in the city, what had set him apart and made him Faisal al-Baylani, stripped away from him. His renunciation had carried more truth than he could handle. During the third night, he woke in a sweat, fearing he was just hands, just spit, just the slow thump of a heart that resembled everyone else's. This made him afraid, but it also gave him comfort. He went back to sleep to the sound of the others breathing.

During the day, Majid stayed with the hostages in the customs building while Faisal stationed himself atop the highest rampart to watch for approaching cars, helicopters, tanks, a thousand horsemen, the masts of an armada, the dripping, warty tentacles of a kraken come to sweep them out to sea. But always, the still wash of blue, the infinity of brown. He longed to take a swim in the bay, to let the salty water float him along on his back, to feel the pressure of the water against his eyes and ears as he fell into the familiar rhythm of the strokes.

Faisal was glad to get out of the cool darkness of the building's interior, away from his mother and Dan. After days spent looking everywhere except at Rosalie, Faisal had finally turned her around to face the large, empty room. She looked younger there in the desert, out of her house, away from her fine clothes. Her face was smudged with dirt, and the sight made him sad. He wanted to go to the water and bring back a bucket of the warm shore water to bathe her face, but instead, he decided to go stand watch outside. Seeing her at his mercy was too much.

From his watch, he could feel the cool, wet air off the water fight the hot, dry air off the desert just above his head, and it energized him. He counted the sea birds, the flying and diving gulls and the stick-legged storks that waded far into the lagoon. At the horizon tankers heaved slowly, moving to and from the refinery down shore. Occasionally, wandering camels moved to break the desert's stillness, their bodies tiny but unmistakable from that distance, their movements so languid that it seemed to take them the entire day to move a pencil's length.

As Faisal got hungrier and hungrier, thirstier and thirstier, he began to feel as weightless as he did during the Ramadan fasts—so dizzy and insubstantial that a sudden gust of wind might lift him out over the shallows of the bay. He began to see shadows moving in and around the customs building. From his perch, he watched patches of darkness move over the sand below him, and he felt sure that they were ghosts of the tradesmen and pirates and colonizing armies. Should he warn his mother about them? She spent most of her days sleeping, pitched in the sand like a beached dhow. Sometimes, he wished the ghosts would come and speak to him. Sometimes, he wished his mother would come and speak to him. His was a silent watch, an hourless watch, a cloudless watch. Sometimes, he wondered if the earth had stopped turning.

FIVE TIMES A day, he removed his knife and turned inland to pray, to confront the desert's vastness, which unnerved him more than that of the sea. Perhaps because it was fewer than three hundred kilometers to Iran across the water but more than a thousand to Mecca over the scorching, indifferent sand. Since they'd arrived at Wisoum, he had prayed twenty times already. At first, he had been nervous, thinking that every click or shuffle was the secret police padding across the desert between the road and the fortress. Now, a calm had descended on their small camp. Inside the building, away from the radio, every sound was natural: mouths breathing, sands shifting, water lapping, birds calling, men praying. The nights were cold and clear, and during Faisal's allotted five hours of sleep he huddled beneath a rough woolen blanket. In his dreams, he leaned over a man-sized cauldron of seleek, and drank the milky broth until he was warm.

ON THE EVENING of the fourth sunset, after saying the Maghrib prayers, Faisal meditated with the purples and reds of the dying sun filling the sky around him and the Gulf breezes billowing his shirt. God felt very near to him, and he was certain that Ibrahim was alive. He felt a wash of spirit, had the feeling that the sheikh was there, watching over them. It had made his skin prickle and his heart beat quickly.

Even though the announcement was taking longer than expected, at least their actions would mean days of life for Ibrahim. The police were probably trying to figure out how to react to the message, how to release the sheikh without looking as though they'd negotiated. Still, he was growing alarmed; supplies were dangerously low, their plan disintegrated as easily as sugar in tea. When he tried to approach Majid to discuss what might have gone wrong, Majid preempted these attempts with a curt shake of his head and a scowl: "God has a plan for us, brother." And because there was nothing else to do, Faisal proceeded with his daily tasks.

At night, he and Majid took turns sleeping. Majid preferred to sleep out in the sand, his back pressed against the rear tire of the car, and Faisal watched him just like he watched everyone else. On their fourth morning, a loud banging roused Faisal from his contemplation of Dan's face (ruddy, square-jawed, a substantial nose through which he snored at night). He peered out the archway to the car, where Majid was beating his fist against the hood and kicking at the tire. To his right, Dan and Rosalie were sitting up straight, ears cocked toward the sound. The noise rose disharmoniously in the dawn's quiet, and the sea birds fled in a flurry of squawks and beating wings.

"Brother, shway shway," Faisal started, but Majid was already huffing toward him, sand spraying out beneath his stomping feet. When he spoke, his words were muffled by his ghutra, which he had wrapped tightly across his mouth to keep himself from breathing in the dust. His eyes were raw and tired.

"I'm going for water. We're down to the last of it. We didn't bring enough. They were supposed to answer us sooner."

In a whisper, he added, "Why haven't they answered us?"

The question startled Faisal. Majid was a man of answers, not questions.

"I . . . I don't know. Perhaps they're waiting for us to run out of supplies? Or they're searching for us? Perhaps they've already released Ibrahim?"

"Or perhaps he's dead. Perhaps they ignored our warning and killed him. Perhaps it's time for us to retaliate."

"No, I felt his presence when I said my prayers yesterday. I know he's alive." Faisal glanced in at the two captives.

"You don't know anything—we won't know anything until we hear from them. Khara."

"Then we must continue to wait. God led us here and he'll lead us home again."

Faisal was hungry, and his throat was dry with dust despite the care he took wrapping his ghutra. The desert always found a way in. Now, when Faisal urinated, it was a dark yellow trickle.

"The springs are a few kilometers to the northwest," Majid said. "I shouldn't be gone more than a few hours."

"What if someone comes while you're gone?"

"We can't be sure that they won't respond, but I do know we'll die if we run out of water. Remember, Faisal—be strict with them. No talking. And if they have to relieve themselves, they'll just have to go where they're sitting because I won't be here to watch the other one. Remember their sins against your family and against God, Faisal."

Majid gave him the pistol and picked up two of the empty gallon containers. "Masalama, Ibn Muhammad," he said. "I'll be back soon, inshallah."

"Why don't you take the car? It'll be quicker, and you can carry more water back."

"And risk being seen from the road? La. Every policeman in the Eastern Province might be looking for our car. It wouldn't be safe to drive in the dunes, let alone on the road. Better for me to go on foot, where I can hide if need be. The springs are close. It won't take long."

Faisal watched him as he made his way along the hard, wet sand near the water, his stride assured and long, the slap of his footsteps at first audible, then lost to distance. After a while, he saw Majid cut west into the softer sand of the Dahna, a dark spot moving slowly away. Faisal felt the pistol at his side. Walking back into the archway, he took a seat on the step that was now so familiar to him. He took a long breath in and then exhaled, slowly. He scratched his beard. He wondered how many times his stomach had folded in on itself in hunger. He thought of what he would eat once he got home—a giant shwarma with lamb spilling out of the top and sauce dripping all over his hands. He wished Jadd Abdul Latif were there, because he would teach them how to survive in the desert—something that he and Majid had not considered carefully enough as they'd made their plans.

But in the next instant, he was glad his grandfather was not there to see the mess they'd made, or his own grandson at the mercy of the desert that Jadd and his family had lived in, at times mightily, at times timidly, for generations. Certainly, Jadd would not have approved of this treatment of his mother. Faisal felt gnawed by guilt. Even if she was going to leave them, she deserved better than a bed of sand and bound wrists. But now they were in it, in deep. In their preparations, he and Majid had focused too intently on the glory of their ideas. They'd forgotten the basics—that in order to realize an idea, a person must have water, protect his tender skin from the sun's blazoning. Though he hated to admit it, they were city boys. Faisal took another breath and waited.

"FAISAL."

After three hours of quiet, the voice startled him. It was Dan, who spoke to him without sitting up, without even raising his head. How strange to see such a large man lying vulnerable like that.

"Faisal," Dan said again. "I have to . . . relieve myself."

"What?"

"I have to go to the bathroom."

"Just go where you are."

"I don't think you want me to do that. Because if I do, you know you're going to smell it for days."

Faisal considered what Dan said. If Majid came back soon, they could clean it up and be done with the issue, mafi moshkela. But what if he took longer? What if it took him a day or more to find water? It wouldn't do to have the hostages turn the shelter into a hamam. In the midday heat, it would be unbearable.

"Fine. You can go by the water. But she has to move outside where I can see her." He looked at his mother. "Get up, please."

Rosalie stumbled to their feet and walked toward the archway. Dan rose more slowly and moved in behind her. His white sneakers were brown with dust, his Polo shirt rumpled.

"No talking. Face the building," he instructed his mother.

Rosalie dropped her eyes and gave the slightest shake of her head. It was the kind of gesture he'd seen people make at funerals, as if to say *What a shame*. Nonetheless, she moved to the spot in the sand that he had indicated. Faisal turned back to Dan. "OK, yallah!" He walked a few paces behind Dan until they were a respectable distance away.

"Don't turn around," he said over his shoulder.

He felt his blood surge. Here, he was in control. It was a good feeling, one he had not experienced in quite a while. Though he regretted his mother getting in the way, if it meant the sheikh's freedom, it would be worth it. They stopped at the water's edge, twenty meters from where Rosalie stood, still as a boulder. Clearing his throat, Faisal turned to face down the coastline so that the man could have his private moment, and he was annoyed to have his politeness overlooked when Dan began talking as his urine caught the breeze and blew out over the sand.

"It's not too late," Dan said. "No one's been hurt. Think about it. That's your mother up there."

"No talking."

"Son . . ."

"I am *not* your son, thanks be to God. And you are in no position to advise me, after what you've done to my family."

"Be honest with yourself, just for a minute." Dan zipped his pants and turned to face Faisal. "They're people. It's a messy business."

"This is about Sheikh Ibrahim. He would have been killed if we didn't act. The prince told my father."

"I was there when they discussed it. Abdullah didn't mention anything about anyone getting killed. He said something about re-education and . . ."

"No, my father told me specifically that Ibrahim would be tortured. That he might not live much longer."

"I'm telling you, I was there and your father didn't say anything about that."

Faisal considered what Dan said. Was Ibrahim even in danger? Could it turn out to be a routine arrest that ended with a slap on the wrist? No. His father had spoken with such conviction. There must have been danger.

"What exactly did you hear?" Faisal pressed. "I need to know the prince's exact words to my father."

Dan shook his head. "They were speaking in Arabic. I . . . I couldn't understand."

"Please, think! You must have a basic idea of what they said."

"I remember hearing the prince say 'fitna' a few times. That's it. That's all I've got. I'm sorry."

"You're telling me that you've lived in this country for more than twenty years and 'fitna' is the best you can do? Ya Allah!"

Dan's ignorance was an insult, but worse than that, it meant that Faisal had no access to those crucial moments between his father and the prince. He believed his father to be a lot of things—a drinker, a showman. But a liar? He had never known Abdullah to lie. Of course, there was Isra. Hadn't he lied to Rosalie for years?

"She loves you, Faisal. Even though she's upset with your father, she's staying here."

"Just be quiet. Please, no more."

"Let's leave before Majid gets back. No one thinks you're a terrorist, Faisal. You're a good boy. You mean well. Like your father."

At this remark, Faisal pulled his pistol out. His face was hot, his teeth clenched tightly.

"I am not a boy. And I am nothing like my father."

He raised the butt of the gun above his head—yes, he felt he would relish bringing this man low, finally—but before he could move, he heard a distinctly foreign sound, not the birds or the waves or the wind to which he'd become accustomed. He looked around and it took him a moment to realize: the car. Rosalie was gone from her spot, and the low sputtering he'd heard was an engine. He ran hard to the edge of the customs building, where Majid had parked the car four days earlier.

"Hey!" Faisal shouted, waving his arms.

The car had begun to crawl over the soft sand. Faisal stopped running. Twenty meters. Thirty meters. She was moving farther and farther away, gaining speed. His feet stuck deep in the sand, and he felt the drift and pull of the distance between them. This was what he wanted, wasn't it? It would be so easy to let her go. She didn't belong there with them.

But then he thought of Majid, the way he let the desperation take hold, hammering himself into something hard in order to save Ibrahim. Faisal couldn't let her go. She would tell where they were, and then it would be over. Faisal took aim at the rear tires, bracing his body for the recoil. He fired. Nothing. The car kept moving. He aimed again, sending off a volley of shots. Again, nothing. With a mounting sense of panic, he fired a final time. His ears rang with the noise, but he heard another sound, a distant thunk. One of the shots had landed, and he saw the car slow to a stop. It was stuck in the shallow basin of a small rise of dunes. The door opened and Rosalie tumbled out.

"Jesus Christ!" Dan was standing behind him.

"She was leaving," Faisal managed.

Sand coated his throat and the weakness of hunger made his legs leaden. The sun was high and clouded with dust. It had lost its distinct borders, heat spilling down on them. Faisal was suddenly tired, more tired than he had ever been. He wanted to lie down in the sand and sleep. He thought longingly of the blue tiles in the courtyard of his home. How often he had sat there in silence, grateful for God's presence, which made it somehow less lonely in the empty house. He would like to be there now, feel the fountain's water setting around his bare feet while he formulated his private prayers.

Dan broke into a run toward the car, lumbering awkwardly because of his bound hands. Faisal could not let him get to his mother first. Though he was weak with fatigue and thirst, he sprinted forward. He fought the give of the sand, finding reserves of fury in his legs that catapulted him forward. When he got to the car, his mother was kneeling in the car's shadow, crying. Her nose was running and she struggled to breathe with the tape over her mouth. In that moment, he was terrified, for he felt that if he gripped the gun less tightly or relaxed the muscles that ran like iron through his shoulders, he might cry too. He might never stop crying. He turned to his mother, whose head was down, her nose dripping into the sand. Kneeling beside her, he gently peeled off the duct tape. She choked a little and wiped her face with the back of her hand.

"Untie my hands, Faisal. Let me hold you."

He hesitated. For a moment, he felt as if it were the best idea in the world. Here was the woman who might make his mistakes seem OK, as she had so many times before, just by taking him in her arms.

"Umma." He let the tears fall down his face. "They are going to kill him. Baba said so. I just want Ibrahim to live. We are going to make it so he can live. It's why. I had to stop you from leaving."

She made a shushing sound. He wanted badly to free her hands, to feel the cool of her palm against his sweating forehead like he was a boy with a fever. But if he untied her, then he would have to untie Dan, and he was not prepared to do that. It would mean abandoning their plan.

He left Rosalie's hands bound. She searched his face, and this time, he stared back. He reached out and moved her hair away from her wet nose. It was midafternoon and the sky was a pitiless white. Dan walked toward them. When he arrived in front of them, he glanced at their faces.

"We'll go back inside now," Faisal said.

"You're really going to continue this?" Dan asked.

"Faisal, let's go home. You don't need to explain why. We can work it out, just our family. We'll figure it out together. Your baba can protect Ibrahim," Rosalie said. She spoke in Arabic, as if it was a little secret they would share. But he was tired of her secrets. He was tired of his father's secrets, of the Kingdom's secrets.

"Please," she continued. "We've made mistakes, both of us. I'm so sorry I've disappointed you. I've been out of my mind with grief, habibi. I love your father the way you love your God, and . . ."

"That's blasphemy," Faisal said cutting her off. "We will go inside and wait for Majid's return." He did not want his father's help with Ibrahim. He did not want a man of Ibrahim's pure spirit beholden to his father, who seemed to forget that a man's purpose on the earth was to strive for the glory of jannah, not the false triumph of the dollar.

"Faisal, please," Dan said.

"I said that's enough! I've been tested once already today. Yallah, let's get to the shade."

He steered them toward a side archway that led back into the vast and cool room where they had spent much of the last four days. He drained the water into a thermos cup and took a sip before taking it first to his mother, then to Dan. They had drunk too much on the first day, rationing only for one or two days. On the third day, they were down to a few sips per day per person. Light-headed with thirst, Faisal floated back to his familiar spot in the archway. Every so often, he fought a spell of dizziness that threatened to send him face first into the sand. It had been six hours since Majid left. The water was gone. The waves thrummed. The gulls shrieked. No one had answered their demand. No one seemed to miss them at all.

ELEVEN

ABDULLAH WAS ANNOYED when his cell phone rang. It was Mariam—the third time she'd called him that day. He was not in the mood for plaintive messages, so once again, he ignored the call and message. He had gone to play the State Oil golf course specifically to get away from his connections to the world. After his conversation with Faisal two nights earlier, it was a world he wasn't sure he wanted to inhabit for the next few hours, possibly the next few days. He was not well-equipped to deal with vexation, and Faisal's intimations about Rosalie and Dan had been vexing in the extreme. Abdullah was a rich man in a country ruled by rich men. He got what he wanted from people, and that news was, quite simply, not what he'd wanted.

Unfortunately, at the course, Abdullah had quickly discovered that anger wasn't good for his stroke, the abused ball falling sullenly into every trap or rough until he'd moved to the driving range, where he could hack away artlessly. It was cool and gusty under the midday sun. He had told no one where he was going. Let them wonder about him. Let them grow worried when he didn't show up at the office or at home.

With a sharp swing of his club, Abdullah sent the ball flying. He lost it against the white sky, then caught sight of it as it came down on the deep brown of the oil-weighted sand course, where it joined the hundred other balls he'd sliced out over the range. Another bad shot. Finesse was not in his blood this afternoon. He should have confronted Rosalie first thing yesterday, but when he woke up in the morning, he found he didn't have the strength, and Isra had been there, soft and beckoning. Rosalie and Faisal would sort themselves out, he decided. He despised argument and apology, and had found that if given enough time, most personal matters handled themselves—the passage of time meant diffusion through disinterest, healed injuries, or provided the chance to return to one's senses. He was certain Faisal's accusations against Rosalie were nonsense. A woman only had her good name, her life spent preserving it. Rosalie was not stupid. She wouldn't destroy that so casually.

In between the *pock* of his club connecting with the balls, it came to him: The Rosalie he had married was gone. The adventurer, the gypsy-souled livewire searching for a home in the world. That woman in her wildness was gone, replaced by someone who wanted him and everyone else around her to follow the rules of good conduct. She'd become a stickler, a nag, a preacher of right behavior. Where was that half-feral girl, the one who'd smelled of cigarettes and bourbon, who wore torn black tunics and dirty moccasins, the one who did her homework by the light of the liquor display at the Lazy Lion? The girl whom he had wanted so desperately to bring into his life despite all the living forces working against him because she was so different from any iteration of woman he'd known—she'd gone missing somewhere.

Abdullah glimpsed a flash of color from behind the row of oleander bushes that shielded the course from the parking lot, and soon Ayoub emerged, trotting down the path toward him. He was waving both hands, laboring despite his substantial bulk in an attempt at swiftness.

"Sir! Sir!" Ayoub called out.

It was more difficult to ignore the flailing, calamitous Indian than the repeated phone calls from his daughter. Abdullah wished he'd driven himself, but when he'd considered it earlier, he found that his pride wouldn't allow it.

"Mariam just called me, sir. Found my number in your datebook. It seems your wife hasn't been home in twenty-four hours. Faisal, too. I told the miss that we'd come home, but I don't know if she heard me. She was crying, sir. She asked me why no one wanted to live with her anymore. She said she was sick of Yasmin's cooking, and . . ."

"All right, enough. I understand. We'll go." He paused, then shouted, "We'll go!"

Had God answered his foolish, furious prayers from yesterday evening, airlifting them straight out of his life? No. On earth, he was a powerful man. In heaven, he doubted it. Rosalie had probably gone to Lamees and Khaled's, trying to teach him a lesson, and Faisal was camped out on the dirty floor of Majid's basement. He would go to them and they would return home. A request, granted. It was how he had always done business.

He stuffed his club in his golf bag, then thrust the bag at Ayoub. The carob trees and palms whispered to them as they walked down the concrete path. The sun was lost behind haze, the afternoon already succumbed to dust's monotones. Out on the browns, the forgotten golf balls stared up into the empty sky like a hundred lidless eyes.

AT THE BIG house, Mariam and Raja, Rosalie's driver, sat on opposite sides of the kitchen.

"Raja knows something, but he won't tell," Mariam said, her eyes red and swollen.

"Sir, a moment in private?" Raja was a small man, his shirt stretched tightly around his narrow shoulders. He did not meet Abdullah's eyes.

"Of course."

In the soft light of the study, Raja kept his body angled toward the door, as if he might flee at any moment.

"Funny, sir," Raja said, "but Rosalie did not wait for me at Biltagi Brothers' last night. I sat for nearly an hour outside the store. I thought perhaps she had gone down the street to another shop. Perhaps she called a taxi?"

"I don't think I understand you, ya Raja. Are you telling me you left my wife on the streets of Al Dawoun at night?"

"Sir . . ."

"And you had the audacity to return here and sleep peacefully in your bed?"

"Sir . . ."

"And where is my wife now? Did she go to another shop? Did she take a taxi?"

"No, sir. She isn't here."

Abdullah stood, his ears hot. He turned his back to Raja, ran his forefinger along the spines of his books, quickly, so it made a snapping sound.

"And why in the name of Almighty God did you not call me, when I was a short walk away?"

"Sir, you said never to bother you there. You said I was never to come there for anything."

Quickly, Abdullah was at Raja's side, his hand around the man's elbow—so bony he felt he could snap it if he leaned into it.

"Not in an emergency." He squeezed. Raja yelped.

"Sir, have mercy! I didn't know it was an emergency. The madam has been so upset, I thought maybe she wanted to be with friends, to disappear for a while, smoke shisha, I don't know."

Abdullah held Raja's arm a few beats longer, teeth clenched. He was not usually an ill-tempered man, except when afraid. When his mother was dying while he was still a teenager, he had tormented an old, tethered goat, throwing pebbles at it though it had nowhere to run.

"Get out of here." He stepped back. "You're back to Sri Lanka in the morning."

Abdullah stared at the green lampshade on his desk until he heard the door to the garage slam. He exhaled, closed his eyes. Moving to the overstuffed chair in the corner, he sank down, drew his feet up onto the ottoman. That she wouldn't even call, for Mariam's sake.

"Baba?"

Mariam stood in the door of the study, her hand on the doorknob, her dark hair falling in her face.

"What is it?"

"A'm Nabil has been calling for you since this morning. He wants you to come to his house this evening after work. He says it's urgent."

"Everything's always urgent to Nabil. He's a newsman." Abdullah massaged his hairline, felt where the hair had thinned, felt the movement of his loose skin against his skull.

"Why didn't you answer your phone, Baba? I tried calling you a hundred times. And A'mi was upset you weren't in the office or at home. He said it must be nice to be a man of leisure."

"I'll meet him. If he calls back, tell him I'll be there at six p.m. Now please, give me some peace. I have a lot to think about."

"Where's Umma?"

"I'm sure she's with Lamees and Khaled. Nothing to worry about, Mimou. She'll be home soon."

But he wasn't certain. Raja's news troubled him. He knew Rosalie loved Mariam too much to leave without a word.

THE *SAUDI TIMES* offices were on the outskirts of Al Dawoun, just inside the freeway that looped the city like a modern fortress wall, a thin edge between civilization and everything else. Though it was dinnertime, half the building's windows were still illuminated, and Abdullah imagined the stories streaming through the telephone lines, pinging into inboxes. Nabil had worked there since his return from Texas, where he and Abdullah had overlapped by a few years, their scholarships identical, their productivity markedly not. Within five years, Nabil was editor-in-chief of the paper and though the royals financed it, he was fearless in his coverage. In the Kingdom, the *Saudi Times* had become the paper of record. Editorials grew denser, more involved. One of his reporters had his car destroyed after questioning the methods of a radical cleric. When Nabil had married Abdullah's sister, Nadia, the Baylanis had wondered how it would affect their relationship with the al-Saud. But the machine churned on—the contracts flooded in, the foreign dignitaries continued their elaborate, well-rehearsed visits to the big house. The royals knew that bullying did not look good to the outside world.

In a small office on the third floor, Nabil sat waiting for him. He had the shrewd face of a carnivorous bird, all beak and intensity. His hair was dark gray, salted through with white. He was both harried and distinguished as he sorted papers on his desk, his thobe still crisp and immaculately white at day's end.

"Ahlan, brother," Nabil said. "Close the door." He removed the phone from its cradle, placed it down on the desk.

Abdullah sat, already feeling the soreness in his arms from the hours of golf.

"There was a note, slipped under my door last night. A janitor brought it to me. I thought you should see it before anyone else, since it's your man they're talking about." Nabil thrust an envelope at him.

Scanning it quickly, Abdullah tossed it back among the papers on the desk.

"A prank," he said with a snap of his fingers. "I'm going to kill Dan, that son of a bitch. He's trying to get back at me."

"No, I don't think so. I checked with my sources. Ibrahim is in prison, taken a few nights ago. And Coleman wasn't at work today, in case you didn't notice while you were out on holiday."

"You have no idea the kind of week I've had. And I'll tell you, this is nonsense. Somebody's writing a bad screenplay with other people's lives. Be careful here, Nabil."

"Abdullah, yanni, I know this is hard, but I'm going to ask you once, and if I don't get a proper answer, I'll be forced to take this matter to the police. Faisal studied with the sheikh. Is this your son? Is this his note? Now, think, Abdi. Be honest with me."

Abdullah clasped his hands together tightly and thought of his son, of his feverish words at the feast, his defiance, obstinacy, and contempt. And then he thought of his own words, said to his son in anger: *The light of day won't look good on a dead man's face.* Those words, hiding under his tongue, tasting of bitter tea leaves. Nabil was a man who traded in words, whose very livelihood depended on them. The royals feared words nearly as much as they feared bombs.

He felt chastised by the fluorescent light, the chair beneath him, the rug at his feet. To know one had done something terribly wrong. To face it. Did he have the strength?

"Is it him, Abdi? Is it Faisal?"

"Yes. And his friend. Majid al-Urbutiin."

The evening had deepened outside the window of Nabil's office.

"I know your family," Nabil said. "I know the last thing you'd want is police involvement, especially if this is about Ibrahim Ibn Sayid. Since Abqaiq, they're keening for arrests, any arrests." He paused. "I know a man who can help you. Ghassan. A former police officer. He knows Hasa. He knows the towns. And he owes me a turn. He was a source for me. Remember the story we broke after Palm Court? About some police allowing the killers to slip away?" Abdullah nodded. "I kept his identity secret even when I had government men in here leaning on me. He's trained in counterterrorism."

"That's not what this is."

"He's good, Abdi. He'll help you find them, get to the bottom of whatever this is."

"All right," he said. "I'll call him."

All Abdullah heard was the unusual quiet of the city below. His mind a riot in the stillness.

Rosalie. Where was she?

. . .

AT THE BIG house, Mariam sat in the living room, blinds drawn, no light except what escaped underneath the kitchen door. There, where he couldn't see her face, Abdullah told her that everything would be all right. It was what fathers said to daughters. He would dome himself around her, keep her safe and unseeing. They sat together in darkness. She cried; even without details, she understood that her mother would not be back that night.

"Come here, Mimou." He gestured to the spot next to him on the couch.

She shook her head no and went upstairs.

AFTER MARIAM WENT to bed, Abdullah got in the car and drove to Biltagi Brothers'. He parked at the edge of the store's lot, startling when he heard the scramble of wild dogs as he stood and slammed the door. There was a small flashlight on his key ring. He went to the concrete steps and flashed its narrow beam along the seams of the stairs. He wasn't sure what he expected to find—a piece of ripped cloth, a smear of lipstick on the sidewalk? One of the dogs howled, a high, lonely sound that prickled the hair on his arms. Perhaps Rosalie was watching nearby, sniffing him out as he stooped gracelessly by the stairs. His desperation would please her, so would his guilt, his melancholy. He turned quickly toward the black of the abandoned lot, searching for the giveaway, the whites of her eyes.

"Rosalie!" he called after the fleeing dogs, running like a fool to the edge of the parking lot. In his chest, a painful unfurling. He would do anything to please her again. Less a choice than a realization, it was not calculated for any purpose. It was truth.

And then he saw it, partially obscured by the Dumpster: Dan's Hyundai, its B-Corp decal reflecting the thin light from his flashlight's beam.

They were together, then: a boy resembling his son, a woman resembling his wife, a man resembling his best friend. They had gathered in this parking lot, deciding fates, and where had he been?

He asked himself, *Why had she been here?* He waited for anger, a sense of betrayal. Instead, he only found one thought: Protect her, Dan. Bring her back to me alive.

THAT NIGHT, ABDULLAH lay down on the bed Rosalie had recently refused to share with him. He did not sleep, but he did dream, or at least his thoughts unspooled in that dreamlike way of memory. It was a nervous exercise, one he did when anxious about losing certain people. It started with his mother's death, so young when she left him. After she passed—her soul tumbling out into the desert to seek the highest jebel, where Abdul Latif said it would be lifted to heaven—Abdullah had stayed awake in their tent for days, committing every mundane detail of her appearance to memory: the mole like a teardrop at the corner of her left eye, the soft protrusion of her stomach beneath her robe when she leaned forward to stoke the fire or shift the kettle. And then he had worked on the events of their days, the way her voice sounded when she scolded him or his sisters and brothers, the memorization games they would play with suras. The child who missed the fewest words from a verse received the second-best cut of meat at the evening meal.

But where were memories of Rosalie, Texas, and a love that, like most loves, came from nowhere to become, suddenly, everywhere? He waited for the montage of their love to flood his head. He lay on his stomach as he always did, his face pressed into the pillow, which was freshly washed, no trace of Rosalie, and rubbed his palm over the smooth surface. He rolled to his back and tossed the covers off his legs. He closed his eyes, held his breath, felt the quick movement of eyeballs against eyelids. Still, he couldn't conjure any image of her. Could he not have even the torment of memories? Or had he, in the years with Isra, pushed them so far from his mind that he could not now recover them?

"Have some mercy," he said to the darkened room as he sat up.

He dashed down the stairs, away from the scentless pillow and the emptiness of his head.

• • •

IN THE COURTYARD, he found Mariam, who sat facing the pool, chest pressed against her folded legs, chin resting on her knees. Water dripped from her shorts, from the ends of her long hair.

"Faisal used to swim at night, when he thought no one was watching," she said. "Stupid boy. My window looks right out to the pool. Did he think I wouldn't hear his splashing?"

Faisal, the imposter-son, now sleeping or not sleeping under the dirty light of the shrunken moon.

"Idiot boy," she said. She put her head down on her folded arms, croaked a half-stifled sob.

She looked up.

"Do you even remember how it was?" she said.

No, I don't, he thought. Remind me. Help me.

She paused, looked away from him. "I remember when you stopped going on vacation with us. It was because you wanted to be with her, wasn't it?"

"Please," he said. "Things are too difficult right now."

"They're not coming back, are they? They had to get away from you. But they left me here."

"Tell me something you remember about your mother. Please."

She was silent, and he couldn't tell if she was thinking or ignoring him. The pool filter gurgled. She wiped away the water that had gathered at the point of her chin.

"She wore this white bathing suit while we were in France last summer. You weren't there. Neither was Faisal. It was just us. She wore it every day, and each day, her skin got more and more brown. She bought a huge pair of sunglasses from a postcard shop. When she wore them with her bathing suit, she looked like a movie star. A man approached her, even though we'd paid extra to sit in a private area of the beach, underneath a canopy. But he saw her from way down by the water, and he walked right up to our chairs. He gave her his card. At first, he spoke a language I didn't understand; he must have thought she was from his country. Then they switched to

English. She seemed angry, but after a little while, she was laughing. He had a broad face and some gray in his hair. His shirt was very thin cotton, pale blue like smoke. I remember because I had been searching for a dress just that color. His tan was even better than Umma's. When he walked away, she looked over at me, and I looked up from my book like I hadn't been listening. I knew it wasn't polite to eavesdrop. She blew out her cheeks and shook her head. Then she crumpled up the card and tossed it out into the sand. Later, our waiter picked it up and threw it away."

She looked at him, her head tilted to one side. The electricity behind her gaze surprised him.

"What about earlier? When you were a little girl?" He felt desperate. Mariam's story stung, and he welcomed the pain.

"My teacher says it's not healthy to think only about the past. She says that about Palestine. Whenever a girl gets angry, the teacher says, I am not interested in dwelling on the past. It's not healthy. Draw me the future of Palestine."

"It's unrealistic to think about Palestine's future without acknowledging her past."

"Baba."

"I'm sorry. Nothing?"

Another long pause.

"You and Umma going to Tarek's wedding. You were in the kitchen eating peanuts, your mouth was full of peanuts, and you were trying to tell her something. She said, 'The food won't be *that* bad, will it?' and you made your eyes really wide and nodded. She reached over and pinched your ribs, and you spat the peanuts out everywhere, all over her dress and the floor. I thought she was going to scream at you. She'd ordered the dress special from the White Rose, and she'd had Jibran do her hair and makeup. But then you started singing, clapping your hands and sitting back on your haunches like you were trying to do a wedding dance. She reached down and pushed you over, and both of you were laughing. She leaned over the sink trying to catch her breath, and then she washed all the peanuts off her face. I went up to her room with her when she changed. You were so late leaving, and her makeup was ruined, but she didn't seem to care. She rested her head on your shoulder as you walked out the door."

Yes. He remembered that night. The food had been delicious. He'd had bad intelligence from his friend at the Gulf Hotel, who'd told him the family was skimping on dinner. And Rosalie's dress, a gold lace sheath, had smelled of spit and peanut butter, and had to be thrown away. She'd said, mock-scolding, that she'd found peanuts in her undergarments for weeks afterward.

"I've got thousands of things I could tell you about Umma, and a thousand more I couldn't tell you because I can't write or speak them. They're mine. I can't give them to you." She paused. "I won't."

She told him she was hungry. He took this as a hopeful sign. They went inside. Should he wake Yasmin to make them something?

"Umma always cooked my dinner when it was just the two of us."

"Oh."

He'd never known. He was seized by the extreme tenderness of this gesture, imagined his wife slicing onions and chopping garlic, making the kitchen fragrant in his absence. She didn't have to cook—Yasmin had a book of all the family recipes—yet she had chosen to feel the sting of the onions in her eye, smell the pungency of the raw garlic, nick her nails and burn her fingertips, all to feed her daughter. How often? If he were in an honest mood, he admitted he spent more than half his days with Isra. He had never excused himself for these absences. Rosalie understood the sacrifices he needed to make for the business, for their lifestyle. But all along, she was the only one sacrificing anything. Do the sacrifices we make without knowing we are making them count toward heaven? He wondered. If so, Rosalie would be crowned three times over in the gardens of janna.

He put water on to boil. In silence, they waited, his daughter facing away from him on one of the tall kitchen stools that lined the counter. At the first sign of bubbling, he dropped in a package of pasta that he found, almost by mistake, as he combed through the kitchen for something to make. He hadn't cooked once since returning to the Kingdom, a small change he had hardly noticed as they'd settled into their new lives in Al Dawoun.

Mariam swiveled around slowly.

"What would you like on your pasta?" he asked.

"Butter and red pepper flakes, please."

She stared at him with her smooth face, features in just the right places. He and Rose had made this from their union; shouldn't beautiful children beget beautiful life? If only Faisal had fiercely loved his mother as Mariam had, then perhaps she would have been more inclined to generosity. Instead, the boy had been miserly, the love for Rosalie existing in his heart as it does in the hearts of all children for their mothers, but quietly, hidden behind the swell of his newfound ego, the self that was forming each and every day without any help from either of his parents. It was terrifying, and had reached the worst possible outcome: a child turned back against his originators. The stuff of myth, not of life. At least, not of their lives.

He pulled out the butter to let it soften while the pasta cooked. It was a gesture from another lifetime. He and Rosalie would cook together in her tiny apartment on Rio Grande. Neither of them had much talent for it, but they liked to crack open a bottle of cheap wine and brush up against each other in the cramped kitchen. She had liked to make a ridiculous coq-au-vin—said it made her feel sophisticated—though the chicken was always tough and bland, the wine overcooked to a thickening vinegar. Still, they ate it and were happy.

"The spices are over there," Mariam said, pointing to a tall central cupboard.

"I know," he said, though he didn't. He was embarrassed by how little he knew the house.

"Not that one. To the right. The pepper flakes are on the middle shelf, toward the back."

He fumbled past the za'atar, the white pepper, the ground cloves and cinnamon. The shelf smelled like Rosalie returning from the marketplace. The Hadrami jeweler was not accountable for Abdullah's betrayals, though he wanted him to be. Abdullah would go to the shop, buy up his entire inventory. He would shutter the storefront, scatter the jewels in the dirt behind him. Let the women who would collect them from the dust and wear them on their breasts, ears, wrists, necks, feel the weight of his regret.

Using the lid of the pot, he drained the water, let a handful of pasta slither out into the two waiting bowls. On the steaming noodles, he placed a pat of butter. He handed the pepper flakes to Mariam, watched as she dumped what seemed like an unkind amount first into his pasta, then into hers.

"Habibti, that will burn."

"It seems right," she said.

He waited until she had eaten a few forkfuls of the pasta before speaking. She slurped the noodles up into her mouth, and he was reminded that she was still a girl, a child whose brain was rapidly shaping itself with each passing day. But he had to tell her the truth. In case she knew anything at all.

"Mimou, I'm afraid Faisal and Majid have taken your mother somewhere. And Dan Coleman, too."

"On a trip? If they went camping . . ."

"No." His heart fell. She knew nothing. "They left a note with A'm Nabil. They're in hiding somewhere." In the background the boiling water did its hushed work. "Think, Mariam. Do you have any idea where they would be?"

"No." She frowned. Her eyes filled with tears. "Faisal's been so grouchy these last few weeks. We've barely spoken."

She slid off the stool and rushed over, colliding with him in a forceful hug that knocked him back a step. She was crying now, her face buried in his side, her arms tight around him. He squeezed back, stroked her head. He didn't know what to say. Reassurances meant nothing if you couldn't make them real.

After a few moments, she pulled her head back and looked up at him. "I know how we can find out."

"How?"

"I'll post something to my blog," she said, her eyes widening with excitement. "I won't use any names, and I won't mention the situation, but I'll describe them, their cars. It will be like a missing persons report. I'll ask everyone to link to the post, or repost it. I've got four hundred followers."

He nodded, but he wasn't hopeful. Four hundred people were nothing in a nation of twenty-five million. Faisal and Majid could be anywhere, and the Peninsula was vast, but Mariam was already bounding for the stairs. "Come help me write it, Baba. Come on."

The look on her face—plaintive, eager, desperate—made Abdullah put one foot in front of the other until he was upstairs in her room, sitting on a chair by the computer. He would give her this pipe dream, allow her to believe she could write her mother back to her. She wrote using her brother's most obscure nickname, Zizi, and she called Majid only "M," but her physical descriptions of the boys and the cars were vivid and meticulous. For a moment, Abdullah could picture his son exactly as she wrote about him: thin, swimmer's shoulders, large green eyes with heavy lashes, skin the color of wet sand. Sixteen years old. Missing. Wanted back at home. Family worried. If you have any information about his whereabouts, e-mail sauditeen@blogworld.com.

IN THE MORNING, Abdullah went to Isra's to tell her what had happened. He had Ayoub drive him the short distance between the houses, something he had done a hundred times before, but now he asked the man to park in the street, which he never did.

Isra was watering the flowers in the courtyard, wearing jeans and a navy sweater. She'd been wiping her hands on the front of her jeans; dirt and water formed imperfect handprints there. She kept watering while he spoke, but when he came to the part about the kidnapping, how Rosalie had been taken too, she stood up, her mouth gaping, water spilling out of the watering can and drowning the seedling it hovered over.

"You're killing it," he said.

"What?"

He leaned forward and righted the can, then took it from her hand and set it down.

"Your jeans."

"No matter," she said, her long fingers brushing her hair behind her ears. "They're old. You're upset. Let me make you some tea."

She put her hand on his arm.

"Bring Mariam to me. Let me watch her here until you find them."

Slowly, he lifted her hand, placed it gently back by her side. She was so beautiful. He thought of Rosalie, missing somewhere out there, in danger. He couldn't stand to look at Isra.

"Go to your family for a few weeks," he said. "There's no need for you to be part of this mess."

If she stayed, looking as she did, acting as she did, his Isra . . . it would be too much for him. He needed all his energy for Rosalie. He owed her that.

"My love, you're distraught . . ."

"Have Aziz arrange it today."

"Abdullah, be reasonable. I don't want to leave you like this. Your daughter needs someone. You need someone."

"I'll tell you what she needs. She needs her family, and you are not that."

He walked to the courtyard gate and buzzed it open. He turned back toward her. She was magnificent, her generous features even more pronounced in the honest light of early day. Her eyes—topaz, deep-set, and wise—looked at him now as if at a stranger. Perhaps it was what he should have been to her all along. How easily he had called the number on the real estate flyer in Dubai.

How easily she had answered the phone and shown him the two-bedroom flat with the floor-to-ceiling windows that looked out over the glittering city. How easily he had invited her to dine with him. How easy to fall in love with someone. How easy. And then, how hard.

"You can stay here," he said, turning back toward her. "But I don't want to see you. I don't want to see the lights of this house. I don't want to hear you take a single breath."

The sound of it, he thought, would have me back here in a moment, leaving Rosalie to whatever fate God had for her.

ABDULLAH MET NABIL'S contact, Ghassan al-Badeen, in front of the concrete fish at the public beach. Ghassan was kicking at a wax soda cup and examining his cell phone. He was not a garrulous man; they had made their plan in fewer than five sentences. They would start in Al Dawoun and move outward in circles until they had covered the entire Province. It could take weeks, but perhaps the boys would give up after a few days.

"Was he trained?" Ghassan asked. "Some of these boys have been trained."

"I don't think so."

"Don't think, or don't know? It can mean life or death."

"I don't know."

"Do you think he means anyone any harm?"

"No. I don't think . . . no, Faisal would never harm anyone." Quiet boy, studious boy, a boy who wouldn't harm anyone. Abdullah hoped that boy was still there in his son's core.

BEFORE STARTING THE search, Abdullah sent Mariam to stay with her aunt Nadia. He told her to phone him if she received any news from Faisal or her mother. "Or the blog," she said. "Yes," he said. "Or the blog."

Abdullah and Ghassan drove south along the Corniche, past the poor neighborhoods on the outskirts of Al Dawoun. Laundry lines hung along the roofs of the shabby apartment buildings, the clothes waving like faded flags.

"I grew up there," Ghassan said. "Twentieth Street."

He waved his cigarette in the direction of the buildings, which had grown tea-colored with age. The narrow, spider-webbed streets; the small windows in apartments dark as fortresses. It was like being in another country, one whose traditions Abdullah did not understand. The Diamond Mile was as distant from these people as Houston. In the car, there was only the sound of Ghassan's exhalations. After a time, they left the city and entered an open stretch of desert road.

FOR TWO DAYS, Abdullah rode next to Ghassan in his battered white Datsun truck. During their time together, Abdullah had tried to disabuse Ghassan of his assumption that the situation was a kidnapping or an act of terrorism. "Please, Faisal is a good boy," he said again and again. Ghassan listened well. He had a way of acknowledging what was being said, in the occasional tilt of his chin and the way he removed his cigarette from his mouth, exhaling slowly, weighing each word in his mind. He had fine features: a small, pointed nose and sharp, dark brows that gave his eyes a serious quality, and his goatee-framed thin lips disappeared completely when he smiled. He had a calm that Abdullah envied. If only Abdullah had summoned a moment of composure before his outburst to Faisal. If only. The knowledge of his lie about Sheikh Ibrahim sat darkly in Abdullah's heart.

During the search, Abdullah barely slept. They ate ful mudamas and drank Pepsi that Ghassan had packed in a cooler they kept in the truck bed. At night, they stayed with Ghassan's family, scattered north to south along the coast. They were poor people, their air-conditioning units unreliable, their children barefoot as they played soccer in the salty, soggy flats of dirt that stretched between the houses and the sea. Abdullah told them only that his name was Abdullah, and that he was a friend of Ghassan's. In turn, they didn't ask questions beyond what was polite—Where was he from? Would he like coffee? The walls of their houses had large, dirty gashes running floor to ceiling where the water leaked. The children were round-faced and grinning, happy to have a visitor. He patted their heads, showed them his stump, told them the stories of Sadun. At night, alone on his pallet, he thought of their brown eyes like Faisal's, of their loving mothers who stayed in the kitchen while he was there. A simple life; a simple, wretched life. If Rosalie died, he, too, would have a simple, wretched life. Simple because again he would have one wife, one home. He would not have to tell Rosalie about Isra's rounding belly. At the thought of her death—it was true—he felt a small bit of relief. He caught his breath at the realization. That he had done such things that could only be simplified through death; the shame of it was too much. In the morning when he woke, his eyes were sealed shut by the salt of his tears. He cried for her life, that she might live. In life, there could be explanation and apology. In death, he would have only his assumptions, his bitterness, his guilt, and a love with no object but ash and salt.

IN THE TRUCK, Ghassan and Abdullah spent hours rolling slowly through the alleyways of Hofuf; they tracked by foot across Tarut Island; they skimmed the outlying villages asking if any out-of-towners had been by. The Gulf off Dammam was a dizzying blue, the dhows all roped together as the fishermen pulled in their catch and went boat to boat to say good morning, hear the good stories of the day, trade cigarettes. Husbands and wives walked along the Corniche. Children fell from the monkey bars, got back up, and fell again. All this life going on around him as if in a movie—he and Ghassan, lone audience members gliding by, removed from it by steel and glass and purpose.

"When we see them, we'll tell them that Sheikh Ibrahim has been released and then hopefully, they will let Dan and Umm Faisal go, as they promised to do," Ghassan said one afternoon. "Until we can get them into our care, we will let the boys believe that their note precipitated his release."

"But has he been released?"

"Who knows. The way the Family takes and releases political prisoners, it's impossible to keep track."

"I should call Abdul Aziz . . ."

"No, sir. For your son's sake, you cannot. Too much interest in the sheikh could prove dangerous."

"If there is one shot fired, I promise you . . ."

"Sir, you must trust me. I know what I'm doing."

"Yes. Sometimes you policemen know too well. I remember what happened to the men who beheaded Johnson."

"That couldn't be avoided, Sheikh. But as you've said so many times, your son is a good boy. I'm sure he will give us his gun without firing a shot."

"We're talking about a boy who's only fired guns in video games."

"Come, let's go to the car. How old did you say your boy was?"

"Sixteen." Abdullah stood up and for a moment, the blood left his head and swelled his fingertips.

"Hm."

"Why?"

"It's just that you speak of him like he's still a young boy. But then, it is always a little bit shocking. One day they're men, and it's as if you weren't right there in the same house with them."

"I suppose," Abdullah said.

How many times had he been in the same room with Faisal over the last two years? A few times at Iftars and Eids, once for his graduation party, the occasional family wedding. When they found the boy—the stupid, selfish boy, the dear boy—Abdullah would be a father to him. They would walk together down the streets of Al Dawoun, and people would see them and say, *There are the Baylanis. Look how the one grows out of the shadow of the other.*

They left the cool dark of the house where they had stayed the night before and stepped into the bright morning. Abdullah felt insulted by the sun's cheerful blazing.

"I only smoke when I'm nervous," Ghassan said, placing a cigarette between his lips and lighting it. "That's why I keep the pack in the car. I'm often nervous when I drive, when I'm going somewhere I shouldn't be." The cigarette bobbed up and down as he spoke.

"You're nervous now?"

"Yes, I'm a little bit worried for these boys."

"I feel like that's maybe not the best news for me to hear right now."

A truck crawled by; the driver dipped his bearded chin to acknowledge them.

"Why not?"

"For one thing, you just told me to trust you."

"And you can. I think it's good, and necessary, to be a little bit afraid. It means you respect the situation. I felt this way when we got called to Palm Court. I smoked half a pack on the way there. I didn't want to shoot my countrymen, even though I knew what they were doing was wrong. I wanted God to come down and solve the problem for us, to just send away the hostage-takers. In the end, that's what He did, alhamdulillah. A lot of them got away in the confusion. People blamed us afterwards, but it was God's will."

They climbed into the cab of the truck, which smelled of old food, cigarette smoke, and sweat.

"That's not what they wrote in the *Saudi Times*," Abdullah said.

"The truth is often complicated."

"I hope God is with us today."

"You know, I was so surprised the first time my son disagreed with me," Ghassan said, nosing the truck forward in the direction of the main road. "We were talking about the Intifada, and he spoke with such eloquence that I couldn't see him as a child anymore. But he talked, and I listened. I suppose that's what it's about, once they grow up. It's human, that need to be heard."

Abdullah stared out the window. Ghassan's words tapped a

hollow place in his chest, where the memory of conversations with his son should have been. It was a small, egg-sized holding place surrounded by the larger memories of contracts won and degrees earned and dignitaries hosted. His family had been the backdrop to all of the other things. He had become husband and father because that was what men did. A man without family was nothing. He felt the pinch of the egg-sized cavity and scratched at his chest. He would have them back in the car in a day, maybe two. Then, they would go home and let the relief make them giddy and closer than they had been before. When they awoke tomorrow, they would talk and he would listen.

IN HIS EXHAUSTION, Abdullah started to see strange things. For instance: his mother's hands, bloodied from plucking and gutting a chicken. These were not dream images. He knew because, over the preceding days, he had not slept long enough to earn dreams. As an escape from the fact of their mission, Abdullah relished the delicate visions that appeared to him fuzzily, as if transmitted through the Kingdom's early television waves. But then, in his less subdued moments, in a kind of muddy terror, he imagined that his son and wife had conspired to leave him behind—that they weren't hiding somewhere in the Dahna but instead on a plane to London or Dubai, concerned only with putting distance between them and him. His stump ached. He had removed the prosthesis because it had chafed him badly from being left on too long.

Somehow, amidst the sleeplessness and seeming hopelessness of the search, Ghassan managed to smile. Rather than annoy Abdullah, this habit struck him as being the sign of a man who had found some peace in the world's tumult; who was unwilling to give up on joy entirely. Given what he had likely seen as a policeman—the worst of people, the blood of people—this fact was remarkable. "Yes, surely, your Faisal is a good boy," Ghassan said.

But as the third day drew to a close, Abdullah found himself wondering: Who was Faisal? What was he capable of? And aren't fathers owed some kind of intuition, if only to help with the shock of their children's individual actions? Eyes smarting, Abdullah rolled down his window so that the dry air off the Dahna could evaporate the wetness on his cheeks. A cluster of small purple blooms growing from a tangle of desert weed along the roadside bent with the wind. The yolky sun cast its cellophane light off the peaks of the low dunes, creating half-circle shadows, a landscape of closing eyes. Blood, it seemed, was not enough to bind men.

IN THE MORNING, before dawn, he awoke to the incessant buzzing of his phone. He rolled to his side and fumbled for it, pressing it to his ear with his eyes still closed.

"Baba, I know where they are."

It was Mariam.

"What?" He sat up, clutching the phone with both hands.

"They're at Qut al-Wisoum. On the bay."

"How do you know? Are you sure?"

"I just got an anonymous comment on my blog. He said he was a friend of Zizi's, even gave me his birthday as proof. He knew about Umma. Said it was awful and sad. He asked me to delete the comment as soon as I read it."

"Did he say anything else?"

He heard her breathe in, then exhale loudly through her nose.

"He thanked me for my blog. He said he tries to read every post."

He heard the pride in her voice.

"I did it, Baba. I found them. Can I go with you and Ghassan?"

He wouldn't believe it until he had them all piled in Ghassan's truck. They would leave immediately. Wisoum Bay was an hour and a half away. He felt a supreme sense of urgency. He had to hold Rose again. They had not let go completely. Not yet.

"You've done so much already, habibti. Keep A'm Nadia company, and I'll call you as soon as we have them. No, better, I'll have your mother call you."

So they were at the old customs building where he'd taken Faisal as a boy, back when he had still tried to make an effort at fatherhood. Did Faisal remember that trip? Did he think of it now, and did it make him hesitate?

Abdullah prayed that what little he had given his son would be enough to keep him connected to this world, to their family.

TWELVE

MEMORY GATHERING: VACATION. The summer at the château near the Pyrenees. The cold, freshwater pool fed by the springs beneath the ancient farm. She's making a tomato salad for a late lunch. Abdullah has gone to town for a baguette. She looks out the small, old window, peering through the mottled glass to see where the kids are. Mariam has her porcelain doll, the one she's carried all summer. Faisal's waving at her. No, he's falling backward into the pool, his thin arms flapping like bird wings. Mariam screams, drops the doll. Its face cracks in two as if it's been built to shatter all along. Slamming open the shuttered door to the patio, Rosalie slaps barefooted toward the pool. Plunging beneath the bitter cold water, she feels her heart come into her throat. She fumbles in the murk, her toes slipping on the moss. That moment of blind reaching. In the water, his eight-year-old body is light as a wafer. His limbs are caught in the creeping vines that spill into the pool. After she gets his head into the air, she pushes him out into the dirt and climbs out after him, scraping her knees on the rough concrete ledge. When he spits up into her mouth, it tastes like bread spread with sour butter. She clutches him close, thumps his back as if to pound the memory out of him. Umma, I need to learn to swim, he says, choking. He is still so small, she thinks. And for all of my careful watching, darkness found its way to him.

ROSALIE LAY BACK in the dirt and stared at the ceiling of the customs building, where yellow circles of water damage expanded outward from a concentration of mold like rings around a small, rotten planet. She'd been late to Biltagi Brothers' because she was contemplating whether to go. At last, and out of a sense of obligation to Dan, she'd gotten in the car with Raja. These decisions we make in a moment, trying to achieve a desired outcome. Didn't she know better by now? That control is elusive and, almost always, accidental?

When she'd made her escape attempt, she hadn't hesitated. She'd started for the car, turned over the engine, and taken off in the direction of the road. It had taken a great deal of resolve to move at all, given her dizziness and the fact of the gun. But what, in the end, was she struggling toward? The road, yes. But beyond that, what kind of freedom was available to her anymore? She had made the choice to stay in the Kingdom, and choosing required a certain freedom, but once she made the difficult choice, the selfless choice, after the momentary heroism, she realized that the self-sacrifice had only just begun—that more would be required.

The sand was cool at her neck. She listened to the wind moving through the doors. After giving Dan a brief grace period to eat, Faisal had taped Dan's mouth to get him to be quiet, and she could hear him breathing through his nose, a slight whistle with each exhalation. When she looked over at him, she saw he was asleep. She thought of the times she'd gone camping with Zainab and Dr. Salawi when she was a little girl living on the compound. She remembered the dead baby and the khat-chewing village girl, and the moment she had first experienced the fear of being deep in the desert with nothing but Dr. Salawi's jeep linking them to the world. She did not want her time in Arabia to end with that fear. It did not represent the country, or her life there. She needed to know that Saudi Arabia was what she had been searching for those years in Texas. To admit anything else was to reveal the soul's caprice in choosing its direction.

Her body felt light, as if she could close her eyes and float, nose first, to the ceiling. She was barely anchored there. The air was heavy enough that she would just rise and rise, using her bound hands as a rudder. Levitation as escape. She would watch Dan and Faisal and Majid grow very small, until they were dots on the lip of the desert, where it met the Gulf in a sloppy kiss. Then, they would be nothing at all, and she would puncture clouds, sucking in their moisture, bathing her face in their cooling mist, all the while barely breathing, high from the thin air, and forgetful.

Her son, her Faisal. He resisted erasure. He was the reason she had chosen not to flee with Dan, because she knew that in his absence from her life, he would be more powerful than any living, breathing child. His eyes, the color of the flesh of a cucumber, or even the paler seeds within that flesh, always closed tightly when he stepped into the desert sun. She had imagined that his blood vessels were perhaps too active, that they expanded too readily and absorbed too much so that the merest thing—a fleck of dust, a friend's sneeze—would send him into a fit of ill health. But it wasn't just a matter of the body. His heart was overlarge; he expected too much of people, even the world. A few weeks before, she'd come across him crying at the call to prayer. His teenaged moods were unpredictable, or predictably sour. He felt easily wronged, but by turns was easily lifted by approval. Somewhere, he'd started channeling those vulnerabilities into shows of strength. No longer was he the porous adolescent at the mercy of his environment. To dust, to germs, to teasing, to her pleas, he was now impermeable. His heart was a diamond of righteousness.

By the car, she'd seen him falter, an exuberant panic spreading over his face. It was the fear that follows a mistake—a mild consequence compared with the encumbering yoke of guilt that would come with time. She knew, for she now felt those things deeply when she considered her son, a boy made to feel so far outside his family that he would take up a gun before asking any of them for help. It must have been harder for him than she had ever imagined.

Then, of course, after seeing she was unharmed, he'd assumed an eerie calm he had been cultivating since his return from Switzerland. Somewhere, Faisal had learned a stoicism that made her feel as if all the years spent coaxing words from him were a wash. Boys and men and silence—its false, beguiling strength.

"Faisal, I need water." She spoke to his outline in the doorway.

"There's none left," he said without moving.

He sat back on his heels as if he were preparing to eat or pray. For several minutes, he stared out to the water. Rosalie closed her eyes to steady herself but it only intensified the dizziness.

"Please, habibi. Bring me water. I can barely breathe. I've made mistakes, but I don't deserve this. Please. You can't make everything right this way. Our mistakes are only our own."

"This isn't about your mistakes. It's bigger than that."

"I know you have forgiveness in you. I didn't raise you this way." Her tongue was dry, so that she struggled to shape the words.

"No, you didn't raise me to be this kind of man; a man who stands for what he believes in. This is about beliefs."

"Maybe it was, but now it's just us."

"*'Let those who would exchange the life of this world for the hereafter, fight for the cause of God; whoever fights for the cause of God, whether he dies or triumphs, on him We shall bestow a rich recompense.'* "

"Yes," she sighed. Her eyes drooped shut. "Aren't the verses beautiful? Like poetry or songs. Read me verses, please. Read to me, Faisal. I'm tired." She heard his muffled footsteps on the sand.

"Umma, open your eyes." He paused and then palmed her head, giving her a shake. "Wake up."

"Everything is small," she said. With difficulty, she opened her eyes and scanned his face. "Let's go back, Faisal. Let's go home."

"Why did you come here?" he asked. "Didn't you know? Didn't Baba tell you what it would be like?"

She felt as if she were someone very famous and this was a moment in the interview to be dramatized for the sake of her viewers, the ones who longed to know the intricacies of her love life, her simplest domestic choices.

"I was in love." She let the last word float the pitch of the sentence higher. She wanted to make the accompanying gesture—run her hand through her hair, put it on her hip, to punctuate this simple phrase that excused everything. And didn't it? Whether that love was for a place or a person, and regardless of whether that place or person deserved to be its object?

"Promise that you and Baba won't make me go to America."

If she concentrated very hard, she could follow his meaning.

"You're our son. You're our only son. Remember that book we read? The son left the wadi in a caravan, and the mother went crazy. Remember? Her name. I wish I could recall . . ."

"*'Forgiving those who wrong you is a good thing.'*"

"There," she said. "It's the only true thing. Please, get me water."

Faisal shook his head. He took a step inside the customs building, then back out again.

Before she could see him, Rosalie heard Majid returning, the slap of his feet resounding against the hard sand of the beach. Water; she had prayed a hundred blue prayers for water; Muslim prayers, Baptist prayers, yogi prayers. Arabic, English. She knew they were desperate for grace, and she asked for it any way she could.

The two sips a day were barely enough to keep her heart beating, and she could feel her whole body slowing down. Majid would pass the water around and it would taste of the jug's plastic and she would not care and she would not spill a drop. Outside the portico, she heard Majid shouting for Faisal.

From where she sat in the cool shadows of the building's interior, she watched Majid and Faisal standing by the shore. Majid yanked the gun back, and she was glad that her son was no longer responsible for it. Sand crusted her ears, rimmed her nose, and cracked against her teeth. She wondered when and how she would feel clean again.

"What happened to the car?"

"My mother . . . she took it." He hesitated. "She tried to escape."

"Where are they?"

"It's fine. Everything's fine. They're inside." He spoke slowly, each word like a boulder he had to push out of his mouth.

"It's not fine. How could you let this happen?" Majid gave Faisal a shove that sent him stumbling backward.

Majid turned to face through the archway. He grinned at her and his teeth glowed white in the dusk, which had cast the beach in purple shadows. "I think we need to start teaching lessons today."

"Where's the water?" Faisal asked. He sounded as if he would cry.

"There was none. The drought must have dried up the spring. I went as far as I could. So we will be like Hagar and Ishmael. We will ask, and God will provide."

Rosalie's legs felt leaden beneath her. She shifted to try to get the blood flowing. When she pinched her calves to reawaken the flesh, the skin remained in little peaks. Her thirst had become something huge, a space within her body that roared with need.

Majid looked at her and laughed a long, wheezing laugh, so that Rosalie wondered if he were a bit touched by the sun. It didn't seem hot enough for heatstroke, but he had been gone all day. Faisal shifted his weight, a half-smile on his face, a look equal parts eagerness and doubt.

"Can I stand up, please?" she said.

"Yes," Majid said. "Yes, actually. Stand. Both of you stand up, now." He moved toward her, the sand from his steps landing on her arms and neck. He grasped the crook of her elbow and, wrenching her shoulder, pulled her to her feet. He was a full head taller than her, his body like a looming building. She stepped back, swooning a little. Across the room, Dan struggled to stand.

"Move outside," Majid said. "No more hiding. We're going to take care of something right now. We're going to do something that we should have done when we first got here."

Majid dragged her past Faisal and out into the fading daylight.

The Gulf was the color of a new bruise, edged in dark blue. Rosalie scratched her scalp, felt the sand lodge beneath her fingernails. What would it be like to dive into the bay and swim along the seafloor, clutching at the cool mud and feeling nothing but the movements of the Gulf: the whisper of fins, the silent pirouettes of jellyfish. She would open her mouth and swallow bathtubs full of water. She would move through sunken gardens of seaweed.

"Where are you taking her?" Faisal said.

"You stay here and watch Coleman. I'm going to make sure she doesn't try to escape again."

Majid tightened his grip on her elbow. Hours before, her whole body had begun a slow shaking—shivers of hunger and sleeplessness and a low-grade fever. Now, fear. She hoped that Majid could not feel the pulse of her delirium, which moved through her body to make her feel that she was standing up out of a chair too quickly, her surroundings turning black as she waited a moment for the blood to reposition itself.

Majid continued, "And I'm going to give her plenty of time to consider the crimes she committed against your family."

"Wait, Majid," Faisal said. "I think maybe you misunderstood. It's not like I thought . . ."

"I understand what happened; you told me yourself. Remember your anger, brother? I won't let anyone treat you that way, not even your mother."

"But she wasn't even supposed to be here. It was an accident."

"No, I think God has arranged it this way. We were meant to discover them at the market. It was the only way to get you to act."

The waves continued their shushing. Yes, thought Rosalie. Quiet. Please, just be quiet.

"Please, Majid. I didn't actually *see* anything at the house."

"You saw the ticket and the visa. They were going to run away together."

Majid's face had a yellow tinge to it, the color of chicken fat pooling on the surface of a boiling broth.

"I'm telling you, leave her out of this," Faisal said. "What she has done or not done is for God to judge."

Rosalie watched Faisal's face twist into an angry knot. With his free hand, Majid reached down and grabbed the shovel that sat among the other supplies along the wall of the building.

"Let's go."

"Ya Majid, you're making a mistake," Faisal said. "They're not coming for us. We should go home."

"Don't try to interfere, friend. You've obviously forgotten our purpose here."

"Our purpose? It's been five days and still you talk about purpose. You're fooling yourself if you think that anything we do here has meaning anymore." He was close to shouting, breathing heavily as he spat out the words. "They're not coming, Majid. No one's coming."

It surprised her to hear Faisal raise his voice, especially to Majid. In all sixteen years of his life, she had never heard him be gruff. He had learned to talk a year later than most children, and even then, he spoke so quietly that she had to lean in close to his tiny mouth to catch the whispered words. His Arabic was like sheets tumbling in the dryer—the language of poets and soothsayers. When she found herself close to his face trying to hear him, she would kiss his cheek and breathe in the smell of his soft baby skin. She'd heard that softness again after he'd fired on her in the car; a boy calling for his mother to lean in close. He was a boy, a searching boy. She saw it in his face, which was not prepared to reflect tragedy; she saw it in his shoulders, which were not prepared to bear tragedy.

Majid looked at Rosalie and smirked. "Come on." He yanked her toward the water, pushing the shovel into the sand like a walking stick. She looked back at Faisal, whose arms were folded across his chest. Dan was standing, but he was swaying gently back and forth like he was starting a samba or a faint. Although the sun was setting over the desert, the air was still hot. Now she was moving forward, stumbling along toward the ruins of the Ottoman fortress that stood adjacent to the customs building. She wanted to put her tongue to the chalky stone, taste the salt of four hundred years of sea air. Her brain was in a fog. A gulp of water per day. How long had they been on the Bay? Days? Weeks? She was no longer sure, time spooling out in a dizzying zigzag.

"Hey! Ya Majid. Shway shway. Where're you taking her?"

Faisal had caught up to them and trotted beside Majid. He was pulling Dan along beside him; Dan had been given the least water among all of them, when he probably needed the most. His skin was ashen, and before his mouth was taped, he hadn't spoken but to ask for something to drink.

"I'm going to make sure things don't get out of control again," Majid said.

"You're not going to hurt her?"

"La. Just a lesson, as I told you. To remind her that, by her actions, she's made herself lower than the dirt on the ground. Go back to the customs building."

But Faisal did not go back. He hovered a few steps behind them. Rosalie glanced back, but Faisal's gaze was fixed on Majid. They arrived at the fortress's crumbling wall, and Majid leaned Rosalie against it. He began shoveling the sand. The corners of his mouth were white. The dry surface layer of sand caught the wind and blew away from them, but as he went deeper, the sand became moist, clumped together in heavy shovelfuls.

"There," he said after a few more minutes. He threw the shovel down and dusted off his hands. In one swift movement, he was in front of her. He picked her up, his arms so tight around her that she couldn't breathe.

"Please," she gasped. "Please."

He placed her on her knees in the pit he had dug, and all around her was cool sand. She was eye to eye with the bay's small, breaking waves, and for a moment, she felt protected, tucked into the earth and away from Majid. But as he started to dump sand in around her, a sense of panic returned, and she flung her bound arms out onto the sand, desperate to hold on to something.

"Bismallah, Majid," Faisal said. "Stop. Bas!"

Majid turned to him and whacked him on the throat with the side of his hand. "She's been with someone who wasn't your father!" he yelled. "And you're *defending* her? Where's your sense of honor?"

Gripping his neck, Faisal gasped for breath.

"Ya Allah!" He tried to swallow. "I don't *know* what happened between them! That's just it. I . . . all I know is that she was leaving."

Rosalie felt very hot, and briefly, her vision blanked so that the water and the customs building and Majid's feet were just an empty, whitewashed room. She closed her eyes.

"Perhaps Coleman can explain. Perhaps, then, there's a perfectly good explanation, eh? Is that what you think, ya Faisal?" Majid tore the tape from Dan's mouth. Immediately, spots of blood appeared along his lips. He was silent.

Majid turned back to her triumphantly. "It's truly a miracle that Faisal came to be the way he is, living in your household."

She opened her eyes, and the images separated out again.

"You have no idea about our household. We had love in our household. That boy was loved; he is loved."

"Children need more than love. They need examples."

"This isn't part of our message," Faisal said. "We can't try people for morality crimes."

"Leave her and follow me back inside. If you still believe in our message; if you still believe in Sheikh Ibrahim's right to live."

"Faisal," she said.

She watched her son. He was an obedient boy. For those in power—parents, teachers, imams, kings—obedience was a good trait. But to the weak, the oppressed, the subjugated, obedience only meant more of the same, the continuation of the status quo.

Just then, Rosalie did not want her son to be obedient, a good foot soldier. She wanted him to be a human being, to draw upon the strength of his own instincts to say *no*.

"Come now, yallah," Majid said. "For the sheikh."

Dropping the shovel in the sand, he nodded in the direction of the customs building. He took Dan by the elbow and began walking away. Rosalie felt the sluggishness of her blood as it moved thickly through her veins. Would the desert take them all? With all the breath left in her chest, she groaned. Faisal turned around to look at her. .

"Zool . . ." She needed to get out. Immediately. The pressure of the sand was unbearable. With every remaining bit of energy, she heaved against it, felt her eyes bulge with the pressure, but there was no give. "Zool!"

She heard retching, saw Majid doubled over, wiping his mouth with the back of his hand.

"You need help," Dan said to him. "We all need help."

"Don't talk to me," Majid said.

Rosalie let her head loll to one side; she was too tired to hold it upright any longer. In the distance, she saw the blinking red light of a tanker. The blinking light moved in time with her heart, but she knew—knew with cold certainty that it was moving away from her.

And then Faisal's feet appeared in front of her. She strained her neck upward, saw him holding the shovel suspended in front of him like a pendulum, as if he weren't quite sure what to do with it. Biting his lip, he started to dig.

"Yes," she said. "Please."

"Faisal, stop!" Majid said. He turned toward them, tried to run back while still holding on to Dan and gripping the gun. "They will listen to us. Somebody will hear us, have patience. I have seen too many people die—so many of our innocent brothers and sisters. This will send a message. Stop!"

Now Faisal knelt in the sand, the shovel fallen at his side. With deliberate movements, he scooped the sand away from her neck and shoulders and then leaned in close, burying his face in her hair. He drew a long breath and, through the dirt, smelled her as she had always smelled—like skin and soap, and more faintly, like a kitchen full of cooking things: salts and oils, a faint smell of garlic. *Mother*, he thought.

Inside his boot, Faisal felt his grandfather's dagger cold against his leg. That night he'd taken it from his father's study seemed millennia ago, from a time before his family, before his tribe, when the sea covered the peninsula. From a time when he was a mollusk waiting to be buried under a thousand layers of earth, waiting to sludge into something more valuable. Everything that happened before this moment in time did not matter. He scooped the sand away from his mother's neck. Her eyes were closed, her head tilted to the side.

He was telling her to wake up when he felt the blow of the shovel against his back. With a grunt, he fell forward, and then Majid was on top of him, shoving his face into the sand. "*I told you to stop!*" Majid said. They rolled over, pushing each other away and drawing each other close as they moved. But Faisal had the dagger in his hand and then it was only a matter of physics: Majid's belly, and Faisal's left arm long and taut like a catapult—a slash, and then Majid's red blood. The gun fell into the sand. Faisal dropped the dagger and closed his hands around Majid's neck, feeling the slick blood between them as he pressed closer. Majid was weak and getting weaker. Faisal's fingers dug easily into his throat, and he watched Majid's bloodshot and tearing eyes bulge with the pressure.

With his hands bound, Dan could do nothing more than pummel the tumbling bodies. *Oh God*, *please*, Dan thought. An elbow to the chin sent him reeling backward. They might have just been two boys wrestling, but for the blood that stained their clothes. Dan grabbed the half-buried knife and sat back on his haunches, trying to maneuver it against the tape on his wrists. He dropped it and picked it up again several times before placing the handle between his shaking thighs and moving the tape against the blade. Once freed, he pumped his elbows to rock himself to his feet. Now the boys were on the sand, each struggling to pin the other down. Majid had the size, but Faisal the fury, and so they rolled and grunted, slapped and spat. Again, Dan moved forward to try to split them apart. Faisal was sitting on Majid's chest and had nearly submerged his head in the rushing tide. Majid made gurgling baby sounds and did not move his arms. Dan grabbed Faisal under the armpits and pulled with all his remaining strength.

"Stop!" he shouted. "Stop, Faisal." But the boy wouldn't let go.

Dan yanked down hard on Faisal's hair, so his head jerked back.

"Let go," Dan said. "You don't want this." He pulled Faisal up and away from Majid, who lay still, the water floating his hair around his head. Dan put his hands under Majid's body and lifted him up, his back straining beneath the weight of the wet boy, who was no longer a boy but a body. He placed his cheek near Majid's mouth. He did not feel breath.

But Dan had not predicted the whispery rush in his ears, the cascading words of Majid's lifetime of prayers, a sound like eucalyptus leaves moving with the wind as they left his mouth, not words, but an unmistakable wave that was beyond language. Dan did not know that Faisal also heard the sound. At first, they heard only the familiar swishings of a young man's prayers for his family; that they might be secure and safe. *Please, God, make my wife beautiful and good and full of love for You; let me know true love as you have given it to us here on earth;* and *please, Almighty God, I know that the Prophet, peace be upon Him, has said there is no shame in poverty, but please show me how to find dignity within it, at least for my mother.* Then, they heard specific pleas—*Oh please, God, do not let me hit my shin on this chair one more time!* And for a toilet that worked, for enough money to buy meat for all of them, not just the youngest children; that he might be a provider, *a leader for this family, so that we might not be lost.* As they heard the word "provider," both Dan and Faisal saw a figure cloaked in gold spreading its arms, but they would never know they had both seen this, simultaneously, while at the beach at Wisoum, for they kept it to themselves, attributing the visions and the strange whisperings to their hallucinatory dehydration.

Finally, they heard the rattlings of fear, a young man praying for guidance as he and his older cousin found their way from Yemen to Syria, then across the Syrian border and into Iraq; the prayer of pain when he spilled cooking oil down his arm as he made dinner at the camp near the banks of the Euphrates, the oil leaving a pink, banana-shaped scar from his wrist to just above his elbow; and then, three weeks later, more prayers as he scrambled back across the border of Iraq and into Syria, in flight from those men who would have made him nothing more than a puff of smoke inside a Shi'a mosque, as they had his cousin: *Brother, they are not Muslims; they are with the occupiers now, not with God. They must be stopped. You must stop them. You will do it at the noon prayer, the busiest time.* Together, Dan and Faisal felt his disgrace when he arrived home without the martyrdom money that would have provided for his mother and siblings for the rest of their lives, but as Umm Jalal never knew such money existed, she kissed him and cried out to him. Dan and Faisal felt her kiss as a breeze prickling their skin. Then they felt the weight of Majid's cowardice as it had felt to him. They knew his shame at being a poor man in a rich man's country. And at last, they both felt death surge through them, and then the silence of life's end.

Dan set Majid on the sand, out of reach of the tides. Faisal's face was a blank, but his shoulders were square, even proud in the dwindling light. Faisal would have to learn the posture of tragedy. To be young was to be arrogant about how much one could bear. Faisal ran back toward Rosalie, placed his fingers at her neck where he thought her pulse should be. It was strong, but her eyes remained closed when he took up the shovel and began to dig.

He did not think of the violence he had committed. He did not see the gun or the dagger. He did not see the crosshatching of tiny veins on his mother's eyes. There was no immediate world. There was only the memory: his mother, her red hair shining like its own sun, sitting at the edge of the courtyard fountain. *Faisal, come and see.*

He was not more than two years old, and still, he hadn't said a word. Her hands lifting him up. The cool, still surface of the fountain. A water bug's spindling legs, six pinpricks on the mirror of water. He had known to be quiet, to let the sun grow hot on his back, to hear the sound of his mother breathing, to watch the delicate thing as it did the impossible and walked across the water. Together, they were so quiet and so alive. When it moved away, she drew her white fingers through the water and it made a sound like coins jingling in a pocket. She touched the side of his face with her wet finger and drew him close so that he could smell her clean blouse, feel its smooth silk against his cheek.

With Dan's help, he pulled her from the earth. He placed his wet hands on her forehead.

"Umma."

Her eyes opened slowly; she blinked several times, as if she had been sleeping.

"Majid's dead," he said.

Faisal took her arm and together, they stood and moved to the water's edge. There, she shook the sand from her clothing, rinsed her arms and legs clean. He bathed his bloodied hands, wet the back of his neck. He removed the soiled white T-shirt he had been wearing since their arrival five days before. He set the T-shirt on the sand and knelt down, his back to the water. His mouth moved, but no sounds came out. He stood and kneeled, stood and kneeled, his eyes open. Then, he turned and ran out into the small waves until it was too deep to run. Diving forward, he swam, his face bathed in the salty water, his arms churning the surface that had turned pale pink with the dawn. He felt the familiar rhythm of his strokes. When you cannot sleep, swim. When you cannot live, swim. Turning onto his back, he floated there, looking into the sky that held the shrinking day.

BACK ON SHORE, Faisal supported his mother as they walked toward Dan. In his arms, she seemed insubstantial. She was small in a way he had never noticed when she stood erect in front of him, her chin held at that insistent angle. He had allowed himself to be annoyed by her habits whether or not he understood them, just because they were hers, American. How he had hated her difference, for it meant one thing: his own.

At the near horizon, pearling boats moved like wooden toys. The ruins continued their silent erosion, the wet salt air drying on the porous stone, insinuating itself into the tiny fissures that spelled the structure's doom. The three of them stood looking at one another in silence. After several minutes, Dan set his hand on Faisal's shoulder.

"Let's go home," he said.

Faisal stepped away, then swayed to one side before toppling over. Behind his eyelids was starred blackness, occasional colors moving across his line of sight as if refracted from a crystal lodged in the center of his skull.

"Here. Take my hand." Dan leaned over him and saw that his face was an unnatural red. He glanced up and down the shoreline, then inland toward the Dahna. Once, he had felt that all that sand, all that blankness, meant freedom; it had represented a chance for the rewriting of self. Now Dan knew that the desert would kill them if they didn't leave immediately.

"We've got to start walking for the road," Rosalie said.

"We should put him inside until we can come back for him." Dan nodded toward Majid's body.

"Let the gulls have him," Faisal said.

"Let us give him some dignity in death," Dan said.

"Only the lucky few have dignity in death," Faisal said. He paused and tried to swallow, but his throat was too dry. "We'll leave him."

"Life doesn't offer us many moments of grace, Faisal. We have a choice."

"Yes, and I choose to leave him out there."

Faisal hung his head and put his thumb and forefinger to his temples, gently massaging them.

"I'm so tired," Faisal said.

"I know." Dan paused. "Let's bring him in."

They laid Majid a few feet inside the door, careful not to disturb the wound that threatened to open up like a glistening, bloody flower. Faisal took a moment to look into his friend's face, where the mouth had relaxed into a scowl. Bruises had formed at his neck, and the blood had crusted across his abdomen. In making his plan, Faisal had not considered that violence could be senseless, the instrument of nothing at all.

Squatting down, he took Majid's hand and examined the nails, which were ragged and dirty. Once, those hands were folded in prayer. Now, the nails would blacken, the skin would melt away, and the bones turn to dust. And for what?

Dan crossed Majid's arms over his chest, then covered the boy's face with a T-shirt. Faisal didn't watch him as he did this, instead looking out at the water.

When they left, they did not look at one another, and they did not look back. They left the body. They left the propane stove and the shovel, the empty gallon containers and the crumpled rice sacks. They left the rotting dhow and the crumbling walls of the Ottoman fortress. They left the customs building with its lighted archways and dank walls. They left the ghosts of traders and tribesmen, soldiers and emirs. They left the fine dust of a century of insects. And they left other things along the bay of Wisoum, things too delicate to name—subtler than the movement of the waves along the shoreline, invisible as the spirit of a boy rising over the Gulf.

THIRTEEN

ABDULLAH WATCHED GHASSAN as they barreled down the highway. The man was a marvel of concentration, his hands pale where he gripped the steering wheel, his eyes focused on the road as he wove in and out of traffic. Abdullah's heart beat more rapidly as he thought about the possibility of finding them. Dan's car at Biltagi Brothers', Faisal's accusations—none of it mattered now. In his days with Ghassan, Abdullah had felt jealousy and anger slipping away from him, felt his very self disintegrate in the homes of Ghassan's people, where he was only another Abdullah. To them, Baylani was just a word they saw on buildings, on ships. Here, it was no longer about possession or power. It was about survival, his family's and his. Did he want to see Rosalie again? The answer was yes. The answer was always yes.

"We've wasted our time in those Hofuf alleyways," Ghassan said. "All this time, they've been at Wisoum." He shook his head. "How did you say your daughter discovered their location?"

"Her blog. Someone wrote on her blog."

"Eighteen years as a police detective and now a computer can do my job. Unbelievable. Beautiful. Your daughter should join the force."

"She's not very good at following orders," Abdullah said. He laughed weakly.

They drove the last hour in nervous silence.

"I see Wisoum," Ghassan said. "Do you see it, sir? Just off to the left." He pointed toward the Gulf.

Abdullah's breath was coming in shorter now, his heart hammering in his ears.

"It's another ten kilometers to Wisoum from here," Ghassan said. "We're going to park out of firing range and use the megaphone. You must stay inside the car, no matter what happens."

"I understand," Abdullah said.

Abdullah shut his eyes and prayed. The car slowed, the tires catching on the road's loose gravel. He opened his eyes. He saw them before Ghassan could point them out. They were a kilometer or so away. They did not show any sign of having seen the car. Ghassan rummaged under the seat and pulled out binoculars.

"Here, you look and tell me if that's them."

Abdullah got out of the car. He ran to the driver's side and yanked the binoculars from Ghassan's hands. It was Dan, Faisal, and Rosalie.

"Yes, yes, it's them," he said. "Please, drive me there."

"I apologize sir, but we have to proceed according to the plan. They might have weapons."

"No, it's just them. You don't understand. It's only them."

Abdullah dropped the binoculars and took off down the slope that led from the road into the basin of the desert. As he ran, his sandals slid off his feet. *Sir! Sir!* Ghassan called. The sand was hot on Abdullah's feet. He hiked his thobe up in one hand. He felt his ghutra and aghal slide off his head. Bare-headed and thudding across the desert, Abdullah kicked up sand in great brown splashes.

"Hey!" Abdullah called. "Hey!"

As he ran, he waved his hands back and forth over his head. The car started up behind him; Ghassan honked, but Abdullah continued his tear toward them, closing the distance until he could see their dirty faces. They had stopped moving.

Abdullah yelled out, though there was no longer any need. They did not answer back, just stood there mutely. He stopped. The car stopped behind him, the door opening and shutting, sharp sounds in the absorbent desert. There was shouting. Faisal moved into Abdullah's arms. Baba Baba Baba, he said. I'm sorry I'm sorry I'm sorry I'm so sorry. You told me they would kill Ibrahim. You told me.

Only Faisal's head on Abdullah's neck told him that it was not a waking dream. The boy sobbed but no tears fell. "It's OK," he said. "Everything's OK."

"But Majid . . ." Faisal said, the sounds muffled by Abdullah's collar.

Abdullah pushed his son to arm's length so he could see his face. "What? What's happened to him?"

"He's dead." A pause. "I killed him."

Abdullah stared at his son, then looked left over his shoulder as if to make sure the desert was still behind him. Finally, he looked back at Faisal, who was only a dark outline against the pale sand behind the blur of tears that had gathered in Abdullah's eyes. He put his hands on his knees and hung his head.

"It shouldn't have come to this," he said.

Faisal, unaccustomed to seeing his father in any sort of yielding posture, rushed at Abdullah and gave him a hard shove. Abdullah fell to his knees. He was so tired.

"You told me they would kill Ibrahim." Faisal moved both hands through his hair and glanced around in desperation. Then he sat down in the sand and folded himself down over his knees. "Beat me!" he shouted. "Tell me I've done wrong."

Over Faisal's bent head, Abdullah met Rosalie's eyes. She was alive. They would have their apologies, their explanations. They would go on. They would all go on, together.

. . .

GHASSAN DROVE THEM to the customs building, where Faisal had said that they would find Majid's body. Faisal and Rosalie rode up front, Abdullah and Dan in the bed of the truck. When they arrived, when he saw the body lying still in the dark of the building, Abdullah's stump throbbed, and for a moment, he felt that it was 1967. It was one memory of pain, and to that stockpile, a lifetime's accumulation, he would now add this: the salt from the sea stinging his nose as he watched his son crouch over his friend's lifeless body, lay his head on the boy's bare chest and sob.

He watched Rosalie, her hand pulling at her collar. He would be more careful with his threats; he would be more careful with his promises. He would not want as much. Rosalie. His wife. A shadow of gold at the inner eyelid. The faint heat of another body in the bed. He covered his mouth.

Ghassan looked out to the bay. It embarrassed him to see this powerful man whom he had once only read about in the papers made silent by grief. Gulls dove to peck at cuttlefish dry and bleached as bones. Ghassan crushed his cigarette into the sand next to a large black beetle, lit another one.

AT THE HOSPITAL, the ragged group received bags of fluid from careful doctors who knew only that the party had spent too long under the desert sun. While he waited for them to finish their treatment, Abdullah decided he would make no mention to Dan of Biltagi Brothers' or Faisal's accusations. In the truck, beneath a tarp, Majid lay stiffening. With death still so close, Abdullah understood jealousy to be a concern for people who had the time to be injured, to entwine themselves in all the impossible postures that surrounded love but were not themselves love.

BACK IN THE truck, Faisal asked: "And the sheikh? What about Ibrahim?"

"I'm sure he is safely at home," Ghassan said, though he was not sure of anything. A man arrested for crimes of dissent could go missing for years, until his family forgot the features of his face. Then, when the interrogators grew tired of bouncing him from prison to prison, they would turn him out into the street, stunned and blinking. With all of the years of freedom they had stolen from the wrongfully imprisoned, the al-Saud could build an army of centenarians.

Night had fallen. Dan and Abdullah rode in the back of the truck on either side of Majid's corpse. Lights blinked from the tops of the electricity towers, which were staked into the sand from horizon to horizon. Abdullah did not bother to pull his ghutra across his face to protect it. He closed his eyes and let the strong wind push and pull the skin of his face. Dan watched the darkness, content to let his eyes swim over the invisible passing landscape. Occasionally, he looked over at Abdullah. He could be a camel herder coming home after a long day spent manipulating the unruly beasts and drinking camel's milk with his Sudanese workers. There were simpler ways to live than what Abdullah al-Baylani had chosen for himself. For all of them, there were simpler ways to live.

Feeling Dan's eyes on him, Abdullah glanced up.

"We will pay the family reparations," Abdullah said, placing a hand on the tarp. "Even though Faisal was defending his mother, we will pay. The boy is still someone's son. We won't go to the authorities with the note. No reason for the families to bear that shame in addition to this tragedy."

Dan nodded, but he wasn't thinking of Majid. He was thinking of Rosalie and what was left for her.

AFTER HE LEFT the family in the driveway of their home, where Abdullah leaned in and made his request for Majid, Ghassan drove Majid's body to the al-Urbutiin home. At the door, he rang the bell. While he waited, he looked over the note that had been dropped at the *Saudi Times*. Was there anything more futile than a demand, with its sad showmanship, its desperate arrogance? Countries demanding; people demanding; kings demanding; armies demanding; terrorists demanding; and guns demanding. And always met by silence or aggression, never solutions.

A fat young man answered the door. He had a softer face than Majid, but it was clear they were brothers. Ghassan unfolded the note, held it where the brother could read it.

"Your brother has died for his cause," Ghassan said. He heard a woman cry out—the mother, hidden in shadows. He swallowed, then continued. "He kidnapped innocents. It's what the authorities would call hiraba, an action against the state. Sometimes, in the courts, this gets the sword. In a way, your brother is lucky; he will not bring you shame. You can bury him in privacy."

"Will there be blood money to pay for my brother's life?"

The mother shouting bitterly, no, no, la, la. A rhythmic pounding on the walls.

"He was killed by an act of self-defense. There are witnesses. There is no diyya owed, but the Baylanis will pay your family for the loss. A gesture of good faith. Let us keep this between families."

The brother looked down at the floor, his mouth slightly open. From within, the long whine of an exhaled sob. Ghassan wondered if he had understood him. At last, the boy looked up and nodded.

"I will help you with the body," Ghassan said.

Jalal walked with him out to the truck. A few cats had found their way into the truck bed. The boy hissed and pounded the side of the truck to disperse them. He pulled the edge of the tarp down to reveal his brother's face, now sunken and dull-skinned.

"Ya Majid," Jalal said in greeting, the second syllable of the name swallowed by his cracking voice. My brother, he thought. You rode your passions down the wrong street. And now. Now.

WHEN HE CLOSED his eyes at night, Faisal dreamed in the white of mourning clothes, in the silver of the blade, in the red of his own blood. When he awoke, he felt the chill of his deeds settle around him. He prayed five times a day, and in between those prayers, he prayed more. He prayed for forgiveness from God and from the families, including his own. When he felt particularly lonely, he prayed for Majid—prayed that he appear to him in his room so that Faisal might hear his bossy, teasing voice again—so that he might be made to feel important, like his destiny would somehow take him further than Al Dawoun and the big house and the small pleasures of his car and his video games. With Majid, Faisal had gone further than his own thoughts. He supposed that was what friendship was, in the end.

Didn't you wonder how they found you? Mariam asked one day.

No, he answered. It was God's will.

It was Hassan, she said.

It was God's will, he repeated.

I missed you, you foolish boy, she said.

I missed you, too, he said. He clutched her close to him.

FOR A WEEK, Rosalie did not leave the living room of the big house except to relieve herself and shower. On the embroidered couch, she slept, took her meals, watched television with Mariam and, occasionally, Abdullah. At first, she had considered going to her bedroom; she was so tired she wanted to sleep for days. But then she had been jolted by fear. If she went to her room, all the living would take place around her. Abdullah and Faisal would use her absence as permission to go on as they had before. So she stayed in the living room, in the heart of the house.

On the couch at night, she pulled the blanket up under her chin, watched the moonlight filter in through the linen curtains. For a brief moment at Wisoum, she had wanted to die, so she would not be forced to return to the indignities of her life. But now, here she was, and what would change? She could not float on as if nothing had happened. Her son had thought he hated her enough to take her by force into the desert, and he had killed another boy, his best friend, when he realized he did not. In the aftermath, their family was living under the same roof like warped puzzle pieces that once fit together. What to do? What on earth was she to do?

ABDULLAH GATHERED HIS sisters together at the big house. Dina, Nimmah, and Nadia were to tell their sister-in-law about Isra's pregnancy. Abdullah thought that, if the words were spoken among women, Rosalie would see that a baby meant only love and happiness for a family, no matter how it found its way into the world. When they first met Rosalie, the sisters had not liked her, but over time they came to love her after seeing the galloping way she adored their brother and her children. Secretly, they had sympathized with her after hearing about Isra, but their husbands had told them to mind their own business, so they had not taken sweets to her, as they had wanted to do, nor had they invited her over to take tea or coffee, for fear that this would be seen as interfering. Instead, they had kept close watch over their own husbands until they regained the certainty that their men would not make the same reckless choice as Abdullah. Their pity and sympathy for Rosalie was like a flower that the women of the family had tended.

"A baby," Nimmah said between bites of a biscuit.

"Your family is growing," Nadia said. "Think of it as your family growing."

"After all that has happened," Dina said. "A baby means so much. It means life goes on."

The sisters were surprised at her calm.

"You're not angry?" Nadia said.

"I am," Rosalie said. "But anger is useless to me now."

DAYS PASSED, FEBRUARY became March. Rosalie remained in the living room. One morning, Faisal came to see her. He looked thin in his thobe, his eyes grown too big for his face. As she looked at her son, Rosalie felt the same tenderness she had always felt for her boy. Though for a period, she would love him but without fondness. She was permitted that. She saw traces of her face in him—the light eyes, the high cheekbones. She opened her arms to him and he moved close to her. He let himself be held—it was the only way he knew to be forgiven.

"Sweet Faisal," she said. She kissed his temple.

When she stepped back from him, he would not look her in the face, and she knew: They had to send him away. The prince had called Abdullah to check in. He wanted to make sure his instructions were taken seriously. Rosalie was glad Faisal would have to go. How else does one learn compassion than through suffering? To have your mother's love no matter what, your family's love no matter what, to be always among your own people, like surrounded by like, to be always in the majority and loved. These things weren't good for a man's spirit, not if the man wanted to learn humility, or how to give love, or tolerance. After Wisoum, perhaps he would be ready to learn.

She steered his chin in her direction. He blinked, hesitant, then met her gaze.

"You're going to leave this house," she said. "You're going to leave this country."

She understood that she must empty their lives, hers and Abdullah's, in order to see what was left between them. She knew Abdullah would agree to it because she sensed a change in him—a willingness to listen, a desperation to please her.

"We'll find a school nearby for Mariam. She needs it too—the leaving. We'll send her before summer. I know the perfect place. You can visit from time to time. You'll take good care of her, won't you, Zool? You'll need to take good care of her."

A breeze came in from the courtyard, where he'd left the sliding-glass door open to the cool morning. He felt it, her quiet withdrawal. The air blew right through his thobe.

WHEN DAN FIRST arrived back at Prairie Vista after Wisoum, he had picked up the phone and called Carolyn because she was the only person in the world he could imagine talking to at that moment. He'd told her what had happened and she had cried for them. She had asked him, did he remember when they were all young and indomitable, borne up by their belief that life held for them a singular destiny? They had believed that, the four of them: Rosalie, Abdullah, Dan, Carolyn. They were young, and they believed in their unimpeachable greatness. On the phone, he'd asked Carolyn: What if I had died? Would you have cried? And she'd said my God, Dan, what kind of a question is that? And there was a comfort in that. He told her that he would arrive in Austin in six weeks' time and she said she would drive out from Santa Fe and be there to pick him up at the airport. He knew they would not be together in the real sense, that there had been too many hard things said in the intervening years, but goddamn if it didn't mean something to have someone there to pick you up at the airport.

FAISAL AND ABDULLAH got into the car and drove to Majid's grave. Banyan and fig trees shaded the site, where the dirt still possessed the darkness of being recently turned. The wind had picked up, bringing with it a host of billowing gray clouds. It was mid-February and had not rained in more than three months, an anomaly in wintertime. The newsmen had promised a cold front—rain, perhaps a shama'al first. But for now, the heat weighed heavily on the men's shoulders, the clouds casting shadows whose edges bled like wet ink around the graveyard.

"Baba," Faisal said quietly, his voice barely audible above the rising wind. He did not look up from the grave.

"Na'am."

"I'm so sorry. For causing this."

"You were defending your mother. Before God, you are free. You must live like it. You must stop apologizing. We are both responsible for what happened."

"Na'am, Baba."

"Sheikh Ibrahim is still in prison somewhere. There's no record of his arrest."

"He's a good man," Faisal said. "He gets carried away sometimes, but he's a good, faithful man. I'll start a petition for him."

"No. They might withhold your passport. Let me. I will see what I can do." Abdullah paused. "You're not the first young man to let his anger get the better of him."

Abdullah thought back to that day in June, the heat like an act of violence against his thinly sheathed body, the crackle of burning cars and pop of firecrackers and the stickiness of the road's melting blacktop on the bottom of his sandals and then the sudden cold of the air against his exposed blood and bone. A flash of fire warmed his eyelids. A long-ago fire, kindling his bones, prickling his skin. Anger was in the air the day he'd lost his hand. It had been mixed with the acrid smell of burning rubber, of noisome summer heat.

"Let me tell you how I really lost my hand."

"I know, Baba. It was Italy . . ."

"It wasn't. It was far from Italy. It was just down the road from here. It was so close to home that your grandfather would never let me speak of it. I was an angry boy that day. It was the Six-Day War, and on the compound, a riot had broken out at the American consulate. Everyone was angry that day. The loss of those lands . . . it was devastating. Americans were the easy target, with all the money they gave Israel.

"I was an accidental participant in the protests. I was angry for other reasons, reasons that had nothing to do with Nasser or Hussein or Eshkol. It was easy to let myself get carried away by the day's events."

Even though, at Abdul Latif's urging, Abdullah had spent decades pushing his memories far from his consciousness, he found that the details of his last day with two hands came back to him with vivid ferocity. Carefully, slowly, he recounted those details to his son. He had not spoken them aloud to anyone but his father, not even to Rosalie.

Abdul Latif had sent him to the State Oil compound to deliver a package to officials regarding a new contract between B-Corp and State Oil—he hadn't had time to go himself, so he sent Abdullah, who was working for the company in the afternoons after school. Abdul Latif had warned Abdullah not to get mixed up in anything—that people were agitated about the war and doing foolish things that would only harm their own country. With the windows rolled down, the wind blasting his face, carrying late summer's sweet, dying smell. Abdullah made it to the State Oil office twenty minutes late, and a man named Larry met him at the door, looking with vexation at his watch.

"Son, we've been waiting for you. Need to get this project rolling."

"Yes, well . . ."

"How are you people going to manage a country if you can't even make a delivery on time? Just think on that, son."

You people. Who people? he'd wondered, though the man's tone told him to be angry. The soft, sensitive cavity that had settled in his molar caused him to open his mouth and grimace, which the man interpreted as a smirk.

"Just give me the package," Larry said, grabbing the manila envelope from Abdullah's hands and turning back into the office.

As the door closed, Abdullah felt a brief, welcome rush of air-conditioning. He stood and stared, not knowing how to react. After a minute, his ears hot with the June sun, Abdullah walked slowly back to his car. Khara. He couldn't believe he'd let himself be treated like that by a man whose jowls dripped down his jaw like candle wax. After only a few minutes in the sun, the car was a furnace. He raced back toward the security gates, determined to put as much distance as he could between himself and Larry. The Americans behaved like they owned the country. All because they knew how to stick a pump down in the earth and button up a dress shirt. He thought about going to the next majlis to complain to King Faisal.

As Abdullah drove back down the compound's main road, he saw a flash of light off to the right. When he looked over, a car was being upended, turned on its back, its windows violently reflecting the sun's glare. There was a crowd of people in front of the consulate. Abdullah slowed to a stop and rolled down his window. They were chanting loudly: "*Israel-lovers get out! Go home Amreekees!*" Several people were spray-painting the building's exterior, sloppy Arabic script condemning the people inside. Abdullah felt a sudden surge of energy, felt his heart beating fast in time with the chants. *Go Home Thump Thump Get Out Thump Thump.* He stumbled slightly getting out of the car before breaking into a run, galloping sure and fast toward the consulate, toward the smell of burnt rubber and the sound of crunching glass.

As he neared the throng, he saw a young boy light a firecracker and throw it at a consulate window. That Larry bastard, yebnen kelp. The Americans and Israelis, thinking they ran the world. He reached into a pile of firecrackers. They were big, more like miniature rockets. He closed his hand around one and grabbed the boy's lighter. Sparking the fuse, he squeezed the firecracker tightly, as if his anger would somehow propel it farther. He reached back to blast it toward a window, but before he could send it sailing he heard a popping noise. As he swung his arm forward, he looked toward the building to watch his hurled bomb. Instead, he saw a splatter of bright red ribbon across a man's white thobe and felt a searing pain up his arm. It was the last conscious thought he would have that day. He spent the night under anesthesia as a surgeon at the al-Salama Hospital wrapped and shaped the grafted smirk of skin that permanently replaced his hand. After the surgery, he'd called his father from the hospital, and he could hear the fear in the old man's voice as he tried to understand the day's events.

"You'll go to Italy for a week or two, stay at the Naples apartment," Abdul Latif said. "By the time you come back, the government will be done making examples of people."

• • •

ABDULLAH LOOKED AT his son, waiting for a reaction. The sun had retreated behind a bank of buildings and the air was chilly.

"We're all victims of our own anger sometimes," Abdullah said. "It is so powerful, it must be respected. Sometimes, it should be squashed."

"It was awful, Baba. She wasn't supposed to be there in that parking lot."

"She forgives you. Your mother will always forgive you. She loves you too much. Before it happened, she asked me how she could get you to love her again."

"When she looks at me, she has this expression on her face. Like she doesn't quite know me. And she's sending me away."

"You're going away because you have to. Because of choices you made. Now we have to let the government play their games."

Faisal's face contracted, and he turned so his father would not see him cry. How could he have ever felt love to be dispensable? Now, without it, or without it in the easy form he had always known, he felt as if he were walking with only one shoe. It was something he only noticed once it was changed.

"Please. Will you leave me here? I'll walk home."

Abdullah nodded, walked back to the car, the soles of his shoes scraping the concrete path. Leaves, wax Pepsi cups, and bits of newspaper rustled around his feet. The thin metal peel-off tabs from soda cans pinged metallically as they blew through the gutters. He wanted his son to remain with him. So much time that should have been theirs had already been lost to business, to foolishness. Perhaps it was too late for them, and he had already made up his mind to do whatever Rosalie asked of him. It was not yet evening, but for Abdullah, the day was over.

Over Majid's grave, Faisal prayed: *Allah, do forgive him and have mercy on him and make him secure and overlook his shortcomings, and bestow upon him an honored place in Paradise, and make his place of entry spacious, and wash him clean with water and snow and ice, and cleanse him of all wrong as Thou dost clean a piece of white cloth of dirt, and bestow upon him a home better than his home and family better than his family, and admit him into Paradise, and shield him from the torment of the grave and the torment of the Fire.*

THE LIGHT OF *day won't look so good on a dead man's face.* This phrase held up Abdullah's dreams. Dark dreams in which he had no children but a thousand wives, or pieces of them—torsos, hair, fingers grasping at the edge of his thobe.

He called Abdul Aziz.

"What of Ibrahim?" he asked.

"What Ibrahim? Who Ibrahim?" Aziz said.

"I know you have him. The man's a scholar, not a warrior. Release him. Mercy is a virtue in kings."

"But I am not a king, ya Sheikh."

"Mercy is a virtue in men."

"We'll see."

Abdullah placed the phone back in the receiver. The Kingdom was the Kingdom was the Kingdom. These were the ways of the state. The poets knew it. *Against* was a tired word in the Arab canon. The skyscrapers stretched toward the heavens. The kings put their hands in their bulging pockets. They counted three barrels per subject. They pardoned when it suited them. They tore up petitions and closed the door on their people. He had taken part in it for too long, a silent and willing partner. He had sacrificed everything to stand alongside kings.

ROSALIE PLACED DOZENS of calls to arrange the terms of Faisal's stay: to the Saudi consulate in Houston, to the American consulate in Harran, to her brother, Randy. She did not say anything about Wisoum. And so Randy arranged for Faisal to be admitted to the local community college, where he worked as an accounting professor. Another call to Aziz, and Faisal's visa arrived within the week.

The king was dying and the country was abuzz with talk of the Crown Prince, who was thought to be honorable and forward-thinking, who knew the value of tradition and the necessity of modernity. Abdullah could practically feel the country holding its breath, awaiting the rise of this new sovereign. It was what Saudis knew how to do best: wait. Abdullah did not tell Faisal that his heart ached to think of him leaving—at the moment God had returned his son to him. Would Faisal be as lonely as Abdullah had been, decades before, when he had first arrived in Austin just before his nineteenth birthday? In the days before Dan and Rosalie?

ON THE DAY of Dan and Faisal's departure, Abdullah told the driver he would take them himself. They filled the trunk of the Range Rover, and Faisal, Mariam, and Rosalie climbed into the backseat. In silence, they drove across the causeway to Bahrain. Dan followed the shoreline off to the right until he spotted the sandpaper and cinderblock rubble of the clubhouse. On the breeze, he imagined that he smelled the familiar sourness of the hundreds of empty beer bottles stacked on the kitchen counters. He didn't think that Abdullah would be spending much time there anymore. Faisal also looked to the south along the shoreline, but he craned his neck back so that he was looking at Saudi Arabia. He knew he would not be able to see Wisoum from there, but he looked anyway. The sky was a pale, winter's blue, the clouds propelled by the powerful wind moving down from Iran. He pulled the folded-up photo of Jadd Abdul Latif from his pocket and stared at it. It was the only family he would take with him to America.

Now they were crossing the causeway into Bahrain, which was still a Gulf country, still a Muslim country, though there were a few churches scattered around; Faisal had heard that the whorehouses outnumbered both the churches and the mosques. Was it going to be that bad in America? Would his uncle attempt to convert him?

Mariam had shifted into the center seat and pressed herself against him, tucking her arm beneath his as if he were escorting her on a stroll somewhere. He thought she might be crying but he didn't look because he knew that if he did, he would not be able to stop everything from spilling forth out of him—his love for her, for his baba, for the stifling, troubled place he was leaving behind, for the mother whose body he had once inhabited. He squeezed Mariam's arm tightly and looked straight ahead. Moving fast over the causeway, Faisal felt his home stripped away like the thinnest raiment. He had never imagined it could be taken from him so easily.

At the airport, Abdullah parked and everyone walked in together. Faisal's hand shook. He had never left the Kingdom alone; he had only traveled alone once, when leaving boarding school. His father took him in an awkward embrace, and Faisal realized that he was now taller than Abdullah. Faisal felt the scratch of his father's goatee against his cheek. Was there still time to learn from him? Mariam grasped onto them from the side, and the sweet smell of her lavender shampoo raised in him an inchoate sadness. "I'll come in a few weeks," she said. "I'll be there soon."

"Say hello to my brother for me," Rosalie said to Faisal. "Say hello to Texas."

And then Dan and Faisal were through security and waving from the other side until the people around them began to get annoyed and mutter unkind things. Before turning away, Dan paused to look at Abdullah. His iron-gray hair was combed back in an unruly wave, and he'd cocked his head ever so slightly to the right, as if assessing a painting on a museum wall. With deep-set black eyes, the cynosure of his elegant face, Abdullah watched him, too. Dan understood that they might not continue to be friends. Their friendship had survived difference for decades—they'd built their bond simply on essence—but it could not survive what had happened in the last weeks. What came between them now was not religion or language or homeland, or any of the other false barriers that humans erect between themselves in their search for order and identity. Rather, what now diminished their friendship, which had become something so utterly a part of both of them that its removal would leave them keening with a phantasmal ache that would last until their deaths many years later, was the fact that their bond had become entangled in the same woman.

Finally, Faisal and Dan turned away to find their gates.

"Good luck, Faisal," Dan said.

They didn't shake hands or touch. They merely turned in opposite directions and walked away from each other. This parting was not done in coldness or anger; it was done out of necessity. They were going different ways.

DAN BOARDED HIS plane to Marseille and later caught the ferry to Corsica, where he drank sweet pink wine and hoped for rain so that he could stay indoors by the fire listening to Miles Davis. If the sun came out, it would require him to put on his boots and venture down to the water, to smell the gorse and lilac and be in the world. For Rosalie, for what she had survived, he would never forget the blessing of another day. Dan knew that he had missed the point for too long. After tragedy, you must still undress your heart and send it naked into the day, where it would be battered and expanded. Wives left, husbands cheated, floods came and took everything out to sea. But if you were left alive, there should be gratitude for that, always. He knew you could relearn those things. How to put on your boots. How to walk. How to love. By the time he got to Texas, he would be ready to run.

ON HIS SIX-HOUR layover in Amsterdam, Faisal bought a Toblerone, wandered though the terminal counting the number of Arab faces that he saw (thirty-eight, including one man who was possibly Greek or Spanish), and changed from his thobe into a pair of suit pants and a white button-down shirt. He listened to all of the languages around him and heard Persian and Turkish and Urdu and Arabic. He wondered what it would be like to be in a place where he might not hear Arabic every day. While he waited to board, he watched an English-language news program. A Moroccan named

Youssef Belhadj had just been arrested in Belgium in connection with the Madrid bombings and was awaiting extradition to Spain. He looked like a professor—his face had that learned quality to it. Faisal wondered what could move a man like that to kill. It was something other than God. Faisal had held Majid's twitching neck in his hands, he had seen his death tremors. They were things Faisal could not bear to see again.

Outside the glass walls of the airport, the sun of late morning had ignited the water-slick runways; the tails of departing planes bandied the light back in bright, surprised O's. The whole world seemed alight, and Faisal recalled a quote that Imam Sa'ad at his masjid liked to repeat: *Muslims, in their dealings with others, should appear like the sun that shines and melts away darkness.*

Now, sitting in the Schiphol Airport in Amsterdam, he was concerned with one thing, and that was the frozen blue in his heart; the pain and regret that might never leave him, not as long as he lived, maybe not even in heaven. Would heaven be his? He felt a darkness in him—a shadow that had not been there before.

After twenty-eight hours in transit, Faisal landed at the George H. W. Bush Intercontinental Airport in Houston, Texas. As the plane flew low over the city, he was stunned by the orange lights that seemed to stretch on and on in every direction. He was nervous, as if he would be asked to do something for which he had failed to prepare. The plane taxied to the gate, and Faisal felt calmer. It was darker along the runway, the city panorama gone from view. Fat men in vests waved their orange sticks.

Inside the terminal, he slowed his step. There was no reason to rush. In fact, he wanted to prolong his time in the airport as much as he could. Again, he tried to count the Arab faces that he saw, but he found only one—a woman who looked Egyptian, wearing a pink headscarf. Several times, he thought he had seen another one, but when he moved closer, he heard them speaking Spanish. Maybe he would call Abdullah after he went through customs. He knew that his uncle was waiting for him beyond the divide, maybe his aunt, too, but the thought of seeing them made him very tired. He would be a guest in their house, in their country. How would he fill up his days? How would he move from the kitchen to his bedroom? Would he be watched? Where would he pray? It was not his house. This was not his country. Even the sign at the customs line reminded him: ALL OTHER COUNTRIES. As Faisal moved toward the front of the line, he could see a man with a face like his mother's waving at him from behind the glass panel. The man was tall and blond, his face ruddy. The man had German cheekbones. His mother's. His own. Here was this man to meet him, this man who shared his blood. Faisal caught his breath. Surrounded by all the people, the brown and the beige and the yellow and the pink, the spotted and the smooth, the stooped and the heroically tall, Faisal was entirely alone. He should go back; he wanted so badly to go back. He could barely bring himself to edge along the blue carpet toward the Exit sign and the expanding and consuming fluorescence of the strange, whirring world that lay beyond it. The people who belonged went streaming by; they treated the transitional place with ease. They spoke English more quickly than his mother had. He tried to picture Rosalie making her way down the tiny airplane staircase and onto the tarmac in Al Dawoun that first time, her pale face already burning in the September sun. Imagine. To live out your life in a country not your own. Imagine it.

IN AL DAWOUN, the sun rose and set in a flawless sky, the rain saving itself for a more blessed time. Spring arrived, then summer. Faisal was gone, Mariam had started at St. Stephens in mid-spring; when she arrived in Austin, she'd written to Rosalie right away: *Umma, the highways here are lined with flowers, purples and reds and yellows. The man who picked me up at the airport said that I came at the best time, wildflower time, and that soon, the flowers would be gone and the grass on the shoulders would brown and die. It reminded me of our time in France, with the sunflowers and all the lavender, when the whole earth was color. I want you to visit me at exactly this time next year. I will try to take a picture so you can see it, or remember it, if it was this way when you and Baba lived here.*

In the past months, since the children's departures, Rosalie and Abdullah had lived easily together. Together, they talked of the children, missing them, wondering who they would become. The love was there. Remember the Qabbani, he said. He began reciting the old poet, trying to take them to a simpler time.

When I love you, the Arab cities leap up and demonstrate
against the ages of repression
and the ages
of revenge against the laws of the tribe.
And I, when I love you,
march against ugliness,
against the kings of salt,
against the institutionalization of the desert.

She interrupted him: And how does that poem end? You never recited the ending.

He looked perplexed, as if he had never considered that the poem had an ending, so consumed was he by the passion of the beginning.

So she recited for him.

And I shall continue to love you until the world flood arrives;
I shall continue to love you until the world flood arrives.

IN THEIR TIME together, Abdullah was tender and eager, and only occasionally did he disappear from the house. She did not ask if he went to Isra's or to B-Corp; she did not want to disrupt the harmonious passage of days. She sensed his regret, and, as she was not a cruel person, she did not try to intensify it. On any day, she could have said: Our son kidnapped me because of your outburst. On any day, he could have said: You were going to leave our family, our country, with my best friend. So she did not say anything, only accepted his touch, his words, because she understood that his affections were turning more and more back toward her, and this was almost enough. Almost.

THAT EVENING, THEY lay together on their bed for the first time. They touched each other tentatively. At dusk, they stood at the window, watching the desert flood with copper light. They remarked the eroding landscapes of their aging bodies. This is how two bodies orbit each other after decades together, when the gravitational pull of love is properly in place. They had been out of orbit for too long, Abdullah recognizes. His love has been too diffuse, not enough to center them.

Abdullah thinks with exhaustion of watching two women grow old—of differentiating their habits, their particularities—and he is angry at Isra for the first time in their short love. Angry that she will not stay fine and firm; that she will one day need him to love her despite her infirmity, her dementia, her stooped and brittle body. After all, it was her fineness that made him think his heart capacious enough for two women. That it should fail her, fail them, one day, was too much for him to bear. And beneath his anger and exhaustion is doubt: Two women have given everything to be with me. Am I worth two lives? He tries to bury this thought back in the shadows, but it will not be buried. It is lodged where, now, he will always consider it.

ROSALIE SEES WHAT is left of her love. It is as if a switch has been flipped. She can touch without being consumed. She can remember without sadness. She is not bitter, and she is not afraid.

AT THE HOSPITAL after the baby is born, Abdullah greets his sister Nadia, who has come up to offer her assistance.

"Mashallah, my brother," Nadia says. She watches Abdullah clutching awkwardly at the baby. In her brother's world, helpless things have no place. It is why, she thinks, he married the American, the Palestinian; women tough enough to stand with a foot in two worlds, as he did.

FROM HER BEDROOM, Rosalie listens for the front door. She stands at the dresser and surveys the room; she imagines the bed pushed all the way into the corner, as it was off Rio Grande. She sees their young bodies stretched across the mattress. They are not yet engaged. She wants to return to that moment and steer herself differently. Not away from him, but not so fully into him.

She hears the click of the bolt easing out of its place, the swoosh of the door's rubber liners against the tile. With both hands, she smoothes the map she has placed on the dresser top. She found it in a desk drawer, the socialist's map from the bar all those years ago. He cannot know how well he paid her that night, when he gifted her with the entire world. She runs her fingers over the boot of Saudi Arabia, feels the crinkle of the paper. She remembers the ache of homelessness she felt when they flew out of the desert, she, Maxine, and Wayne. Sometimes, the cure for nostalgia is return. She knows she will leave.

She puts her finger on Texas, moving it from west to east until she arrives at Sugar Land. For her, it is a heavy place, the blinds always drawn, her mother cranky without her supply of Yemeni khat, the swampy Gulf air rich with decay. She has never been nostalgic for Sugar Land, and she will not start now. A new place is what she is after. She feels the Urals rise up under her open palm, the unfurling of the South China Sea at her fingertips. She knows there is an island where she can catch slick, muscled fish that glitter more brightly than all the jewels of Gold City. She knows there is a place where she can sit too long in the sun and shed the layer of skin that clings to her now. She will find the place, lose herself, lose memory. The children will visit her there, in this place beyond language, beyond nation; they will laugh and laugh and laugh, a sound like bells echoing into the sky.

You will search everywhere for her,
you will ask the waves of the sea about her, the
turquoise of
the shore . . .
Your heart's love has no land, no homeland, no
address.

Life does not permit even the greatest love poets to write only love poetry.

At night, she and her children will fall asleep like foundlings, glad of each other, only as far apart as the salt skin that keeps them separate seas of blood and bone.

ACKNOWLEDGMENTS

I AM INFINITELY grateful to my editors: Allison Lorentzen, who chose this book as her own and guided me to its best end; Sally Kim, the consummate professional whose wisdom and generosity continue to amaze me; and Maya Ziv, whose passion, energy, and insight have been invaluable. Thank you, also, to Priscilla Gilman, who sold the novel in North America. Thank you to the Iowa Writers' Workshop, a place that changed the course of my life, and all of the talented teachers there who helped me refine the book and better my craft: Anthony Swofford, Elizabeth McCracken, Charles D'Ambrosio, Scott Spencer, Lan Samantha Chang. Thank you to the Workshop's dedicated staff: Connie Brothers, Jan Zenisek, Deb West, Kelly Smith. Many thanks to the Truman Capote Literary Trust, the late James Michener, and the Copernicus Society of America for generously funding this project. I would be lost without my critical readers: Richard Rodriguez, Julia Fierro, Jennifer duBois, Victoria Kelly, Adam Krause, Shannon MacCleery, Carolyn Nash, and Rebecca Gradinger. I started writing this book in large part due to the guidance and encouragement I received at the Sackett Street Writers' Workshop, and for both of those things, which came at such a crucial period, I'm ever grateful. Thank you to the Sloan family, the Settles family, Janice and Malcolm Robertson, and John Parssinen and Laura Bernstein, for your support and kindness, and for being the storybook family I thought a girl could only dream of having. Thanks to the ARAMCO Brats, for the memories. Thank you to my readers and friends in Saudi Arabia, who cheered me on and helped me to get it right. Finally, thank you to my beloved husband, Michael Robertson, who is my most dedicated reader and gentlest critic, and to my parents, Jon and Cathie Parssinen, who have delighted all of us with the enduring strength of their love. Without you, I wouldn't have had the courage.

Insights,
Interviews
& More . . .

About the author

About the book

Read on

About the author

Meet Keija Parssinen

KEIJA PARSSINEN was born in Saudi Arabia and lived there for twelve years as a third-generation expatriate. She earned a degree in English literature from Princeton University and received her MFA from the Iowa Writers' Workshop, where she held a Truman Capote Fellowship and a Teaching and Writing Fellowship. For *The Ruins of Us*, her first novel, she received a Michener-Copernicus award. She lives with her husband on the edge of a quarry in Columbia, Missouri, where she directs the Quarry Heights Writers' Workshop.

A Country Not Your Own

WHEN I WAS IN MIDDLE SCHOOL in Texas, I was deeply troubled by the question "Where are you from?" I was born and raised in the Eastern Province of Saudi Arabia, where my mother had also lived since she was four years old. I had lived more than half my life in that country, and it was listed on my birth certificate as my birthplace. My mother and maternal grandparents had lived there before me. And yet when I answered that question about my origin by saying "Saudi Arabia," I got incredulous looks. I was blond, the child of two Californians, and American by citizenship. But I still claimed Saudi Arabia as my homeland even though I might never go back, thanks to the strict laws governing visitor visas. Unless you have an immediate family member living there, or you're a journalist working for a major newspaper, it's impossible to secure a visitor visa. And for a while, I felt comfortable with my answer to the question. After all, what other criteria aside from being born in a place must be met in order for you to belong?

But then I got to college. At my mother's urging, I went to international student gatherings. Missing Arabia while she was at college in Southern California, she'd sought out Saudi students and became a part of their raucous social circle, and I think she hoped I would find a similarly satisfying experience ▸

A Country Not Your Own *(continued)*

waiting for me at school. To the first meeting, I wore my mother's Arabic name necklace—it spelled out *Catherine*—which I had come to cherish as a symbol of my Middle Eastern past. A student read it back to me before I could introduce myself. "Catherine," he said. "Hi." He was from Syria. In that moment, I felt incredibly foolish—I wasn't *from* Saudi Arabia; I couldn't even read the name necklace that I had so loved.

I didn't go back to the international student gatherings, and from that point forward, I told people I was from Texas, even though I'd only lived there for seven years, not nearly as long as I'd been in Saudi. But I started to understand that much more comprised national identity than mere presence upon a country's soil. But where did that leave me? Texans seemed to require at least a decade of residence before allowing you to claim their state as home. I kept up a quiet nostalgia for the Kingdom, a place that bloomed with all the mystery of memory in my imagination.

Several events precipitated the writing of *The Ruins of Us*. First, I learned that a Saudi friend of my parents had taken a second wife—it shocked my parents deeply and, as a result, shocked me. It was not something they had expected of their friend, and their other Saudi and Arab friends looked on plural marriages with mild disdain. My young mind pondered the details of such an arrangement: Why did

"I kept up a quiet nostalgia for the Kingdom, a place that bloomed with all the mystery of memory in my imagination."

he do it? Emotionally, how did everyone in the family survive the fallout? Logistically, how did he manage it?

And then, September 11, 2001, came and went. Fifteen Saudis (my countrymen, a part of me still thought) flew themselves into the Twin Towers just a few miles north of where I lived in my college dorm room, and I wondered, did I know the country of my birth at all?

> “I wondered, did I know the country of my birth at all?”

Finally, in the summer of 2003, my father, now divorced from my mother, moved back to Saudi Arabia, even though the country was wracked by terrorist violence and had experienced its bloodiest months since the 1979 takeover of the Great Mosque in Mecca, when hundreds of soldiers and rebels were killed. Al-Qaeda in the Arabian Peninsula had formally and gruesomely announced itself, and my father, a six-foot-three blue-eyed half-Finn, was thrusting himself into the middle of it. Was it suicide, or was it willful ignorance? My parents had always had many Saudi friends, so growing up we often left the compound to socialize with their families. Perhaps my father felt he was safe because he knew the lay of the land, knew and trusted his neighbors. After all, he had lived in the Kingdom for decades; he had written his doctoral dissertation on the Palestinian Diaspora; his best friends were Saudi—perhaps he felt that this gave him a pass. That he was somehow protected from the violence because he had always ►

been sympathetic to Arab struggle and had built a life and community in the Middle East.

But for me, his daughter, who was no longer sure she knew anything about Saudi Arabia, it was frightening. While my father was overseas, Paul Johnson was beheaded on videotape. A group of French tourists were shot while visiting Mada'in Saleh, the historic site in Southern Arabia. Terrorists tried to blow up the Abqaiq refinery. Because I was not living there and could not observe the more mundane details of my father's life—the kabsa feasts, the late-night carousing with his buddies, the thousands upon thousands of nonviolent Saudis who were equally threatened by the outbreak of violence—I was left only with what was reported to me by the BBC and the *New York Times*. Anxiety limned my dreams.

In 2005, I started writing *The Ruins of Us* to assert some control over my father's story. I was tired of feeling fearful, and I wanted to better understand exactly what was going on in the country I had called home for so many years. In a note at the end of his novel *To the End of the Land*, David Grossman wrote that he began the novel to protect his son once the young man was called to the frontlines in Lebanon, and so I began to explore through fiction the violence that plagued my mind, and the fear it inspired. If I could control the story, my father would be safe. I read

“I began to explore through fiction the violence that plagued my mind, and the fear it inspired. If I could control the story, my father would be safe.”

dozens of books about the history of Saudi Arabia, about al-Qaeda and September 11, about Saudi ARAMCO, where my father and grandfather had both worked, and about the al-Saud. I read every newspaper article I could find about the Kingdom. I spoke with journalists and human rights experts. At the University of Iowa library, I pored over scholarly papers. I read blogs written by young Saudis, Saudi women, American women married to Saudis. And I started to feel that, at last, through the writing and research, I was coming to terms with the complicated country where I had spent my childhood. My father survived the violence in a way that Grossman's son, tragically, did not; fiction, it seemed, was an unreliable bodyguard.

The research was, of course, an exercise in disenchantment. When you realize that you spent your entire childhood in a carefully guarded bubble—where people did not live by the same rules as the citizens of the country, where Arabic was not taught in schools—you get a little sad, you get a little angry. You feel robbed of authentic experience. You feel like a phony. My research was an education, and the knowledge it delivered did what knowledge always does—it enlightened, but at a cost. When I talked about my new feelings with one of my oldest ARAMCO brat friends, she didn't really want to hear it. "I don't think that's all it was," she said. And she was ▸

“My research was an education, and the knowledge it delivered did what knowledge always does—it enlightened, but at a cost.”

A Country Not Your Own *(continued)*

right: I possessed the cynicism of the newly informed, and I was letting it kill my happy childhood memories. So I tried to let my friend's nostalgia, her pleasant memories of a tight-knit community of people surviving as best they could in a harsh, strange, and marvelous place, return me to my original, simpler sentiments about the Kingdom.

In 2008, I traveled back to Saudi Arabia. I was able to secure a visa because my father was still working there. I rode a bike around the Dhahran compound, stopping by all my old haunts—the snack bar, the Third Street pool, my school, the white clapboard ranch-style house where my family lived for years. On a drive out to the oasis town of Qatif, Dad and I stopped to gas up the car. I rolled down the window and leaned out to take a photograph of a beautiful pink neon sign flashing brightly against the oncoming dusk. Some young men hanging out in the back of a pickup truck stared at us. "Put it away, roll up the window," Dad said nervously. He got in, we drove away quickly, and I noticed him checking the rearview mirror a couple times. I could see, then, that my fear and paranoia about my dad's existence in post–9/11 Saudi had not been misplaced.

At Half Moon Bay, I stared out at the darkening Arabian Sea. I had celebrated countless birthday parties on that beach. I'd caught jellyfish, built sandcastles,

"I possessed the cynicism of the newly informed, and I was letting it kill my happy childhood memories."

jumped from the pier that stretched far into the clear, salty water. At that moment, I realized that for all my research, for all my years living there, Saudi Arabia would forever remain a mystery, just beyond my grasp. Yes, it was true: it was not my country, and it could never be my home, at least not one I could return to. But it was more than merely a place I had lived, once. It was the mythic, wondrous land of my childhood.

Journey to the Middle East
Author Recommendations

Literature Related to Saudi Arabia

1. Cities of Salt Trilogy (*Cities of Salt, The Trench, Variations on Night and Day*), Abdelrahman Munif

In the epic trilogy that got him stripped of his Saudi citizenship, Munif explores a fictitious Gulf country's evolution after the discovery of oil beneath its sands. Set over several decades, the books scathingly assess Western influence and exploitation, as well as royal pandering and greed, during the subsequent period of rapid change that forever alters the desert kingdom's landscape, physically, politically, and socially. A gifted storyteller, Munif unfolds the tale with all the heart and bitterness of a man who feels he has lost his home to the inexorable, unforgiving push of modernity—these books are a lament for a way of life forever lost.

2. *Girls of Riyadh*, Rajaa Alsanea

Upon publication, Alsanea's book caused a scandal in the notoriously private Kingdom, where people would do just about anything to prevent the airing of their families' dirty laundry. Though it is a work of fiction, this fact did little to protect Alsanea from being condemned for exploring the taboo subjects of romantic love, marriage, and sex in the Kingdom. A fun, frothy peek behind the closed doors shielding the sequestered daughters of Saudi Arabia's elite, and an interesting examination of the dual lives those daughters are forced to live depending on whether they are at home or abroad.

3. ***Arab Women Writers: An Anthology of Short Stories*****, ed. Dalya Cohen-Mor**

In this anthology, Cohen-Mor includes several stories by Saudi women writers Umayma al-Khamis, Sharifa al-Shamlan, and Khayriya al-Saqqaf. Some of the other contributors are famous in the Arab world and abroad—Hanan al-Shaykh, Alifa Rifaat—but I had never heard of the Saudi contributors and enjoyed their odd, well-imagined stories. After years of reading articles and books written about women in Saudi Arabia, it was refreshing for me to hear some of them tell their own stories, in their own creative, insightful, and powerful voices.

“After years of reading articles and books written about women in Saudi Arabia, it was refreshing for me to hear some of them tell their own stories.”

4. ***Eight Months on Ghazzah Street*****, Hilary Mantel**

This book, recommended to me by Kelly Smith, the librarian at the Iowa Writers' Workshop, joins ranks with other works of what I'll call "expat gothic": horror stories that unfold in strange lands, where part of the horror is the alien qualities of the land itself. Think Alex Garland's *The Beach*, Peter Carey's *My Life as a Fake*, or Paul Bowles's *The Sheltering Sky*. Mantel tells the story of Frances, a Brit venturing to Saudi Arabia to join her husband, who works there. Through Frances's black humor and paranoia, Mantel shatters romanticized portraits of expatriatism ▸

in Arabia—Lawrence of Arabia, Frances is not, and her story makes for an unsettling read as Mantel explodes the myth of easy multicultural understanding.

5. *Finding Nouf*, Zoë Ferraris

Ferraris married into a Palestinian-Saudi family and lived with her husband in Jeddah for a year. *Finding Nouf* is a riveting mystery that follows a wealthy Jeddah family after their daughter, Nouf, goes missing. In Ferraris's book, you have at once a compelling detective story as well as a transporting work of literary fiction.

6. *Changed Identities: The Challenge of the New Generation in Saudi Arabia*, Mai Yamani

When I brought up Yamani's book with an older, conservative Saudi friend, he said, "She doesn't know what she's talking about. That book is silly." Rather, I think "that book" hit a nerve with the older generation in Saudi Arabia, perhaps because it exposes the changing beliefs of a people in flux. Using an anecdotal style bolstered by extensive research, Yamani, the daughter of famous and controversial former oil minister Zaki Yamani, gives us a fascinating glimpse into the lives of young people in the Kingdom.

> "[*Changed Identities*] hit a nerve with the older generation in Saudi Arabia."

Arab/Middle Eastern Literature

1. *Season of Migration to the North*, Tayeb Salih

First published in Arabic in 1966, this book by Sudanese author Salih was ahead of its time, considering that Edward Said's seminal work, *Orientalism*, was still more than a decade away. It turns upside down traditional notions of the Orient by tracking the journey of the keenly intelligent unnamed narrator, who ventures to London and proceeds on a violent mission of reverse-colonialization by bedding naïve British women entranced by his otherness. He exploits their fantasies to devastating effect. Poetic and brutal, this book takes you by the throat and doesn't let go.

2. *The Septembers of Shiraz*, Dalia Sofer

I wept at this novel's conclusion. Though the story ends hopefully, Sofer examines the injustices of revolutionary Iran with such mastery and humanity that you can only weep for the terrible things we do to one another in the name of religion, the state, and beliefs. I found it so thoroughly engrossing that I continue to dream about the family at the heart of the story.

3. *The Media Relations Department of Hizbollah Wishes You a Happy Birthday*, Neil MacFarquhar

MacFarquhar, the longtime *New York Times* bureau chief in Egypt and a former Libyan oil brat, has a unique perspective on a complicated region. An Arabic speaker who has travelled extensively in all parts of the Middle East, he turns a critical but compassionate eye on recent events ▸

“[MacFarquhar] turns a critical but compassionate eye on recent events there and helps his Western audience better understand the intricate social and political dynamics underlying them.”

there and helps his Western audience better understand the intricate social and political dynamics underlying them. Sometimes funny, often heart-wrenching, always honest, this book is a master class on the modern Middle East.

4. *In the Country of Men*, Hisham Matar

With this striking debut, Libyan Matar gives us the story of the el-Dawani family told through the eyes of nine-year-old son Suleiman. In the terrifying aftermath of the 1969 revolution that brought Muammar Qaddafi to power, the family struggles to find its way. The secret police are menacing and omnipresent, and the father and mother clash on how to best exist in their brutal new reality. Suleiman reveals much to readers through his guileless yet keenly observant narration, through which Matar examines the day-to-day impact of despotism on a people, as well as the heartbreak of losing a homeland to vile forces.

5. *On Entering the Sea*, Nizar Qabbani

Qabbani, Syria's unofficial poet laureate, writes such sensuous, large-hearted love poems, you'll need a cold shower after reading this book. But more than writing love poetry, he also rallied in a famously conservative region on behalf of sexual freedom, particularly that of women, whom he viewed as the unfortunate victims of stifling and old-fashioned tribal mores.